Sam Reeves is back with the Portland P.D. in this third martial arts thriller, *Dukkha Unloaded*, by veteran police officer and martial artist Loren W. Christensen. This is as good as it gets if you're looking for an action packed authentic martial arts cop novel. Christensen's years of experience shine through in his writing, keeping the reader both on the edge of the seat in anticipation of what will happen next and nodding in approval with the realistic descriptions of police work and violence. Full of action, suspense, and a little romance, *Dukkha Unloaded* is an engaging and entertaining continuation of the series. This is the best cop fiction around!

—*Alain Burrese, J.D., author of* Lost Conscience: A Ben Baker Sniper Novel *and others*

These books just get better and better! Great characters, rock-em-sockem plot with a perfect blend of police procedures and martial arts action from an author eminently qualified in both fields. Don't miss out on the action! Essential reading for any fan of martial arts, police or action novels!

—*Dave Grossman, author of* On Combat and On Killing

Dukkha Unloaded is a fast-paced thriller written by an author who's been there and done that. Loren W. Christensen takes his experiences as a veteran, law enforcement officer and martial artist, and creates a well-rounded character in Sam Reeves. The outstanding action scenes are obviously heavily grounded in reality, and it shows in their depth. Everything that happens is realistic, making it that much more real for the reader. If you are to read any action series, pick up the *Dukkha* series, you won't regret it for a moment.

—*Bert Edens, avid reader and martial artist*

Detective Sam Reeves experiences life changing events that would destroy most of us: involvement in police shootings which cause major uproars in the community, finding his Green Beret father long thought to have been killed in the jungles of Vietnam, a beautiful and capable "sister" which stir emotions and confusion, a war with Southeast Asian organized crime which involves his newly discovered family and results in non-stop action and death.

Loren Christensen has produced another non-stop action novel in the Detective Sam Reeves series. What makes his work unique from others in the genre is the detail and heart stopping reality based on first hand experience. Christensen worked the dangerous streets of Portland, Oregon during the hay day of the White Supremacists Movement, the rise of gang violence and racial turmoil. Although fictitious, his police and community characters are real for those of us who shared those responsibilities with him. That he is an accomplished martial arts student and instructor is without question. The fight scenes had me always on the edge of my chair. He understands the impact of PTSD and the stresses of the day to day job of both the soldier and the cop.

When I came to the last page of *Dukkha Unloaded* I almost yelled out "NO!!! It can't end here!!!" Fortunately the story continues. I can hardly wait.

—*Robert E Kauffman, Commander (RET), Portland Police Bureau, Lieutenant Colonel (RET), USAR, US Army Special Forces (Abn)*

Dukkha Unloaded is a fast-paced, riveting tale that deftly handles deep subjects like violence, PTSD, and race relations in a compelling yet unpretentious manner. Christensen's experience as a soldier, law enforcement officer, and martial artist lends a gritty realism that's sadly lacking in similar stories. It's enthralling, entertaining, and consequential, so good you may not realize that you're actually learning something when reading it.

—*Lawrence A. Kane, best-selling author, martial artist*

Loren Christensen peels back the veil on police work in his newest book in the *Dukkha* series. Some action writers would have you believe that violence is just one more literary technique to move the plot along. Christensen draws upon his career as a cop to show violence in all its many facets, both its allure and the toll it takes on the lives of victims, perpetrators and law enforcement professionals. *Dukkha Unloaded* is an edgy story that places an honorable man between haters and the society they would harm. If you find yourself relating to detective and martial arts instructor Sam Reeves, don't be surprised if you finish the book with a bit more starch in your spine and an itch to go out and find a heavy bag to work.

—*Susan Lynn Peterson, author, martial artist*

As Sam Reeves is disembarking at the Portland airport, he is thrust into the middle of a riot. The action begins fast and doesn't let up. He soon learns that his friend and former boss has been the victim of a hate crime and the hunt is on for the perpetrators.

Christensen's characters leap off the page and his narrative sounds like reality. I've been a cop for thirty-five years. When I read most books in the genre, they don't get a lot of things right, like the way cops talk to each other and to the public, the way cases are actually put together, the way cops really investigate crimes, etc. I don't have that problem with Loren's books. The cop banter sounds authentic, the characters act like real cops, the cases are solved in a manner that is reasonable. As with [his] previous books, the action sequences shine. In one instance I got so angry with someone in the book I had to stop reading. I then realized that I'd been totally sucked in to the narrative. That is very rare for me.

If you've already experienced the *Dukkha* series, I don't need to encourage you to grab the newest installment. If you haven't, and you enjoy realistic and action-packed police work set in a well-written book, do yourself a favor and pick up the whole series.

—Steve Holley, Chief of Police, HSPD

Sam takes dukkha to a new level. While he struggles with his demons, he finds true love but it doesn't keep him out of problems. The events in this book are loosely based on real events of the Portland Police Bureau. They are at once believable and unbelievable in their raw descriptions of the realities of police work.

—*C. W. Jensen, Captain (Ret.) Portland Police Bureau; TV commentator* World's Wildest Police Videos

DUKKHA
UNLOADED

LOREN W. CHRISTENSEN

DUKKHA
UNLOADED

A SAM REEVES
MARTIAL ARTS THRILLER

YMAA Publication Center, Inc.
Wolfeboro NH USA

YMAA Publication Center, Inc.
Main Office
PO Box 480
Wolfeboro, NH 03894
800-669-8898 • www.ymaa.com • info@ymaa.com

ISBN Paperback	ISBN Ebook
9781594392535	9781594392825

Dukkha Unloaded was edited by Leslie Takao, and its cover was designed by Axie Breen. This book has been typeset in Adobe Premiere Pro and printed on 55 LBS FSC-Env100 Ant EDI Creme paper.

10   9   8   7   6   5   4   3   2   1

Publisher's Cataloging in Publication

Christensen, Loren W.
    Dukkha unloaded / Loren W. Christensen. -- Wolfeboro, NH : YMAA Publication Center, c2014.
        p. ; cm.
        ISBN: 978-1-59439-283-2 (pbk.) ; 978-1-59439-284-9 (ebk.)
        "A Sam Reeves martial arts thriller."
        Summary: Police detective and martial arts instructor Sam Reeves learns that during his two months absence, a number of hate crimes have rocked Portland, including a lynching. Still undecided if he will continue in police work three months after his "bad shoot," Sam accepts reassignment to the Intelligence Department. He is quickly consumed as he works to find racist killers, a hate gang that attacked his friends, deal with his 'issues' about carrying a loaded gun, help a new martial arts student cope with PTSD, and offer comfort to his special friend Mai who is in town grieving a lost parent. It all comes to a climactic clash when Sam discovers the killer's hideout. He's right, and the engagement is explosive.--Publisher.

        1. Reeves, Sam (Fictitious character)--Fiction. 2. Police shootings--Psychological aspects--Fiction. 3. Firearms--Psychological aspects--Fiction. 4. Hate crimes--Oregon--Portland--Fiction. 5. Hate groups--Oregon--Portland--Fiction. 6. Gangs--Oregon--Portland--Fiction. 7. Post-traumatic stress disorder--Fiction. 8. Police psychology--Fiction. 9. Martial arts fiction. 10. Mystery fiction. I. Title.

PS3603.H73 D858 2014   2014937531
813/.6--dc23   1406

This is a work of fiction. Names, characters, places, and incidents either are the product of the author's imagination or are used fictitiously, and any resemblance to actual persons, living or dead, businesses, companies, events, or locales is entirely coincidental.

Editorial Note: *Dukkha:* a Pali term that corresponds to such English words as pain, discontent, unhappiness, sorrow, affliction, anxiety, discomfort, anguish, stress, misery, and frustration.

Printed in Canada.

To my parents

Thank you for reading my short stories when I was a kid and for laughing at the "funny" stuff and trembling in fear at the "scary" parts. I will always hold dear the memory of the pride on your faces when I began selling magazine articles and penning nonfiction books. I wish you could have read my fiction—the tamer parts, anyway.

PROLOGUE

A rush of wind sent debris skittering along the empty sidewalks, filthy gutters, and streets long in need of repair. Though few vehicles passed through the darkened skid row intersection of Northwest Third and Couch at three a.m., its lone traffic signal, swaying in the wind, continued to cycle its colors, casting hues off the sides of old buildings and the cracked windshield of a decaying station wagon propped up on four rusted wheels.

A lone dog, a white mutt with protruding ribs, a broken ear, and a two-inch stub for a right rear leg, hobbled along the sidewalk, sniffing at a wino's puke and startling on every noise. On an especially dark southwest corner of the intersection, it stopped and looked up one of the city's few remaining turn-of-the-century lampposts, a fifteen-foot high, paint-chipped black column crowned with four skeletal arms reaching outward in cardinal directions, as if holding court over the sad, decaying streets.

A rope, one end looped over one of the lamp's arms, the other end around the neck of an old man, rubbed and creaked against the flaking metal with each gust of wind that lurched the body. Red, amber, and green played on the bloody, black face.

The three-legged dog emitted a low growl, and backed up two or three irregular steps, sniffed right, left, and looked back up at the limp figure silhouetted against the night sky. He cowered against the building wall and began a trembling whine.

About a quarter of the way down the block, two sets of eyes peered around the edge of a graffiti-covered alcove of a long, empty building, watching and smiling as the body slow danced in the wind.

CHAPTER ONE

"Where to, weary traveler?" the black man asks, as he stuffs my two pieces of luggage into the back of his green cab. He's in his sixties, bald, big happy face, and a monstrous belly. I give him my home address. "Won't be a problem," he says, slamming the trunk. "No sir." He opens the backdoor for me. "Where you flyin' in from?"

Oh, good, he's a gregarious sort—just what I need with a jet-lagged brain, hairy and mushy from the twenty-six-hour flight. "Saigon," I say. "Vietnam."

"Oh goodness!" he laughs, his big shoulders shaking. "Saigon. Know it well. *Beaucoup*. Number ten. Our hot day here probably don't mean nothin' to you right now, right? When I was there in the war, we used to say 'If you can't take the heat we shouldn't have tickled the dragon.' Get it? Land of the dragon and we tickled it? 'Course they tickled us right back and some." He guffaws, which makes his big belly shake and quake. He shuts my door and calls a loud greeting to the cabdriver in line behind us.

I retrieve my cell, tap in Mark's number for the fourth or fifth time, and listen to it ring and ring. Where is he? We chatted for a couple minutes when I was boarding the plane in Saigon, and he confirmed he would pick me up at five p.m. in the new Lexus he bought a couple days ago as a retirement gift to himself. I told him he sounded as giddy as a cheerleader.

"I am, indeed, Sam," he laughed. "Lots to be giddy about. I bought my dream car, I decided to take the PD's early retirement offer, David is thinking about retiring too, and you're coming home. Life is good."

Mark and I have been friends for most of the fifteen years I've been a cop and for the three years I've worked the Burglary Unit in Detectives, he's been my boss. We've been through lots together, especially these last few months with all my shootings and the horrific aftermath. He's been a wonderful friend; me, not so much, and I desperately want to change that.

The driver, laughing at something the other cabbie said, struggles to squeeze his bulk behind the steering wheel. "Yes, sir, spent eighteen months in Saigon back in nineteen sixty-eight and sixty-nine," he says, as if our conversation hadn't had a two-minute break. He turns up the fan. "It's hot here, eh? Eighty-six today. Thinking of changing my policy to 'No shirt, no pants, no problem.' So hot I saw a funeral procession stop at a Dairy Queen for ice cream. But hey," he laughs, "don't mean nothin' compared to Vietnam's heat. They probably don't say 'don't mean nothin'' over there. No, probably don't. But the heat over there, it was somethin' for sure." He shakes his head, and guides the car around the long line of cabs and takes the ramp out of the airport pick-up area. "*Tet* is their New Year celebration, you know. When New Years happened in nineteen sixty-eight, it was one crazy-ass time. VC hit us so damn hard from so many directions we didn't know if we was comin' or goin'. Crazy-ass time, for sure."

"Thanks for your service," I say. "It's a beautiful city today. Most of the population now weren't alive during the war." I see a folded newspaper on his dash. "Is that today's paper?"

"No, sir," he says, retrieving it, though he can barely reach it because his belly is already pressed to the max against the steering wheel. "It's two days old, but I've been savin' it 'cause of what happened. You been gone for a spell, right?"

"About two weeks."

"Crazy-ass thing happened right here in Portland—my hometown, no less. Sadness for sure, right there on the front page. Never thought I'd see such a thing again. No, sir. Didn't think I'd see it again. Not in my hometown."

I unfold the paper. The large font headline reads: AFRICAN AMERICAN FOUND LYNCHED.

> An elderly African American man was found hanging from a rope tied to a light post at NW Third and Couch Street early this morning, according to Portland Police Spokesperson Darryl Anderson. An early morning jogger found the body. Anderson says foul play is suspected in the hanging. There are no suspects at this time, and the name of the victim is being withheld until notification of next of kin.

It must have happened right at press time because the piece is short but definitely not sweet.

"What have the follow-up stories said," I ask.

"The po-lice aren't sayin' much. Must be gettin' their ducks in a row or somethin'. Yesterday they didn't say his name, only they thought he was in his seventies. Po-lice got no suspects, or least they aren't sayin'. I think it's 'cause it's sensitive, you know. Some folks had a rally outside the downtown po-lice station last night demanding to know what's goin' on."

I refold the paper. This is going to be huge. I know the local press and every other major news organization across the country, and probably every black church, black community leader, and civil rights organization are swamping the PD with calls right now.

"The shit's about to hit the fan," the cabbie says. I nod, looking out the side window. When I look back toward the front, I see the cabbie's eyes studying me in the mirror. "You're a po-liceman, right?"

Oh man. I'm back in Portland less than an hour and I'm recognized. It's been almost two months since my mug was splashed all over the bloodthirsty news and everyone wanted to kick my butt, and I was hoping being out of sight meant I'd be out of mind. Guess not. I look out the side window again and wait for him to order me out of his cab.

"Yes, sir. I thought it was you when you walked up to my cab. I got an eye and a memory for faces. Recognized you from the TV news. I'm a news junkie, you know." I keep looking out the window. "Remembered your physique too. You must be a lifter." Out of the corner of my eye I see him look back at my arms. I'm wearing a dark blue polo shirt. "Lordy," he says, shaking his head.

We ride in silence for half a minute, and I can feel him looking at me through his rearview mirror.

"Hey, man. The shit hit the fan for you didn't it? Lots of people sayin' bad stuff about the po-lice when you killed the little boy. Me, I wasn't one of them. I saw a lot of shit in 'Nam and I got a cousin back in Baltimore who's on the PD—city cop. I know personally how somethin' can go down and how it can turn to shit in a quick hurry."

He doesn't say anything for a minute, which I'm thinking is hard for him to do. I look toward the rearview mirror, and into his eyes.

"Yes, sir. Everybody says I talk too much, especially my wife. Guess I do. But do you mind if I say something—just a little worthless advice from a man who's been where you are. For me it was during the war, a short ways outside of the city you just visited."

"I don't know. I'm pretty tired. Actually, I'm very tired."

"Just a quick comment, sir. For what it's worth, that's all. My sweet mama, God rest her soul, used to say to me and my six sisters, 'If God sends us on strong paths, we are provided strong shoes.'" He shakes his head and does the loud guffaw again. "I was barefoot for a while after I come home, yes sir. Then I found me some strong shoes." He looks into my eyes. "I've been driving a cab for thirty years and I know how to read people, probably better than some of these shrinks getting a hundred dollars an hour. I can tell you're a good man. I wish you luck, brother."

"What's your name?" We're on the freeway now, heading west toward the city. "Rudolph Abraham Lincoln, the third. I go by Rudy."

"Well, thank you, Rudy," I say softly. "I'm Sam. You're very kind."

"You are most welcome, Sam. Mind if I ask you your take on this lynching?"

"I don't have one yet. I've only been back an hour and just now read this. My educated guess is if the perp isn't apprehended quickly things are going to get bad. And if it turns out to be racially motivated, things are going to get even worse."

"Yes, sir. I hear you."

"It's fastest if you take the Forty-Seventh Street exit and head south ... Oh, sorry. I guess if you've been driving for thirty years you know your way around."

"Yes, sir," he says, taking the exit. "Tell me, there been many crimes like this lately? They call 'em hate crimes, don't they? Were you on the department when all the skinhead nonsense was going on in the early nineties?"

"Came on in ninety-five, but I know what you're referring

to. There were lots of hate crimes back then. Of late, I don't know. I was off for nearly two months. Kinda kept my head buried in the sand for a while, plus I've been in Saigon for the last several days. I haven't a clue as to what's happening."

My cell rings. It's Mark.

"Mark! What's going on? I landed at five and called you several—"

"Sam ..." Voice weak, strained.

"Mark? What is it?"

Long pause—ragged breathing.

"Mark? What's going on? Are you okay?"

His words come in a nonstop rush. "David and I were attacked. We were just sitting by the river and he's unconscious. I'm okay. We're at Emanuel Hospital can you come here?"

* * *

Rudy could easily be a Saigon cab driver. I ask him to take me to Emanuel Hospital as quickly as he can, and he pulls a one-eighty so fast, if my seatbelt wasn't fastened, I would have been thrown against the door. We're heading south on North-east Thirty-Third now and breaking multiple traffic laws. I'm glad I didn't say "really fast."

I ask Mark what happened and all he says is they got jumped by several people, and beaten. He barely manages to say it before erupting into a coughing fit, followed by a lot of moaning. I tell him to stop talking. I'm on my way.

Mark is a tough guy. Almost thirty years as a cop, a hardcore jogger, bicyclist, and swimmer. He competed in Hawaii's Iron Man event at the age of fifty-two. He's fifty-eight now and still fit and strong. David is a dentist and trains just as hard on the same three events. None of those things makes them fighters, but it does give them an edge over a pot-bellied couch potato. How could this have happened?

Mark has always been a good friend but I had strained that bond. Just before I left for Saigon, I had been swept into actions in Portland that while in defense of my family's lives and my own, were nonetheless illegal. I didn't tell anyone, but Mark is a good cop and he guessed I was somehow involved. I should have trusted him and told him. Instead I had lied to him, lied by omission, anyway. He called me in Saigon and we worked it out. It's still not over but I'm relieved Mark and I are back on solid ground.

Rudy makes a hard left on Knott Street, blowing through the yellow traffic signal and taking the turn nearly on two wheels.

"Three miles, sir. We're makin' good time."

"Thank you, Rudy."

"Excuse me, but I heard part of your conversation. Is this person who is hurt a good friend?"

"Yes, a longtime friend, and my boss."

"Any arrests?"

"I didn't ask. He was hurting pretty bad."

"He black?"

"No, why?"

He shrugs. "It just popped into my head there could be a connection to the lynching. I get feelings about things sometimes." He shrugs again. "Doesn't sound like it, though."

Connection? Not unless both turn out to be hate crimes. Mark said they were walking by the river but didn't say if it was the Columbia or the Willamette. I'm guessing the Willamette since it has walkways on each side with a nice view of the downtown area from the east side. Why would someone attack them? They're not a threat to anyone. They're both nearing sixty and are more about exploring museums and antique stores. Neither one is effeminate so it's hard to imagine they were selected because someone just guessed they're gay.

As we cross Martin Luther King Boulevard, Rudy says, "Two blocks, Sam. You want me to wait?"

"I don't know how long I'll be. I'll pay up so you can go about your business."

Rudy nods as he crosses Vancouver Avenue and heads toward the entrance to Emanuel. "You're goin' to need a ride home, right? It can be hard to get a cab this time of the evening on a Friday. I'll wait for you." When I start to protest, he says, "I got a break comin' so I'll just take it here. They got a nice cafe. If you take longer than forty-five minutes, I'll head out."

"Okay, Rudy. You really don't have to do this, but I appreciate it."

"Yes, sir. Besides, maybe someone will do my cousin a favor, the one who's a cop in Baltimore. Being black and a cop isn't always easy for him." He parks the cab on the ER side of the hospital. "Where you meetin' your buddy?"

"Good question. I forgot to ask. The front desk will know where he is."

I'm out of the car and standing by the fender as Rudy works his girth out from behind the steering wheel. "My wife calls me 'Fatty McButterpants,'" he says, standing and catching his breath. "I tell her it's her fault 'cause she's such a good cook."

We wind our way between several rows of parked cars. A KGW News van and a KOIN News van are parked side by side across from the ER entrance. There must have been a shooting or something.

"Always somethin' goin' on here," Rudy says. "Been here lots of times with fares who got themselves sick, shot, or stabbed. One guy got all three done to him. The front desk is to the right just inside the door."

The last time I was here I was cradling Jimmy in my arms. I shudder. I sense Rudy looking at me. Thankfully, he doesn't ask what's wrong.

The glass doors slide open and we hang a right into the air conditioning. The elderly woman behind the desk is talking with a large, Hawaiian-looking woman. The big woman thanks her and heads quickly toward the elevators.

"I'm looking for Mark Sanderson," I tell the woman. "He was brought in some time today with a David Rowe."

"You a friend or relative?"

"Friend."

"Don't need to look them up on the computer. Lots of people interested in them today—police, the TV. Everyone is up on the second floor. I don't know if they will let you see them but it's where they are. Sad about what happened. It's been crazy," she says, looking behind me at someone else needing directions.

"I hope everything will be okay, Sam," Rudy says. He points to a hallway to our right. "Coffee shop is down there. I'll wait 'bout forty minutes, forty-five."

I nod, too stunned to speak, and hurry toward the elevator.

The elevator doors swoosh open on the second floor to reveal a crowd of police brass and reporters. The press doesn't look my way but the cops do, some with blank faces, a few with slow nods. Chief Rodriguez looks at me for a long moment before giving me a single nod, then continuing his conversation with Deputy Chief Glanville. My fans. Gotta love 'em. Only Captain Regan smiles and moves toward me.

"Sam, how are you doing?" he says.

"Captain," I say, shaking his hand. Bill Regan is the Captain of Detectives, my top boss. He's a good one, a hundred percent supportive of his people. He and Mark have been a dream to work for. "I just got back into town. Mark was supposed to pick me up at the airport but he called me about twenty-five minutes ago. Said he and David got assaulted."

Regan nods. "He and David were walking on the River Walk on the east side of the Willamette when some assholes jumped them, don't know for sure how many. Thumped them good. Mark has a lot of lacerations and some torso bruising where they stomped his chest. Docs looked him over and patched some of his cuts. Nothing broken. David is in rough shape. Still unconscious. They're doing all kinds of X-rays and scans."

Adrenaline charges through my muscles, pushing away my jet lag. I don't know what my eyes are doing, but Captain Regan takes a step toward me, his eyes looking intently into mine. His voice is low, his words just for my ears. "This is the time for cool heads, Sam." I don't say anything.

"You hear me?"

I nod. "Yes."

He looks at me for a beat longer, then over at a camera crew. "Just once, I'd like to catch whoever calls the press whenever a cop is involved in something. Anyway, the Fat Dicks caught the case and are still in there talking to Mark. We'll know more details when they've finished their—"

"Excuse me." An Asian nurse smiles at the captain. "Are you Sam Reeves?"

"I am," I say.

She turns toward me. "Sorry. Someone over there pointed

at you two. Mark Sanderson is asking for you."

"Oh, okay," I say. "Captain, I'll let you know what I find out."

Regan nods and I follow the nurse through the crowd.

"Detective Reeves," a female voice to my left calls out before we get to the doors. I recognize the woman as a KOIN reporter. "May we get a comment from you? Why are you here?"

"Does this have anything to do with your shooting?" asks a male voice from behind me. Shoulder mounted cameras that had been sitting on the floor are quickly lifted into place and aimed at me.

I ignore them and follow the nurse through a set of swinging doors and into a large room with a series of small rooms formed by curtains along each wall, some empty, some with their curtains drawn. Men and women in pale green scrubs dart about busily. Mark waves to me from where he is sitting outside of one of the rooms, its curtain drawn.

"Mark," I say, rushing over to him. Grimacing, he scoots to the edge of his chair, tries to get up but his body changes his mind. He looks like hell: bandaged forehead and hand, abrasions on both pale cheeks and chin, and a wide-eyed, confused look I've seen a hundred times on the faces of trauma victims.

"Sam, I ... David is hurt bad."

"Mark," I whisper, kneeling down on one knee next to him. I gently touch his shoulder, not knowing where he hurts. "What on earth? Are you hurt badly? Is David in this room?"

He slowly scoots back until his back is flush with the chair, closes his eyes, and exhales as if it's all he can manage. "No. He's in X-ray right now. I think they're bringing him back here but I don't know for sure. He's got tubes sticking in him, he's hooked up to machines ... God." Mark takes a slow, laborious inhalation and eases it out. "They kicked him ... over and over ... in his head. I tried to help him but two of them were on me. They had me ... down, punching and kicking me."

"They hurt your head," I say, tentatively lifting my hand toward it but not touching him. It's hard for my jet-lagged brain to compute my friend is hurt. Ninety-nine percent of me is still back in Saigon. Stepping off the plane into Portland's airport and the cab ride on the city streets was a culture shock after the chaos and intensity of my ten days in Vietnam. It's hard to catch up. "I mean, damn, Mark. What do the doctors say about you?"

"ER released me," he says. "Nothing broken. Ribs are badly bruised. It's a little hard to breathe and to ... talk. I cough a lot, which really hurts. They stomped on my chest and my side. I hit one of them. I might have fractured a knuckle."

"Are the suspects in custody?"

He shakes his head. "White ... late teens, early twenties. There are these ... benches along the walkway. It was about three this afternoon and Mark and I ... we were sitting on one looking out at the river, having a Starbucks and sharing a muffin. We were sitting close to each other. Guess it gave us away. I saw them coming in my peripheral but I didn't think anything about it. I was aware of them again, out of the corner of my eye, when they were about fifty feet away. When my cop instinct finally kicked in, I scooted away from David a little. But it was too late. The young men were moving straight at us saying things like ... 'faggots' and 'butt rangers' and the like. We stood and ... started walking in the opposite ... direction but they were on us."

"Can you ID them?"

He nods through a cough spasm, clearly in pain. "For sure

the ones who worked me over. Maybe the two who got David, I don't know. They split in the direction they came from. No one else on the walkway, so no witnesses, none I know of, anyway. Fat Dicks are on it. They got my report and left just a couple ..." Mark coughs into the crook of his arm. He takes a deep breath, then, "They left a couple of minutes before you got here. Must have left a back way. Didn't ... want to deal with the press."

"I'm so sorry about this, Mark. I'm so pissed right now I can't think straight."

His scabbed lips smile ever so slightly. "Do I look as bad as you? Jet lag is special, isn't it?"

"No, you win, you look worse. What can I do right now? You want a lift home? I got a cab waiting."

He shakes his head. "Got to wait to find out about David. It might ... take a long time, hours maybe. I think he's going to get a room on one of the upper floors. They said I ... I could stay with him. I'll just sleep. Got me on some crazy meds."

"I'll stay with you."

"No. I just wanted to see you now that you're home. Seeing you makes me feel better. Safer, for some reason." He starts to smile but it ends up being a grimace. "Not exactly cop buddy banter, eh?"

I shrug. "We're friends first."

He pats my hand. "Yes, we are. Go home now and get some rest. I want ... to hear about Saigon when we're both in better shape."

"Okay. Call me when you're ready to leave and I'll come and get you."

He leans his head back against the wall and blinks slowly a couple times. "Deal. Glad you're back ... Sam." His eyes flutter shut and his face relaxes.

I ask a passing nurse to point out another way down to the first floor and she directs me to a stairwell. I find the number for Captain Regan in my cell phone and tap it in. By the time I'm done filling him in on Mark, I'm in the first floor lobby and half hiding behind a coffee cart. I don't want to deal with the media.

"Thanks, Sam," Captain Regan says. "On another matter, you ready to come back to work?"

I knew that was coming. The shooting was two months ago and I haven't been back since. The police shrink Doc Kari's last words before I went to visit Samuel and Mai in Saigon was it was my decision when I want to go back. The unwritten guide for cops who have dropped the hammer on someone is you don't return until you know you could do it again. No cop who has ever been forced to kill on the job wants a repeat of the experience, but the police shrink, the department, and the officer in question need to know he or she can do it again if required. A cop who can't decide, or knows for certain he can't, has no business on the street. The officer's life, as well as those of other officers and citizens, might depend on him doing exactly that.

For the past two months, I've been telling my father and myself I will never again pick up a gun. I kept the proclamation even when I was in Saigon, and I was thrust into the middle of a deadly shooting. But now, after talking to Mark, it's like I suddenly have an itch to get back and do some police work. I want to have it both ways, but I know I can't.

"I don't know, boss. I plan to make an appointment with the shrink tomorrow and talk about it. I'm sorry. I wish I had a solid answer for you."

"I understand, Sam. Just know Deputy Chief Rodriguez wants to put your name back in Personnel as unassigned so we can fill your spot in Burglary. He was talking about doing it last week so it might have already happened. If it has, don't worry about it. If you're ready, I want you back and I'll make it happen."

"Thanks, Captain. I'll call you as soon as I know what's going on." I stuff my cell back into my pocket and, not seeing any reporters, step out from behind the coffee cart. Rudy waves to me from where he is talking to the elderly woman behind the information desk. She is laughing at something he said. Quite the gregarious guy.

"How's your friend?" Rudy asks, leading the way to the cab.

"He's hurting and his partner is in bad shape. Still unconscious."

He shakes his head. "Sorry to hear it, Sam. You said partner. Were they on duty?"

Whoops. I didn't want to get into all that. But why shouldn't I? Mark's relationship with David isn't a secret. In fact, it's been going on for years while most of the hetero marriages I know of on the PD have crashed and burned.

"My friend is gay," I say, watching him for a reaction. He opens the driver's door, not giving me one.

"Ooooh, all right, all right," he says over the roof. "Explains things some. Get in the front seat there if you want, Sam."

I slide in and shut my door while Rudy struggles to fit in behind the wheel again. The seat is pushed back as far as it will go.

"Was it a, what do they call it, a gay bashing?"

I nod. "Looks like it. Perps are still on the loose."

He backs out of the slot and winds us through the lot back

out onto the street. "Another hate crime, right? Sons-of-a-bitches. Three now, if it turns out the lynching is one."

"Three?"

"I forgot, you been gone. 'Bout a week ago some fool threw a firebomb at the Muslim Community Center up in Northwest Portland—the one on Twenty-Fifth. Nobody hurt and the fire went out before it could damage anything on the building. Oh, hold the boat. There was a cross burning too. Southwest, near Council Crest. Make it four."

"Has anyone been arrested?"

He shrugs. "Haven't heard anything except a few TV news stories about Muslims being afraid and sayin' how they are people of peace." He looks over at me. "What do you think, Sam? What does it all mean?"

I shrug. "Hate crimes for sure. Several white guys attacked my two friends. Could they have lynched a black man? Sure. Could they have attacked the Muslim center? Sure. But usually haters focus on one or two groups. But who knows? What do you think?"

"I think there's too much hate in the world. People get intimidated, scared so they turn to hate. Maybe hate gives them some kind of power over what scares them. Don't know if it fits, but my mama used to say church gives some people just enough religion to hate but not enough to love."

"Your mother was a wise woman."

"Yes, sir," Rudy chuckles as he turns right onto Martin Luther King Boulevard. "She was a wonderful ... Uh-oh. I forgot my dispatcher warned us to avoid this part of MLK today and here I drove us right into this mess. Folks demonstratin' again in front of the clinic."

At least two hundred people are blocking the street in front of the Northeast Women's Center, a well-known family planning clinic that performs abortions. Looks like about every other person is waving a sign:

CHILDREN KILLED HERE
STOP ABORTION NOW
BABY GOOD, BABY KILLER BAD
PRO-LIFE AND PROUD

Several are holding long poles with naked, red paint-splattered dolls dangling from them.

There have been demonstrations here by pro-life groups as long as I can remember. The first year I worked by myself, I worked uniform in this part of town for about two months. Got called here twice for crowd control. The first call was no big deal but on the second one a few weeks later, there were pro-choice and pro-life groups clashing hard. I caught the call and like the dumb rookie I was, I waded right into the middle of it before my backup arrived. When a guy pushed me from behind, I spun around and leg swept him to the sidewalk. Who knew he was the national president of "A Woman's Right to Choose," one of the largest pro-choice groups out of New York City? The man had flown into Portland to give a speech only to be launched face first onto the sidewalk by little ol' me. He wasn't hurt badly, but face injuries tend to bleed a lot, which fired up his people into breaking out windows and attacking the police. Since I had waded into the crowd without backup, and it was me who dumped the guy, and since I had less than a year on the job, I decided it best not to mention it was my action that fueled the riot.

Right now, a dozen cops wearing black helmets and black, heavily padded chest and leg protection are guarding the front door, standing stoically unresponsive to the demonstrators surging toward them, backing away, and surging toward them again. The cops aren't about to get suckered into their antics.

Rudy twists in his seat to back us up, but we move only a foot or two before he has to anchor it. "There's a truck on our butt and crazy folks squeezing between the bumpers."

"This demo is bigger than usual," I say, looking at a middle-aged man standing in front of our car and thrusting a sign at us: JESUS FORGIVES YOU. Brother, I hope so.

"A girl died here last week," Rudy says. "I only read part of the story but I think she was about sixteen. Guessin' it's what this is all about."

New arrivals stream around the cab heading toward the clinic. Someone pounds on our trunk lid.

"Hey!" Rudy shouts, unsnapping his seatbelt.

"Stay in the car," I say. The guy with the JESUS FORGIVES YOU sign is thumping the butt of his stick on the hood now. Rudy leans on the horn.

"Don't honk, Rudy. It draws more attention to us. It doesn't take much for an ugly crowd like this to turn real ugly. Okay, the truck's starting to back up. Let's follow it."

But there are people pressed up against both sides of the cab now, so many all we can see are crotches, bellies, and belt buckles. Someone starts pounding the roof and then another and another. It sounds like it's raining baseball-sized hail.

My door opens but only a few inches before the weight of all the bodies shuts it again.

"Lock your door!" I shout, but Rudy's is already open. Mine opens again while I look for the lock button on the armrest.

A hand grabs at my face. I snap my head back and grab the man's pinkie and ring fingers with my left hand and his middle and index fingers with my right. The Japanese call it *yubi tori*, a finger hold, but my students call it "make a wish." I yank the two sets of fingers in opposite directions. Even over the roof pounding, I can hear the hand's owner scream. I push his arm away and pull my door shut, lock it, and turn to Rudy. What the hell?

If my new friend's stomach wasn't so big, the protestor's head would probably be pressed against the big man's lap. But since there's no room, Rudy has braced the side of the bearded fellow's face against the steering wheel with one hand and is pinching a wad of the man's eyelid with his other.

"Which do you like the most?" the big cabbie asks calmly. "When I do this?" He pulls the flap of skin at least an inch away from the terrified man's weeping eye. "Or this?" He twists the skin right and left as if trying to get a key to open a lock. I can't tell if the man is screaming because of the pain or from the utter horror of the technique. It's probably about fifty-fifty.

The weight of the crowd has been pressing the driver's door against the man's lower body holding him in place, but the easily bored mob abruptly abandons their peer for greener pastures, this time to something happening at the front of the clinic.

"Better catch up to your homeboys," Rudy says, releasing the man's eyelid. He palms the bearded face as if it were a hairy basketball and pushes him out of the cab. The guy sprawls onto his back and covers his face with his hands. Other protestors step over him. The roof pounding has stopped now that everyone has rushed off. Over by the building I can see riot police spraying the crowd with pepper spray.

"Back up this unit now!" a cop dressed a little like Darth Vader shouts, slapping his palm on the hood of the cab. His shiny black helmet, tinted visor, and heavily padded uniform are definitely intimidating. "Follow the truck out of here," he barks. "Do it now, driver!" From behind the riot control officer, a female protestor, dressed in a black peacoat, army fatigue pants, and wearing a bandana over her face, smashes the officer across his back with a white cross. Two other black uniformed officers grab her and take her to the pavement.

"The truck is backing, Rudy," I say, looking out the back window. "Let's do it."

"Oh my," Rudy says, backing us up. "This was somethin'. This was surely somethin'."

"It was but it could have been worse. There's a driveway. See it? Back into it and get us turned around so we can head out of here front end first."

* * *

"You okay?" I ask. Rudy has pulled to the curb a few blocks from the women's clinic and is patting his chest with his palm.

"I got to go on a diet, for sure. My old heart works overtime just to pack my ass around and when I got to do somethin' harder than eatin' chips, it feels like my ticker is goin' to bust right out of my chest. The wife and my four daughters are ridin' me all the time to lose some weight."

"Sounds like they love you," I say, watching his face for signs he might pass out.

He laughs, which sends his belly rolling and his shoulders shaking. "Guess you're right. Yes, sir."

"Where did you learn the eyelid technique?"

He laughs even harder, which shakes the cab like we're in a magnitude four earthquake. "You like it? Works every time. Learned it in the army from a ranger. He taught me it was the best way to get a man's attention. He was right too. I've used it many times on ornery drunk fares who didn't want to pay me. What about you? Your friend is going to remember you every time he goes to use his hand or what's left of it."

"I teach martial arts."

"Oh, right. I remember from the news. Some people burned down your school, or somethin'."

I nod, flashing to that awful night watching my school burn. I flinch at the memory of the events leading up to it and of the crazy turn my life had taken. I learned there is a word for it: *dukkha*. Most cops never fire their weapon in their career, but in one eight-week period, I got into two shootings, one in which I accidentally shot and killed an innocent child. The "accidental" part doesn't make it any easier.

Then I met my father. A man I thought had died in the Vietnam War suddenly became a part of my life. With him came a family life I had been sorely missing since my grandfather and my mother passed away. It's been more than wonderful that in one of life's great coincidences we found each other, but along with this joy came more violence. Seems like crazy *dukkha* runs in the family.

But then there is Mai, the most incredible woman I've ever met. I started having feelings for her the moment I saw her. It was devastating at first thinking she was my sister, but happily she isn't. She is an unrelated stepsister and we have fallen, as she says in her rough English, "asshole over tea kettle in love."

"They did burn it down. I'll probably rebuild. Right now I'm holding classes in the basement of a church where one of my brown belts preaches."

"Too cool. Hey, you think I'm too old and too fat to learn the art?" He makes chopping motions on his steering wheel with the edge of his palm.

"Mmm," I say, giving him an up and down appraisal. "Yes."

Rudy looks at me, sees my smirk, and does that whole-body laugh of his. "Okay, okay. First I get it from my wife and daughters and now from you. Okay."

I lightly punch his massive shoulder. "Just messing with you, Rudy. You're never too old. I had a male student in his seventies and an overweight grandmother in her sixties. It would get you in shape for sure."

He's still chopping his steering wheel. "I just might do it. Yes, sir. First there was Bruce Lee and now there's goin' to be Rudy Lee."

I laugh at his antics. "And you can teach me the eyelid technique. I've heard of it but I never saw it in action."

"I'll do it, yes, sir. Right now, I should get you home. My dispatcher is probably wonderin' what I'm doin'."

Rudy pulls away from the curb and chuckles. "Rudy Lee. I like the sound of it. No, no, no. How 'bout Rudy Van Damme?" He hangs a left on Hawthorne. "So how is the chubby grandmother and seventy-year-old man doin'?"

"Not too well. They both died."

"Say what?"

I laugh. "They're both doing fine."

"Okay," he says, pointing at me. "Got to watch you every second."

Ten minutes later we're parked in my driveway.

"What's the damage?" I ask, helping Rudy pull my luggage from his trunk. I wave at Bill, my neighbor. He nods reluctantly. Probably mad because my lawn is overgrown and because of the hubbub here a few weeks ago.

"Let's see," Rudy says. " I got to deduct the time I was in the coffee shop at the hospital, the fun we had at the demonstration, the laughs we had talkin' after ... I'd say I owe you about fifteen dollars."

"We did have a good time, didn't we? It kind of pushed the jet lag right out of me."

"Gimme twenty dollars to satisfy the boss and maybe you can buy me a burger one of these noon hours."

"Let's make it thirty dollars and I'll buy you a salad with vinegar and oil dressing."

He laughs. "Okay, okay. It's a deal. Here's my card."

I hand him mine. "I will call you, Rudy."

*   *   *

I'm sipping a cup of green tea, a two-bagger, which should give me a little shot of energy to get through the rest of the evening. Got the front and back door open to air out the place and I've let all the faucets run for a minute to flush out the rust. No one broke in while I was gone, which I always worry about and, except for the lawn, the place is in good shape. Mai and I washed all my clothes before I left Saigon so I just got to put my things in drawers. It's midmorning in Vietnam and there is where my mind and body are right now. It took me about three days to get over the time difference when I got to Saigon so I'm figuring about the same coming home.

It's a little after eight p.m. and in the time I've been back in Portland, I visited my best friend in the hospital, did a little jujitsu in the front of a cab, and I made a new friend. Can I pack a lot into three hours or what?

Mai is probably in her office working on the jewelry stores' books, or maybe tending to her sick mother. Kim's TB is worsening and though no one has come out and said as much, I don't think she has much longer to live.

I tap in about twenty-five numbers, listen to all the clanking, dead air, some creaks, and finally, ringing.

"This is the devil talking," Mai says, "who do you want?"

I laugh. "That's almost how it goes."

"Sam," she whispers, her voice heating up my face. "Are you in Portland?"

"I made it back sort of in one piece," I say, imagining all five feet eleven inches of gorgeousness sitting by the koi pond in their ornate backyard, the color-splashed, wiggling fish nibbling at her dabbling fingertips—lucky fish.

"I miss you," she says softly.

"I miss you more."

"You are probably correct."

"How is your mother?"

Long pause, then in a halting voice, "Oh, Sam. I am so scared. She talked about dying last night. Father got angry with her and I just cried. This morning she acted like she had not talked about it at all."

"I'm so sorry, Mai. How is Father?"

"He is quiet. When he is not with Mother, he sits by the koi pond. I am worried about both of them. If something happens to Mother ... I do not know what will happen to him. He lost his teacher nine days ago and if he loses Mother ..."

When my father dropped into my life, Mai was attending Portland State University and was about to graduate with a degree in business. My father, who is Mai's stepfather, traveled to Portland to see her graduate. Over the years he kept abreast of his hometown by regularly reading the *Oregonian* newspaper online, and two years ago he came across a story about my mother's death in a traffic accident. The story caught his eye because around the time he went into the service he had dated a young girl with the same last name. When he read she was survived by, at the time, a thirty-two-year-old son, Sam Reeves—his first name—as well as the same number of years he had been in Vietnam, he put two and two together. He was captured after only a few months in Vietnam, and if she had mailed him about being pregnant, he never received the letter. After he read about my mother, he would see my name ever so often in the online newspaper regarding a police case. He also found Internet sites about my martial arts and my competition years when I was younger. A few weeks before he came over, and probably the deciding factor in meeting me, he read I had shot an armed robber.

"Mai, I wish I could say or do something to make all this better. I hate to see you hurting."

She doesn't say anything for a moment, then, "You are doing something by being here for me."

"I can say the same thing to you."

I tell her about what happened to Mark and David, my new friend Rudy, and our run-in at the women's clinic.

"How sad about Mark. I know he is a good friend; I hope to meet him some day."

"When you come."

"With Mother sick, I do not know when I can."

"Don't worry about it right now, Mai. There is where your head should be, with your mother. We'll make it happen when the time is right. And I can always come back over." Neither of us speaks for a moment. Then I hear her sniff. "Mai?"

"What did you call it ... LDR?"

"Yes, we have a long-distance relationship. Some couples say they have an LDR when they live a hundred miles from each other in different cities. We live nearly eight thousand miles apart so we win the LDR. But no two hearts are more together than ours."

She sniffs a couple of times. "That was good, Sam."

"It was, wasn't it?" We both laugh.

"Have you think—*er*—thought more about what you want to do?"

"Sorta. I thought I was pretty certain about resigning from the PD, but after talking with Mark at the hospital, I don't know. My original reasons for joining the PD came rushing back."

"We talked about it before and you said it was because you hate bullies."

"That's the simple reason, yes, although bully is a pretty feeble word for what's going on. It angers me my friend was hurt because of who he is. Also, I've heard there have been a series of possible hate crimes. Most recently a black man was found lynched from a lamppost. I haven't heard yet if it was a hate crime, but I'm betting it was."

"Hate crime?"

"It's an additional charge on someone who commits a crime against another person because of their race, religion, sexual orientation, and other things."

"Oh yes. We talked about it once in a class at Portland State. I think the professor called it a bias? Yes, a bias crime. I think Portland had a lot of it."

"There was a huge wave of it about twenty years ago. It seems like every twenty years or so, it flares up and there will be a lot of incidents for a while, and then it will die down again. To me, it's bullying at its ugly worst."

"It sounds like you decided. I think the protector in you is deciding."

"I don't know. Maybe. I'm just more confused than ever. And there's another not so little issue. I don't want to ever pick up a gun again."

"You have to wear one, right? To be a policeman?"

"Yes, every officer must. There are desk jobs but still you must carry one."

Mai is quiet for a moment, then, "When you were here you said you could live in Saigon."

"I did, and I still think so. But I'm not sure Vietnam is where I'm supposed to be. Samuel, er, Father said he sees my destiny here, in Portland."

"Oh," she says in a small, disappointed voice. Mai holds our father and his beliefs in high regard. So do I.

"He also said you could end up here, in Portland. With me."

"He did?" More perky. "When did he say it?"

"We had a long talk the night before I left. I certainly don't have his ability to see, but I think things are about to change for all of us."

"Mm." Long pause. "Thinking about it makes me happy, sad, and scared."

"Me too."

My doorbell rings.

"Someone come?" she asks.

I scoot my chair back. "A little surprise for you—actually, a big one. Be right back."

"Hey, Todd," I say after opening the door. "Thanks so much for doing this. I would have come after her."

"No problem, Sensei," the big man says, stroking the white cat cradled in his arm. She looks lazily toward me and her eyes widen in recognition.

"Hi, Chien. Have you missed me?"

She meows and reaches a paw toward me.

"Aaw," Todd groans. Then in baby talk, "I sure have, daddy waddy. I missed you sooo much I cwy and I cwy." Todd stands six foot three and is a second-degree black belt.

"Uh, ooookay, Todd."

He laughs and hands Chien over to me. She snuggles into the crook of my bent arm like it was designed with her in mind. "Like I said on the phone, I was coming this way, anyway." He picks up a bag of cat food from the porch. "She went through two of these while you were gone. Eats like a Marine."

Chien is rubbing the side of her face against my chest. "Just let me know how much I owe you for litter, food, and shredded curtains."

"No charge, Sensei. The kids loved her and she didn't hurt a thing. Of course, now I got to get them a cat. Have you ever noticed Chien is more dog than cat? I mean it's like eerie. She even fetches."

We say our goodbyes and I head for the phone. Chien is really Mai's cat. She gave her to me to take care of when she went back to Saigon. I was going to try to take it to her when I went there, but Chien got sick and the vet said she shouldn't travel. Chien means warrior in Vietnamese, a name Mai chose after the cat attacked a fellow student who thought studying together meant he could cop a feel.

"You still there, Mai?"

"No, I have gone to Timbuktu."

"Cute. Okay, listen." I put the phone next to Chien's purring face and hold it there for a moment. Then into the phone, "Guess who?"

"Chien! I miss her so much. How are you my little warrior?"

"She misses you too. You can see her when you come." I

refuse to say Chien "cwyed and cwyed and cwyed."

"Okay," she says softly. "Oh, Mother is ringing for me, Sam."

"I will talk to you tomorrow. I'll get my Skype set up and we can use it from now on."

"I am glad you are in my life, Sam. I love you."

"I love you too. Goodnight."

"It is 'good afternoon,' Sam. It is lunchtime here."

"*Phở*?" I ask, referencing the Vietnamese soup I had there so often.

"Yes. Talk to you tomorrow."

CHAPTER TWO

What a crappy night. I went to bed at ten p.m., which is early afternoon in Saigon, so I mostly tossed and turned and tossed some more until about four when I finally conked out. Woke up at eight with Chien trying to snuggle under my chin. Now I'm working on my second twelve-ounce coffee. I miss having *Trung-Nguyen*, Vietnamese coffee, though Starbucks French Roast is a distant second. My usual English muffin hidden under a ton of peanut butter isn't even close to the fresh Vietnamese fruit and French croissants I enjoyed with Mai.

Today's agenda: buy groceries, a toy for Chien, mow the lawn, call Doc Kari and set up an appointment, call Captain Regan and talk about the job, and call Chris Graham to see how the school is doing. Chris, known affectionately by all my students as "Padre," is a brown belt and a Baptist minister at the Davis Street Baptist Church. He and his church elders have allowed me to hold my martial arts classes in the basement until I can get established again in a place of my own. Which reminds me: I need to call the insurance company and check on the status of the payout for my lost school.

My cell sounds. Where did I leave it and who would be calling so early? I find it on the dining room table. It's a PD number. I answer.

"Detective Reeves?" Female voice, official sounding.

"Yes?"

"Good morning. This is Karen, Deputy Chief Rodriguez's assistant. The Deputy Chief would like to see you in his office this morning at ten."

Oh man. Early call, emphasis on the Deputy Chief's title and name, official tone, precise time, no discussion. How could a fella resist? The hell with any plans I might have.

"See you at ten, Karen."

"I'll advise the Deputy Chief. Thank you."

I can only guess what the look was about he gave me yesterday at the hospital. "Old salt," "old school," "old timer," "kill 'em all and let God sort 'em out" are just some of ways the troops describe him. The scuttlebutt is he despises the social worker approach police work has been moving toward the last fifteen years or so. He thinks police psychologists should be put in the same category as sacrificing goats to the Hawaiian volcano Goddess, *Pele*. At one of our in-service training sessions last year, he said, "You fall off a horse, you get back on. Likewise, you blow some son-of-a-bitch out of his socks, you go back to work the next day."

In honor of Rodriguez's opinion, I call Doc Kari's office knowing it's too early for anyone to be there.

"This is Doctor Stephens."

"Doc Kari! Hi. Didn't expect you in this time of the day. Thought you worked the eleven a.m. to one p.m. shift."

"Sam. How was Vietnam?"

"Hot. Tarzan jungle hot. I'm back and was hoping I could get a session in."

"Today at one. I'll work overtime." Kari is as tough as a Marine drill sergeant and looks even tougher. She doesn't spare words, she tolerates no b.s. and definitely no whining. She invented tough love.

"One it is. Thanks so mu—" Dial tone. Guess we're done chatting.

I tap in Mark's cell number.

"Sam," he says.

"How's it going?"

"David is still out. They're calling it a coma now. Jesus, Sam. A coma."

"Oh man. I suppose it's too soon for them to say what's going on."

Mark doesn't answer for a long moment, then, "An MRI showed blood in his brain and an EKG revealed some kind of an electrical pattern in his heart Doctor Vale said is abnormal. Right now, there's some concern he might lose his reflex for swallowing and ... for keeping his tongue forward. If it goes, his tongue can slide back and occlude his ... breathing."

"Oh, Mark. This is awful." When he doesn't say anything, I ask, "How are you?"

"I don't know. I'm probably hurting but I can't tell, they got me on some good meds."

"You decided when you're going home?"

"No."

"Okay. Just let me know. I got to see Rodriguez this morning."

"Shit."

"Well put. I don't know what he wants. To give me a medal, you think?" Mark snorts. "Then Doc Kari at one. I'll call you after my appointment with her and see how you're doing."

"Thanks, hoss. Good luck with Rodriguez. He'll probably threaten you or something. You know how he feels about officers taking time off after a shooting, right?"

"Oh yeah. Think I should take someone from the union with me."

"Not this first time. Hear him out first. I can't imagine him threatening you with termination or threatening to cut off your pay. He knows it wouldn't hold up in court. Maybe he just …" Mark coughs hard several times. "Sorry. Damn. The throat hit makes me cough, which is a real killer with bruised ribs. Anyway, let me know what he says."

"Will do. Hang in there and I'll call you in a couple three hours."

*   *   *

I don't park my pickup in the garage because the hanging heavy bag, dumbbell rack, and my shadowboxing space don't allow for it. I crack the big garage door about a foot to let in some air. I've debated since I got up whether to work out a little, but after talking to Mark I've got to burn off a little adrenaline. Chien glides over and sits on a gallon can of paint next to the wall, her usual spot when I work out.

I guess no one likes bullies, but I have a personal demon. I was always a little bigger than most of my classmates, so most of the time I wasn't the kid they picked on, except once. When I was in the third grade, three high school kids in a car started harassing me as I was walking home. I don't remember saying anything to them but knowing me I probably did. They jumped out, grabbed me, and dragged me behind a doughnut shop where they pushed me around and forced me to stand with my back to the wall while they decided what they were going to do to me. I remember I was shaking hard, crying, and wanting my mother. They held me there for a couple hours, while their friends came to look at me and laugh. When I had an opportunity to run, I took off like a bat out of hell and didn't stop until I was safe at home.

I can still feel the awful sense of helplessness and stark fear and embarrassment, all because some morons took pleasure in breaking a little kid. And although I know there was nothing I could have done—I was outnumbered and outsized—in my fantasies I go back to that moment and use my martial art skills to kick their butts, erasing the deep humiliation I felt. As I grew older I realized that bullies don't change, they just get bigger and stupider. They're basically cowards who use their power, be it size or money or superior number, to feel important, relevant—whatever they need I don't care, I still want to kick their butts.

I circle my arms to get the juices flowing, and do some leg raises to the front, side, and back. I circle my head a few times in each direction to loosen my neck a little. It still hasn't recovered from the fight we had in the warehouse in Vietnam. We rescued a few girls who had been kidnapped and were being held by sex traffickers. Sadly, they were the tip of the iceberg in the malicious human trading that goes on there, but we did what we could. The battle didn't end there and the owie will go away, but the memories of those events are going to last.

I shuffle around the floor snapping out jabs, rear-hand punches, and front kicks. I still feel like my brain has fur on it, but my muscles are starting to feel pretty darn good. I push the heavy bag away, sidestep, and slam a roundhouse kick into it. Take that Rodriguez. I bob, weave, and sidestep in the other direction to roundhouse kick the Deputy Chief with my other leg. After a dozen reps, I practice hitting in all three ranges by closing the distance with a front kick, cross punch, elbow strike, and a head butt. I move out of range with a two-handed push and a crescent kick. I do twenty reps of those.

I look over at Chien. Unimpressed, she blinks slowly, steps down from the paint can, and examines my old lawnmower.

She loves the smell of an unused lawnmower in the morning. I wonder how she would react to my father's martial workouts.

When I went to visit him in Saigon, he showed me concepts from Temple of Ten Thousand Fists, a style he has studied for two decades in Vietnam, with his Chinese teacher, Shen Lang Rui. Among other things, the style emphasizes extraordinary speed. Thing is, the word extraordinary doesn't begin to describe what appears to be almost supernatural.

One day he had me put my chest against a three-hundred-pound, three-foot thick hanging bag. When he hit it from the other side—I think with a punch, though I couldn't see because the bag was so monstrous—I was knocked back a step or two and my chest felt as if I had been hit by a laser. The supernatural part is the bag didn't move. My father said his goal is to hit the bag so the person on the other side feels it when standing a couple feet away from it. I've been training in the martial arts for twenty-eight years, and he makes me feel like a guy who hasn't even thought about taking his first lesson.

I simultaneously slap both sides of the bag to simulate smacking someone's ears and drop low to hook the lower part of the bag with both hands catching an imaginary attacker behind his knees for a takedown. I do twenty reps and finish with a few minutes of shadow boxing. Yeah, I feel good right now, but it's time to say bye to my high and go visit Deputy Chief Rodriquez.

Chien follows me into the shower. She likes to swat at the water drops on the shower door. I envy her simple life.

*   *   *

An elevator door in the Justice Center lobby opens and I slip in, happy to get the car to myself. When I came into the building a moment ago, cops chatting in groups or walking in and out of the building waved at me or gave me a "Hey, Sam." Others quickly looked away. It's nice to be greeted, and I read into it that they have empathy for me and for what happens to a police officer when he is forced to fire his weapon. I'm not sure what those who look away are thinking. Maybe they don't know what to say. Maybe they're just assholes.

When a cop is forced to use deadly force, he automatically becomes a member of a subgroup of cops, men and women who no longer wonder what it's like to face the dragon and make a sometimes split-second decision to shoot and maybe end a life. Often, those outside of this group are uncomfortable around the members of our thankfully small group, not sure how to act or knowing what to say around them. When they do speak, they sometimes err on the side of thoughtlessness, "Good shooting, Wild Bill," or "Righteous shoot, Deadeye." These officers might mean well but such comments are like salt on a wound. Happily, some officers know exactly what to say. "I'm glad you're okay" is always appreciated. It's simple and says it all.

I push the button for the fifteenth floor. The chief, his deputy chiefs, and their butt boys all reside on the top floor. Easier to piss on the little people from up there.

Oh man, when did I become so bitter?

"Karen," I say walking into the outer office. She was the Commander's secretary when I worked East Precinct about ten years ago. She's got to be in her fifties now, but looks to be taking care of herself. "You look great. Still jogging?"

"Good morning, Sam. I am. Ran with a bunch of other seniors in the Portland Marathon in February. I still do those freehand exercises you gave me when I was at East."

I remember writing up a little workout for her. "Well it shows. You look fantastic. I guess I'm supposed to see Deputy Chief Rodriguez."

"Yes, and sorry about my tone on the phone. My official voice. It didn't dawn on me who you were until after I hung up. Been making one call after the other all morning."

"Well, you got the voice down perfectly. I would have jumped through a fiery hoop, you were so commanding."

"Let me see if he's ready," she says, picking up the phone. "Detective Sam Reeves is here. Yes, sir." She hangs up and reaches for a folder. "Personnel just brought this over, Sam. It's yours but you can't look at it. Please take it in with you. His office is down the hallway, first on the left."

"Thanks, Karen," I say, taking the folder. "Is there a special knock and will he scream, 'Who dares knock on my door?'"

She laughs. "Even the toughest cops shake in their boots when they have to come up to the fifteenth floor. But don't worry, he'll greet you before you reach his door." She looks at me. "Nervous?"

"Should I be?"

"Detective Reeves, come." Deputy Chief Rodriguez is standing outside his office door dressed in dark slacks, a blue dress shirt, and a burgundy tie. He's at least fifty years old with coal black hair and a black, bushy moustache. I always thought he looked like a character from an old western movie, like a Mexican bandit. I'm not the only one. I've heard guys refer to him as *El Bandito*, among his many nicknames.

He doesn't offer his hand so I don't extend mine. "Enter. Ah, your file. I'll take it. Thank you. Sit there in front of my desk." He closes the door. "Talked with your lieutenant a while ago. He's drugged up pretty good. Best thing right now, I would think. Took a good beating. His, uh, partner. Sorry, I've forgotten his name."

"David, Chief."

"Oh yes. He's in bad shape. Coma, I'm told."

"Yes. Do you know how the investigation is going?"

"I don't. I'm to be briefed by Detectives Richard Cary and Richard Daniels at noon. They still call them the Fat Dicks?"

"Yes, sir. They even call themselves that."

"Good men, the both of them. Excellent investigators."

"Yes, sir. I agree."

What's with all the nicey-nice? Rodriguez get religion or something?

"Are they as good as you?"

"Sir?"

"Your captain and your lieutenant tell me you're an outstanding investigator."

Ooookay, I don't know what I expected to happen this morning but for sure I didn't expect to be stroked.

"I work Burglary, or I did work it. I've never worked serious assault or homicide. The Fat Dicks are experienced experts there."

"I know." He leans back in his chair taking my file with him. He crosses his legs and rests the folder on a knee. He scans the pages. "Ah, says you worked hate crimes in Intelligence a few years ago."

"Sort of. I did a month there while I was still on probation. The bureau had a program where rookies bounced around for two weeks to a month in various units. I thought it was good because you learned quickly about all the different jobs. But someone in their great wisdom nixed it for no reason I can fathom."

He looks over the folder at me. "That 'someone' was me."

Shit, shit, and triple shit. He looks at me for a moment, no doubt reading my realization—I just stepped on my Mr. Happy. Are his eyes twinkling? The SOB is enjoying my discomfort. Well, I'm not going to apologize because it was a good program and it shouldn't have gone away.

"Did you like it? Hate crimes?"

"I did. It was different, interesting, and sometimes it angered me."

"Angered?"

"Just knowing there are people who hurt others because of who they are."

"Think your lieutenant was hurt because of who he is?"

"Yes, sir."

"Your thoughts?"

"Sir?"

"Your boss is a homosexual. Your thoughts?"

"My thoughts on the assault?" I snap. "Or my thoughts on him being a homosexual? Chief, with all due respect, if your question is about him being gay, I think you're out of line. But I'll answer it. I don't give one shit damn if Lieutenant Sanderson is gay or green. He's a good detective, an outstanding leader, and he's my personal friend. I find your question offensive and—"

Deputy Chief Rodriguez holds up his palm for me to shut up, and I do. Good thing because when I'm angry my mouth has a mind of its own. His eyes study me.

"Good answer," he says.

Good answer? So far this meeting hasn't gone the way I thought it would. Why isn't he reaming me for the shooting, for embarrassing the Bureau, and for taking so much time off?

Where is the Chief Rodriquez I'd heard so much about?

"Good answer, but I hope you don't always fly off the handle before getting all the facts.

"Sir?"

"Do you have children, Detective?"

"No, sir."

"I have three. All boys. One is a captain in the Marines. Done two tours in Afghanistan. Married, baby on the way. The other is on the Bureau. You know him?"

"Not well. But I hear he's a good cop." Not kissing up. It's what I've heard. "Works nights out of Northeast Precinct, I think."

Nods. "He's engaged. To a woman."

Okay. That was a tad weird. Why is he telling me this? We going to be best buds or something?

"My oldest son, Derek, he's twenty-seven, lives in New York City in the SoHo district. Sells retro clothing, and urban emo stuff, goth, and punk clothing. Lives with a forty-five-year-old man, a fashion designer. They've been lovers for four years."

Face, stay neutral. Don't smile, don't frown, stay neutral. Staaaay.

"He was twenty when he told his mother and me he was gay. Told us from the ER at Good Sam Hospital. He had been walking to the bus stop after a night class at PSU. There were two perps. They broke his jaw and fractured two ribs. Suspects were never found. His mother and I went from being shocked he was hurt, to being shocked he was gay, to being outraged he was hurt for something he is."

"I'm sorry that happened to him, Chief." I mean it but I still wonder where he is going with this?

He nods, and looks at me for another long moment. "I can't

put you back in the Burglary Unit."

Okay. I'm not sure if I even want to stay in police work let alone worry about continuing in Burglary. I'm not going to say anything about it right now, though.

"You're too high profile. It's been nearly two months since the shooting and we're still getting a minimum of two-dozen phone calls a day up here, people wanting your head. Down from a hundred a day. So you need to lay low."

I don't say anything.

"I want you to work hate crimes in the Intelligence Unit."

Say what?

"I understand you've been out of town. In Vietnam, of all places," he says with a shrug as if he can't imagine anyone ever going there. "There's been a sudden spike in hate crimes in the last few weeks. A cross burning, a beating of an Asian man up on Twelfth and Southwest Stark, an attempted arson of a Muslim Community Center, your lieutenant's attack, and a homicide."

"Damn," I say. "The lynching. It's officially a hate crime?"

"Yes to both. We found the word 'nigger' carved into his chest. You don't need a crystal ball to know things are about to explode. So I want to get a jump on the public's demands by beefing up Intelligence and the hate crimes function. I'm transferring the Fat Dicks there part-time and I'm transferring you. You three will join forces with Officer Steve Nardia and Detective Angela Clemmons. Lieutenant B. J. Sherman is running the unit. Your job is to gather intelligence, to ferret out any existing hate cliques, and gather info on any plans to commit other crimes. Right now, we don't know if these incidences were done by one person acting alone, two or three individuals acting alone, or a group of people acting in consort. In short, we don't know shit but that's going to change."

Rodriguez tosses my file on a stack of papers and leans his elbows on his desk. "I think this would be a good fit for you, Reeves. Plus, it will keep you out of sight. As you know, the public has a short memory, but I don't think so with your shooting. The goddamn media will be bringing it up for a long while."

We look at each other for a moment. He lifts his eyebrows as if to say, well?

*   *   *

Doctor Kari Stephens sits down in her well-worn burgundy leather chair, and I take my usual place at the end of a matching sofa.

"You look great, Sam," she says over the rim of her coffee mug, on which there is an image of John Wayne and the words *A man's gotta have a creed to live by*. "How was Saigon?"

Doc Kari, as all the cops call her, is a plain looking fifty-year-old Chinese woman, no makeup, fit, leaning towards muscular, with gun-silver hair a tad longer than a Marine's. A framed photograph on the windowsill shows her with her long-time partner, an attractive blond-haired woman of the same age, standing near a waterfall. They're both wearing shorts and Hawaiian shirts.

"One for the memory books," I say. "Connected more with my father, met his wife, and fell harder for Mai."

"Sounds wonderful," she says, studying my face, looking for the truth. I hate when she does it because she has a way of picking up on the slightest nuances, like a flicker in my eye or the way I hold my mouth. I told her once she should be a detective and she said she was. Got that right. She leans toward me a little. "Something else happened, didn't it? And don't say no."

I chuckle. "You're amazing."

"Why I get the big bucks. Something terrible happened over there."

I sigh. "Yes. But it's not why I'm here today."

"I see. How about you tell me in as few words as you can then we'll talk about why you're here. Sam, everything matters. So please tell me."

"My father, Mai and I, with some old but oh so incredible Vietnamese vets raided a warehouse to free twenty-seven little girls about to be shipped off to Cambodia to work as prostitutes. Sex trafficking. We were successful but several people died in the process. A few hours later, a teenage boy and I had a death match with a man, in a tunnel that threatened to bury us."

As is her norm, Kari doesn't bat an eye. "You directly involved in the deaths?"

I shake my head. "I was present but no one died by my hand."

"How are you dealing with it?"

I look past her and out the window at Portland's skyline. "I don't think I've processed it all yet. Things were pretty fast-paced from the moment I got there until a few days before I flew out. I know you're going to say I need to think it out, and I agree. I just need a moment, or several, to do so."

Kari jots on her pad, then, "This strikes me as huge, Sam, yet you want to talk about something else today?"

"I do. It's because I'm back to where I was before I left for Vietnam. Actually, I'm where I was in the weeks following the shooting, although I may have moved a little in my thinking."

Kari lifts her eyebrows. "I'm good, but you're going to have to explain that."

45

"After the shootings, I knew I could never pick up a gun again. I told myself this over and over. I knew it in Saigon too. I had opportunities there to carry one, but I refused to do it. Knowing I won't do it again, can't do it again, I've been thinking I have no choice but to leave police work." A cop who won't carry a gun or who can't use one to defend himself or others has no business in law enforcement.

I look down at my hands folded in my lap. Out of the corner of my eyes, I see Kari uncross her legs and then cross them again. A minute passes, maybe two. She's giving me space to continue but I have nothing else, or maybe I do.

"Sam, I hear a 'but' in your voice?" I look up at her. When Kari gets her look, the same one a hawk gives a field mouse, there's no escaping.

"It's driving me nuts. I just came from Deputy Chief Rodriguez's office."

"Uh oh."

"Hey, he wasn't as bad as I expected. In fact, the experience wasn't bad at all. The rumors of him being an asshole are overdone."

"I know," Kari says, as if she knows it to be a fact. Might he be a patient?

"He offered me a job working hate crimes in the Intelligence Unit."

"Ah yes. Been a series of bad incidents. A black man was hung down in Old Town. Are they saying it's racially motivated yet?"

"They are as of today. Anyway, he stroked me a little and said the job would keep me out of the public eye and out of trouble. I know a guy who's been there for four years so I know it's true. Most of the time he keeps his weapon in his desk."

"Sounds like a job where there would be little to no opportunity to get yourself into trouble."

"No opportunity, unless the Taliban repelled down from the roof and crashed through the windows on the twelfth floor."

"Any history of it happening?"

I smile. "None. But you know how I attract trouble."

"So Rodriguez has you questioning your declaration."

I tell her about what happened to Mark. "Among the many things bouncing around in my head is maybe this job could be a way of doing something good. My father says while we can't always fix bad things that happened in the past, we can strive to do good now."

"Samuel, wasn't it? You're calling him Father now?"

"Yes, and I'm comfortable with it." No need to tell her all that led up to it.

"Good. So your concern right now is what to do about your job. You know I can't release you until you can tell me you could use your weapon should a situation require it. And you've been pretty adamant to me and to yourself that you're incapable of doing it again."

"*Incapable.*"

"This word bothers you? It means powerless, unable, helpless."

"I know what it means," I snap.

"Why are you irritated?"

I look at Kari. She'd probably call it a glare. "Because I'm a protector—a protector and a fixer—it's what I do. Words like 'incapable,' 'powerless,' 'unable' ... they don't fit into that picture."

Doc Kari chews on the end of her pen, silently, those eyes watching me.

"I know your tricks, Doc." She lifts her eyebrows. "You're letting me weigh my 'I won't pick up a gun' with my need to protect, aren't you?"

"Those internal battles are the best, aren't they?"

"How do you determine the winner?"

She shrugs. "Only you can determine it. Fill out pro and con columns and see which one wins? Or you wait until the battle dust settles between the protector you and the 'I don't want to pick up a gun again' you, and see which Sam Reeves wins."

I look past her and out the window again. Which Sam Reeves wins? I look back at her and into her hawk eyes.

"It just might be the real one," she says.

*   *   *

I'm in line at a Starbucks drive-up, third car back. I called Mark after I got out of the shrink's office. He wanted to stay at the hospital with David, and asked if I would mind going to his condo and retrieving a clean set of clothes. He called his neighbor lady, who met me with a key, and within ten minutes I had stuffed a grocery store bag with things I thought he would need, dropped it off at the hospital, and once more tried to talk him into going home, but he wouldn't have it.

He laughed when I told him about my meeting with Rodriguez, which made him groan because it hurt his throat and his sore ribs. That made me laugh, which made him laugh again, which made for another groan.

"The guy's full of surprises," he said. "I didn't expect him to offer you a job. What do you think?"

I told Mark I wasn't so sure, which was a big change from being nearly convinced these last few weeks I wasn't going back.

I said, "My father and I talked the night before I left about how uncertain I was about what to do. I was wondering if I could live there, in Saigon. But, he said as much as he and Mai would like it, he saw my destiny here, in Portland.

"My father has a quote for everything. This time it was 'No trumpets sound when the important decisions of our life are made. Destiny is made silently.'"

Mark said, "Wise man."

"You don't know the half of it," I said. "Lots to tell you about my new family."

*   *   *

I tell the purple-haired girl with three rings in her lower lip, I'd like a twelve-ounce French Roast with cream and a chunk of their crumb cake. I've always found crumb cake to help the decision-making process. I maneuver my pickup out of the narrow drive-up lane and into the street and head toward Davis Street Baptist Church. I called Chris Graham, "Padre," after talking with Mark and told him I was coming by. He has an office there where he does his minister business.

After my school burnt to the ground, Padre and several of my black belts helped me fix the basement into a passable martial arts school. Padre finagled some old wrestling mats out of one of his parishioners, a high school principal, I found four tattered heavy bags in my garage attic, and a friend who operates a hung gar school in Gresham, loaned us a dozen hand pads, three rubber guns, five rubber knives, and a medicine ball.

Three of my black belts from what I call my "Bloody Dozen" taught the six weeks I was involved in court proceeding after the shooting, as well as during my stay in Vietnam. The drilling and grilling by Internal Affairs and the Grand Juries were so intense I barely had enough energy to stretch a little before I went to bed. I had hoped to train with Mai and my father in Saigon, but except for some demonstrations by my father and his teacher, the only "training" I had were the times I had to literally fight for my life.

"How was Vietnam?" Padre asks, after we shake hands and do the man-hug thing.

"Hot, so very, very hot. Incredible city, though, wonderful people and fantastic food." I'm not about to tell him or anyone else besides Doc Kari and Mark about what went down there. I follow him down the aisle between the rows of pews. "How are things here, the church and the school?"

"Up here, it's going well. Some wonderful families have moved into the area and we're in the black for the second year in a row. Downstairs, the school is going good too. We lost some kids after your ... you know, the incident. But ninety percent of the students you still have. One of your new students is a soldier who just got back from Afghanistan. He's got a black belt in kenpo. Nice enough guy, an American Indian, I believe. Quite intense. If I had to guess, I think he might be having problems from his time in the war."

"Thanks for the heads up," I say, following him down the narrow, wooden stairs to the basement. It's a large room, twelve hundred square feet. The church removed all their accumulated junk so we have the entire room at our disposal. My black belts have made a third of the room the grappling area. They have hung my old heavy bags after duct taping the heck out of them, and brought in a few chairs for spectators and parents. Someone, probably Alan, who we call "the scrounger," got a couple of large mirrors, six by ten feet, at least.

"Must have been fun bringing those down the stairs," I say.

Padre smiles. "We had the white belts do it just in case the mirrors broke and the jagged shards pierced soft tissue."

I laugh, though I know everyone wrestled them down. "You've all done a wonderful job. How about the church elders? They still okay with us being here?" Padre was concerned, especially about one elder in particular, who thought it might be unchristian to teach martial arts in a church.

"We're good. I convinced Ben Waters we were actually teaching people alternatives to fighting as well as self-defense. I told him we teach the proper use of self-defense has to do with wisdom, understanding, and tact."

"Very good, Padre. You're going to make a wise black belt."

"Thank you, Sensei. I have wonderful teachers. Ben liked it too, so all is okay." He smiles. "The elders also like the five hundred dollars a month you're paying us."

"I still say you're charging me way too little. I was paying three times more a month on my school lease."

He shrugs. "It's five hundred dollars a month we weren't getting before. Plus it helps you while your insurance company drags their feet paying you, and it's sparked an interest in some of the young people in the youth group. Three have joined and three from the community joined with the agreement they ..." he grins sheepishly. "Okay, I leaned on them a little. They joined the school with the agreement they would come to church too."

I slap his shoulder. "You're good, Padre, yes you are."

We turn at the sound of footsteps coming down the stairs. A short wall conceals the top of the stairs so anyone descending is progressively revealed. I see feet wearing sandals.

"Oh, it's N uh r t uh n ah," Padre whispers. "Good, you can

meet him."

N uh who?

Next I see legs in blue jeans and a brown hand gripping the straps of a workout bag. Then a black polo shirt covering a hard torso, lean but muscular arms, a strong neck, and a face straight out of a western movie, with cinnamon-colored skin, straight black hair to his shoulders, prominent cheekbones and nose, and a broad face in which sit penetrating dark brown eyes. He's at once extraordinarily handsome and dangerous looking. I'm not sure why I perceive him as dangerous, but I can definitely feel it, like heat off a radiator.

His eyes do a quick body scan of me and settle on my eyes. There is a degree of haughtiness in his bearing, but not like conceit or bravado. It's more stoic, regal. Yes, that's it, regal.

He nods. "Sensei Reeves?"

"Yes," I say, extending my hand. "Call me Sam. Padre was just telling me about you. But you will have to help me with your name." His hands are soft, his grip light.

"Nate."

"Nate?" I look at Padre. "I thought you said something else."

"Nate is a nickname," the man says. "My full name is N-uh-r-t-uh-n-ah. It means 'makes others dance.' Apache."

"Beautiful name," I say, meaning it. "I want to master it."

He nods, studying me. "Nate is fine."

"I'm going to leave you two," Padre says. "I have an appointment coming in shortly and a class down here in forty-five minutes. Will you lead it, Sam?"

"I wasn't planning on it but, yes, I will. It will be good to see everyone and to scrape some of the barnacles off my hull."

"Great," Padre says. "I look forward to it." We shake hands

and he nods at Nate before heading up the stairs.

I toe off my shoes. Nate does the same. "Let's sit for a moment." I indicate a couple of folding chairs along the wall. "Padre says you've been training for a while. A black belt."

"Kenpo."

"Excellent. I've always liked the art. And you're a veteran of Afghanistan?"

He sits ramrod straight, hands on his knees. "I am. Fourteen months in Iraq too."

Minimum responses and he has yet to break eye contact with me. A shy man wouldn't make such intense eye contact. Perhaps he is just a man of a few words.

"How long have you been back?"

"Four months."

Not only has he not looked away, I don't think he has blinked. Okay, this is weird.

"I'm glad you made it home safely. How long were you deployed?"

"Nine months in Afghan," he says, blinking rapidly.

Curious. His manner didn't change, and his face remained neutral, but the eyes reacted. To what? My question or his answer? Best to change the conversation.

"Where did you study your kenpo?"

"Oklahoma City. I trained with Albert Madison for nine years. I earned my black belt before I went into the Army three years ago." No blinking. Clearly, he's more comfortable talking about kenpo than his military service.

"So are you finished with the army?" I ask just to test my theory.

Again the rapid blinking. "Yes."

"I see. Well, I'm glad you're here in my school. As they

probably told you, I've been away in Vietnam taking a vacation."

He nods, his eyes watching me, studying me, not blinking. I can't tell if there is a reason for it or it's just the way he is. He's got the stoic Indian stereotype down, but there's something brewing behind his eyes.

"I know of your ..." His eyes are searching mine now, moving from my left one, to my right one, and back to my left one.

"What?" I urge.

Still without looking away, he takes a deep breath, exhales it.

"Your situation," he says tightly. Then in one exhalation, he rattles, "I know about your situation. I followed it on the news and in the paper. I wanted to study with you because of what happened to you, and because so many said you're a good teacher."

His eyes narrow a little, as if trying to read my reaction. Well, I'm not going to reveal anything. He wants to train at my school because of what happened to me? What the hell?

"You're going to have to explain, Nate. Why would my unfortunate actions be cause for you to want to study with me?"

For the first time he looks off to the side, blinking rapidly. He looks back, his eyelashes wet. He doesn't seem to care if I see.

His voice is tight again, as if he's holding his breath as he speaks. "Because something similar, but different, happened to me."

Nate's prominent cheekbones have taken on sharper lines and the skin across his broad forehead seems tighter than a few moments ago. His deep-set eyes reflect confusion, sorrow, and ... I'm not sure what the other thing is. It's similar to how my grandfather looked at me as he was nearing death from congestive heart failure. He wasn't the sort of man to beg for anything, not even for his life. But there was something in his eyes, a beseeching, a need he had no control over.

"Did something happen in Afghanistan," I ask. "Or Iraq? Something you think is similar to what happened to me?"

Nate looks at me for a long moment before nodding ever so slightly. "Similar."

I wait for him to elaborate but he only looks at me. I can't tell if he wants me to ask him questions or drop the subject.

"Do you have Indian blood in your family?" he asks.

I smile, partly because of the abruptness of his question and partly out of relief he changed the subject.

"Funny you should mention it, Nate. I haven't thought about it in a long time, but my mother told me we have some Hopi blood on her side of the family. A great-great-grandfather or something."

I wish I hadn't said "or something." Makes it sound as if my Indian heritage, however small it is, isn't important to me. Maybe it isn't; I never think about it. But now because I'm sitting with someone who appears to have a lot of Indian blood, I'm feeling uncomfortable.

"Hopi means peaceful ones, peaceful people. It's from Hopituh Shi-nu-mu. Did you know?"

"I'm sorry. I didn't." Why do I feel I need to apologize? Oh, I know why, because I'm ignorant about the blood pumping through my own veins.

"I am one hundred percent Apache. The word is a collective for six tribes from the Southwest. I am Chiricahua Apache. And no, I'm not related to Geronimo or Cochise. But I possess their warrior nature."

I bet he does. He has an aura in constant flux. One moment it emanates a sense of peace and in the next, it radiates ... sorrow? And there is some agitation. Right now, I see something else, something I've seen in our veteran SWAT guys, in my father, and in the old Vietnamese soldiers I met in Saigon. The aura communicates I don't want to fight, but if I have to, someone's going to be in a world of hurt. It's an attitude I know well.

"What do you do now?" I ask.

"I've taken all the tests for the Portland Fire Department and I'm waiting to get hired. I'm told it could be anytime."

"Really? Very good career choice." I smile at him. "Didn't want to take the police test, huh?"

He shakes his head. "Had enough of guns."

I hear that.

*　　*　　*

"Everyone feeling good? Everyone feeling loose?"

"Yes, Sensei!"

"All right. Pair up and do a little light sparring. Don't try to kill your partner but be mindful of moving in and out of range, working your combinations, using body movement to avoid your partner's blows, and using efficient counters. Got it!"

"Yes, Sensei."

"Glad you're back, Sensei," comes from the back of the group. Laughter follows.

"Thank you. Glad to be back. Now get busy."

These are my brown belts, two dozen of them and four soon-to-be browns. I've always said the most dangerous martial arts students are hungry brown belts. They've been at it for over three years and because they're closing in on their promotion, they train like they're possessed; eager to prove to each other and to me, they are black belt worthy to each other and to me. Because I've been away for a while, these guys are extra eager to show me they haven't been slacking off.

Nate asked if he could train with the brown-belt class tonight because he had an appointment and couldn't stay for the following black-belt class. I said sure, plus it would give me a chance to see him move and see how he treats lower belts. I've had black belts from different systems ask to train with my students. There have been a few who possessed excellent skills but treated my lower ranks with disdain. Those I've asked not to come back. The ones who are always welcome are those black belts who are kind to my lower ranks, act humble around my black belts, and listen to my suggestions. Nate appears to be one of these.

As a kenpo stylist, he wears black pants as we do, and he's purchased a black T-shirt from Adam, my senior black belt in charge of supplies. Nate's belt isn't old and tattered but it isn't brand new, either. The ends display two stripes depicting he's a second degree. He didn't mention it when we were chatting earlier. That's a big plus for Nate.

He and Steve have partnered up and are moving about swapping techniques at a nice, controlled pace. Steve is in his late twenties, a little over six foot and skinny as a *bo* staff. However, it would be a mistake to think skinny equates to weak because Steve is deceptively strong. He's tried everything to put on size but instead he gets stronger and stronger, which isn't the worst thing to happen. He's been training off and on for about four years, mostly on for the last year.

Nate is doing a nice job of controlling his speed and aggression but I can tell he's itching to release it. His expressionless face is in direct contrast with Steve's constant smile that spreads even wider whenever he launches a cool move and likewise when Nate throws something nice. Steve likes a good move no matter who does it.

I can see Nate's hand skills are his forte with his kicks coming in a distant second. His front, round, side, and hook kicks aren't bad, they just don't shine as brightly as his precisely delivered hand combinations and his near flawless body mechanics. He's had good training from a teacher who stressed hands over legs.

"Stop!" I call out. "Okay, everyone looks great. You've been practicing hard while I was away, and it shows. I'm proud of you. Any questions?"

Billy Bob raises his hand with phony eagerness to which everyone smiles except Nate who doesn't know what is going on. Every class has their funny man. Mine is tall, lanky and red-headed William Appleton—"Billy Bob"—born and raised in Mississippi.

"Dare I ask, Billy Bob?"

"My question, sir, is what is truth?"

"I got your truth right here," I say, clenching my fist. The class goes, "Oooo" in unison.

"Happy you're back, Sensei," Billy Bob says with a grin and a bow.

"I missed you too," I say, shaking my head at the smiling class. "Okay, switch partners and lets do the four-count dummy drill."

We've practiced this a lot, but for Nate's purpose I demonstrate on Jackson Steele, a short, muscular brown belt, who is testing for his black in the next couple of months.

"You will take turns hitting each other four times, not a flurry, but with half a second between each blow. Each time you hit your partner with a controlled shot, your partner will react as if really struck. For example ..."

I front kick Jackson in the abdomen and he snaps forward holding his stomach as if I'd hit him hard. I follow with a controlled round kick to his right leg and he sags to the right. My third hit is a controlled hammer fist to the back of his neck. He drops to one knee, his head hanging limply. When I follow with a knee strike to the side of his face, Jackson falls all the way over.

"Now it's your partner's turn to hit you back, beginning from his last position. In this case, Jackson went all the way to the floor so he has to start from there."

The muscular brown belt thrusts a controlled sidekick into my knee, and I bend over sharply pretending to be in pain. Up on his knees now, he pretends to hit me with a palm-heel uppercut to jerk me nearly upright. He hops to his feet and snaps a controlled front-legged, lower shin kick to my groin, and I bend over with a theatrical grunt. He finishes with another slap kick to the same target, and I stumble back with a small whimper.

"Oscar performance!" Billy Bob calls out. A few students applaud.

"Okay," I chuckle, waving them off. "Remember, the idea here is each time your partner reacts, you're presented with a different silhouette. This is much more valuable than always striking at a stationary upright one. Okay? Have at it."

The class always has fun with this drill and Nate is fitting right in. He's not smiling, but I can tell he's enjoying himself, especially since his partner, Padre, overacts to each of his blows.

Nate's burden seems to have lifted once he began training, and I know well the feeling. While the martial arts have saved my cute behind on several occasions, it has saved my psyche more times than I can remember. Doc Kari, no doubt, has an explanation with lots of Latin words. I just think of training as blowing out negative carbon buildup.

"Stop! Okay, looking good everyone. Whatever you're doing on your own time, keep at it. Your extra practice is showing. Padre, up front."

"Yes, Sensei," he says, scurrying up to me.

"Let's finish the class with basic reps: jabs, cross punches, backfists, and uppercuts. Then do front kicks, sides, rounds, and hooks. Two sets of fifteen reps each. Got it?"

"Yes, sir."

I move through the rows to the back of the class and stand ready to throw reps with everyone.

"Fighting positions," Padre barks. "Backfists with a front-leg lunge. Ready. One!"

Twenty minutes later, I resume my post at the front of the class. We're all sweating hard and breathing hard.

"Thanks, Padre, good job. I haven't been able to train much lately, and it feels so good to be back. Okay, feet together, stand straight, and place your hands on your belly. Breathe in through your nose and feel your belly expand. Hold it, two, three, four. Blow it out slowly, two, three, four. Hold it, two, three, four. Breathe in, two, three, four."

Two more repetitions and everyone's heartbeat and breathing and more importantly, energy, have returned to normal. It's important to mellow everyone out before turning them loose on the highways and byways.

"Thank *you* for teaching *us*!" Padre barks after calling the lines to attention.

"Thank you for teaching me," I reply. "Ready! Salute!"

Left hands cover right fists, and both are thrust forward. Class over.

*   *   *

Mai laughs when I hold Chien up to the screen. The cat meows and touches the screen with her paw.

"She looks so cute, Sam. Her hair is so white, so clean."

Mai looks tired, drained. Chien lies down next to the keyboard between us.

Mai smiles at her. "You look good too, Sam. Did you work out?"

"Taught two classes tonight and worked out a little with each. Not too much. Got to ease back in."

She's wearing a beige tank top that shows off her beautiful shoulders and arms. Her raven black hair is slightly mussed, which looks amazing. Those green specked, brown eyes look heavy lidded as if it's all she can do to keep from falling asleep.

"You look exhausted."

"Oh, Sam, Mother is doing so bad. Father call doctor to the house this morning because she could not breathe good, and she was coughing blood more than before. The doctor is worried about the ... strain? Yes, the strain on her heart. He says the TB is very advanced and the strain on her heart is worse."

"I'm so sorry, Mai. I wish I was there with you."

She nods for a long moment, looking directly at me. "I wish you were with me too. I am so scared."

"She's a tough woman."

Mai wipes her nose with the back of her hand. "Not ..." She looks away, and I can see her take a deep breath before she turns back to look into the camera. "Not any longer."

I hear a soft knock. Mai looks to the side and speaks in Vietnamese. I can hear the sound of a door opening.

"Come, Father, I am talking with Sam."

"Oh good," I hear Father's voice say. "May I say hello?"

"Of course. Sam, Father is here."

"Hello, Father," I say, as he kneels down so I can see him in the camera. Mai scoots her chair to her left so all I can see is her right shoulder.

He looks trashed too. No surprise, considering he's been battling coercion from the Vietnamese mafia, lost friends in ensuing firefights, and lost a beloved teacher. Now he is watching helplessly as his beloved wife of some thirty years slides quickly toward death.

I grew up thinking my father had died in a North Vietnamese prison during the war. He, in fact, was in prison for several years, but fate led him to the unusual position of teaching martial arts to the prison commander. Through the training their friendship grew, and, as the story grows, my father fell in love with the commander's beautiful daughter Kim. After the war ended, the commander helped my father remain in Vietnam, and my father married Kim two years later, fathered two daughters, and helped raise a stepdaughter. Over the years, the family built a thriving jewelry business, no mean feat given the confusion after the war, the anti-American sentiment, racism, and rampant corruption of government officials and law enforcement. It helped that my father has a charming personality, has tirelessly helped his community rebuild, and he speaks flawless Vietnamese. Interestingly, his slight physique and his Vietnamese-like mannerisms, have led many people to think he is indeed Asian or mixed race.

"You look good, Son. Rested from the jet lag? Oh, there is Chien. Sleeping like always."

"I am, thank you. I'm so sorry about Kim."

"Yes, yes. Thank you." He is looking into the camera but it's obvious his mind is with Kim. After a moment, he says,

"Thirty years ago we were newlyweds. Now we are oldie-weds. In between, the most precious years of my life."

"I wish I could have talked with her more while I was there. I found her to be a beautiful and wise woman."

She was so sick when I was there I was able to talk with her only three or four times. Even in her illness and frailty, it was clear she was a powerful woman who loved her family deeply, and didn't tolerate fools.

"Thank you, Son. I also wish you two could have had more time together."

"I look forward to more times," I say. Silly words. Meaningless, but they convey my love.

He nods; the gesture also meaningless, but it takes in my love. Father knows a thousand quotations for a thousand situations but he is at a loss for this one.

"How is your school?" he says. "You said you were anxious to check on it."

"I taught two classes this evening. Trained a little, worked up a sweat, cleaned out the cobwebs."

"Very good. The martial arts are a constant we can always return to, no? A place for us to take comfort; a place for us to seek; a place for us to find; a place for us to vent; and sometimes it is a place for us to hide. I am sorry we did not train more while you were here."

"I got lots of practical experience," I say without humor. "One of my new students is a kenpo black belt and a veteran of Afghanistan. I think he's troubled by something that happened to him in the war. He said something about choosing my school because he thinks we shared similar experiences. I think he thinks I can help him."

"Then help him, Son. You have been through much. Share

what you have learned with him. Buddha said a thousand candles could be lit from a single one. And lighting the thousand will not shorten the life of the one."

"I'm not sure if I'm ready."

"You are. Chödrön says, 'We work on ourselves in order to help others, but also we help others in order to work on ourselves.' I have told you about Pema Chödrön before. She is one of my favorite modern day Buddhist teachers. She also says, 'Only when we know our own darkness well can we be present with the darkness of others.' I believe you are at the door, Son. There is still darkness in you, but just keep opening the door to let in the light."

"Yes, sir," I say. "I will do what I can. I think he is a good man. Oh, one other thing. I have a tough decision to make. I've been offered a job in our Intelligence Unit. There have been a lot of hate crimes going on here in the last couple weeks and they want to get a jump on it. I'd be out of the public eye doing mostly intelligence gathering. I'd still have to carry a gun but ..." I look away from the screen and Father's gaze for a moment. I swallow and look back. His face is neutral. "I don't know. If I were to pull the trigger again, to use your words, I'd be in darkness forever. But I feel compelled to take the position. Man, I'm so screwed up."

Father lifts his eyebrows as if he's surprised at what I just said. "You want some cheese with your whine, Son? We have talked about this before. You know the answer. You have already decided." He tilts his head as if trying to peer around my defenses, which I'm sure he is. "Have you seen the woman doctor yet?"

"Yes."

"Helpful?"

I nod.

"Son, I can see in your eyes the answer is within you. Reach in and extract it, no matter how painful or frightening it might be. He looks at me for a long moment, his eyes making me feel like a girlyman. "What time is it there, Son?"

"Almost eight thirty."

"Make your decision by ten," he snaps, his eyes loving, stern, a father telling his son to man up.

"Okay."

"Talk to you later," he says, standing. He disappears from the screen. Mai reappears. I hear the door close.

I raise my eyebrows. "He's such a funster."

"I do not know your word, Sam, but so many times he is right."

"When was the last time he was wrong?"

"He did not think you and I were a good idea," she says.

I laugh. "I remember. Gave us a hard time didn't he? And he was wrong."

She smiles, which nearly burns up my screen. "Yes, he was. And he has admitted it to me."

"Really?" I say, feeling like a lovesick teenager learning his girlfriend's father approves.

Mai smiles. "Cool, huh?"

Chien looks up at her on the screen and at me. She meows and settles her head back next to the mouse.

"Definitely," I say grinning. Next, we'll be talking about our big math test on Friday and which brand of acne cream is best.

"But, Sam, all he said to you just now?"

"Yes?"

"For what it is worth, whatever you decide, I'm with you."

I nod, and stroke the top of Chien's head.

*   *   *

I'm leaning on my bedroom windowsill looking out at the night. Over the four years I've owned this house, I've made all my big decisions right here: where to bury my mother; whether I should take the test to become a detective; whether to refinance my school; whether to go through with my promise to Mai and go to Saigon. Then there was the crazy time I decided I would never ever step foot out of this house again. I'd convinced myself if I did I would most assuredly kill again. Not all my decisions have been good ones.

Maybe it's because it's a bedroom window, a place where I'm tired, groggy, and vulnerable in my underwear. Or maybe it's my reflection in the glass looking back and compelling me to decide. With me looking back at me waiting for me to make up my mind, I feel the need to please the face in the glass.

Should be in a country western song. Oh, my wife left me, and took my pickup and my dog. Now I got to please the sad man in the mirror and decide what I want to fight for: my truck or my dog? Needs work but, hey, it's not too bad.

I turn my head to the left and my reflection turns to its right. I turn to my right and my reflection turns to its left. Man, would I crap a brick if my reflection turned in the opposite direction. Okay, I'd better decide before the face looking back at me drives me over the edge of what little sanity I'm using to navigate.

Thinking ... thinking ... Done.

And it's only nine fifty-five.

CHAPTER THREE

Louise pulled her hood tighter around her face so only her patched eye, her good eye, and her nose peeked out. She pressed herself back against the old brick building at Third and Couch in a feeble attempt to stay warm on this unusually crisp June morning.

Since the police cars and ambulance had left a couple of hours earlier—there had been a stabbing on the corner—she had been standing with her back to the wall watching the traffic volume change from sporadic to heavy. Seven blocks to the north, commuters exited off the Steel Bridge onto Third and, though the three-lane, one-way street had a speed limit of 25 MPH, nearly every motorist went at least 35 to get through skid row and on to the chrome and glass high-rise district on the south side of Burnside. Only the old timers still called it "skid row." The modernettes, as she called them, called it "Old Town," as more and more art galleries and unique eateries occupied the former flophouses and ass kickin' taverns.

Ocnod's death had shocked Louise, not because he had died but by the way he died. Death happened almost daily on skid row's streets, and as a long time resident, she had seen a lot of it. Many of her friends had frozen to death or died of tuberculosis, but lots of others had died at the hands of another down-and-outer. Clara's death was from a two-by-four smashed across her forehead; Wade and Johnny got it from knives; Ol' Ed got himself pushed out the 6th-floor window of the Free Clinic; and Big Danny got himself shot to death. She witnessed that one. No, death wasn't anything new to her, but ol' Ocnod's death was horrifying. Hung from a lamppost. She shook her head and tucked her gloved hands into her armpits.

Her eye watched a shiny black BMW pull to the curb. She frowned as the 30-something retrieved an electric razor from a leather attaché case and began moving it about his face.

"Hey, asshole!" she called out, rapping her gloved knuckles against his window. "Get the hell outta here! This ain't no god-damn bathroom. This is my house you're in."

The man stared stupidly for a moment at the hooded personification of ugly death—broken teeth, sprouts of whiskers growing out of moles, and a patched eye. He tossed his shaver quickly into his briefcase, its blades still whirring, and goosed the car into heavy traffic, nearly clipping a passing Volvo.

"Way to go, Louise baby," a gruff voice called from behind her. "You told Mister Pussy what it is."

She turned and snapped a military salute at two winos huddled in a doorway a few feet away. The tall one was Abbot and the short, fat one, Costello. They stood side by side, shoulders hunched against the morning cool, trading swigs from a brown paper bag.

Louise resumed her position against the wall and sucked hard on the last of her cigarette. A few street people passed, some nodding a greeting at her. Some new faces lately, she thought. She alerted on an old black wino across the street, a longtime skid row regular everyone called The Mayor. It was hard to see him with all the cars and trucks stopped at the light, but as usual, he was drunk out of his mind long before most people had their morning coffee. His tattered, brown overcoat was unbuttoned, revealing blue sweat pants, brown slippers, and a bare, bony chest. Hanging onto the signpost with one hand, he leaned into the street and waved his other at a pretty, young brunette in a red Honda.

The traffic signal changed to green for southbound traffic, and the pedestrian signals flashed Don't Walk for the east/west foot traffic. Oblivious to the signals, The Mayor let go of the post and staggered into the street, heading west toward Louise's side.

Abbot and Costello, who had also been watching The Mayor, shuffled from their doorway post and shouted at him to get back to the sidewalk. Louise tried to shout but realized her voice was too feeble to be heard over the passing traffic. She shambled over and grabbed Abbott's arm. "He's gonna get his ass kilt," she cried into his ear.

"Well, I sure ain't goin' out there to rescue his drunkness, Louise," Abbott said, taking a quick pull of wine from the bag.

The Mayor somehow made it across the first lane, accompanied by a cacophony of blaring horns and screeching tires. Louise, Abbott, and Costello moved to the curb's edge, the three of them gesturing madly for him not to move as he precariously straddled the yellow line. Louise mouthed silently, "Stay, stay, stay."

Because of the heavy volume of traffic from the bridge ramp, the signal held green thirty seconds longer than most intersections, extra seconds that seemed like minutes to Louise, as cars and trucks streaked by, some swerving, some sounding their horns, but not one vehicle slowing even a little. The Mayor was fine with it, swaying as if dancing to the sound and the fury. He held open his overcoat, exposing his bare chest and shouting drunkenly, "Ole!" at the charging herd of steel bulls.

Anxious, Louise kept looking from The Mayor to the traffic signal, and back, all the while willing the light to change to red. A city bus passed slowly, blocking her view for what seemed like forever. When she finally could see him again, The Mayor was looking back toward the sidewalk from where he had begun. What was he looking at? Louise strained her one eye to see through the streaking traffic to the other side of the street. She could make out two young men, teenagers, both standing next to the No Parking sign. They look weird, she thought, wearing all black clothes and knee-high boots. Like ... what do they call them? Punk Rockers, or something. One had long, impossibly black hair and the other had not-as-long impossibly yellow hair.

"What are they doing?" Louise asked aloud, watching in disbelief as the yellow-haired one motioned with his right hand for The Mayor to come back to the sidewalk, while holding up the middle finger of his left. The other waved his hands for The Mayor to continue to cross the other two lanes over to Louise's side.

Desperate now, Louise said, "They're confusing the old fool." She started to step off the curb but an angry horn drove her back. "Hey, you dirty shits!" she yelled feebly. "What you think you doin'?" The light finally changed to amber. "Thank God," she whispered.

Traffic in all four lanes accelerated to beat the light. A white delivery truck next to the curb slowed to make a turn, blocking her view. She hobbled sideways a couple of steps closer to Costello to see around it, but still it was in the way. Costello could see, though, and his eyes widened.

He shouted, but his words were drowned out by a riot of screeching tires and blaring horns from the other side of the truck.

The truck moved on and The Mayor was gone.

Off to the right, bluish-white smoke swirled around the tires of a blood-red Nissan sliding sideways into the intersection. Underneath, a human form tumbling. A flash of skin, a pajama-clad leg, a flap of brown coat. Something pinkish shot out from under a tire and bounced across the pavement toward Louise. The Nissan rocked to a stop.

At Louise's feet: a broken denture plate.

Across the street, the teenagers walked quickly away slapping each other on the back.

CHAPTER FOUR

One just doesn't drop in on a deputy chief for a chat. There is a protocol. An officer or detective must ask permission from a superior officer in his unit to talk with someone on the fifteenth floor. But I don't have a superior officer right now because having been off duty for two months my name has been dropped from the duty roster in Detectives and placed back in Personnel. Since I'm in limbo, I head straight up to the Chief's Office.

Karen smiles as I approach her desk. "You're coming to see me again, Sam? You do know I'm married, right?"

I snap my fingers and feign disappointment. "Darn. Hey, you got a sister?"

"An older one."

"Better yet."

"You here to see Deputy Chief Rodriguez?"

"I am."

"Does he know you're coming?" When I shake my head, she keys a button on her phone. "Chief, Detective Sam Reeves is here to see you. Yes, sir. Will do." She looks at me. "Not as nervous this time?"

I smile. "More, but it's not about seeing Rodriguez."

"You'll be fine, Sam," she says like a reassuring mother. Like most personal assistants, Karen knows everything going on in the Bureau. She nods her head toward the hallway, and whispers, "He's waiting."

"Detective Reeves," Chief Rodriguez says, from his

doorway. "Come on in. Sit."

"Good morning, Chief." I sit in the same chair I sat in yesterday.

"You asked for twenty-four hours to decide and here we are at the twentieth hour. You going to take the job?"

Rodriguez is a cut-to-the-chase kind of commander so I'm not going to annoy him with what all went into my thinking. I'm especially not going to let him know about my issues with firearms.

"Yes, sir."

"Very good," he says without emotion. "Your shrink cleared you?"

"It's in the works, sir. We chatted earlier and I'm good to go. She'll be sending her report over before noon."

"Good," he says, picking up his phone and tapping in a number. "Stand by. I'll let Lieutenant Sherman know."

BJ Sherman is the lieutenant in charge of Intelligence. Since a small unit such as Intelligence doesn't have a captain, Sherman probably answers directly to the captain of Detectives or maybe to Rodriguez himself.

"BJ, Tony here," the Chief says. "Sam Reeves is on board ... Right, I'll tell him. The Fat Dicks check in with you yet? Good. I'll have Reeves's personnel file sent over to you, and I'll make sure he's back on the books. Good ... Okay, he's on the way." The Chief cradles the phone.

"Do you know Lieutenant Sherman?" he asks.

"We worked East Precinct together about ten years ago. He had a desk job."

"He's a good lieutenant. Savvy to the sensitivity needed to work hate crimes. He also understands the importance of you keeping a low profile."

My new mantra: Keep a loooow profile.

"You know Angela Clemmons and Steve Nardia?"

"Angela, just to say hello. Steve has been in a couple of my in-service classes. Funny guy as I recall. Coincidentally, I talked to him about Intelligence about six months ago. Said he liked it."

Rodriguez nods. "Sharp guy, knows what he's doing, Angela Clemmons is a good cop—tough woman, very race conscious. Lost her mother and father to homicide about eight years ago, in Chicago, I think it was. Anyway, we just got a vacancy in Intel. You're the replacement."

"Thanks, sir. Appreciate being considered for the job. The last few weeks have been a rollercoaster of ..." I'm not sure where I'm going with this so it's time to shut up.

He looks at my personnel file. "You've been on, what? Fifteen years, coming up on sixteen." He lays the file down and looks at me for what seems like a half minute, though it probably just feels like it He sniffs, and says, "I've been on twenty-five. In my third year I killed a mother and her daughter."

What?

"I was racing to an accident on I-5, going way too fast and zipping between cars like I was in a video game. Clipped a Volkswagen Bug and sent it into a cement pillar. Killed both occupants." The lines around the Chief's mouth deepen and you can see in his eyes the sad place he visits too often. "Witnesses said she jerked her car into my lane as I was passing. Officially, it was her fault, but in my mind, the fault was mine. Still believe it. I was racing to a car accident and there was no need. It had already happened. No need for me to drive over the speed limit with lights and siren. It startled the poor woman and she turned left instead of right, and I slammed into her. It wouldn't have happened if I hadn't been hotdogging."

"I've never heard about this, Chief. So sorry."

He nods, as his eyes come back to mine. "I've never heard a bad word about you, Reeves, but I have heard lots of good. I trained in the martial arts myself when I was younger. Brown belt in judo."

"Very good, sir." Hard to say something nice to a deputy chief without it sounding like you're kissing up.

"This is a good opportunity to get yourself back on track."

"Thank you."

He smirks. "So don't fuck it up."

"Don't fuck it up. Copy that, sir."

"All right. Head on down to twelve and have a chat with Lieutenant Sherman." He looks at his watch. "Today's the first day of the new pay period. It's ten fifteen. You're already two hours and fifteen minutes late for duty."

I stand. "Thanks, Chief."

"I think you'll be a good fit. Any problems, let me know."

"Yes, sir."

Karen is on the phone so we just wave at each other and she gives me a thumbs up as I pass. She probably already knows I took the assignment.

I go into the restroom before taking the elevator down and splash cold water on my face and behind my neck.

Dang, I just accepted the assignment. These past few weeks I've been all over the map as to what to do. Resign and expand my school? Move to Saigon? Take up sheep herding? I smile remembering when I ran into Tom Bashman in the hall after he had signed his retirement papers. When I asked what he was going to do, he said, "Gonna be a sheep herder, Reeves. Wear a robe, walk with a staff, and if one of them goddamn sheep go astray, fuck it. I ain't going after it." It was clearly time for Tom to retire.

Maybe it's time for me too. I can take the elevator all the way down to the lobby, drive home, and call Rodriguez and tell him not only am I not taking the position, I'm resigning.

I won't though. I'm going back to work. I don't know why but I know it's my destiny. Saying it sounds corny, but it's what I'm feeling. When my father told me in Saigon he believed my destiny was to return to Portland, I don't think he was talking about me being a grocery bagger or a mail carrier.

What about not being able to shoot again? Don't know. Have to wing it, I guess.

*   *   *

The elevators swoosh open to the twelfth floor and I nearly bump chests with Clarence Sanders who is one of the academy training officers. He's a black man, early fifties, slight build, greying hair, and wears horned-rimmed glasses that, combined with his facial structure, give him the hangdog look of a younger Woody Allen. Many a street hoodlum made the mistake of thinking he was a pushover. I'm approaching thirty years in the martial arts; he's got close to forty.

"Sam! How the hell are yuh?" he says, extending his small, fragile-looking hand. Earlier in his martial arts career, Clarence was known on the tournament circuit for breaking stones with these gentle-looking hands.

"Good to see you, Clarence," I say slapping his shoulder. When I was working in Detectives, he was always badgering Mark to free me up for an afternoon to help him teach defensive tactics to new recruits. Mark let me go whenever my work-load allowed. Clarence is an excellent DT instructor with black belts in several fighting arts. We always had fun teaching together. "What's going on? How's the Training Division?"

"Excellent, man. Just had coffee with Steve Nardia. Said the rumor was you're going to be working with him. He really likes it there."

"I am. Just going in to meet up with the lieutenant now."

"BJ is ..." He pauses, clearly picking his words carefully, then, "A good administrator." Interesting thing to say. "Steve's great. Angela? Well, you got to tiptoe around her a little. She might be a good-looking sister, but she's got some attitude. If this were nineteen sixty-eight, she'd fit right in with the black power movement." He shrugs apologetically. "I don't like to say anything bad about anyone but take my comments as a heads up."

"Gotcha, Clarence. Well, I better get in there. BJ knows I'm coming down from Rodriguez's office."

"Rodriguez, huh? How was it?"

"It went pretty well, actually. The rumors about him ripping out your intestines have been exaggerated."

"Good to hear. Never had any dealings with him but I've heard the rumors. Hey, you want to come help with a class when you get settled in?"

"Sure. It depends on BJ now."

"My lieutenant's tight with him. I'll make it happen. Get settled in and I'll give you a shout in a couple three days. Good luck with the new gig. Crazy stuff happening out in the mean streets, I hear."

I tap on the glass and Steve Nardia, sitting at the closest desk to the window, buzzes me in the door.

"Norris, right?" Steve says, walking over to shake my hand. He's about six feet tall, one seventy, mid-forties, greying hair.

"Chuck Norris?"

Steve and Clarence have been best buds for years. Clarence is a martial artist and Steve has made a name for himself playing violin with the Oregon Symphony Orchestra. Friendship is a magical thing.

"How are you doing, Steve?"

"I'm doing awesomely." He gestures to the room. "Welcome to, uh, this place."

It's a small, mostly beige office, in which are crammed six desks, each with a PC, and surrounded by file cabinets. The only wall adornments are vintage World War Two posters. Two are close enough for me to read. One depicts a parrot and the words, "Free Speech Doesn't Mean Careless Talk." The one beside it depicts a desperate hand and part of a face sinking below a choppy sea. It reads, "Loose Lips Sink Ships."

"BJ and Angela went over to Records but should be back anytime now. You got the middle desk by the window. Yes, I got seniority and could have it but I got acrophobia. I hate looking down twelve floors to the street, and it freaks me even more to look up at those taller buildings over there. I like my post right here at center front. Angela's got the one in front of you and the Fat Dicks, when they're in here, got the one behind you and the one across from it. The center one in this row is for anyone to use who drops in, usually uniformed guys or dicks. BJ has the one office there in the back."

"Thanks, Steve. I've been in here a few times over the years. Last time was about three years ago, maybe four. BJ was here then, I think he just got assigned."

"Then it was four years ago. I came in right after him and Angela joined us a year ago. Candy Abrams was here briefly but it wasn't a good fit for her. She transferred out a couple weeks ago to Northeast Precinct. I heard your name bantered about right after."

"Really." So I was being talked about at the same time I hadn't a clue what I was going to do.

The door buzzes. "Here's the boss and Angela," Steve says.

"There he is," BJ Sherman says pleasantly, though not much louder than a whisper. He's in his midforties, my height, with thinning brown hair, and a pear-shaped body carrying twenty pounds too much on hips wider than his shoulders. He extends his hand as he approaches. "Good to see you and glad you're on board." I'm not getting a read as to how much he means it, or doesn't mean it.

"Hi, Sam," Angela says, moving around the big man. She's wearing blue jeans that reveal a toned figure, and what I think is called an African Dashiki shirt, with lots of yellows and blues, big pockets, and oversized sleeves. Her wrists are covered with at least a half-dozen multi-colored bracelets. A two-inch high afro haloes a pretty face with almond-shaped brown eyes and a huge smile. "Good to see you with us," she says, gripping my hand as her eyes crawl over me. Hmm.

"Steve give you the layout?" BJ asks in a low voice. I've heard guys refer to him as "Whispers" and I see—hear why.

"He did. Guess I have the middle desk by the window."

"It's settled then," he says. "Everyone back to my cave for a short chat."

It's a small office, cozily lit by two small lamps definitely not department issue. Classical music plays softly from a Bose unit resting on a long wall cabinet behind him. A bible lies next to it. The lieutenant has definitely made the place his. "Understand you were in Saigon, Sam," he says sitting behind his desk.

"Just got back. Talk about your culture shock."

"My father was there during the war," BJ says. "Has lots of stories."

I do too, but I'm not telling them. "I bet."

"Okay," BJ says. "In a nutshell, here's what we're all involved in at the moment. I'll let Angela and Steve fill in the details later. The biker gang wars have mellowed as of late, so we're not doing anything with them except writing up bits of info we get from snitches. Organized crime is quiet as well; there was a series of firebombing rival adult bookstores. They still own most of them, as well as most all of the massage parlors and escort services. The Vice Unit actively works them for violations, of course, and our job is to collect info on threats of violence, mass drug sales, that sort of thing. There are no named politicians or other officials coming to town for a while so things are quiet as far as dignitary protection goes. There was an abortion clinic protest a couple days ago, which Steve and Angela knew was coming up, so we were able to give a heads up to the precincts."

"I got caught in it," I say. "A cab driver and me. A couple of them tried to get in the cab."

"You do your magic on them, Chuck?" Steve asks. He looks at Angela and BJ. "You know when the boogeyman goes to sleep, he checks his closet for Chuck Norris."

"Anyway," BJ says, a little annoyed, "because our other areas of responsibility are quiet, we're able to put our combined energy into these hate crimes and suspected hate crimes. The Fat Dicks will be in here from time to time getting info from us and providing us with anything they learn. Right now, they're assigned the lynching in Old Town and the attack on Lieutenant Mark Sanderson and his friend David Rowe.

"Sam, you've been working in Detectives, but understand

in here we're not involved in investigations of crimes, at least in the way you have been doing them in the past. Our task is to gather information from informants, from crime reports, and from interviews with suspects, witnesses, and victims. We do write up minor reports from time to time and forward them to the respective precincts and the Detective Division. But I don't want you getting wrapped up in an investigation that will interfere with your primary task, which is gathering intelligence."

"Got it," I say.

"Right now we don't know if these recent hate crimes are part of an organized movement, if there is one person behind them, or several people; it could be a militia group, the KKK, some might be copycat crimes. Nor do we know if they will continue." He takes a sip from a water bottle. "Understand Mark is a friend of yours. You heard how he's doing?"

"I haven't talked with him this morning but yesterday he was pretty down in the dumps. Speaking of, I need to ask a favor already. I didn't know I'd be starting work when I came to the Justice Center this morning, and I promised Mark I'd give him a ride home when he's ready to leave. Should he call, may I go get him?"

"Of course," BJ says. "I haven't talked with the Fat Dicks this morning, but I'm sure they're declaring Mark's and his friend's assault as a hate crime."

I look at the bible on the table behind BJ and at an artsy crucifix propped up against the wall. It's about twelve inches high and about as wide and is made of nails, all silver, all varying sizes.

It always concerns me when a copper is so in your face with his religious beliefs. I've worked with two officers who would read their bibles when it was my turn to drive. One would ask suspects to pray with her in the backseat of the patrol car, and the other would give sermons to suspects as well as to complainants. Didn't like working with them because they were on a personal mission, which made them a danger to themselves and others. One is thankfully off the street now and the other quit. But I worked with another guy for several months who had a degree in theology, and he was as gritty and street savvy as any cop I've ever worked with. I'd work with him again in a heartbeat. Seeing this material in BJ's office makes me wonder if his beliefs ever bump heads with what needs to be done.

"Any questions, Sam?" BJ asks.

"Lots," I say.

He smiles. "Well, I'm going to let Angela and Steve bring you up to speed on the computer programs we use, our hard-copy filing systems, how we pay informants, and so on. When the Fat Dicks come in, we'll gather again to hear what they have on the lynching and on Mark's assault. Angela, make sure Sam reads up on the attempted arson of the Mosque, the cross burning, the assaults, and the bullying cases."

"Will do," she says.

"Glad you're on the team, Sam" BJ says, standing and extending his hand. "Let's you and I have coffee after lunch."

"Sounds good," I say, getting up. Probably wants to chat about where my head is and the rumor I was thinking about resigning. As my boss, he has a need to know, but I'm still not comfortable talking about it, maybe because I'm not comfortable with all of it myself.

Steve had to go meet up with a snitch, and BJ left for another meeting in the Chief's office, so for the next ninety minutes Angela, her chair turned around to face my desk, gives me a rundown on the computer, the files, where the keys are to the cars, and the nuances of getting along with the boss.

I have only a passing acquaintance with her. I keep hearing she can be a tad militant about race, but I'm not one to put much faith in gossip. Still, I wonder about the warnings.

Afrocentric. I just heard the word for the first time a few weeks ago when I was cruising the cable channels and paused on a fashion show. A voice-over called a black woman's long, zebra-striped dress, afro hair, and the cluster of multi-colored beads draped around her neck as Afrocentric. "To celebrate her heritage," the voice noted. Funny what sticks in my mind. I look at Angela's African-style top and her multiple bracelets of copper, fake or real bone, and earthy-colored beads. I notice several pictures under her desk blotter of her with two black women, all dressed similarly. Afrocentric.

Regardless of whether it means anything, she would have to be a good cop to be assigned to Intelligence for the last few years.

But there was the blatant way she looked into my eyes when she came into the office, along with the ol' up-and-down appraisal. She's done it twice more since we've been talking. She sizing me up as a potential father of her children, the ones she has now, and the new ones we make together? Nice for my ego, but even if Mai wasn't in my life, this kind of attention could be a problem.

"I'm going to talk with a guy today who lives just above Old Town," Angela says. "He's not an official snitch; he's a second cousin of mine. He's been away for about four days and he's back at work today. I want to see if he knows anything about the lynching. You want to go with me?"

I shrug. "I don't know. I'm kinda swamped, and all."

She smiles. "Grab the second set of keys from the right on

the board next to BJ's office and let's go. You drive, rookie."

*   *   *

We're three blocks back from the main intersection at Second and Burnside. I'd like to hang a left onto Burn but traffic is at a standstill. In fact, traffic is a mess everywhere in the area, including the side streets where drivers are trying to get through the jam or trying to get away from it.

"Listen," Angela says, turning up the FM station. "The news guy said to stay away from the area of Third and Couch. There, hear him? Said there's some kind of police action going on there."

"Info we could have used three minutes ago," I say, cranking a hard right onto Pine and heading toward Tom McCall. "I'll shoot north and then cut back to get us up to Twenty-First. Wonder what's happening there. Probably a shooting or a knifing. I worked the area for a few months way back when I—"

"There," Angela says, pointing at the police radio this time. "A unit said something about a struck pedestrian. Fatality."

"Ooooh, okay. Getting run over is considered a natural death down there with all the drunks staggering around."

"So sad," Angela says, sounding like she means it. No dark humor for her, I guess. She looks over at me. "You up on Ocnod?"

"Oc ... The guy who was lynched?"

She nods. "Street name Ocnod. His real name was Qasim Al-Sabti. The Fat Dicks think he was from Iraq because they found a famous artist with the same name listed in Google, a long-dead painter who lived in Baghdad. Our Ocnod has lived here in Portland for fifty years."

"Wait a sec," I say, cranking a left, which at least gets us heading toward Twenty-First. "So the guy lynched wasn't black?"

Angela shakes her head. "Not an African American and not black the way the GP has been led to believe."

"So the general public thinks he's black because of what the police told the media?"

"Yup, but it wasn't a lie at the time. He didn't have ID on him and he looks like an African American. It wasn't until yesterday the Fat Dicks learned his name was Qasim Al-Sabti."

"Oh man. So our perp killed a man he thought was African American, but he was really a Middle Easterner. Oh man!"

"Yup. Still a hate crime, though. Deputy Chief Rodriguez told BJ to tell us to keep Ocnod's real ethnicity hush-hush."

"I can imagine the African American community is ... concerned." I was going to say upset, but Angela might think it's a feeble word given the gravity of the issue.

She snaps her head toward me. "You think they might be *concerned* because a black man was hung from a fucking light post?" At least she restrained her volume.

"Hold on, Angela." So this is what Clarence and the Deputy Chief Rodriguez were talking about. "Sorry I used the wrong word, or at least one you think is wrong. I was out of the country when this happened so I'm trying to play catch-up here. What I know is a black man was found lynched and there have been protest marches. In my experience, racially motivated crimes in the black community almost always lead to marches. So that's why I was asking."

I break our stare down first so I don't crash us into a parked car.

"All right," she says softly. "I give you that you're trying to play catch-up. What do you make—"

"Wait. You 'give me?'" I say meeting her eyes again. "'*Give* me'?"

She keeps looking at me until I have to look back out the windshield again. Twenty seconds pass. "Wrong word choice. Sorry."

"I'm sorry about my wrong word choice too."

Another twenty seconds pass. She looks over at me. "All right then."

"All right then," I say back. We smile at each other and the tension eases. Thing is, I don't care how sensitive she is to racial issues, I refuse to tiptoe around her. I'm not a racist so I have no reason to watch my every word.

"What I was going to ask, Sam, as someone just learning all this, what do you make of the fact he was lynched and 'nigger' was carved into his chest?"

"At first blush, I'd say hanging him might be a message, same with the N word scratched into him. Hanging someone because of their color or ethnicity is pretty unusual, although they used to do it down in the South. The KKK and similar ilk. But around here?"

"I see," she says, her voice tight again but not angry. Maybe she didn't like me saying 'N word.' What the hell am I supposed to say? Naughty word? Not going to happen. "I agree with one part and disagree with the other," she says.

"Which is which?" I ask.

"I think lynching the man and the carving, oh, by the way, the word wasn't 'scratched' into his skin. The ME said it was cut all the way into his sternum. Anyway, I agree those things were a message. I disagree lynching black folk was only done in the past. Last year in Chicago, a black man walked into what he didn't know was a big-time racist bar. The next morning,

Chicago PD found him hanging from a roof overhang in the alley out back. Last Fall in Boise, Idaho, some teenage white boys raped a pregnant black woman, and then hung her from a tree."

"Damn."

"Yeah, damn," she snaps.

I hang a left on Tenth and look over at her again, and say pointedly, "I didn't know about those hangings, Angela."

She looks back at me. "Okay."

I'm not accepting her 'okay.' "My point, Angela, is my not knowing about them does not make me a bad guy and it doesn't give you a reason to snap at me."

"I never said you were a—"

"You implied it by your tone."

"I—"

"Here are a couple of things about me. One of the reasons I agreed to work on hate crimes is the very thought of someone getting hurt because of their sexual preference, ethnicity, race, skin color, religion, or whatever, pisses me the hell off. Secondly, you're black and I'm white. I don't have one iota of a problem with this. Do you?"

It's called putting the turd in the other guy's pocket.

"What? No, I don't," she says defensively, her eyes impossibly wide.

"Good, now tell me where we're going."

My eyes back on the road, I hear her take a deep breath as if she'd just been smacked in the face. Maybe no one has called her on her attitude before. "Hang a left up there. It's on the east side of the street."

"Thank you."

We ride in silence, which gives me a moment to look at a

part of Portland I haven't seen for a long while. This part of
Twenty-First Avenue has seen some rough economic times in
the last few years. There is a boarded-up storefront and right
across the street is another. I see a building not boarded but it
still looks as if it hasn't been occupied in a while. Here is one
remodeled with a nice all-brick front and big smoked window.

"There," Angela says, pointing at the brick building.

"What is it? There's no sign." The little one over the front
door reads: Enter In The Rear.

"Rose City Steam," Angela says. "Gay bathhouse. Pull in
the driveway there. It takes us to a parking area in the back."

I hang a left. "A gay bathhouse. Your cousin works here?"

"He's actually my mother's cousin, God rest her soul, which
makes him my ... something. Second cousin? Anyway, he's
been living down in Old Town since his wife died about ten
years ago. He knows everyone and everything going on in his
hood. As far as working here, he says they treat him right and
he's his own boss. Head of maintenance." She shrugs. "I don't
think he's gay."

There are about a dozen cars parked back here, which seems
like a lot for a place like this considering it's only noon. But
what do I know? Angela and I walk toward a canopied door.
It's fluorescent purple and guarded on each side by four-feet
high, shiny black panthers sitting on their haunches and looking eager to pounce. They're magnificent stone carvings that
must weigh five hundred pounds each.

Angela pulls open the door and we step into a small foyer
with sparkly purple walls draped with white, twinkling lights.
Straight ahead is a thick Plexiglas teller's window, and to the
right, a heavy-duty door with a buzzer. On the other side of the
window, a man wearing only a white athletic supporter sprays

cleaner on a small window in an open door on the opposite wall. From here we can see about halfway down the softly lit hall where half-a-dozen men are standing in a group talking and laughing. It would look like an office workplace setting except every man is stark naked.

"Angela!" greets the man whose jock strap makes him the most dressed on the other side of the window. He moves up to the teller window. Yowsa! He's got nipple piercings. He smiles at Angela. "How are you, sweet cheeks? Haven't seen you for a ... whoa! Like who's your knock-down-gorgeous-and-sit-on-my-face friend?"

Angela laughs. "This is Sam. He's a detective."

"Detective! Oh my. So he's a dick, on top all of that gorgeousness. Saaaam," he says, crotch gazing me. "My name is Teddy. Remember it, you'll be screeeeaming it later." Angela laughs.

I smile, and say, "Isn't going to happen, Teddy. I'm straight, it's great, I don't hate, and I don't discriiiiminate."

Teddy points at me, and laughs. "You're good, and oh so hot." He looks at Angela. "Want to see Terrance, sweet cheeks?"

"Just for a few minutes, Teddy. Appreciate it."

"Hold a sec," he says. He slips out of the room swinging his bare ass. After three or four steps he looks over his shoulder, and says, "Sam?"

"It's still no, Teddy."

He lets out a theatrical sigh. Down the hall, several of the men, most in the twenties and thirties, turn all the way toward us. I'm not sure if they are really interested in us or just want to pose.

"I love it here," Angela says.

"I bet you do."

A small sign by the window lists the price and the rules:

- No clothing allowed past the locker room except for sandals.
- No alcohol or drugs.
- Condoms will be worn for all sexual activity.
- When you're told "not interested" respect it and move on.

There are about a dozen more, but before I can read them the door opens and a fit-looking, sixty-something black man in a blue tank top and matching shorts steps out, his arms spread wide. "Angie baby. How you be? How you be?"

The two embrace for a moment, then Angie says, "Terrance, this is my partner Sam. Sam, this is Terrance."

"What it is, Sam?" he says pumping my hand "What it is? You taking care of my girl?"

"I got a feeling she can do just fine without my help."

"Sure 'nuff the truth," he cackles, extending his palm toward me. "Sure 'nuff." I slap it.

"Can we go outside, Terrance?" Angela says.

"Let's do it, let's do it." He pulls the door open and gestures for us to lead the way out. "This about Ocnod?" he says as the three of us sit on a long bench at the side of the building.

Angela nods. "He lived in Old Town. Did you know him?"

"Talked to him off and on, off and on. If you squint your eyes he looked like a black man, you know. But he wasn't. Heard he was from Iraq or some such. Don't think he liked real blacks too much. Maybe cuz everyone thought he was one." Terrance cackles. "Sad thing hanging him up. Don't know what to make of it, I don't."

"When's the last time you saw him?" Angela asks.

"Let's see, let's see. I was gone for a few days, but I think I seen him two weeks ago, or some such."

"Where, cousin?"

"At Hung Far Low."

"The Chinese food joint on Fourth?" I ask.

"Yes, sir, yes, sir. Lunch time. Didn't talk. No we didn't. I waved, but he didn't wave back. Don't think he liked real blacks too much."

I nod. "Any reason you know for someone to kill him?"

"Wasn't a friendly sort but don't know a reason to kill him, I don't."

"Any strange faces in Old Town?" Angela asks.

Terrance cackles loudly. "For sure, cousin. For damn sure. You probably mean new strange faces."

She smiles. "I do."

"More in the winter when it's cold and folks stop into Portland to get free food and clothes. Now, not so much. A couple dudes with huge backpacks yesterday, but nothin' too strange about them. Can't think of nothin' else ..." He looks off for a moment.

Angela touches his arm. "What, cousin?"

"Two ladies—last weekend, I think. Yup, Saturday. Saturday for sure. Big women, not fat-fat you know, but big, like they could knock any man on his ass. Both white. They were walking along Fifth and cut down Everett to Third. One had a camera."

"What caught your eye, Terrance?" I ask.

"Something about them, something about them. I only looked at them shortly, very shortly, but I remember thinking they didn't fit in Old Town. Not like folks passing through, or like no tourist, neither."

"What did they look like, Cousin?"

"Well, no prejudice intended, none at all, but if I had to guess, I'd say they was dykes. You know—lesbos—sisters for sure. Maybe twins. Had short hair combed like a man, both of them. One had her damn head shaved here, on the sides but real long in the back. Wearing work jeans. One wore blue ones, the other had black ones. Both had work shirts, sleeves rolled up to the elbows, the both of them. Oh, yes, yes, yes, yes. Just remembered. One had a swastika tattoo. Right here on the back of her hand, left, no, right hand. Right hand. And if I had to guess, it was a Stoney Lonesome tattoo. You know, done down there in Salem at the prison, or some such."

"Prison tattoo," I say. "Good info, Terrance. Good eyes."

"Cousin, where did Ocnod live?"

"I always saw him around Everett. Probably in Rose City Place, old hotel turned into apartments between Everett and Davis."

We chat for a few minutes longer but Terrance doesn't have any more useful info.

"Thanks so much, cousin," Angela says. "They treating you okay here?"

"Oh yes, oh yes. None of them too interested in me, except every once in a while one will make a move when the pickin's slim, you know. But I'm still straight as an arrow. Mostly I tend to the furnace in the winter and the air conditioners in the summer. I clean up things too. Pretty good job, I guess. Pretty good job."

Angela leans across and gives him a hug. "Thanks, cousin. I'll tell Auntie Beth I saw you."

"Thank you, thank you. Got to get over there to see her. I

do." He extends his hand to me. Take care of this girl, Sam. She can be ornery but she's a good one."

"Ornery?" I say with pretend surprise. "No way."

Angela struggles not to smile.

*   *   *

"To be fair," I say, as I guide our car down Burnside, "we should stop at Mary's Club to see if they've seen anything unusual." Mary's Club, located on Broadway, one block south of Old Town, is one of the oldest strip joints in Portland.

"Uh, huh. You want to know if any of those topless girls have seen anything?"

"Well, you just got an eyeful of bottomless dudes."

"There were bottomless dudes there? Why didn't you tell me?"

We're tension free for the moment and I hope it continues, but I'm not betting on it.

"You familiar with Second Chance, an old secondhand store at Two and Davis in Old Town?" I ask.

Angela shakes her head. "No. Why?"

"I know the owner. He's got another store on Southeast Fifteenth and Taylor. If he's not there, he's usually at his Davis store. We can check to see if he's seen anyone around who's caught his eye."

"Let's do it," Angela says. "Will he be dressed?"

"I so hope so."

I find a parking spot a couple blocks away from the store. It's a pleasant, partly sunny June day so there are lots of people on the sidewalk, a mix of down-and-outers and uptowners, the latter braving the two- or three-block walk into Old Town to lunch at No Cows Allowed, a spendy, all veggie eatery.

"In five years," I say, gesturing toward everything in our path, most if not all of the winos, dopers, panhandlers, and low-income folks down here will be a thing of the past, replaced by glossy establishments catering to the high-rise folks."

"Think you're right," Angela says. "But as is always the case, those displaced won't be helped out of their poverty and addictions. They will be shoved somewhere else, the east side of the Willamette River, maybe, or to North Portland. But the one place they won't be allowed to go is to the neighborhoods where the politicians, attorneys, money lenders, and CEOs live."

"So right. It never fails to amaze me why—"

"Hell-oooo salt-and-pepper people," a raggedly looking man says gravelly, stepping out from a doorway and blocking our way. "Help an old altar boy buy a jug of communion wine, will you?" The guy looks to be in his thirties but they've been hard years. He's got grime imbedded into his skin, long unwashed hair, and filthy, mismatched clothes. Panhandling is legal in Portland, but it's illegal to block people's path. When we start to move around him, he sidesteps to block us. "Your donation?" he says, holding out his palm, his mouth smiling, his eyes not.

"You're going to move out of the way," Angela says. "We're the police. Move now!"

"Come on, pepper," he says, reaching for her jacket. "Be a good Catholic and—"

I grab his arm and yank it toward me hard enough to spin him completely around. I reach around and cup his forehead with my palm and pull his head up and over until he plops unceremoniously onto his rear.

"We're the police, pal," I say to the top of his head. "I want you to—"

He kicks at Angela, just barely missing her leg, and reaches behind him to grab my ankle. I jerk my leg away, drop down onto one knee, and slide the inside of my wrist over the bridge of his nose. Before he can bring his hands up, I pull his head back against my chest, grab my fist with my free hand, and pull my wrist in hard against his schnoz, wiggling my hand a little to grind in the misery.

"Aaaah! Sweet Lord!" he bellows, his rough voice now nasal, his hands struggling to pry my crushing wrist away.

"Put your hands behind you," Angela commands, her hand-cuffs ready.

"Do as she says," I say into his ear as I apply more pressure. "Do it or you will never breathe right again." He releases my arm and quickly puts his hands behind him. "Cuff him now." I scoot back a couple of inches to give her room. She snaps on one, then the other.

My cell phone rings. It's got to be Mark. It will have to wait.

I keep my hand on his shoulder as I stand and lean over to look at him. His nose is pouring snot and blood, and tears are making dirty rivers down his cheeks.

"Stay still, altar boy," Angela says. She extracts her hand radio from a holder attached to her pants belt. It was hidden under her jacket. I didn't even think about asking to get one before we left the office. Guess I'm rustier than I thought.

"Four Four Four," she says into her hand radio.

"Four Four Four," dispatch repeats.

"Can we get a uniform car to Two and Northwest Everett to transport a prisoner for us?"

"Eight Thirty-Two, can you do it?"

"Eight Thirty-Two, we're a couple blocks away."

Twenty minutes later, Angela and I are again on the way to the secondhand shop. The two uniformed officers knew him and said his street name really is Altar Boy. He had two warrants for failure to appear, one for an assault on a police officer and the other for aggressive begging.

"You know," Angela says, "I could have handled the man if you'd given me the chance."

"Sorry," I say. "Soon as I saw him reach for you, I just reacted. I didn't know if he was going to grab you or hit you, and I couldn't see if he had a weapon in his other hand."

She laughs. "Well, it was pretty cool. There a name for your nose crush move? It's gotta hurt."

"There is," I say. "It's called nose-oyama crush-azuki. It's a good one because it messes with the recipient's breathing and vision, plus it hurts like holy hell. Not particularly a good police technique unless you got a partner to do the handcuffing."

"Good thing I was there to save your ass," she says with a smile.

"Yes, ma'am."

Oh, man, are we flirting with each other? Don't need it. Don't need it at all.

My cell rings again. I pry it out of my pocket, thankful for the distraction, and check the screen. "Mark," I say. "How are you doing?"

"Sam. Did I catch you at a bad time?"

"It's good. I'm actually working. Rodriguez put me to work in Intel today and already I'm out serving and protecting. At the moment I'm in Old town with Angela Clemmons. We just pinched an aggressive panhandler." Angela smiles at me. "It's Intel's secondary mission, you know." I expect him to laugh but I get only silence. "Mark? You okay?"

"Yeah. Just so tired. I was going to bother you for a ride but I'll grab a cab. Got to get home and check on the place, and get a shower."

"Listen, buddy. We were about to interview a man but I can get over to the hospital after and—"

"No, no, no. I'm good. A cab's fine."

"Hold on a sec," I say, retrieving my wallet. I find Rudy's card: RUDOLPH ABRAHAM LINCOLN. WORLD'S BEST CABBIE. "I got people, Mark. Putting you on hold. Don't go away."

I tap in Rudy's cell number.

"Rudy, where to?"

"Still pulling on innocent folk's eyelids?"

"Ha ha. It was a hoot, wasn't it, Sam? How you doin'? You goin' to buy me a burger?"

"Hey, Rudy. I'm working right now. Let me give you a shout in a couple of days."

"Listen to this. Weighed in this morning and sure enough, down one."

"Excellent. Wife happy?"

Oh, yeah. Says the thought of me with a six pac makes her feel warm all over." He laughs uproariously.

"Well, gotta say, thinking of you with a six pac kinda does it for me too."

"Uh oh. Uuuuh oh. I got 'em comin' at me from all directions."

I laugh. "Listen, Rudy. If you're free, can you swing by Emanuel and pick up my friend Mark Sanderson? I'll have him meet you in the lobby."

"Consider it done. Just gassin' up and I'll be there in ten."

"Thanks, Rudy. I'll call you in a couple three days for a

burger."

"Ten four, Sam."

I click back to Mark. "Hey, me again. Got a cab coming for you. He'll meet you in the lobby in ten. His name is Rudy, black man, huge belly. I guarantee he will cheer you up before you get all the way home."

"Thanks, Sam. Appreciate it. How's it feel to be on the bricks?"

"Weird, good, fish out of water, exhilarating. How's David?"

Long pause, then softly, "The same. I'm ... scared. Got a bad feeling."

"I think you'll feel better after eating some nutritious food and sleeping a solid eight in your own bed."

"Maybe you're right."

"I am. You heading down to the lobby?"

"Almost there. Thanks, Sam. Talk to you later."

Angela has been standing a few feet away fiddling with her cell. When I pocket mine, she asks, "How's the lieutenant doing?"

"Hurting physically and hurting more mentally. He's really worried about David."

She shakes her head. "Sons of bitches," she says through gritting teeth.

"I concur."

"Is Second Chance on the corner there?" Angela asks. Before I can answer, she does. "Yes, it is. I can see the little sandwich board on the sidewalk. What's the man's name?"

"Mister Efrem Axelbrad."

"A mouthful," Angela says, pushing open the door. "Sounds Jewish."

"Detectives Reeves!" the seventy-four-year-old man shouts

from the back of the cluttered and dusty second-hand store. "Come in, sweet man. And your friend too." The old man clasps his hands and shakes them vigorously above his head as he twists and turns his way through all the old crap lying about. He points upward as he approaches, and says, "Praise God I can see you today, my sweet detective." He grips my arms and looks at me, his head nodding. His face shows hard years of worry and strain, his large nose and elongated ears sprouting more hair than his mole-covered, balding scalp. "Praise God. How are you, my friend?"

I laugh and touch his arms. "I am well, and you, Mister Axelbrad?"

"I am alive! Because of you." He looks at Angela. "Young woman, did you know? Detective Reeves saved my life. Four months, eight days, and," he looks at a big clock over his door, "one hour ago. He saved my life. Not at this store, my other one on Taylor, on the other side of the river. A hero. No, no, an angel," he says, jabbing his finger heavenward. "Sent from God himself. I'm seventy-four years old and Detective Reeves gave me a few more years."

Realization spreads across Angela's face as she looks from the old man to me. "Ooooh, so this is the man ..."

I nod, wondering if either of them can hear my pounding heart. Four months, eight days, and one hour ago, I interrupted an armed robbery in progress. A doper was pressing a gun against Mister Axelbrad's head—he was about to blow a hole in it, but I shot the tweaker first, right under the nose and into his medulla oblongata, which stopped all his body functions instantly, preventing him from reflexively pulling the trigger. A couple months later, I would shoot two more people.

"I am so happy to see you, Detective. But such terrible

nightmares I have. You too?"

"Yes," I say, and pocket my trembling hands. "This is Detective Angela Clemmons."

The old man bows several times, his hands still clasped. "So happy to meet you. You are a very pretty lady." He wags his finger at her. "Be careful of my friend here. He is most handsome, is he not?"

Angela shrugs indifferently, then smirks at me.

He points at her again, laughs. "Ooooh. Detective Sam. I think it is you who should be careful.

"We are investigating the hanging over on Third," I say quickly, wanting to terminate the uncomfortable moment." Mister Axelbrad shakes his head. "Ocnod. So sad. He was in here last week, you know? Bought a ... what was it? Oh, yes, a clock." He shrugs his thin shoulders. "Buys a clock and the poor bastard didn't have much time left. God has a sense of humor, no?"

"Did you know him well, sir?" Angela asks, looking at a dusty Darth Vader helmet.

"Ocnod? Not at all. He came in a few times, just looking around. He looked my age, you know, so I tried to engage him in conversation, but he didn't make an effort. Turned down my offer for some tea." He shrugs. "Shy maybe, or just not sociable."

"Too bad," I say. "He say anything about anyone bothering him, harassing him?"

Mister Axelbrad shakes his head. "Hard enough getting a hello out of him."

"How often are you at this store, sir," Angela asks.

"My brother and I rotate between the two stores. So I'm here three days a week usually." He closes his eyes and shakes his head. "I don't like so much working at the other place ... ever since ..." He pats my cheek and smiles, and I take a deep breath to slow my heart, which has been in the red zone since we walked through the door. "And my brother doesn't like working there anymore either. Might shut it down and work here for another year or two. My Hannah wants me to retire." He shrugs. "Maybe she is right. It is about time."

Angela touches his arm. "Have you seen anyone around who's caught your eye? You know, someone who didn't look right among all these other people who don't look right?"

"Yes, a woman!" he says, angrily swatting at the air. "An awful woman. *Oy-vey*! A big man-woman. Had a fucking swastika here." He jabs his finger at the back of his hand. "*Farshtinkener*! I saw it and my stomach ..." He clenches his fist ". . . it did like this." He steps over to a counter loaded with old, dusty junk, and picks up a foot and a half-long bone, bleached, chipped, from an animal's leg, or a human's, maybe. "I lift this up in my hand like this, and I tell her, 'You *nafka*! You whore. You get out of my shop or I will beat your ugly face in.'"

"What did she do?" I ask, thinking he looks like Samson had he lived into his senior years.

"The bitch left," he says with a shrug. "Who wants their face beat in with someone's bone?"

"What day?" Angela asks, eyeing the weapon. "What was she looking at in here?"

"A week ago, I think. Looking at knives, under the counter there. I felt like giving her a knife," He smacks his stomach. "Right in the *kishka*."

I put my hand on his shoulder. "You're all right, Mister Axelbrad."

"I see you have two video cameras in the corners back

there," Angela says. "Do you have tapes of when she came in?"

He shrugs. "Sorry. They are empty. For show only."

"No problem," I say. "How is business?"

He shrugs. "Could be better. But I don't worry so much about it. A *bi gezunt*, eh? So long as you've got your health."

I hand him my card. "I think you already have one but here's another. Call me if anything catches your eye. For sure call me if you see the woman again."

"That *nafka*!" he says loudly lifting the bone over his head. "If I call you, you better hurry before I bone her."

"Promise me you won't do any boning," I say, gently taking the bone from him and setting it on the counter.

"I will, my boy. But you should know I live by this, "Call on God, but row away from the rocks." He shrugs. "I have a temper, I'm sorry to say. My dear Hannah has been telling me for fifty years I need to control my temper. I try. It's all I can do."

I squeeze his shoulder. "Try real hard, okay. For me?"

He pats my face again. "I will try hard for you, my sweet boy." He looks at Angela. "You take care of him."

Angela smiles.

*   *   *

Turns out, Angela is quite the health food enthusiast. She takes me to her favorite lunch place, a vegetarian joint where most of the customers look like they are in dire need of protein and Vitamin B-12. Angela says she eats meat but likes the sandwiches here. She orders one so stuffed full of vegetation it would overdose a rabbit. I order the same thing but to be funny I ask for four slices of ham with extra mayo, which couldn't have shocked the skinny hippie dude behind the counter more if I'd slapped his mother.

Angela says she has been doing yoga three times a week for about six years and weight training twice a week for about ten years.

"Well, it's obviously working for you." Oh man. That sounded like flirting and could even be construed as sexual harassment.

She blushes, as much as a black person can blush, and says, "Thank you, Sam," all sweet and coy-like.

Angela is an attractive woman and there is where the thought ends. The slow body scan she gave me in the office made me feel uncomfortable as did the smiles we exchanged in the car after our getting-to-know-you spat. Of course, it didn't help we looked at naked men together, nor did Mister Axelbrad's teasing. Now my comment about her having a nice body is like a gusting Santa Ana wind buffeting an out-of-control fire in a southern California canyon.

Am I over thinking this? Hope so.

It's two p.m. by the time we finish lunch. We head toward the river walk where Mark and David were jumped, but there is construction in the area and not a parking place to be found, even for a police car. It's getting late anyway so we head back to the office, and fill out reports about our conversation with Terrance at the bathhouse and with Efrem Axelbrad at Second Chance. I call down to Central Precinct duty sergeant and ask her to have the Old Town beat cars keep an eye out for the two women we were told about and get their names and other vitals.

Angela and I fill in Steve and BJ on what we learned. Steve loves hearing about our arrest of the panhandler, especially liking the fact I used a couple of martial arts moves. "This is what I've been saying," Steve says to the lieutenant. "Did you know ghosts sit around campfires telling Chuck Norris stories?"

BJ isn't amused by any of it and asks me to remain as Steve and Angela leave the office. Guess I'm in trouble already and I have yet to work a full day, but in trouble for what?

BJ straightens some papers on his desk that don't need straightening and clears his throat that doesn't need clearing. "Sam," he says, in his whispery, Alec Baldwin voice, his face still angled down as if reading a report, though his eyes peer up at me from under his eyebrows. "Between Steve, Angela, and me, we have ten combined years in Intelligence, during which not one of us has used physical force. You're here one day and you're doing your kung fu thing on a homeless person."

"He was about to grab Angela," I say, sounding like a little kid alibiing his actions.

"You couldn't have backed away? You couldn't have sternly warned him to leave you alone?"

Is this guy for real? Now I'm pissed off. I control it, though, and reply calmly, "I hear what you're saying, boss, but if you've looked over my personnel file you won't find one complaint for excessive force, and I have been in many beefs on the job. I do not abuse people and I do not insult my art or my teachers by using my skills unnecessarily. Check with any of my previous partners and they will tell you I am the last guy to use force."

"I'm glad to hear it," the lieutenant says, his face still angled toward his desktop. I notice for the first time he has a serious comb over. "This position isn't about jumping fences, doing karate chops, and shots fired. It's a low-keyed job about gathering information. Period. And I don't need to remind you this is especially important for *you*."

"Understood," I say, gritting my teeth, and standing. I want to tell him next time I'll do exactly the same thing if I think another officer is about to be grabbed, punched, or whatever, but I refrain. His little speech isn't about me dumping a guy on his butt, at least I hope he's enough of a cop that that isn't what this is about. No, this is about him letting me know he isn't about to be embarrassed and put on the spot by me.

I'm well aware some cops dislike me intensely for what I did nine weeks ago. Well, welcome to the club because I hate what I did too. I destroyed a family, I shamed the PD, I instilled fear of the police in the people I'm sworn to protect, and I scarred my soul. I've been through hell over it and now after two months of confusion as to what I should do next, I made the decision to come back here to do what's right. If my boss has trouble with it, and if anyone else has trouble with it, well, screw 'em. And if my coming back gets to be too much—for them—I'm out of here.

"I'm done, Sam," BJ says, giving me all of his face. "Questions?"

"None, Lieutenant."

"Good. It's quitting time. See you tomorrow."

Steve and Angela ask if I want to have a beer with them and I decline, telling them I have to teach. Angela seems disappointed. Oh well.

I get my pickup and head toward my school, stopping first to get a Whopper. I give Mark a call while chowing down in my truck.

"How are you doing?"

"Hey, Sam," he says, with more life in his voice than I've heard since I've been home. "Your advice was all good. Your friend Rudy brought me home. What a live wire he is. Even had me laughing. He helped me in the house and with getting settled. And he volunteered to go to the grocery for me."

"Great, Mark. You sleep at all?"

"I did. Got about five hours in and I feel pretty good. Well, maybe not good, my ribs are killing me, but I feel awake."

"Heard anything on your case?"

"Nada. The Fat Dicks were in court all day so they didn't work it at all. Babcock and Tyler checked on surveillance tapes in the area and talked to some construction workers, but they didn't turn up anything. Hopefully tomorrow. How was your first day back?"

When I tell him about my day with Angela, he laughs and then groans in pain. "You better watch out," he says. "She is a looker. I've heard she's a bit of a racist, but apparently she's made an exception for you."

"You're funny. I'm not even remotely inter—" Mark's phone bleeps. "Sounds like you got a call, Mark. I'll let you get it. I've got to get over to the school."

"Okay, pal. Thanks for taking care of me."

I head on over to the church and park in the lot.

"Sensei," someone says from behind me as I climb out of my truck. It's Nate, the new black belt. He pulls his workout bag out of the trunk of a black Honda.

"Hey, Nate, good to see you," I say, extending my hand. Last evening when we chatted before class, he seemed subdued, as if he hadn't an ounce of energy. But he came alive during class. As soon as it was over, though, he slipped back into the same lifeless, quiet demeanor. Before he left, he came over to where I was talking with a couple of brown belts and thanked me. He hesitated for a second, as if he wanted to say something else, but he didn't, and left without uttering another word to anyone. I haven't known him long, but it's apparent he is a troubled man.

"You're here early," I say. "White belts are at six and black belts are at seven."

Nate nods. "I was going to work on stretching while the white belts trained." He's wearing all black again, a long-sleeve button shirt this time. A large turquoise ring adorns the index finger of his right hand.

"Sounds good," I say. We look at each other for a moment, break eye contact, and then look back at the same time.

He clears his throat. "You teaching the white belts?" he asks, his tone more like, "Do you have to teach the white belts?"

"The padre will teach it if I'm not there." He nods, looks at the passing traffic, sniffs, and then looks back at me. "Nate, you want to sit in my pickup?"

He tightens his lips, blinks several times, nods.

I move my truck just off the lot and park at the curb a few feet away from the church entrance. "The arriving students shouldn't interrupt us now."

He sits stiffly, holding his workout bag in his lap, like a woman on the bus clutching her purse. He unconsciously squeezes the fabric with both hands.

"You looked real good in class last night," I say to get the conversation going. "It was clear you had good teachers." He bows his head slightly, the gesture reminding me of my new Vietnamese friends in Saigon. "You've trained with my black belts already, right?"

"Yes," he says. "They are very good, strong, fast. I especially like their attitudes. No one shows off. I have seen too much of it at other schools."

"Thank you. I'll take that as a compliment. I have always taught that besides self-defense, the martial arts should teach you to respect the struggle, respect it in yourself and respect it in your training partners. In my school, there is no place for strutting peacocks."

He nods.

When he doesn't speak, I ask, in an attempt to establish a comfortable connection, "It's been my experience most kenpo practitioners are hand specialists."

"My teacher is a very good kicker but he is amazing with his hands. So I lean toward hand techniques more than kicking."

"Most street encounters are settled with the hands, anyway. I don't think I know what weapons are used in kenpo." Actually, I do. Just trying to encourage conversation.

"The usual: staff, Chinese sword, chain. My teacher helped me adapt my family's war club to the martial arts."

"Really. You mean the hammer-looking weapon with a rock attached to one end?"

Nate smiles, no doubt at my ignorance. "I have mine," he says, unzipping his bag. He rummages through his training gear to the bottom, and extracts a thick cylinder of rolled brown and white cowhide.

"As near as my father can tell," Nate says, unwrapping it, "this has been in our family for over a hundred and fifty years. He told me another family might have owned it before, and it was either lost in battle or maybe dropped when its owner fell injured or dead. He lifts it up with reverence. He doesn't offer it to me to hold.

The twelve- or fifteen-inch-long handle is some kind of hardwood with black cowhide wrapped in the middle, a clump of brownish fur above it, then another band of black cowhide, and near the top one more clump of fur. I've seen photos of war clubs with a fist-sized rock secured to the end, but this one has about a ten-inch-curved piece of something black and hard looking. It's not steel and I don't think it's a rock. One end looks a little like an axe and the other end a blunt snout, like a hammer. Whatever it is, someone has carved about a dozen shark-like teeth into the axe end.

"This would leave a fella lonesome for his skull," I say. "What is the head made of?"

"Jawbone of a buffalo. See how this end has been ground to give it teeth?"

"Nasty," I say. "Guess you could hit with the blunt end too? Like a hammer?"

"It's all good." He spins it in his hand so the hammer end is forward, and then snaps his wrist a couple times as if pounding in a nail. "You can bash someone's head or any other body part with the hammer end." He spins the blade side forward, snaps his wrist again to hit an imaginary target, then rips the blade downward. "I like to hack with it like it's an ax and then slice downward a few inches to rip flesh with the teeth."

"Gee, I was going to ask you to teach it to the tiny tots class until you mentioned the ripping flesh part." He smiles. "Impressive. How often do you train with it?"

"Three or four days a week. I've created a routine of strikes, blocks, and combinations. There is no one to test me, but my father and grandfather approved when I demonstrated my skills."

"You'll have to show me. Not on me, of course, maybe on one of the white belts."

Nate laughs, the first time I've heard him do so. It fades quickly. Silently he rewraps the club and puts it back under his training gear. He folds his hands on top of the bag. When he doesn't say anything, I crack the window a little to let in some air. I'm not going to force the conversation this time. The ball is in his court.

Awkward silence. More awkward silence. Then, "How did you do it?" he asks softly, looking out the windshield.

"Meaning?"

Thirty seconds pass. "How did you survive what happened to you?"

I know he's not referring to the shooting in the secondhand store. He means the one in the house, the hostage taker ... and the hostage. Three cops have asked me this same question. They had been involved in deadly force encounters, all good shoots. Still, they were haunted by their experiences. I told them every day is a challenge because every day I wake up, I'm a killer. Alcoholics have the twelve-step program. There isn't anything out there for cops who kill innocent children.

On two occasions, people who recognized me at the grocery asked the same thing. Actually, they asked how I could live with myself. My first impulse was to strike out at them. My second was to hope they'd strike me. In the end, I walked away without doing or saying anything.

When I tell Nate it's mostly the ol' one-day-at-a-time thing, he nods, as if he knew already knew it, but knowing wasn't helping. "Do you feel like telling me what happened?" I ask.

He shrugs.

"I'm sorry, I thought you were wanting to talk about—"

"Sensei, have you heard the expression, 'Men are at war with each other because each man is at war with himself'?"

I shake my head. "I haven't but it's interesting." I wonder if my father knows it.

"I'm not sure if it applies to what is going on between our countries around the world because, as has always been the case, the grunts, the one's doing the fighting, aren't privy. Their job is to put on the war garb and go into harm's way. Some go mindlessly into the fray, others go like wound-up robots, others go with a sense of doing something right for the indigenous people. Lastly, there is a small percentage who go in with the anticipation of getting to kill. I went two times with all those reasons except for wanting to kill."

He shakes his head as he looks out the side window. He mindlessly drums his fingernails on the glass for a moment before clutching the fabric on his gym bag again. He takes in a deep breath and lets it out. "I killed during my first tour ... three times. The first was two months after I'd been in Iraq, the second one after six months there, and the third man I killed during my eighth month. All of them were firing at us and all were armed. I ... didn't feel good about killing and I didn't feel bad. I guess I felt ... nothing. I kept thinking I should feel something, but there was nothing there. It was like white noise. Even when my captain told me that those I killed would not kill any more of us, still, I felt nothing."

Can't say I had the same experience. After I shot the tweaker who was about to shoot Mister Axelbrad, I felt horrible. I remember collapsing against the plate glass window outside of his store and losing my breakfast on the sidewalk, and losing it again when I got back to the office. For the two months I was off duty, I'd fluctuate between feeling giddy one moment and sinking into a deep funk the next. Doc Kari always says whatever I feel is perfectly normal because I experienced an abnormal event. It's hard to keep that in mind sometimes.

Nate continues, "I was home for a few months and then I was ordered to go back over for a second tour, to Afghanistan this time. My wife was extremely upset, my four-year-old daughter was inconsolable, and I was having problems facing the possibility of having to kill again."

Nate looks down at his bag for a moment and turns to me. "I said last night I'm not related to Geronimo or Cochise, but I possess their warrior nature. And I think being a member of the warrior class is an honorable thing. But somewhere along the line during my second tour things ... my belief in acting honorably got ... buried. I became miserable, anxious, angry, full of hate, and I wanted revenge—desperately."

He pauses, his eyes focused on mine but his mind off in some dusty rock pile in the Middle East. My sense is he has had these thoughts before, but this is the first time he's verbalized them.

"I don't know, Nate. If I've learned anything about violence it's that everyone processes what they see and do differently. Some have issues with it right away; others might not feel the impact for a long while; some never have a problem with it; some suffer all their life. There's no wrong or right about how you feel. "

He shakes his head, but I don't think it's directed at what I just said. It's more like he's trying to shake out something revolving in his mind. He's silent for a moment, his eyes on his hand as it slides the zipper over and back on his workout bag.

"It's not what happened in Iraq," he says. "It's what happened in Afghanistan. It's what I ... allowed to happen."

I start to ask what he means but I decide not to intrude. Sometimes not responding can be a powerful tool to get someone to talk.

"Do you know about the dust there?" he asks, his eyes wide, his body almost vibrating with ... What? Anxiety for sure. Fear maybe.

"In Afghanistan, you mean? The dust in Afghanistan?"

"Yes," he says. He's working the zipper faster than he was a moment ago. Back and forth, back and forth.

"I'm ..." I shrug. "I guess I don't know anything about—"

"It's a constant," he snaps. "It blows all the time. It gets in your eyes, ears, mouth. You breathe it in with each inhale but you don't breathe it all out when you exhale. See the problem?" Nate is talking faster now, one sentence flowing into the next, the zipper sliding back and forth, back and forth. "I researched it online while I was there. I knew it couldn't be good for you, the dust. I just knew it. I breathed it in when I was in Iraq, and I didn't breathe it all out there, either. I read the dust is made up of a thousand particles, some so small they can sit on the head of a pin. Aluminum, lead, tin, manganese, and other shit. All of it causes neurological disorders, and stuff like cancer, lung problems, heart disease.

"But that's just what the Army tells us. Here is what they aren't saying. Some of the particles are from humans. Particles are flaking off the skin of millions of diseased Afghanis. Dead ones too. They just bury their dead in the dust and under rocks. They don't put their coffins in concrete liners like we do. So their bodies decompose and become part of the dust, part of those particles on the head of a pin, and it blows and we breathe it in. But we don't breathe it all out."

"So you're saying—I guess I don't know what you're saying, Nate."

"The dust," he says irritably. "I'm saying it's part of it. The Army admits we're breathing it in and it's making the troops sick. And the heat. Who knows what the awful heat does to you—the heat—and, you're packing eighty pounds of shit on your back. Then there's the IEDs. They're invisible, see? You can't fight them because you can't see them. Not until they blow. Not until they explode and take your legs and feet and balls." He nods his head rapidly. "Yes, improvised explosive devices take your balls.

"I've seen six vehicles get hit by IEDs. Two times, there were indigenous people on the road when it happened, like they were waiting for it to happen. They laughed. They laughed when the vehicle blew and the legs blew off, and when the one guy lost his balls. They laughed."

The zipper—back and forth, back and forth.

"I hated the indigenous and I hated the dust. Both were killing us. You understand? The dust and the IEDs. The heat was miserable, the constant tension was miserable. But the IEDs and the dust ..." He snaps his head toward me, his long hair swishing about, his eyes looking wild, his face dark with blood. He jerks his head toward the windshield.

"Nate, look at me for a moment." He does. "Breathe with me, okay?" He frowns a little. "Humor me, Nate, and follow me as I count. Please sit up straight and close your eyes. Straighter. Good."

I wish my father were here. He is a master at guided meditation. His voice hypnotizes, takes you in, takes you under.

"Okay, Nate, now breathe in slowly, two, three, four. Hold it, two, three, four. Exhale slowly, two, three, four. Hold it, two, three, four. That's one cycle. Now let's do it again. "In, two, three, four. Hold, two, three, four ..."

After three more cycles, Nate's complexion lightens and his breathing has returned to normal. He looks at me, nods. "I'd forgotten about it," he says, his voice mellow, again under his control. "They taught it to us in my unit."

"Helped me a few dozen times these past couple of months. Do you want to continue talking? Or we can always do it later."

"If I may, I'd like to finish."

"Sure."

Nate takes a deep breath, lets it out. "Here goes," he says, more to himself then to me. "My best buddy in Afghanistan was another Indian, Jay Butterfly, hundred percent Blackfoot from Montana. Jay had been hurt in the COP, a combat outpost, unloading a vehicle. He'd been sleeping in his bunk when they told him to go out and help unload some heavy fifty-caliber ammo cans. So, crazy guy that he was, he went out barefoot, and one of the cans fell on his right one and crushed four of his toes and some major bones in the top of the foot. The last time I talked to Jay, he was about to get shipped stateside and he said he had to tell me something. Said he needed to unburden himself."

"Unburden himself?"

Nate nods. "Yes, but it ended up burdening me. Says he knew about two guys, both sergeants, who were killing civilians. Fun kills, thrill kills, whatever you want to call it. The people weren't a threat; they weren't even the enemy. They were people we were supposed to be helping. Killed them just because they were Afghanis. He knew for sure of two. I don't know if he saw it happen or what, because all he said was he, 'knew for sure.'"

"Damn," I whisper.

"He told me the sergeants' names. They weren't in my platoon. They were in another one in the COP. I knew them, or of them, although I hadn't seen them in a while. Loud mouths, obnoxious. Or at least they had been. Because when I saw them after Jay told me what they had been doing, they weren't so loud anymore, they kept to themselves, talking quietly, sitting together all the time.

"A couple weeks after Jay shipped out, I heard the sergeants were getting an attaboy for killing two other Afghanis who were about to attack them with pistols. The two troops claimed they were quicker and blew away the young men, teenagers, before they could get off a shot. Their story was different than the one Jay had told me.

"Then it happened again about three weeks after they got the award. This time the two tossed a grenade at an old man. They said he had a pistol on him too. The two got another attaboy, and they were strutting around like banty roosters. Then someone, I don't know who, found some photos. I think they were on one of the sergeants' computers, but I'm not sure. Anyway, the photos showed these guys with the two dead teens and the old man. They had taken pictures of each other so only one guy was in each shot. In one, one of the sergeants was smiling and kneeling next to one of the dead teenagers, and lifting the kid's head by his hair. Another shot showed the other sergeant pretending to kiss the old man's forehead. In another pic, the same sergeant was pretending to have sex with the old Afghani."

"Oh, man," I say, shaking my head. "I think I read about it. The two were charged, weren't they?"

Nate nods. "Yes, they were eventually figured out. The Army is talking about the death penalty."

"So sad," I say. "Atrocities happen in every war. For every hundred great, righteous warriors, there is one criminal psychopath."

"These two killed five people," Nate says, his eyes penetrating mine, the skin across his forehead and around his mouth impossibly tight. "The sergeants planted the weapons on the people they killed. Jay told me about two of them. The other three happened after ... *after* I knew about what they were doing."

"I'm not following."

"What I told you before about the heat, the toxic dust, the IEDs, the laughter, the constant tension ... I ... my ... craziness ... it peaked. I was so filled with hatred for the Afghanis. I pushed them around, insulted their culture, called them 'dune coons,' 'camel jockeys,' 'towel heads,' 'dead meat.'"

"Nate, I would think under such horrible conditions it wouldn't be unusual for a guy to ..."

"Thing is ... I knew what those two sergeants were doing—and I didn't report it. Instead, I applauded it."

*   *   *

Mai hasn't answered my calls on Skype or my cell phone calls since I've been home tonight. I tried at eight p.m., eight thirty, and again at nine. It's midmorning tomorrow in Saigon, so she should still be in the house. Plus, we agreed to chat at eight at night my time each day. I could call our father, but I don't want to come across clingy and desperate, which I sort of am right now. Mostly I'm worried, remembering how crazy things were before I left.

I'm sitting in my kitchen eating a yogurt blended with protein powder, blueberries, and a little Cool Whip, my usual post-workout meal. The black belt class went well, though Nate and I were a little down for a while after our talk.

I think I did a convincing job of hiding my feelings about what he had told me as I greeted my black belts, many of whom I hadn't seen for a few weeks. They have been my friends for years and have been infinitely supportive during all my troubles and in keeping the school going while I was in Saigon. I started the class and within a few minutes, Nate and I were enjoying the endorphin rush of hard training.

The guy is carrying an enormous burden. He said his intense hatred for Middle Easterners has mellowed since he's been home, but the feelings come back in a red hot flash whenever he sees a reference to Afghanistan, Iraq, or any of those other countries over there. The feelings don't last long, but they bother him so much he doesn't watch the news or read the paper. Still, no matter where he goes, there is always a magazine cover, a movie trailer, a TV playing, and there it is again.

We discussed his seeking professional help, but unfortunately his insurance doesn't provide for mental health, and there is no way he would confide in anyone in the Army. He will have a medical plan after he joins the fire department, but he needs help now. Doc Kari comes immediately to mind, and I told Nate I would ask her for recommendations.

I try Mai again. Nothing.

After a shower, I put on baggie pants and a T-shirt, and call Mai again. Damn! I try to read an old National Geographic magazine but I can't focus. I head into my bedroom and lift the window to a chorus of barking dogs, sirens in the distance, and jets streaking overhead. I close the window.

I must admit my first day on the job went pretty well. I'll have to tip toe around Angela and hope her crush passes. Police officers work virtually shoulder to shoulder for eight hours and we share a variety of intense experiences. Sexual tension occurs sometimes. In fact, I've had a crush or two on female partners. Fortunately, I've been able to keep my cool and wait for the crush to work itself out.

BJ, I don't have a good read on yet. I've heard guys say he is a good boss, which, they always add, makes up for his lack of street experience. Supposedly, the lieutenant, who has been on three years longer than I have, only worked the street for a couple of years before getting promoted to sergeant in Records Division. Five years later he made lieutenant and was assigned to Community Affairs for a few years after which he transferred to Intelligence where he's been ever since. I'm not sure what to read into his accusation that I *chose* to use force on the street guy. Talk about jumping to conclusion without having all the facts. Guess I'll have to tiptoe around him too.

I try Mai once more. Double damn!

Being back on the job felt okay. I didn't feel bad and I didn't feel out of place. It was like slipping on a favorite pair of shoes, easy, comfortable.

Hell, tomorrow I might even carry my gun.

CHAPTER FIVE

Yolanda Simpson laboriously made her way up the litter-strewn stairs, grasping hand over hand on the splintery handrail that threatened to rip from the stained wall with her every tug. Her brain was swimming from a thumb-thick joint and the however many pulls from the jug of wine she shared with Candy in her car. Sharing a little wine after they'd call it quits for the night was a two-month-long tradition for the two of them. The fat joint was an extra bonus she found at the bottom of her purse next to the Vaseline. On top of her brain fog, her legs were tired as hell from walking on concrete for the past several hours in high-heel shoes way too high and way too tight.

Reaching the third-floor landing, she stopped to adjust her white headscarf, and to fight back the nausea from the exertion of climbing the stairs loaded. She leaned against the wall to pry off her pearl white shoes, lost her balance, and fell to one knee. She remained there for a moment to make sure she wouldn't fall all the way over or heave up all the wine, and then palmed her way back up the wall.

A statuesque black woman, Yolanda stood an inch shy of six feet and possessed a body that slowed traffic at her usual corner, especially when she had on the outfit she wore tonight. A regular gave her the full-length, fake-fur coat last winter, which was way too warm for June, but was always a real showstopper on Eighty-Second Avenue. More than one customer had told her that when she opened her coat to flash her butt-cheek-revealing gold satin hot pants, and the clinging pink camisole over her unencumbered breasts, they had to have her right then and there.

At ten feet away, she looked like the 25-year-old she was, but up close, her eyes and face revealed years of dope, booze, and the countless johns who had frequented her body and then gone home to their wives and children. Normally, she wore a red wig to hide her alopecia, a disease that caused her to lose most of her hair. But a couple of weeks ago she had a hell of a fight with Rosie, the bitch, which Yolanda won, but not before the Mexican whore tore her wig off and chucked it into one of those big storm drains under a sidewalk curb. Now she had to wear a scarf until her new wig came in. Twelve hundred bucks, but there was no way she would wear some cheap over-the-counter thing.

Yolanda counted aloud each apartment door, since most had long ago lost their numbers to vandals and thieves. She stood unsteadily in front of the sixth door, pulled a single key from her big coat pocket and fumbled it into the lock. Before opening it, she looked fuzzy-eyed to her left and right to ensure no one was in the hall. Unlikely at 1:20 a.m., but better safe than sorry, a philosophy that's kept her alive in a dangerous job.

She shuffled in, managed to click on the lamp, and butt-pushed the door shut. She sagged against it. "Shit," she breathed. "Got to count the money before Lee shows up."

Lee wasn't a bad guy, except when he'd hit her in the stomach, sometimes really hard. He never hit her in the face because it was important she look good to bring in the money.

She reached into her coat pocket and retrieved a fat, orange clutch purse. She pulled out a wad of tens and twenties, dropped them onto the pink sheet at the foot of the bed, and did a quick count.

"Damn, two hundred twenty dollars," she said aloud. "Must have done ten ... no, eleven blow jobs tonight. Not the busiest night but above average."

She made two piles, 110 dollars in each. Sometimes Lee let her keep more than fifty percent, especially when she brought in a good haul. It would be nice to get a little extra to buy some dope, maybe get a couple nights off to rest and spend time with Chelsea.

Chelsea! She raised her heavy eyes to the head of the bed and smiled drunkenly at her four-month-old sleeping peacefully between two oversized pillows.

"Chelsea," Yolanda said in a baby voice, swaying over the infant. "Have you been sleeping like a good little angel while mama was at work?"

In the bathroom, Yolanda leaned against the sink to examine her face in the mirror. It was always this time of night, when back in her place, stoned, and looking at her reflection, she would have one of her guilt trips about having to leave Chelsea all alone while she worked. Some nights, the wine helped push the thought out of her mind, or at least numbed her feelings about it. Tonight wasn't one of them. Guilty, guilty, guilty.

Yolanda brushed her teeth and studied her face some more. Damn, I look old, she thought. And the damn scarf wasn't helping. She even wore it at home because it pained her so to look at her hair, or what was left of it. The scarf hadn't slowed down business, though. Even when she was pregnant, she was busy right up to the last week. She pulled off her camisole and hot pants, and turned on the shower.

Looking in the mirror again, she jiggled her breasts and giggled, "Big boobs. Where would I be without 'em?" She turned to adjust the water.

The shower door rattled. Lee's here. Now he could get his money, and she could get some much-needed sleep. She slipped into a blue robe. I hope all he wants is the money, she thought. I'm too trashed for anything else.

She stepped out into the living area ... something was wrong.

Before she had gone into the bathroom, she had turned off the lamp by the door and left the one on in the kitchen. Now it was off too.

A long rectangle of light from the bathroom fell across the floor and draped over the end of the bed. She instinctively looked over at Chelsea, struggling to focus her eyes in the semi dark. Chelsea? Where is ... Her heart thumped against her throat; her hands reflexively covered her mouth. "Chelsea?" she whispered, tentatively stepping toward the bed, terrified of finding the makeshift cradle empty.

"Oh!" she whimpered. Her darling baby still slept soundly on the other side of the biggest pillow. "Oh, thank God," she breathed, closing her eyes in relief.

She looked into the dark kitchen and back toward the door. Closed. Then what—

A noise behind her.

"Lee?" She turned toward the kitchen.

"Moooo-slum." A female voice.

Yolanda's eyes widened then narrowed as they struggled to focus, to understand. "What ...?"

Light from the bathroom reflected off a long knife blade floating, or so it seemed, in the darkness, arms reach from her face, its tip pointing upward as if wanting to be seen.

A moment passed in which she couldn't move, and then

the blade made a wide arc and sliced deeply across the front of her neck.

Time, confusing. Space, swimming. Lots of blood, arcing.

Time, confusing. The red arcing from her neck, diminishing.

Hard to think now ... so sleepy.

A floating knife. A smile behind it. Strange smile.

It was ... a white woman's smile. And it was ...

Evil.

Who?

The sick, swimming sensation, increasing now.

Chelsea crying ...

Oh, ... can't hear her now. The roar is too loud ... in her ears, in her brain, in her body.

It's the sound of ...

... death ...

... approaching.

CHAPTER SIX

Tears are streaming down my face and falling on my keyboard. I've got one hand on my mouse and the other touching Mai's flushed, tear-streaked face. Her eyes are squeezed closed, her mouth covered with her palm. We've been frozen like this for several minutes. It's three thirty in the morning.

"Where's Father?" I ask softly, looking into the monitor.

Mai's head jerks. She struggles to open her eyes and wipes at them with the back of her hand. New ones roll down her cheeks. "With ... Mother. He is ... un ... incon ... damn ... I do not remember how to say the word."

"It's okay, sweetie. Inconsolable?"

She nods and wipes at her tears again. "I want to be with you, Sam."

"And I want to be there. I will ask my bosses—"

"Bosses? You go back to the police department?"

"Yes. Long story. I called you last night to tell you."

"We were at the hospital. Everything happened so fast. They don't know if Mother had a stroke or heart attack. I was in her bedroom when ... "

Mai begins weeping uncontrollably into her palms. After a few minutes she looks up, her beautiful face a mess. "Don't come here, Sam. It is too expensive and will take you too long. We will probably bury Mother tomorrow."

The PD allows for death leave but I just had six weeks off and I've been back one day. I'm sure they'd say no. I could file a grievance but how long would it take? No matter. I need to be with Mai and my father. I need to be there to—

"Sam," Mai says, looking into my face. "I need to be with Father and my sisters today and tomorrow."

"Of course. I will talk with my new boss first to see what he—"

"I want to come there, Sam."

I look at her.

"To Portland. I will be with Father and Linh and Anh for the next two days and then I will fly to Portland." She shakes her head. "My head is full of craziness right now so I cannot think right, but I think it will be Friday. Or Thursday. Wednesday ... shit, I do not know,"

"Are you sure? Don't you ..." I almost ask her if she thinks she should be there but I hold my tongue. Everyone handles these things in their own way, but the selfish part of me would like her to come. "Don't make a decision right now, sweetie. Do what needs to be done there and be with your family. I have my cell with me even at work, so you can call me anytime." I'm still going to check on the death-leave issue.

Mai nods and takes a deep breath. "Father and I talked last night about what we would do if Mother ..." She squeezes her eyes shut. "We did not know it would happen in a few hours. We thought we had more time." She struggles to get her breath before continuing. "He said Linh and Anh have their husbands and I have you. He said he would stay with Linh for a few days and I should go to America to be with you. I had not thought about any of this before because I did not want to think of Mother ... It was like Father knew what I wanted to do before I knew what I wanted to do, before I thought about it." She shakes her head. "Sorry. I do not know if what I say makes sense."

"It does, because I know Father." Mai doesn't smile but does give me a nod. "Okay, sweetie. Why don't you go and take care of things. I won't call you; you call me whenever you want. Keep me posted about your flight. By the way, can you leave Vietnam so quickly? Isn't there a lot of red tape?"

She nods. "Father has friends who can help."

We place out hands palm to palm on the screen. "I love you, Sam."

"I love you, Mai."

*   *   *

I got into the office a little after eight, a tad groggy since I didn't go back to sleep after talking with Mai.

We all knew Kim was very sick but it is still a shock. I can't imagine the pain my new family is going through. The woman was the love of my father's life, Mai and her sisters worshiped her, and I was looking forward to getting to know her more. She was so ill when I was in Saigon our visits never lasted longer than fifteen minutes. She was a feisty, smart, and beautiful woman, qualities she passed on to Mai.

No one else is in the office yet, so I set about making a pot of coffee. I thought Steve told me the day begins at eight but maybe it's eight thirty.

What's going to happen to my family? Before I left Saigon, Samuel told me that should Kim pass away he would turn over their chain of jewelry stores to Mai or, if Mai wanted to move to the Portland, he would sell all the stores and put more work into helping homeless Vietnamese veterans. Oh man, lots for everyone to think about.

"Hi, Sam," Angela says, coming through the door. "Did you think you had the shop to yourself today?" She's wearing tan khaki pants, a blue polo, and a brown jacket to conceal her weapon. No African garb today.

My weapon! Damn. Got to remember to bring it. My grey jacket covers the fact I'm not carrying.

"Where is everyone," I ask.

"BJ, Steve, and I just happened to be coming in at the same time when we ran into the Fat Dicks down in the lobby. They got called in early on a homicide and were heading out to the scene. Uniform told them it might be a hate crime so they will give us a call as soon as they look it over. BJ and Steve had to go up and talk with Rodriguez first thing so it will be you and me if they want us out there."

"Where'd it happen?" I ask, though my mind is on how Mai and my father are doing.

"Apartment building on the west side of PSU."

I nod distractedly. I hear the last sputtering of the coffee pot. "Coffee's ready."

"You okay?" Angela asks, as she hands me a cup and fills it.

"What? Oh," I say, shaking my head a little. "Yes, I'm fine. Family issue. Didn't get much sleep."

"Everything going to be okay?" she asks.

"It's complicated but in short, my father's wife died last night, in Vietnam. It was a long illness but still everyone is shocked."

"Oh my God," Angela says, touching my arm. "Your step-mother. I'm so sorry. You sure you want to be here? I know BJ would give you some time off."

"Thank you. I'm okay here. There is nothing I can do at home, plus I've only been back one day."

Angela nods, touching my arm again, letting her hand linger. "Well, let's make it an easy one. If you want, I can give you my binder of reports on things I've worked on in the last few months. It will give you a flavor of what we're doing and also show you how we write things up. It's quite different than standard crime reports."

"Sounds good," I say, as we head over to our desks. "An easy day would be great."

Angela extracts a ten-inch-thick binder from her bottom drawer, spins her chair around, and sets it on my desk with a heavy thump. It's marked CONFIDENTIAL on the cover.

"Some light reading for you," she says. Then with a smirk, "You should get through it by noon. After lunch you get to advance to a bigger binder." Her phone rings.

I force a smile and pick up the binder. "So much for an easy day." As Angela takes her call, I open it to the first report, take a sip of coffee, and again wonder how Mai and my father are doing. I wish I could be with them.

"The Fat Dicks," Angela says, setting down her phone. "They want us to come to the scene."

"They think it could be a hate crime?" I ask, gulping down the rest of my coffee.

"I think so. All I know is they said the vic is black."

*   *   *

"Wonder how the Fat Dicks managed the climb?" Angela says, as we walk up the final set of stairs to the third floor. "The 'Out Of Order' sign looked like it's been there since the Second World War."

I smile at Angela and nod at a middle-aged uniformed cop, leaning against the cleanest part of an otherwise filthy wall, his big arms folded. "Hi, Jerry," I say.

"Yeah," he says around a fat cigar that looks like it's been resting in the corner of his mouth as long as the elevator sign's been posted. He's got heavy jowls, squinty eyes, balding grey hair, and a belly hiding his gun belt buckle. I'm surprised the climb didn't do him in. Judging by the look I just got, he's probably wishing it had finished me. Another hater.

"What's up?" Angela asks. "This your call?"

Jerry blows out a cloud of cigar smoke. "Got the cover, Miss Kitty got the call. She and her rookie are knocking on apartment doors." He looks only at Angela as he talks. "The vic's name is Yolanda Simpson, a hooker. I've popped her a half-dozen times myself. The perp did a job on her. You had breakfast, Angela?"

"I have," she says.

So have I, Jerry, in case you're wondering. Had an English muffin overloaded with peanut butter. My usual. You probably wish I had choked on it, right? By the way, do you know a cigar is a breath mint for people who eat shit?

Chill out self. You can't get angry at all of them.

"Richard Cary did his usual look-and-puke," Jerry chuckles, his big belly shaking like a jarred bowl of Jello. "He and his pard will fill you in."

Richard Daniels and Richard Cary have been partners for ten or twelve years and have been given the moniker "The Fat Dicks," since both share the same first name, both are detectives, and both weigh over three hundred pounds. They are in their early forties and even look alike under certain lighting conditions, though Richard Cary has thinning red hair combed forward to hide a bald spot, and Richard Daniels has a full head of brown hair, combed straight back. They are good investigators who love food as much as they love a good case. Ironically, Cary has a weak stomach, not a good thing for a homicide detective. He routinely walks into a new scene, looks at the body, dashes outside to throw up, and returns to never again be bothered by it. Just as I start to wonder where he did his upchuck up here, I see an open window halfway down the hall. Nasty. Richard Cary steps out of a room across from it and looks our way.

"Angela," he calls from the doorway. "Sam. Come on down."

"Have fun," Jerry says, looking only at Angela.

Bite me, Jerry. I follow her down the hall.

"How you doing, Sam?" Cary says, nodding a greeting. "Glad you're on board."

"Hey, Richard. Thanks."

"You guys have breakfast?" he asks, with a pained expression.

"Jerry asked the same thing," I say. "Bad one?"

"Yes, sir. Seen worse but it's bad. Follow me. I want you two to see something."

"Detectives!"

We all turn toward a female uniformed officer walking toward us. Kitty Stafford, six feet tall, one eighty at least. I know because I read in our monthly newspaper a couple of years ago she won the women's one-hundred-eighty-pounds-and-over division in the Oregon Power Lifting Championships. I saw her once get pissed at a teenage motorist and yank him out of his car through the driver's window. Her husband, a Northeast Precinct sergeant, is a lifter too. She nods at Angela and me.

"Learn anything?" Richard asks.

Kitty looks at her notebook. "My trainee is watching a guy downstairs in the lobby. Name's Lee Brown, black dude, says he's the vic's boyfriend, but I'm guessing he's the pimp. Says he came into her apartment and found her on the floor. Said he lost his lunch in there."

"Saw it," Richard Clary says weakly.

"This Lee character was holding her baby," Kitty says. "Says it's not his. One of the troops has it now, waiting for CSD to come pick it up. By the way, there are a couple of TV stations down there."

"Your call, right?" I ask.

She nods. "Like I told Detective Cary, Lee Brown called nine-one-one. My trainee and I went in to make sure there was no one else in there, then we backed out. We touched nothing. There's fresh knife marks around the flimsy door latch, so I'm guessing the suspects pried their way in. Lee Brown said the bathroom light was on. He didn't see anyone."

"Okay, good," Richard says. "Make sure Brown doesn't go anywhere and please don't talk to the media."

"No sweat," Kitty says. She nods at me and looks at my chest. "How's your bench, Sam?"

I shake my head. "Haven't had much time to lift lately. I'd probably max with your warm-up." She laughs.

Richard gestures with his head for us to follow him in.

"Paco Martinez and his team are on the way," he says, referring to the crime scene people. "So don't touch anything and walk only where I walk."

There isn't much to the apartment. A bed on the left, a couple of wooden chairs against the wall to the right, and a cheap dinette table between the bed and a small kitchen. I'm assuming the bathroom is to the far right.

"Hello, folks," Richard Daniels says, looking up from his spiral notebook in which he's been jotting observations. He's standing on the other side of a female body crumpled next to the dinette. Her robe is askew, exposing her breasts, abdomen, and one brown thigh. There is a large volume of blood around her head and more has streamed toward the kitchen area. The floor must be uneven.

"Come no farther than right there," Daniels says, indicating a spot near her bare, extended leg.

The front of her throat has been cut, the slit slightly curved and open, like a smiling, crimson mouth without teeth. But it's her forehead that churns the gut. Looks like an old pumpkin starting to collapse in on itself. Pink matter and bone chips have oozed part way down her face, stopping at the side of her nose.

"My God," Angela whispers. "What did ..."

"A hammer, I think," Richard Daniels says. He's too big to kneel down, so he has to spread his legs and bend over awkwardly. He points with his pen. "A knife slit the neck, of course, severed a big artery, and to add insult to injury the perp used a hammer, or something like one. See the round indentations over the left eyebrow? Perp struck her about four times. ME will tell us for sure."

"Show them why we called, Richard," Cary says from behind us.

"Indeed I will, Richard," Daniels says. "Before the ambulance people moved her a little, you could see it better. But it got smeared when they were jockeying her about." He points with his pen again. "On her right breast, see it? Lines carved with a knife."

I see them. The rest of the breast is covered with blood, some of it drying.

"The letter M," Richard Daniel says. "Before the blood was smeared about, we could see two letter Os, an S, a capital L, a capital U, and another M."

"Mooslum?" I ask.

Richard Cary nods. "Maybe the perp can't spell Muslim or maybe he was deliberately being disrespectful."

*   *   *

"Mister ..." Angela glances at her notepad, "Brown. Lee Brown, right?" We're standing in one corner of a large lobby on the ground floor. There are a couple of officers near the glass doors to keep the small crowd and the news media out on the sidewalk from getting in. A female officer, holding a sleeping, light-colored baby, talks quietly with Kitty. Another officer comes through the front door and smiles at Kitty. Must be her trainee.

"Yeah," the man grunts.

"May I have your date of birth and address?"

Brown screws up his face as if Angela had asked him for his liver. "I gave it to that other po-lice? Don't you talk to each other?" The man who says he is Yolanda Simpson's boyfriend but is probably her pimp, stands about six foot, skinny as a rail, wearing dark slacks, spit-shined Italian loafers, and a tan jacket over a black, skin-tight silk T-shirt. Stereotype pimp.

"We do talk to each other," Angela says sweetly. "Thank you for asking

Brown shakes his head as if we were impossibly stupid. He provides his date of birth and home address as if it hurts him to do so.

"Thank you, sir," Angela says with a sweet smile. I had a training coach way back who told me police work was ninety percent bullshit ability. Angela is very good at it, a much-needed trait when one is in the intelligence-gathering business.

"You the poor girl's pimp?" she asks. Angela also cuts to the chase.

Lee Brown sputters his indignation and flops his arms around as if he'd never heard anything so outrageous in all his twenty-eight years. When he finally comes down from his affected indignation, Angela is still passively waiting for his answer.

"I'm her business manager," he says. "Business."

"Of course you are," she says, tilting her head like a beauty pageant contestant. "Tell me, was Miss Simpson a Muslim?" Uniform already confirmed Brown's whereabouts, which the Fat Dicks will follow up on. Right now, we want to know about the etching in the victim's chest. If this murder is another hate crime, and I'm guessing it is, things are about to get hot in the ol' town tonight.

"A mus who?" Brown says, his confusion seemingly real this time. "A Muslim?" He looks at me. "She mean like those Taliban muthafuckers over there in eye-raq?"

"Did Miss Simpson follow the faith?" I ask.

"Hell no," he says, as if such a thing would be worse than being a prostitute.

"Any reason why someone might think she was one?" Angela asks.

Brown shakes his head for a moment before the dawn of enlightenment flashes across his face. "Wait, wait, wait. I get you now, sister."

Judging by the now twitching muscle over Angela's left eye, I think she would have lambasted the man for the "sister" if she weren't trying to get info from him. Instead, she tilts her head sweetly again.

"Yolanda had something wrong with her hair," the pimp says. "Started losing it when she was twenty, I think she said. Lost it fast, you know. Wore a wig most of the time, but sometimes she would wrap her head in a bandana or cover it with a scarf. Sometimes people would ask if she was from India or Baghdad or one of those places." He looks away and shakes his head as if saddened by the loss. His loss. "Thing is, she was so hot the tricks didn't give a shit."

Angela and I look at each other.

"So no ties to the Muslim faith at all?" Angela asks to confirm.

Lee Brown sputters a laugh. "Hell no. Born and raised right here in Portland. Started turnin' tricks when she was a junior in high school. Ain't never stopped ..." He bunches his eyebrows and looks up at the far wall. "'Till now," he says softly. "'Till now."

*   *   *

We're sitting in our car in a Wendy's parking lot having a two p.m. lunch. Before we left the crime scene, Angela and I walked around the neighborhood to get a feel of the area. Across the street and a half block down, we noticed a place called Big Ed's Tires and on its roof a mounted video camera and another perched on a high fence. On a hunch, I suggested we check to see if there were others. We scored because Big Ed has one in the lobby aimed at the front doors that likely captures the entrance to Yolanda's apartment building. Fortunately, Big Ed gladly handed over the tape without us having to get a warrant. We returned to the apartment and gave it to Richard Cary.

I chomp another bite out of my burger and wonder if there were burger joints in Saigon. I didn't see any but then I didn't see the entire city. I sort of remember reading something about Vietnamese not liking American-style hamburgers. I never asked Mai if she liked them.

Man, I miss her, and it's only been a few days since I last saw her, held her. I so want to hold her again.

Angela's cell rings. She answers, listens, and mouths to me, "The Fat Dicks."

"He what?" she nearly blares into the phone. "Oh no. Did Kitty ream him a new one? Did you?"

I mouth "What?" at her.

Still listening, she tilts the mouth end of her cell up, and whispers, "Richard Daniels said Kitty's trainee told Channel Eight News 'Mooslum' had been carved into the vic's body."

"No."

She lowers the phone back to her mouth. "Okay, Richard. "Let's have a meeting when you're able to get back to the office. Right. Sounds good. Bye."

"It would have gotten out eventually," I say. "But timing is everything."

Angela shakes her head. "Rookie took a dumbshit pill for sure. I guess the commander back at Central is berating him right now. Richard told BJ and he's giving the Chief's Office a heads up. To state it simply, the excrement is about to make physical contact with a hydroelectric powered oscillating air current distribution device."

"The media is going to go nuts."

Angela nods. "And the community."

"Everyone's going to be demanding action from the police," I say.

"And there will be accusations we're behind the killings."

"The feds will come a calling."

"Most likely."

"The last thing we had even remotely close to this was

when a white security guard killed a Mexican kid a couple of years ago. Remember?" I ask around a bite of burger. Some in the Hispanic community accused the guard of planting a weapon on him, but when it was easily disproven, they accused the police of doing the planting. Marches on City Hall and on the Justice Center followed.

Angela sips from her ice tea. "This is going to be worse."

I nod, and take another bite. "So Ocnod was born and raised in Iraq and was lynched with the N word carved into his chest. Yolanda Simpson was born and raised in Portland and 'Mooslum' was carved into hers. The do-ers have to be the same but could they be any dumber? Next they're going to kill a Mexican illegal and carve 'Vietcong' in his chest and kill a Chinese dude and carve 'Viva Zapata' in his."

Angela switches from a plastic fork to a plastic spoon to dig out the innards of her baked potato. "I've talked with Intel people from other PDs and the universal agreement is most perps who commit hate crimes are some of the dumbest son-of-a-bitches out there. I interviewed an old KKK man once when I was in uniform. It wasn't a hate crime deal, but I took the opportunity to peek inside his head." She shrugs. "Empty. Even had an echo."

I chuckle. "What did he think of you?"

"He didn't know what to think. I purposely drew on my Ivy League education to use every five-dollar word I could think of just to watch his stupid face scrunch up, and hear him say, 'Whachoomean?' It was pretty funny."

"Three fries short of a Happy Meal?"

"A few peas short of a casserole."

"A few clowns short of a circus?"

She smiles. "No, these people are a complete circus." She

tosses her potato skin into a trash bag. "The ones I've had contact with are losers with a capital L. They're united by their white skin. It's all they got going on, as well as being mental midgets and hillbilly Hitlers. And they raise their kids to think, and 'think' has quotes on each side of it, just as they do. So a belief system based on stereotypes and ignorance gets perpetuated. No, ignorance is giving them too much credit. Stupidity. A belief system based on absolute, unadulterated stupidity."

"Well, I think it's true of all races that perpetrate a crime based on the victim's race, ethnicity, or whatever."

Angela looks at me sharply, probably because I sounded a little more defensive than I intended. Before she can say anything, we both look at the police radio.

"Sounds like a chase," I say, turning up the volume.

"I got 'em running northbound on Sixth Avenue from Northwest Everett."

"Copy Eight Three Two. Car Eight Three One, can you cover?"

"Eight Three One, no can do. We're out on a fight at Fourth and Oak."

I look at Angela. "We can hop on Tom McCall and be down there in three minutes, traffic permitting."

"Let's go," Angela says, snatching up the mic. "This is Four Four Four. Can do backup."

"You got it, Four Four Four."

"Car Eight Three Two. They've cut westbound on Everett, running right down the middle of the street. Two white males, teens or early twenties, wearing all black clothes and knee-high boots. One's got long, coal black hair and the other has shorter yellow hair."

"Four Four Four. We're on Tom McCall at about Taylor.

No traffic. We'll be there in less than a minute."

"Car Eight Three Two, did you copy?"

"We copy. They're nearing the intersection at Broadway. Have Four Four Four come north on Broadway to cut them off. Oh my, one of them just slammed down an elderly woman in the crosswalk. Better start an ambulance just in case."

"Ten-four, Eight Three Two. One's being dispatched. Four Four Four, where are you?"

"One block shy of Burnside," Angela says. "What you got on these guys?"

"Eight Three Two. They match the description of the people involved in the fatal pedestrian at Three and Couch. Okay, they're heading straight toward Burnside on Broadway."

I get onto Second, shoot up to Burnside, hang a hard left onto it, and floor it west toward Broadway.

"Eight Three Two. They're about fifty yards short of Burnside.

We streak by Fourth Avenue, Fifth, Sixth. Next one is Broadway.

"There!" I say, jabbing my finger at two black-clad young men ripping around the corner, arms pumping, faces flushed. I anchor the car in the lane. A truck behind us blares on its horn. The yellow-haired one takes the corner wide and rams into an opening car door, slamming it back into the shins of the man about to get out. The runner spins a three sixty and keeps on beating feet without missing a beat.

Angela is out of the car shouting, "Police! Freeze!" and takes off like a sprinter off the blocks. I bail out of the car just as two uniforms, Bill Rhyder and Kathy Sullivan, round the corner running hard.

Angela is a half block away now gaining on Yellow Hair

who is a stride or two behind his buddy. I dash around the truck and head down the thankfully empty lane thinking if the two try to cut across Burnside, they'll pass right in front of me. I'm actually gaining on them, not because I'm a fast runner, but because the two thugs are tiring.

Angela runs like an Olympic track athlete, and she's close enough to Yellow Hair now he could pass a relay baton back to her. She shoves his upper back, an oldie and a goodie police technique—it throws his stride off and sets into motion his downfall, so to speak. Angela wisely moves beside him as his arms flail desperately to stay upright. She pushes him again to hurry his fall, and his thrashing arms inadvertently tangle in Black Hair's pumping legs. They both splatter to the sidewalk in a grunting, yelping snarl of arms, legs, and nasty skin abrasions.

Officers Bill Rhyder and Kathy Sullivan leap on Black Hair, and Angela and I pin Yellow Hair's arms to the pavement.

"Nice job," I say to Angela. She shrugs indifferently before smiling. She's barely puffing.

"Nice job?" Yellow Hair grunts. He's a slender kid with short legs. "Really?

I press his wrist into the pavement with one hand and use the edge of my palm to press the leverage and pain point an inch above his elbow into the street. Angela is just pushing down on his wrist. When the kid starts to bend his arm, I tell her to do it like I am. She does and the kid yelps, curses, but doesn't move his arm any more.

"Cool," she says.

"Cool?" he shouts. "Really?

I look over at Bill and Kathy who have Black Hair cuffed. I call over, "Hand me your cuffs, someone, and we'll chain up his buddy here." Angela and I have handcuffs but he's their prisoner.

"Oh, hi, Sam," Kathy says with a big smile. She's still breathing hard. We worked together out at Northeast Precinct a few times several years ago. Petite, but tough as nails. "You're back at work, I see." She leans down and snaps on the cuffs after Angela and I muscle the kid's hands behind his back.

"I am. How are you?"

"Doing well. Transferred to Central Precinct last summer. Love it, especially when we get shitheads like these off the street."

"Bitch!" our kid shouts, then grimaces when Angela applies a wristlock on his cuffed hand.

A uniform car pulls to a stop and the door opens.

"Hey, Dave," Kathy says to the lone uniformed officer. I don't know him. "Would you transport these guys back to the precinct for us? Bill and I dumped our car way over on Everett."

A small crowd has gathered a few feet away, several of them capturing the moment on their cell phone cameras.

"Can do," Dave says. He nods at Angela and me, his eyes lingering on mine a moment longer. Probably recognizes me. "How you doing, man?" he asks.

I nod. "Fine thanks."

He nods too, like he's glad I'm fine. I guess it's the way it's going to be. Some coppers are going to be supportive, some won't be.

Dave asks, "These the guys who coerced the Mayor into stepping out into traffic?"

"AKA the guys who are going down for negligent homicide," Bill says, as he and Kathy get their guy to his feet. Black Hair's hoodie reads EXECUTIONER in large letters across the front. Yellow Hair struggles as we pull him to his feet, but stops abruptly upon seeing Angela for the first time.

"A nigger!" our man bellows. Executioner says it a second after, mindlessly following his buddy's lead.

I sense more than see Angela tighten her grip on our man's upper arm. I give her the eye, hoping my look conveys she needs to take it easy.

Bill yanks on Executioner's cuffed hands and pushes him toward the marked car.

"What you lookin' at, you Jew cow?" our man screams, his eyes boring into a woman wearing a light blue business suit. "Listen up, Jews and niggers," he shouts at the crowd. "There's a new movement comin' down. We're just the beginning. Be afraid. Be very afraid."

Executioner fakes a loud laugh and looks toward Yellow Hair as if for approval.

Another uniform car pulls up behind the first one. A female officer gets out.

"Let's separate them," Kathy says. "Sam, put yours in her car."

"No problem," Angela says, jamming Yellow Hair's arm up his back. But before we can get to the unit's back door, he braces his foot against the fender and pushes back against us. We nearly all go down save for our quick footwork.

"Almost fall down and go boom, nigger? How the hell did you get to be a puppet? The cops need a quota on Watusis?"

The female officer, another one I don't know, opens the back door for us as Angela grabs a wad of Yellow Hair's hoodie to force him to walk backwards to the opening. We spin him around at the door. "Bend forward," I say.

"Sure," he says, and spits into Angela's face and follows with a knee strike at me.

I turn just enough so his knee only brushes my hip. "Get his ass inside," I say, reaching to pull his head down.

Angela blocks my hand. "Step behind me," she hisses, so intensely I automatically obey her, blocking her and Yellow Hair from the watching eyes of the noonday crowd. The female officer is on the other side of the open door and has an obstructed view.

Angela slaps her palm into the kid's crotch, squeezes hard, and rotates her hand as if trying to rip the handle off a faucet.

The kid belches out a noise as godawful loud as it is strange, something like a goat would make if Nate hit its snout with his war club.

Yellow Hair, screaming like a Banshee now, falls into the backseat. The female officer shoots me a scowl.

"This is being filmed," Executioner shouts, a second before Bill and Kathy push him all the way into the other car. "We want your names and badge numbers."

Angela shrugs innocently at the crowd as if she doesn't know why our prisoner is fussing so. "Sorry for disturbing your day, folks," she says sweetly to them, doing her head tilt thing. "These are a couple of desperate criminals wanted for homicide. The streets are a little safer today." She ought to run for office.

Our boy's voice is muffled now in the backseat and not loud enough for the crowd to hear. "You almost tore off my dick."

We move over to the other police car where Dave and the female officer are listening to Bill talk to Executioner. "Why did we stop you? Because Traffic Division wants to question you about something that happened at Third and Couch this morning."

I can't see Executioner's face from where I'm standing, but

I can hear him. "The wino? You serious? Puke and me didn't do nothin' to him."

Yellow Hair's street name is Puke? Aptly named.

"Did I say something about a wino?" When Executioner doesn't respond, Bill says, "Hey, why would we doubt anyone named Executioner?"

*　　*　　*

"You got files on Puke and Executioner?" I ask Angela as we step out of the elevator.

"If I do, I don't remember them," she says, slipping her card-key into the slot. The door buzzes open. "I'll take a look."

"Mister and Missus Norris," Steve says looking up from his PC. "How'd it go?"

"Cute," Angela says. "Helped The Fat Dicks on a homicide and helped uniform catch a couple of scrotes who are likely responsible in a death at Third and Couch. And how was your day? Get a paper cut?"

BJ steps out of his office. "Sam? A word?" He goes back into his room before I can answer.

Steve shrugs an I-don't-know at me as I head back.

BJ has turned off his small lamps and the Bose, and turned on the hard overhead lights. "Shut the door," he says in his soft voice, sounding like the announcer on a TV golf match. The ol' 'shut the door' is never a good thing when uttered by the boss. He points at a chair in front of his desk. He remains standing applying the superior position gimmick. "Did I stutter yester-day when I explained the philosophy and mission of Intel?"

"You didn't," I say, not sure where he's going with this.

"Are you a brutal man, Sam?"

My temper flares like a camera flash and I struggle to keep

my mouth shut. How dare this desk-riding, paper-pushing doughboy judge me. Son-of-a-bitch! Where does he get off ...

Take a deep breath ... take another.

There is a certain power in having chosen the option of returning to work. I chose to come back because not only did the Intel job sound interesting, but also my gut instinct told me I should be back. Nonetheless, I'm not married to my gut instinct. After everything that has gone down these last few months, I don't know if I want to be married to anything other than my new family.

"I'm offended by your question, lieutenant," I say evenly.

"You're what?" he asks just above a whisper.

I don't break eye contact as I take a breath to maintain my calmness. "Lieutenant, maybe you don't like the idea I got assigned here. If so, I get it. Lots of people don't like me now because—"

"I don't have a problem with you being in this unit. What I do have a problem with is you hurting people unnecessarily. Yesterday it was a homeless man and today a handcuffed suspect. *Handcuffed*, Sam."

"What are you talk ..." Is he talking about Puke? We just popped him. How did a complaint—?

"I see you're remembering what happened an hour ago. Officer Liz Tracy just called and complained you struck or did something to a prisoner about to be placed into her car. In her words, you 'assaulted her prisoner.' The man is now being checked out by the jail nurse."

My grandfather used to say, "Never attribute to malice that which can be adequately explained by stupidity." I'm having trouble believing this guy is commanding an intelligence gathering unit. Well, I'm not saying anything and I'm definitely not going to dime up Angela. The fact I know what happened is power and I'm holding onto it.

"I'll be reporting this to Deputy Chief Rodriguez. You had better pray this kid you hurt doesn't sue the department. I back my people, Reeves, but not when they act outside the law."

"Understood, lieutenant," I say tightly.

"Here's the thing, Sam. I abhor violence. Call me a pacifist, call me Gandhi, call me John the Baptist, I've heard them all. But it's how I think and how I believe through my faith in the Lord. I never got into a fight growing up, and I managed to get through my two years on the street without getting into one. Does it make be a bad cop? People think what they want, but I don't think it does. I got off the street as soon as I could and I've not regretted it. I think I'm a good supervisor because I do what I can to support the cops who are willing to do what I detest. But I believe violence is always—*always*—a last resort.

"Understood," I say. I flash to Jim Donnelly, a training coach I had back when I was a rookie. He had served in the Army as a prison guard, I can't remember where. He said there was a major in the unit, a man who seldom ventured out beyond his desk and loved to go after the guards for what he perceived as excessive force. On one occasion, Jim had to use a sleeper hold on a prisoner who had kicked him in the stomach. The major decided to use the incident as an example and bring Jim up on charges. But when the major went to interview the convict, the so-called abused prisoner threw his feces through the bars splattering the major's face and uniform. Disgusted, sickened, and embarrassed, the major stumbled back to his office, cleaned up, and ordered the guards, including Jim, to beat the man senseless.

I agree it's wrong to abuse prisoners, but there's abuse and there's the human reaction to a repugnant act. Angela responded to Puke's spit attack from her gut, from a place of revulsion. If she had planned her revenge for two weeks, it would have been wrong. In this incident, her reaction was almost immediate. I think she would have lashed out even if the cuffs were off. I know I would have. My philosophy has always been if someone spits on me—and it's happened three times—it's now personal and the rulebook goes out the window. The three people who did it to me can attest to that.

BJ moves around to his side of the desk and sits. "Go write up your reports and put them on my desk before you go home."

"Ten-four," I say and exit his office without saying another word.

Steve and Angela are busy typing.

Angela swivels her chair around as I sit in mine. "Everything okay?"

"Fine. The boss was just telling me how much he likes me."

"Really," she says, eyeing me, not buying it. "Ooookay. By the way, I looked and I don't have anyone in my files with Puke or Executioner monikers. As soon as we get their real names, I'll check again. I also called Detectives and left a message for Traffic's investigators to let us know when we can talk to them."

"Sounds good," I say.

Angela points at her desktop. "Right now I'm scratching out a Special Report on my part in our assist." She places a three-ring binder on my desk. "When you're done with your report, you might want to look through this. A little more info for your hate crimes one-o-one crash course. It contains hate crime reports from the past twelve months. Eighty-four of them. Keep in mind many go unreported."

She places a small stack of photos on my desk. "These were

taken by uniform a few weeks ago in Forest Park when they interrupted a beer party." She spreads the photos across my blotter. "They are the only known organized group in Portland. Call themselves 'Warriors for Hitler.'" She points at two pics. "Notice there are only two of these dummies with shaved heads. Maybe they're skinheads from twenty years ago or maybe they're just like lots of young men today who shave their skulls."

"Skins totally out of the picture?" I ask.

"At least around here. Of course, it could change tomorrow. A few Intel officers in other cities report only occasional skinhead activity, dudes who actually shave their heads and wear flight jackets and big oxblood-colored boots. Mostly, hate crime activity is being carried out by normal looking dickheads."

"These guys in the pics down for anything racial?"

"Minor stuff, all seven of them. Tagging swastikas, writing 'Niggers go back to Africa,' graffiti, and shouting racial epithets at people. This guy here," she says, pointing at a young man glaring at the camera and bugging his eyes, "was arrested for scaring the crap out of a Japanese family over by the Convention Center. Called them racial names as the people were walking to their car and then beat on the windows after they got into it."

Angela touches the right side of her face where Puke spit on her. She must have scrubbed it in the restroom because only the other cheek is rouged. "Hate is what they're about. They hate Blacks, Asians, Arabs, Jews, gays and lesbians, Latinos, and the police. They think the cops are puppets for the Jews and Jews control everything." She shakes her head with disgust. "Pretty stupid but it's being stupid that makes them so dangerous. Lately they've been harassing a lot of Middle Easterners, or people they think are Mid Easterners. They even hate white people who don't believe as they do. In fact, they assault more white people than nonwhites."

"Whites? Really?"

Angela chuckles. "There's more of you around when they get all liquored-up and want to mess with someone. They say, 'If you ain't with us, you're part of the problem.' They'll walk up to a white guy and ask what he thinks about niggers and ragheads. If he doesn't answer to their liking, they harass him, terrorize him, kick his ass."

"Way back in the nineties," Steve says, shutting off his PC, "the skinheads were getting fed by the KKK and a whole assortment of white supremacy groups, including churches with a white supremacy base. Now, it's these militia nutjobs feeding them."

"I've read about them," I say. "We got them here?"

Steve says, "Not in the city, we don't think, but they're in southern Oregon near the California border, in Montana, Idaho, and Washington—all around us. These are just the ones we know about. We've gotten scuttlebutt about others and we're looking into it. But until a good source of info presents itself or they do something overt, we remain short on intel."

"So we got nothing?" I ask. "We don't know if any of the perps are associated with any of these groups."

Steve shrugs. "No one has been arrested to date for the cross burning, the fire bombing of the mosque, the harassment of the Japanese family, and we got no doers for the two homicides. In our defense, we're in learning mode."

I look at the hate crimes binder. "Any heartburn over me taking this home?"

"No," Angela says. "Technically, the stuff marked

'Confidential' is to stay in the office but we take it home sometimes."

"Okay, thanks."

Angela says, "I'll call Detectives and see what's up with those two shitbirds."

Steve stands and retrieves his jacket from the back of his chair. "Meeting the wife for dinner and a play downtown. I'm outta here. Check your act out in the morn."

After Steve leaves, Angela turns around again in her chair to face me. She looks out the window for a moment and then back, her expression abruptly sheepish. "Sorry about what happened, Sam," she says in a low voice, "about losing it."

I wave her off. "The man spit on you. I thought you showed amazing restraint."

"Still shouldn't have done it. Didn't think about him being cuffed at the time."

"It's past. Do not dwell in the past, do not dream of the future, concentrate the mind on the present moment."

"Heavy, brother. David Caradine?"

I laugh. "My father said it to me once."

"It's a good one," she says, thinking about it. "Makes sense." She smiles. "But you're lucky Steve didn't hear you." She spins back around and picks up her phone.

I begin writing up my role in catching Puke and Executioner.

Angela hangs up and turns. "Bing over in Traffic is working our boys. Said the two guys caused quite a commotion down in the jail, so he's waiting until morning to talk with them. We can interview them after. Actually, maybe you and Steve should. I'm thinking Puke won't be too chatty if I'm there."

I would have to agree. "Understood."

She makes a few notations on her Special. "There. We got

names from Davis. Got a case number too. The names don't ring a bell but I'll double check in the morning. There's no rush right now. You teaching tonight?"

Hmm. Her tone is like she's asking: If you're not teaching tonight do you want to get a beer? I'm not teaching but I don't want to go get a beer. Not a good idea, not even a little bit.

"I am," I say. "Three classes tonight."

She nods, though I don't think she's buying it. I'm a bad liar and she's a cop with a finely tuned b.s. detector. "I'll see you tomorrow, then. Thanks for your support."

A few minutes after Angela leaves, I finish my Special and leave it in the REPORTS box on a table outside BJ's office. He looks up at me without expression. He has the overhead lights off and his cozy lamps back on. Classical music wafts from the Bose. I head back to my desk, pick up the binder, and leave.

*　　*　　*

I stop at the grocery and pick up some veggies and chicken, a bottle of Excedrin—my neck still hurts from my time in Saigon—and head home. I wave at my neighbor Bill, who's doing a little weeding in his yard. He acknowledges me with a barely perceptible nod. He doesn't like me, and his wife dislikes me even more. I guess they have a good reason. I brought my job home a few times, complete with fistfights, and shots fired.

In my kitchen, I unload the three bags, pop two Excedrin, change into sweatpants and a tank top, and head out to the garage to pump a little iron. Chien assumes her post on the paint can. I've got a rack of dumbbells, ten pounders to one hundred pounders, a bench, a Total Gym (Christie Brinkley sold me on it, not Chuck Norris), heavy-duty hand grippers, and a hanging bag. I've got as much muscle size as I want so my weight workouts are mostly to maintain what I have. I don't jog because I don't plan on ever running three miles to defend myself. I favor anaerobic exercise, all-out bursts on the heavy bag and fast combos in the air to work my explosive speed and power, qualities needed for a fast and furious fight.

It's six thirty in the evening, early morning tomorrow in Saigon. The day of the funeral. I hope Mai calls soon.

After warming up, I pick up two forty-pound dumbbells and lay down on the bench. I press both up, lock out my right arm and pump out six reps with my left, thinking *punch* on each one. Then I lock out my left and punch out six reps with my right. I replace the dumbbells on the rack and step over to the heavy bag to throw medium-hard kicks for thirty seconds. Without pausing to catch my breath, I grab a pair of fifties and repeat the single-arm punches for seven reps. I do the next thirty-second set of kicks on the bag hard and fast with all-out intensity as if my survival depends upon it. My last set of dumbbell punches I do with fifty-fives.

To finish my arms, I grab a forty pounder and lay on my left side holding the weight straight up with my right hand. I knock out eight reps of backfists, roll over onto my right side and repeat with my left arm. Good for the backfist strike and good for the triceps. I jump up and shadow box like a crazy person for thirty seconds and then repeat the backfist exercise using forty-fives. After another thirty seconds of high-intensity shadow boxing, I do one more set of backfists with the forty-fives.

For the next twenty minutes, I work my back with dumbbell rows, my shoulders with lateral raises, and finish with two hundred Hindu squats while holding two fifty pounders. As before, I do high-intensity bag work and all-out shadow sparring between each weight set.

Done, I stagger into the kitchen, mix a couple scoops of protein powder with a quart of water and collapse onto one of my kitchen chairs to sip.

My cell rings. "Mai?" I say without looking at the screen.

"Sam Reeves?" the female voice asks.

"It is."

"This is Officer Bev Yalden. District Six Eighty."

I've seen the name on reports but I can't put a face to it. "Hi, Bev," I say, remembering the last call at home I got from a uniformed officer was to inform me my school was in flames. Six Eighty is on the east side, around Eighty-Second Avenue.

"Sorry to bother you at home. I got a guy here who said he's a martial arts student of yours. You know a Nate Whitehorse?"

Nate? I don't think anyone told me his last name. "Long dark hair, Indian features, late twenties?"

"Uh huh. And he's been drinking. We're at a family beef, nothing physical, just loud. A neighbor complained. Your student was on the sidewalk when we got here so I can take him for public intoxication, but he mentioned you, and getting hired by the fire bureau, so I thought I'd do him the courtesy."

"Appreciate it, Bev. He's a military veteran wrestling with some serious issues. I don't know him well but I think he's okay. He didn't hit his wife, you say?"

"No. Actually, he's the one saying he's drunk. If he is, he's a quiet one. She's the loud one. Says none of his friends are answering their phone. You want him?"

I just met the guy and only talked with him twice, but my gut tells me he's okay.

"I'll take him," I say. "Where are you?"

"Southeast Eighty-Fourth and Yamhill. Any chance you

live between here and downtown?"

"I do," I say, and give her the address.

"Okay, I'll carry him to your place. I got to go to the Justice Center, anyway. Give me twenty minutes. And thanks. Seems like a good guy and he doesn't need a drunk tank record if he's getting hired by PFD."

I hit the shower, put on clean sweatpants and a T-shirt, and get the coffee going just as I hear the squad car pull into my driveway. I open the front door to see the officer opening the backdoor of her car and my neighbor Bill glaring at me from his yard.

Bev is an attractive thirty-something officer with a brunette ponytail. Nate gets out of the car effortlessly and leans against the open door. His polo shirt is hanging out of his blue jeans and his long hair looks like he combed it with an eggbeater. It takes a moment for his sleepy eyes to find me. He gives me a short nod. Looks more like a guy who's been hanging around his house than a drunk. Bev opens her trunk and pulls out the same black bag Nate had in my pickup yesterday.

"How you doing?" I say meeting him at the edge of the driveway. He's walking okay, just very slowly. I look over at Bev. "Thanks for bringing him by."

She knuckles her eye to pantomime crying. I nod.

"Sorry, Sensei," Nate whispers. "I'm not supposed to drink firewater."

I pat his shoulder. "I got the anecdote inside, coffee, cop style, strong enough to make you lose an eyebrow. You want a cup, Bev?"

"Thanks, but I like my eyebrows," she says. "Besides, I got to get downtown. Here's his bag. He insisted on bringing it. There's some smelly karate clothes in it and a tomahawk or something wrapped up in cowhide in the bottom."

"Thanks. Like you said, he's a good guy and doesn't need this on his record."

"How are you doing?" She extends her hand. "We've never formally met but I've followed your situation. I hope you're doing well."

I shake her hand, happy she's not another hater. "Day by day. I'm back to work in Intelligence doing hate crimes."

"Good for you. Just know the majority of the troops are behind you. It's the ol' shit happens, right? Let me know if I can do anything."

"Thanks so much, Bev," I say as we shake again.

Nate is standing like a statue in the middle of my living room, his head down as if in prayer. If I hadn't been told he'd been drinking, I wouldn't have guessed.

"You doing okay?" I ask.

Long pause, his head still bowed. Then, "I embarrassed myself in front of my wife."

"That can be painful. Come into the kitchen, Nate, and I'll pour you a cup of coffee. You hungry?"

"Just coffee," he says, following me slowly. "I'm sorry to intrude."

I tell him to sit and pour him a cup. I put a mug of water into the microwave for green tea. "I'm all ears if you want to tell me what's going on. If not, it's okay."

Chien hops up on a chair and looks at Nate.

"Name's Chien. Means warrior in Vietnamese. Chien, Nate."

She turns her back on Nate and lies down on the chair seat.

"Everyone's a critic," Nate says, before sipping from the cup. He grimaces, and sings, "*They say that in the Army the coffee is so fine. It looks likes muddy water and tastes like turpentine."* He takes another sip. "It's an old army marching cadence. Your coffee is worse, Sensei."

I laugh, retrieve my cup, and drop in two tea bags. "Like you said, 'everyone's a critic.' But strong is good." I sit down opposite from him. Chien moves to the edge of her chair and leans her head toward me. I rub it. "If you're not supposed to drink, why were you?"

Nate runs a hand through his hair and looks skyward. "In the words of the great Chief Sidewinder, 'I fucked up.'"

I sputter a laugh. "Was there really such a chief?"

He shrugs. "No doubt." He takes another sip and pretends to chew. When I laugh, his eyes smile. "I drank to reduce the pain. When one drink didn't help, I drank another. Some bar on Eighty-Second. I was smart enough to leave my car and walk home. My wife wanted to scalp me."

"Smart move not driving. Your wife going to be okay?"

He nods but doesn't say anything for a long moment. Then, "She's a good woman. Klamath Indian, but still okay," he adds with a grin. "I'll call her in an hour."

I pour him another cup and fix another two-bagger green tea for me. I put a handful of kitty treats on Chien's chair and sit back on mine, angling it sideways to the table. Nate leans forward, his elbows on the surface, fingers steepled, eyes focused on his hands. Neither of us speaks for several minutes. Oddly for our short acquaintance, it's a comfortable silence.

"My father," I say, punching through the quiet, "has a quotation for every occasion. He said once, quoting Elisabeth Kubler Ross, if I recall, 'There is no need to go to India or anywhere else to find peace. You will find a deep place of silence right in your room, your garden, or even your bathtub.' Peace is inside of us, eh?"

Nate nods. "I read her a lot in college," he says, surprising me about college. I feel bad for being surprised.

"Where did you go?"

"Got a masters in English literature from the University of Oklahoma, minored in Native American folklore. I started outlining a path to a doctorate but I went into the army instead."

"Impressive. Very. An English lit scholar who packs around a war club." He laughs.

We sit in silence for about ten minutes. Chien and I glance at him intermittently. Don't know what the cat is looking at, but I'm noticing how he seems to be transitioning into the guy I talked with before. I know caffeine doesn't sober a person, so maybe he wasn't terribly drunk to begin with or maybe alcohol leaves his system fast.

He clears his throat. "One of the things I appreciated yesterday after I told you about my experience in Afghanistan is you didn't offer advice. An elder once said, 'I want to know if you can sit in pain, mine or your own, without moving to hide it, or fade it, or fix it.' Not every problem can be fixed."

"I agree. My father has never tried to fix me, at least not directly. He's a former Green Beret in Vietnam, with fourteen kills, several years incarcerated in a North Vietnamese prison, and has decades of martial arts training. He has given me ways to think about my ... event, so I can go on."

"An amazing history. And a wise man."

"You don't know the half of it."

He leans forward. "What did you say? Fourteen kills?"

"When I had the same reaction, he said they didn't give desk jobs to Green Berets in Vietnam."

"I bet."

Nate's eyes appear clear now and he's no longer slumping into himself. "How much did you drink? If you don't mind me asking."

"Three beers."

"Only three?"

"Actually, I didn't finish the third one. Drank about half of it. I'm a cheap drunk. The good part is I sober quickly."

"Incredible. I rarely drink but three I think I can do."

Again, we sit in silence. After about five minutes, Nate asks, "May I show you some war club moves?"

I scrunch my face. "Not sure about the wisdom of mixing beer and war club moves."

"Really?" he says with a smirk. "But alcohol makes me heap more braver and faster." He laughs when I drop my chin and lift my eyebrows like an old schoolmarm. He unzips his bag. "I'm fine, Sensei. The beer has long worn off ... I think."

"You think?"

Chien leans out from the chair seat to watch Nate remove the cowhide and wrap his fingers around the fifteen-inch-long handle. Nate lets her smell it for a second before standing and moving back from the table. He loosens a couple of his fingers and rewraps them around the weapon, much the same as a firearms expert adjusts his hand on a pistol grip. He touches the black cowhide wrapped around the handle and brushes his index finger back and forth through the clumps of hair.

"Before you ask," he says, looking lovingly at the war club, "the hair isn't from a scalp." He looks at Chien. "It's from a kitty cat." Chien takes a step back. "Kidding. It's rabbit, used to distract the enemy." Nate smiles. "And to make the club pretty."

He lunges forward, striking horizontally from right to left, then quickly rotates his hand to strike left to right. The movement is fast, smooth, and deadly.

"When done with great speed," he says, aiming the head of the weapon toward me, "my right to left blow smashes the opponent's head toward his right shoulder, and when you change direction and strike left to right, his head is knocked over toward his left shoulder. You must change direction quickly to hit him twice before he falls down."

Now he's shadow sparring with the club. "If you strike too deeply with either end, the weapon might get stuck in the skull, preventing you from doing part two of the move. To prevent that, I strike so whatever end I'm using rips across the skull instead of sinking into the bone. When I use the jawbone end, it leaves a deep slash."

"Damn!" I say. "Our SWAT guys would love this, but the public relations nightmare would be colossal."

He spins the weapon in his hand and cuts the air with figure eights. "Some people prefer heavy war clubs, but I like light ones so I can hit multiple times with greater speed. And I can control the impact. I can punch into the target deeply, or I can inflict multiple superficial wounds so he bleeds out slowly."

Fun guy.

Nate moves to the center of my kitchen and glances about to ensure he is away from my refrigerator and stove. He drops into a crouch similar to a wrestler's, his weapon arm slightly forward, and begins moving forward, back, and to the sides. He turns a one eighty and repeats his footwork. He turns toward me—happily he is a few feet away—and lunges forward, striking downward. Next he rotates his hand to strike upward. Every move is quick and smooth. Chien jumps off the chair and disappears around the wall leading to the living room. Maybe I should follow her.

Now he's moving the war club from his right hand to his left, and back again. He does it in front of him, behind him, and between his legs. He's very fast, shifting the weapon from hand to hand as quickly as a slick magician performing the cups-and-ball trick. The difference is Nate is using the jawbone of a buffalo.

He says, "If you want to be less lethal, you can rotate the weapon like this so you hit with the handle end." He jabs it forward several times, as he advances. "You can grip with two hands like this and drive the butt end into the target with all the force of your body behind it." He lifts the handle head high. "Or you can rip the end of the handle down the adversary's face. My cousin back in Oklahoma, who is much better at the war club than me, likes to forcefully drag the butt end down his opponent's ribs, like a pianist moves his fingers across the keys."

"Did they let you carry it in Iraq and Afghanistan?" I ask to be funny.

"They didn't *let* me," he says with a wink. Never has closing one eye conveyed so much.

He's moving again, throwing medium-speed kicks and war-club combinations. Now he's punching the air with his empty hand followed by a war-club blow.

"As I mentioned in the truck, I can bury the buffalo jaw's teeth into the target, or I can hit shallow and slice downward, upward, or to the side." He demonstrates a few hit-and-slice moves. "I know Padre told you my full name, N-uh-r-t-uh-n-ah, but did he tell you what it means?"

"Yes, uh, one who dances, I think."

"Not quite. It means 'one who makes *others* dance.' May I show you how I've worked it into my war-club art?"

"On me?"

"If I may."

"Since there are no white belts here I guess I have no choice."

"I'll be careful, Sensei. I just wish the room would quit spinning and I had my glasses."

"Hilarious," I say, centering myself on him.

"Okay, please throw a medium-speed jab at my face."

I do as he asks. He backhand blocks my punch, knocking my hand toward my chest, moves to my side, and raps the hammer end of his war club on the floor a hair-width away from my big toe.

"Yow!" I blurt, reflexively lifting my foot. He follows with a second rap that just misses my other foot. When I reflexively lift it, he bangs the club to the side of my first one again.

He straightens and smiles. "'One who makes *others* dance.' I'm the 'one' and you're the 'dancer.'"

"Man it would be brutal," I say, shaking my head.

He nods. "It's much worse when your feet actually get hit. Worse still if I were to target your shins and kneecaps. I've done it and people dance like they've never danced before—for a second anyway. Then they fall down."

I laugh, then wonder what people he is talking about.

"So that's a little of my war club," he says, rewrapping his weapon in the brown and white cowhide.

"You have excellent skills, Nate, and unique. Here's a question. Do you believe the warrior's spirit is absorbed into the weapon? You know, like the samurai believed the spirit of the swordsman lived in his weapon?"

"I asked the elders the same question once. One said I was silly and starting to believe all the folklore nonsense surrounding us. He said the old warriors never got too attached to their weapons because they were often lost in battle or were broken. Most of the time, the fights were too furious to stop and retrieve a dropped war club. When they would find someone else's, they would simply pick it up and use it."

"Interesting," I say.

"I have heard Geronimo might have believed his rifle contained his spirit. But as far as tomahawks and war clubs go, maybe some believed their weapons held their spirit, but I think most didn't. I do know some Apaches believed if a woman touched their weapon it was no longer any good."

"Really?" I say smiling. "I can see it. You let your wife touch your war club?"

"Touch it?" he laughs. "She's chased me around the house with it. Twice."

I smile, though I'm not sure if he's joking. "I think it's great you're keeping your heritage alive. I would guess by combining war-club moves with your kenpo, as well as applying modern training ideas and new innovative techniques, you're probably far more skilled than Indian warriors were a hundred fifty years ago."

Nate shakes his head. "No way am I on their level. Their skill could make the difference between life and death and they applied their knowledge on a real battlefield."

"You're too humble."

"I hope so," he says. He looks at me for a moment, before he asks, "Do you know the story of the two wolves?"

I shake my head.

"One evening an old Cherokee ... wait, let's make him an Apache. So this Apache tells his grandson about a battle that goes on inside people. He said, 'My son, the battle is between two wolves inside us all. One is Evil: anger, envy, jealousy, sorrow, regret, greed, arrogance, self-pity, guilt, resentment, inferiority, lies, pride, superiority, and ego.

"'The other is Good: joy, peace, love, hope, serenity, humility, kindness, benevolence, empathy, generosity, truth, compassion and faith.'

"The grandson thought about this for a minute and asked, 'Which wolf wins, grandfather?'"

"The old Apache replied, "'The one you feed.'"

"Excellent," I say.

"Thank you, Sensei. I strive every day to be humble. My parents taught me this path and I will never disrespect them by being anything but. My father said the humblest man he knew always puts others before himself, so much so he became chief. Well, I don't want to be chief, I just want to live my life by doing what's right." He looks off to the side and shakes his head as if it was the dumbest thing he could have ever said. "There's some funny irony for you, Sensei."

I know he's thinking about what happened in Afghanistan. "Nate, you can beat yourself up over—"

"*Hey, howareyuh. Hey, howareyuh.*" A male voice sounding like an Indian chant emanates from Nate's pocket.

"Wife," he says, looking at the screen. He lifts his eyebrows at me and inhales through his teeth. "Allie, dear. Yes. Yes. I'm sorry. My fault. No, it won't happen again. I'm on the way. Bye. Love you."

I'm not touching that conversation with a twenty-foot pole.

"You know, Sensei," he says, pocketing his phone. "One time in Oklahoma I got jumped by a couple of two-hundred-and-fifty-pound Comanches. In the Army, I survived some of the roughest training they offer, I faced withering machine-gun fire in Iraq, and I drove on IED-infested highways in

Afghanistan. But out of all of those experiences, my eighty-five-pound wife scares me the most."

I laugh. Wait. Eighty-five pounds?

CHAPTER SEVEN

Newsrooms in a dozen AM and FM radio stations, four TV stations, and the city's primary newspapers, the *Oregonian* and the *Tribune*, were frantic about the beginning of a story that had the potential to rock the city. They were concerned and yet morbidly excited. Although Officer Kitty Stafford's rookie had told only one reporter from KOIN TV about the carving in Yolanda's chest, an anonymous police records clerk, the same one who had day's earlier leaked information that "nigger" had been carved on the lynched man's chest, called Channel Eight and Channel Two News, the *Oregonian*, and the small black community newspaper, the *Scanner*. She told them the black prostitute was stabbed to death and the word "Mooslum" carved into her chest. She said the police consider Ocnod's and Yolanda's murders racially motivated.

After someone from an FM radio station snitched to the PD about the leak, the department's Public Information Officer was called back to the station to prepare an official statement. It was a typical media release, giving limited information, but enough to keep most reporters from calling every few minutes.

At ten forty-five, during one TV station's identification break, a male news anchor with heavily sprayed hair gave a near hysterical tease of the eleven o'clock news. "Tonight at eleven, we'll be looking at the grisly slayings of a local Middle Eastern businessman and an African American woman, a single mother of one. Were the killings racially motivated? Are the police worried white supremacists are rampaging in Portland?

Details at eleven."

The Scanner sent a reporter to the morgue to interview the night crew medical examiners while another telephoned black community leaders to get their take on the killings.

The *Oregonian's* morning headline had been decided: "Two Slain: Police Insiders Say Murders of a Middle Eastern man and African American Woman May Be Racially Motivated." The *Scanner's* headline will read: "Racial Attacks Kill Two: Are the Police Doing Anything About It?"

At 11 p.m., every television news program led with the story, milking what little information they had. One station ran an interview with the president of the Coalition Against Racial Violence. The white, self-righteous-looking man said hate crimes against minorities and homosexuals had been on the rise and, although he was "personally outraged" by the murders, it didn't surprise him people were being killed.

KOIN TV concluded their story with a tape of a field reporter named Toni Dunn interviewing an elderly black woman named Bertha Washington. The old woman said teen-age white boys had harassed her at a bus stop a week earlier. The boys had called her terrible names and warned if they saw her on the sidewalk again they would string her up from the nearest tree. The camera zoomed in on her tired face as she described her sleepless nights and how worried she was for her grandbabies who walked to and from school each day on the same sidewalk.

"Bertha Washington is now frightened of her own neighborhood streets," Toni Dunn's voiceover said as the woman trudged down the sidewalk. "Have the streets of our city become a breeding ground for racial violence? Toni Dunn, KOIN TV News."

CHAPTER EIGHT

What better way to celebrate TGIF day than to have to push my way through a crowd of about a hundred mixed-race protestors singing, "We will overcome" on the sidewalk in front of the Justice Center. Most are holding signs and banners:

STOP HATE

BLACKS ARE HUMAN

FIRE RACIST COPS

BEHEAD THOSE WHO INSULT PEACEFUL ISLAM

WHITES AND BLACKS TOGETHER

There is a smaller group across the street holding up signs too:

PROSECUTE BLACK SUPREMACY HATE CRIMES

NO MOSQUES

And my favorite:

GOD HATES SIGNS

No doubt there are a couple dozen riot officers standing by in a holding room inside the Justice Center or more likely in the parking garage across the street. Things are going to get hairy before all this is over.

In the lobby, I hear his sandpaper-on-chalkboard voice before I see him. "Hey, Reeves." I turn as Sergeant Koch barges out of a Central Precinct door.

"Sarge. Long time. How're you doing?"

Koch is a tall, lean strip of leather who looks a little like Clint Eastwood when the actor was in his early fifties. But Clint is a girlyman next to the old sarge. Koch has a grey buzz cut and possesses a long, deeply lined face that looks as if it were chipped from basalt. He's also got a mouth that would make a sailor blush.

He shakes my hand. "Gettin' so short I can play handball against the curb. Sixty-three more days and I'm retirin' to Arizona to play golf and slide up next to some of those wealthy, blue-haired widows."

"You've earned it, Sarge. Thirty-some years, right?"

"Six, thirty-fucking six. But who's counting? Hey, you helped Rhyder and Sullivan bag those two shitbirds yesterday down on Burnside." He looks over my shoulder toward the lobby windows facing Second Avenue. "Looks like the troops are pushing those assholes off the sidewalk."

Officers dressed in black-padded riot gear, or what the media calls "Star Wars trooper uniforms," have formed a line between the building and the protestors. Something hits the glass with a bang, an orange, I think. It doesn't break the window but it leaves wet splatter and seeds drooling down the glass. Central Precinct's desk officers and secretaries move into the lobby to watch the action.

I look back at Sergeant Koch, wondering if he's about to jump me for squeezing Puke's cookies. "Yes, I was there," I say.

He shakes his head, his face grimacing with disgust. "Rhyder and Sullivan lodged the two douches in a holding room down here while they did their paperwork." He shrugs. "Thought I'd see what was in their heads before they were taken up to Dicks. Fuckin' nothin', that's what was in their goddamn heads. Nuthin'. A couple of card-carryin' assholes."

"Did they say anything about—?"

"The piece of shit who calls himself Puke is the worse. He oughta be chucked into a tree-limb shredder." The sarge always has great *oughtas*.

A couple of secretaries, temporarily diverted from the action out front, share a laugh at our expense. They work for him. Outside the windows, the riot squad is pushing the crowd toward the curb so the protestors have to step out into the street or move to either side of the building.

"Any luck with the other guy?" I ask.

"Executioner, the scum-eating turd bag?" Koch practically shouts, causing everyone in the lobby to turn toward us. I shoot them a weak smile. "His mother, if he ever had one, shoulda smothered his little ass when he first whimpered." Koch has a lot of *shouldas* too.

I purposely lower my voice hoping it will make Koch lower his. "You have a chance to form an opinion, sarge?"

He stabs his finger at me and says through gritted teeth, his voice low and intense. "You know what really frosts my ass about these two shitbirds? I don't think we can hold them."

"We can't hold them?"

"What I said, goddamn-it!" Koch blurts, nearly making me jump. I give a little wave to all the faces looking our way. Outside the windows, the sidewalk is clear. "Lousy witnesses," Koch says, his voice a tad lower. "A bag lady and two falling-down winos. They were across the street and couldn't hear what the two shitbirds were saying to the victim. The witnesses saw the boys wave, nothin' else. It's going to be tough for the DA to convict them for waving."

"Did Puke and Executioner say anything at all?"

Koch's face tightens even more. "Said they were *concerned* about the man's safety and just wanted him to stay put. This Puke asshole had a smirk on his face the entire time he was talking about it. I shoulda driven a nail into his forehead."

I say, "Puke spit on Angela and one of them mowed down

an old woman."

Koch shakes his buzz cut. "Citations only, the DA says, plus the woman wasn't hurt. Not a scratch. Jail's full and the weekend's coming up. They'll boot everyone out who isn't a killer or a rapist. Assaulters? No way."

I shrug a what-are-you-going-to-do. "It's the only system we got, right? Listen, I got to get up to the office. Hope they're haven't been released yet. I'd like to talk with them."

"Okay, Reeves," Koch says with a nod. "Maybe the loving kindness approach will work on them." He glances toward the lobby windows. "I got a feeling these protests are going to get hairy before all this over, especially if someone else dies. We oughta just push 'em over the seawall and into the sewer-infested Willamette River."

"Think you're right, sarge, about the protests," I say, shaking his hand. "Wish you weren't."

I almost get to ride the elevator up by my lonesome but a hand slips between the closing doors, bouncing them back open. BJ steps in.

"Morning," he whispers, making only brief eye contact before turning toward the closing doors.

"Morning." We ride in thick silence. To reduce the tension, I say, "It's Friday, eh?"

He nods, watching the numbers above the door. "The media is having a Mardi Gras." He looks at me. "Someone in the PD fed them a lot of information."

What's with the look? He thinks I'd leak information to the media? This guy either doesn't like me or working Intel has made him suspicious of everyone.

"There are always leaks," I say, unnecessarily. He doesn't respond. I should ask the old sarge if there is room for one more in the chipper. And I agreed to take this assignment.

The doors swoosh open and we step out into the hallway. Steve sees us through the glass and buzzes the door. Angela is already at her desk. There are good mornings all around.

"You two are meeting with the feds this morning, aren't you?" BJ asks them.

"At nine thirty," Steve says. "They want a briefing of what we have so far. The Fat Dicks are going too."

Angela says, "Sergeant Bing called from Traffic just as I got here. Said he talked to, or tried to talk to, the two guys we helped capture yesterday. Said they're real assholes and he couldn't get much out of them."

"I ran into Sergeant Koch downstairs," I say. "He tried to talk with them too, but didn't get far."

"Koch, huh?" Steve says, chuckling. "Did he do the bad cop/bad cop routine?"

Angela looks at me, smiles. "Maybe the rookie can try to get something out of them."

"Not a good idea," BJ says.

I stare down his comment. I've about had it up to here with this guy. He looks away.

Angela says, "The two are still up in Dicks. Bing says to let him know. Says they got a substantiated alibi for Yolanda Simpson and both were in Seattle when Ocnod got it. He also said the witnesses to the struck ped on Third are poor to bad. He's still going to present the case to the DA, but right now they can walk with citations. I think Sam should talk to the racist bastards to see where they're coming from before they're cut loose."

BJ thinks for a moment, before looking at me. "Okay, Sam. But I'm going with you."

*   *   *

"These two are serious dickheads," Sergeant Bing says, as a way of greeting my babysitter and me. The sergeant, looking fit in his uniform, has worked the Traffic Division as long as I can remember, specializing in fatal accidents and hit-and-runs. His usual calm demeanor seems a tad ruffled right now, though. "It was all I could do to hold my temper," he says. "They called me a string of racial names, some I haven't heard in all my forty-five years of being Chinese."

"Which room?" I ask.

"The one called Puke is in three and Executioner is in four." He hands BJ a copy of his report. "My sense is Executioner might be the weak one, but I couldn't get far enough to play on it. I'll come with you."

"Thanks, Bing, but we got it," BJ says abruptly. Bing nods, though it's his prisoner and he has every right to be in on the meeting. He tells us he will stay right here if we need him. We head around the corner to the six holding-room doors. "Should we do Puke first?" BJ asks. Can't believe he's asking me for my opinion.

I shrug. "Six of one, half dozen of the other." It's BJ's show. Who am I to argue?

"Okay, I'll do the talking, understood?"

I nod, wanting to say, "Much to learn, I have. Follow your enlightened guidance, I will."

Without looking through the peephole first, BJ unlatches the sliding lock and pushes the heavy door open. Puke is sitting on the wooden bench at the rear of the twelve-by-twelve room, his long legs extended, the heel of one boot resting on the upright toe of the other, his hands cuffed behind his back, and his face shows a sleepless night. I stand slightly behind BJ so the kid can't see my face other than one eye. He probably remembers Angela more than me, anyway, but just in case.

Puke looks up at BJ lazily, wrinkles his nose as if smelling something foul, and snarls, "What you lookin' at, pear body?" He looks back down at his boots, to show how bored he is.

"Good morning," BJ says. "I'm Lieutenant Sherman." He looks at the report. "And you are, uh, Jason Tibbitts. I wanted to ask you—"

"It's Puke, you Jew puppet," the kid spits, looking up. "Enjoying your little dance for your Kike masters?"

BJ moves over to the bench and sits a few feet away from him. Uh, Boss, not a good idea at this juncture.

"Puke, I wanted to ask you a few questions about—"

"How many goddamn puppets are going to talk to me? First the old intense dude, then some gook motherfucker, and now you two." He looks up at me, drops his eyes back to his boots, then snaps his head back up. "Hey, I know you. You're the big asshole who was with that Watusi princess yesterday. Yeah, it was you. Where's she at? I hope I meet up with her again when I don't have handcuffs on. She nearly crushed my balls. Made me puke in the Jew cop car. I'm gonna sue the black bitch."

BJ looks up at me, confused.

"Sorry, Puke. I talked to her about it and she's very sorry. Wanted to tell you herself but she had a meeting this morning." A little honey might help us get some info.

BJ blinks rapidly, clearly thrown by this new piece of information.

"Yeahyeahyeah, I bet she feels real tore up." He looks down at his stacked boot.

The lieutenant, distracted by the information that Angela was the one who tweaked the punk's balls, almost reluctantly turns to the prisoner. "I uh ... I don't want to ask you anything about the pedestrian. I'm more interested in hearing about your beliefs. Do you belong to some kind of an organization?"

"Why?" Puke snaps without looking at BJ.

BJ shrugs. "Curiosity. Your beliefs are interesting to me. Are you a white supremacist?"

"Why? There a law against it? We got thought police now?"

"No, just curious."

BJ is trying the soft approach with this character, but he isn't good at it. It's coming off timid and weak, not an approach to use on this guy.

Puke looks at him. "Blacks spout their hatred for whitey but no one calls them black supremacist. Why?"

BJ shrugs. "Why do you think, Puke."

"Because the system is unfair. It caters to the jigs, the spicks, the kikes, and the gooks. The system believes only the white man is bad. And you know what? The fact you, a white man, knows this is true but you don't do a damn thing about it, is effin' sad. Dance for the mud people, you sad motherfucking puppet." Puke places both feet on the floor and scoots to the edge of the bench. "If you got something on us, put us in jail. If not, take these cuffs off and let us go." His glare is a flame-thrower. BJ doesn't break eye contact, though it looks like he wants to. Puke shakes his head from side to side as if disgusted. "Fuck it!" he spits, standing quickly. He takes a step toward me.

"Sit back down, Puke," I say. "We'll let you know when you can go."

He backs up toward the bench, his glaring eyes never leaving mine. When his heels hit the seat, he bends forward as if to sit, but instead, he quickly slips the handcuffs over his butt and steps over the chain so his hands are in front of him. He does the move fast and unexpectedly, and he's swinging his chained fists at BJ before I can reach him.

The lieutenant has only enough time to turtle his head a little, so the two-handed club slams against his shoulder and barely clips the side of his head. Still, it's enough to knock BJ's other shoulder into the cinderblock wall.

I plunge my hand into the kid's hair all the way to the dark roots. Before he can react, I snap my elbow downward and drive him straight down to the concrete where he lands with a bone-jarring thud on his chest and abdomen, his cuffed hands stretched out beyond his head. I drop my knee onto his shoulder to pin him to the floor. He tries to struggle but stops quickly when I twist his hair more, the acute pain convincing him I'm about to rip his scalp open. His curses are loud and unintelligible.

"You okay, BJ?" I ask. He's cupping his ear with one hand and his shoulder with his other.

Yeah," he says weakly, dazed.

"Listen carefully, Puke," I say, adding more weight to my knee. He groans and kicks his legs as if having a tantrum. "Pull your hands back toward me. A little more. Okay, stop." I grab a couple of his fingers with my free hand and bend them toward the back of his hand. "Do not resist or try to fight me. Understand?" He doesn't respond. I bend his finger back another half inch.

"Owowowowo!" Muffled. "Yeah, I understand."

I lean back a little to take some of the weight off his head. "Good. Now, I'm going to remove your left handcuff. If you try to fight me, I will break your fingers like twigs, and I will put all my weight onto the back of your head and crush your nose. Any part of this you do not understand?

"Yeah. I mean no."

"Once I remove the left cuff, you will move your left hand to the small of your back. Then I will move your right hand to your lower back. You will not fight me and you will not utter a word. If you choose to resist, I won't just break your fingers, I will do it in such a way your hand will be useless to you the rest of your shitty life. We clear?"

"Yeah," he says weakly.

BJ sits at the edge of the bench and watches the process, all the while holding his owies. I'm guessing he's never been hit on the job and his years of insulation from the street makes all this a little hard to comprehend.

With his hands on his lower back, I thread the chain through Puke's pant's belt so he can't step over them again, and cuff his free wrist. I have to admit his maneuver took me by surprise. It's not unusual for skinny prisoners to do it but Puke isn't that slim. Must be extra flexible.

"Smooth move, Vomit Boy," I say, standing up. I nod my head toward the door indicating BJ should leave. "You were going to get a walk, but now you're under arrest for assault on a police officer." I'm not telling him the jail won't hold him on the charge, let him sweat a little.

He waits until I shut the door and slip the latch before he starts bellowing. I look through the peephole. He's already rolled onto his side. "Things are happening, puppets," he shouts, the sound especially loud because of the echo effect in the cinderblock room. He maneuvers himself onto his rear and stands. "It's going to suck big time to be a nigger, a raghead, or a fag. And it's going to suck especially big time to be a puppet cop. Hail Victory." He kicks the cinder wall. "And tell the Watusi princess she hasn't heard the last from me."

He's still yelling as I move over to where BJ is leaning against the far wall.

"What happened," Bing says, coming around the corner. The lieutenant waves him off and the sergeant leaves. BJ touches his fingers to his ear and checks for blood.

"I don't see anything," I say. "It's pretty red, though. Fortunately, he hit your ear with his hand and not the metal cuff."

"Sam ..."

"No need to say it, BJ."

"Yes, there is. I owe you an apology."

I don't say anything because, well, he does.

"You didn't correct me when I got on your ass last night. You didn't deny it. You didn't say anything."

"'Cause you didn't ask me anything."

He snorts a laugh and shakes his head. "Ouch," he groans, touching his ear. He looks at me. "Fair enough." He extends his hand. "Lesson learned. I apologize."

We shake. "Accepted. Like I said before, I've never had an excessive force complaint in fifteen years."

As soon as the words come out of my mouth, I think of the little boy. I don't know what my face just revealed but BJ touches my shoulder.

He says, "Also for the record, Sam, the Lord knows what was in your heart that day. He's the only one you have to answer to. So take it from a guy who talks with Him, I know He isn't blaming you."

Wow. Didn't expect him to say those words. "Thanks, Boss."

"Let's talk with this other guy," he says.

"You up to it?" He nods.

I move over to number four and examine the peephole.

Occasionally, a prisoner will take a screwdriver or some other kind of instrument missed by arresting officers, and pry out the magnifying glass. I've always had the morbid mental image of looking into the peeper just as a prisoner rams a rusty nail through the hole and into my eyeball.

The glass is in place and I can see Executioner standing against the left wall, arms behind his back. He is at least thirty pounds heavier than Puke, his long dyed-black hair falling to his mid-back, EXECUTIONER in bold, white letters across the front of his black hoody. He is big, but he's shaking like a nervous Chihuahua.

To psyche him further, I slap my palm against the door, which sounds like a twelve-gauge shotgun blast in the echo-producing holding room. The big kid nearly jumps out of his skin.

"Sit on the bench," I say through the door. "Do it now." He sits, knees together, his entire body trembling like a fall leaf. I push open the door and barge in. "Stay seated, son. Do not move. Any part of my words you don't understand?" BJ remains by the door letting me run the show.

"Yes, sir," he says meekly. "I mean, I understand."

The ol' enter a holding cell like a SWAT team works every time.

"What happened to Jason?" he asks in a small voice that belies his broad shoulders and thick neck. If this guy wanted to fight he'd be tough. A muscular neck, thick forearms, and an athletic butt beats out big biceps anytime. He's got the neck and he's got the ass. I'm guessing he's got some beefy forearms under his sweatshirt.

"We had a little communication problem. He lost, and he earned a nonstop downstairs to jail. Now we're going to talk to you. We will not have a problem. Any part of this confusing?"

"No. I mean, I understand, sir."

"Your name is Carl Findorff, right" He nods. "Tell me about your involvement in this white supremacy stuff."

"Well, Puke got me into it. He's been doing it a long time. He started talking to me about how unfair things are to the white race. How we're oppressed."

"Meaning?

"Like how niggers get all the breaks, and the Jews run everything and control everything. How the Mexicans are taking over, and how Muslims are starting to make all kinds of demands, and how our government kisses their ass. Puke says lots of people are sick of it, big people wanting a change and willing to pay to get it done."

"How? With violence?"

"That's what the talk is. My personal philosophy is to make the change without violence, but I'll fight if I'm attacked."

Kid sounds like a parrot, repeating things he has heard rather than speaking from some deep commitment. If this is the case, there might be a chance we can use him. Save him, maybe.

I ask, "You think the white race is superior?"

"Of course," he says, as if it were a stupid question. "Don't you?" When I don't say anything, he says, "Me and Puke believe there is going to be a race war soon and we will prevail."

"We?" BJ asks, stepping farther into the room. He must have collected himself. "Whites?"

"Of course."

"You associated with a militia group?" I ask.

"Mil what?" He looks genuinely puzzled.

"Militia. Guys who maybe wear military uniforms—love guns—build fortresses, drive pickups, plan for doomsday."

He shakes his head. "No, I don't know anything about them."

"Okay. You hear about the man who was lynched last week, not too far from where you guys were messin' with the wino?"

He shakes his head. "Nothing. The tall pissed-off sergeant asked me about it." He shrugs. "Don't know anything, though. Puke said somethin' about it a couple days ago, but I didn't follow what he was saying. I don't watch the news too much."

I've been fooled before but I don't think he's lying. I pull out my wallet, extract a card, and stuff it into the pocket of his hoody.

"My phone number. Call me should you need anything. Wait, let's do it this way. Call me Monday morning about ten. We'll chat a little."

BJ looks at the police report Sergeant Bing gave him. It got crumpled in the scuffle. "Who lives at Twenty-Seven East Lake Avenue?" he asks.

"Me and my mom," Executioner says.

"Be sure to call me," I say. "Call me or I'll go to your house. Talk to your mother. Be a regular in your life. You want that?"

He shakes his head.

"Good. Then be sure to call. And take some free advice." He looks at me. "Make better choices. Start with getting rid of the sweatshirt."

*   *   *

BJ is so subservient to me on the elevator ride to the office it's almost embarrassing. Almost. The good news for him is the lesson he got about being too quick to judge is less painful than the one he learned about using sloppy interviewing tactics.

Back in the office, Steve and Angela haven't returned.

BJ rattles around in his office then goes back out to the hall restroom to check out his ear and shoulder. I begin writing up the limited information we got from Executioner. A few minutes later, BJ comes in, says sheepishly, "Guess I'll live," and heads back to his office. I finish my report, drop it into BJ's box, and get a cup of coffee. Instead of sitting, I stand by the window, looking out at the City of Roses, and think about its thorns.

Portland is a pleasant city for the most part, though a tad too liberal for my taste. One pundit called it "a large middle-sized city." It enjoys a diverse mix of races and ethnicities, especially a rapidly expanding Hispanic community. The Asian population is growing too, but not at the same rate as the Hispanics. The black community is large but I don't know if it's growing very much, though more and more are leaving North Portland, a predominantly black community, and moving into the predominantly white suburbs.

As a uniformed cop, I handled many calls in which a person of one race had a beef with a person of another. The initial cause of the clash might have been a car accident, a bumped shoulder in a bar, or an accusation of some kind. But all too quickly, the initial reason was lost to the ugliness of racism, the situation escalated, and things got nasty in a quick hurry.

One thing I've noticed, and other cops have said the same, is fights motivated by race always seem to be especially violent. When two white guys fight because one of them cut in the line at McDonald's, it's usually nothing more than a pushing match. When two black guys get into it over a girl at a party, there is lots of name calling and pushing. But should a white guy and a black guy get into a fight over line cutting or over a girl, fists fly, feet stomp, knives stab, and rounds are fired, lots of them,

DUKKHA UNLOADED

often long after one is down and out of the fight.

An old partner used to say our veneer of societal graces is tissue paper thin. It doesn't take much to tear it and let out whatever ugliness lies underneath. So what is under the thin veneer?

Fear perhaps, deeply ingrained from primitive times when man feared a tribe different from his own, one that was savage, cannibalistic, or at least believed to be so. Ignorance begets fear. It begets insecurity too. I read once the KKK was founded in the late nineteenth century because ignorant Southern white men were afraid black men were going to take their jobs and, to add a little sexual insecurity to the mix, take their white women too.

When people bond, they can easily see who is in their group and who is outside of it. Those outside become a receptacle for the group's frustrations. We see it with the KKK, militia, white supremacists, and black gangs.

Of course, racism isn't limited to easy-to-spot groups. It goes on in corporate America too, in those big high-rises right outside my window, and in our neighborhoods, our schools, and in our churches. Members of every race are guilty. Fortunately, most aren't violent.

I wonder what my new friend Rudy has to say on the subject? I find his card in my wallet and reach for my phone.

"This is Rudy. Where you want to go?"

"What? I can't understand you. You're getting too skinny."

Rudy lets loose his big laugh. "Detective Sam! What's cookin'?"

"You ready for a burger today."

"Lost three pounds so I'm ready to celebrate. Where? I just dropped a fare off in Northwest."

"I can meet you somewhere there, or there's Joe Bob's across the street from the Justice Center on Fourth. But the parking might be a problem for you."

He laughs. "I got people, man. Know a guy at Third and Main Parking who lets me park there when I got business downtown. Thirty minutes?"

"Looking forward to it."

I hang up. A passing helicopter catches my eye and I watch it descend onto the roof of a building. Far below on Third Avenue, the sidewalks should be filling with workers heading to lunch, but they are unusually bare. Street is empty too. Strange.

It's probably naïve but I wonder how many of our problems would go away if we all focused on improving ourselves as people instead of tearing down the next guy? I remember reading about a lesson kenpo founder Master Ed Parker taught a new student who had just been trounced in sparring by a superior opponent. The student was frustrated because he had attempted several moves to trick his opponent, all of them easily blocked and countered.

"Why are you so upset?" Parker asked his student.

"Because I couldn't score."

Parker got up from behind his desk and with a piece of chalk drew a five-foot-long line on the floor. "Tell me, how can you make this line shorter?"

The student offered several ideas, including cutting the line into pieces.

Parker shook his head and then drew a six-foot line next to the other. "How does the first line look now?" he asked.

"Shorter."

"Yes," Parker said. "You see, it is always better to improve your own line than to try to cut down your opponent's."

*   *   *

"Hey, Sam," Angela says coming through the door. "Boss still back there?"

I shake my head. "Said he was going out to lunch. Our interviews were only half fruitful. Puke, your new bff, was uncooperative and attacked BJ."

"Oh no," she says, leaning against her desk. "You're kidding, right?"

I shake my head. "Puke jumped his cuffs and clubbed BJ on his shoulder and ear. Kid's in jail now. But please don't say anything to BJ and especially don't tease him about it. It was a lesson for him and I'm sure he'll do better next time."

She shakes her head in disbelief. "I love BJ as a boss but he doesn't get out in the field. He pretty much lets the troops do the work, and he handles all the admin stuff and coordinates info sharing in-house and with outside agencies." She shakes her head laughing. "I think we've had more violence over the last two days than we've had in the last four years. You bring it with you?" She instantly sobers. "Sorry, Sam. I wasn't talking about ..."

I wave her off. "I know. Not a problem."

"Steve had a lunch date with his buddy Clarence in training. You want to go grab something?"

"Actually, I was about to leave to hook up with a friend at Joe Bob's. Hey, why don't you come along? I was going to ask what he's hearing in the community."

"Okay, but why would he know what's going on?"

I tell Angela about Rudy on the elevator. As soon as we land in the lobby, I see there are only about a dozen or so sign wavers out front walking in an endless loop. It's illegal for protestors to stand and block the sidewalk but they can protest as long as they keep moving. I think some legislator with a sense of humor came up with the law to make protestors look stupid walking in a circle.

I say, "I'm not in the mood to be yelled at today. Let's go through Central Precinct and slip out the back way." Angela agrees.

After the desk gal buzzes us in, we move down a long hall to a side exit to Madison Street, halfway between Second and Third Avenue. I push open the heavy door. The street is clear, but there is a cacophony of shouting, police sirens, and drumbeats coming from around the corner on Third. Something is happening in Lownsdale Park. We can't see what it is because the Justice Center takes up the entire block, but we can see a line of police officers between Third and Fourth—all wearing their black riot gear—facing in the direction of the park. Behind the riot control officers are several parked police cars and a handful of brass standing about talking on cells and portable radios. This is why I didn't see anyone on the sidewalks from out the office window.

"Damn," Angela says. "I saw a few uniforms up there when I walked back from the Fee-bee office on First, but it's grown to about seventy-five now."

"Let's move up and check out the park. We just might not be able to get to Joe Bob's."

As we pass by the side of the Justice Center, Angela says, "They must be expecting a demo ... whoa! Check out the park."

At the north end of the block-long park of fir trees, manicured lawn, and shaded park benches, a mass of about two hundred protestors mill about, waving signs and calling out insults at the riot cops on this end. In the center of the park, an old hippy man beats on a large drum while a half-dozen people dressed up like clowns dance silly-like to the percussion.

I say, "There are pedestrians walking over there on the far side on Third. You want to head on over or bag it?"

Angela nods. "Let's go, but let's go behind the police line."

As we cross Third Avenue, the closest uniformed officer in the line gestures for us to pass behind them. With his helmet shield down, I can only see his black hands.

"You in there, Benny?" Angela asks.

"What are you doing out here, Angela?"

"You know, protecting and serving the general public."

"I got your P and S the G P," he says.

"Those folks going to attack?"

He shrugs. "Who knows? Just wanting attention mostly. They say the police don't care about the murders because the victims weren't white."

"Well, watch yourself, Benny."

We walk behind the line, nod to the brass standing by the cars, and head over to the sidewalk. Halfway down the block, I see a couple of businessmen types come out of Joe Bob's and a nicely dressed woman go in.

"Good," I say. "It's open."

The drum beat stops. The drummer and dancers rush back to join the crowd as it begins to move in a solid mass through the park toward the officers. The drummer takes the lead and begins a rhythmic pattern like he's leading a Civil War army company.

"This is Commander Jonathan Weigert of Central Precinct," a voice booms from a police car PA system behind the long line of officers. "By order of the city of Portland, Lownsdale Park is now closed. You have five minutes to clear the area. If you remain in the park, you will be arrested for Trespass."

Angela chuckles. "Weigert laying it down for the people."

"No one's leaving," I say, stating the obvious as the advancing protestors near the center of the park. From the police end, I hear a command barked, though I can't make it out. The line of officers simultaneously takes three steps forward and lifts their shields to form a solid wall. Some of the protestors, apparently surprised the police are prepared to clash with them, stop and backup, while others peel off toward Third and others head our way. A dozen or more launch themselves into an all-out run toward the police.

The protestors moving in our direction dash across Fourth and onto the sidewalk, a couple of them near us, the two shouting curses at the officers. One is wearing a bandana over his face.

In the park, the charging protesters leap into the air like track and field high-bar jumpers and crash into the unmovable police shields. Most of them land on their feet, a few fall onto their butts.

"Gestapo!" the tall, skinny kid wearing a bandana over his mouth and nose shouts. He grabs his buddy's arm. "Come on, let's move up and hit 'em from behind."

"Whoops," Angela says, as Bandana Boy stumbles over her extended foot. Only by touching the sidewalk with his hand does he avoid sprawling. "My bad," she adds.

"Hey!" he says, turning toward us as if seeing us for the first time. "You did that on purpose." When Angela stands mute, he says, "This is all for you," he says waving his hand at the park where those who charged the officers are being pushed back by the line of shields. His buddy—maybe twenty, Whoppers and fries chubby, and with a righteous indignant expression held by so many protesters—eyeballs me.

"For me? Really?" Angela says,

"Yes," the kid says, as if it should be obvious. "Because of the murders of the African American and Middle Easterner. Because the cops aren't doing anything."

"I see," Angela says. "So you're my white savior. Thank you soooo much. And thank you for diverting the police department away from finding the killers so they have to deal with you. And thank you for uprooting those newly planted trees over there and turning over those trash cans. These things will go a long ways toward solving the crimes. Will you be marking graffiti on windows and on city property too? That always helps."

"You're a cop, aren't you?" his chubby friend asks me, his righteous indignation turning into contempt.

"I am," I say, looking into his eyes.

"You too?" Angela's friend asks.

"Yup," she says.

Bandana Boy and Chubby Boy look at each other, then back at us.

"The ball is in your court," Angela says.

Bandana Boy cackles a fake laugh. "You guys aren't so tough when you don't have backup." In the park, the police line has moved the protesters back ten yards.

"Trust me, your ass-umption is going to hurt you," I say.

Angela smiles. "Look around boys. You don't have backup either."

Chubby Boy steps toward me.

"Before you take another step," I say. "Ask yourself this: 'Can I deal with the pain?'"

He frowns. "What do you mean?"

"What part was unclear to you? The 'can I' part or the 'deal with the pain' part?"

Chubby Boy's eyes blink rapidly. He looks over at Bandana Boy. "Let's go, Darren," he says, his voice trembling.

Darren is about to head in a southerly direction that would take them behind the officers. "Wrong way, Darren" Angela says. She points toward the north. When he hesitates for a moment, Angela adds, "Go now, before I arrest you for jaywalking and for wearing a mask in the downtown core area."

"Shiiiit!" Bandana Boy says.

When he doesn't move, Angela says, "Again the ball is in your court. Listen, Darren, regardless of what you're being fed, the police are working hard to solve these murders. So don't waste your time and ours by fighting us. If you want to be an activist, fine. But choose your battles. Right now, make the smart move and go."

Bandana Boy looks at her for a long moment, then nods.

"Come on," he says, grabbing his friend's arm. "Let's go." Chubby Boy shoots me one last look—I'm not sure if it's his righteous indignation look or the contemptuous one—and the two walk off together arguing. Chubby Boy points toward the park and Bandana Boy vigorously shakes his head.

"You made a difference in a young man's life," I tell Angela. "We otta put up a plaque in your honor."

The two are a couple of strides away from the end of the building when Rudy bounds around the corner. He sees us and waves, just as Chubby Boy spins around and screams, "Gestapo motherfuckers!"

As if he'd planned it well in advance, Rudy smoothly extends his waving hand straight out to his side and clotheslines Chubby Boy across his face. Because the kid was intent on calling us a name, he doesn't even see Rudy's arm. Mid-stride the fat kid's head snaps back and his feet actually go airborne. He slams onto the sidewalk, fortunately not hitting his head on the concrete. If he had landed on a gravel road there would have been a large cloud of dust from the impact.

"Saaaaw-ree," I hear Rudy Van Damn say. "My bad."

* * *

"Please tell me it was an accident," I say, trying not to smirk.

"It was, Sam," Rudy says with phony earnestness. "I was waving at a friend over in the park and the unfortunate young man ran into my arm." He shrugs. "I do hope he's okay."

We have moved around the corner onto Main. We can still see the park and the mass of protesters, though the building corner is blocking our view of the police line. A roar emits from the mob as they suddenly scatter in every direction.

"Gotta see this," I say, moving back around the corner to get a complete view.

The police line has advanced to the middle of the park. Several of the protesters who charged the police are now wearing plastic Flex-cuffs and being walked or carried behind the police line for processing. Though scattered, the mob begins chanting "shame, shame, shame" and pointing toward the police line.

I turn back to Rudy and Angela. "They just learned they can't assault the police without repercussions." I point toward Fourth. "There's a Starbucks on the corner up there. I think Joe Bob's is out as long as this thing is so volatile."

"Rudy," Rudy says, extending his hand to Angela as we proceed up the sidewalk. "I can see why Sam wants to hang with you, but I don't get why you're with him. Last time I was with him, he got us caught smack in the middle of another one of these protests."

"Nice to meet you, Rudy. Trouble does seem to find him, doesn't it?"

"I'm restraining my laughter," I say.

At Starbucks, the only indications of a protest are the sounds of distant shouting and police sirens. We order coffee and sandwiches. Angela and I get the sandwiches. Rudy gets a yogurt.

"If I can't get a burger, I may as well stick to my diet," Rudy says sadly, as we sit around a table. A Leonard Cohen CD rumbles from the sound system. Love him. Rudy looks at Angela. "Girls like six packs, right?"

She lifts her eyebrows. "Uuuuh, yes."

"Soon," Rudy says. "A few more yogurts and I'm all about a six pack."

"Angela is teaching me the ropes in Intel," I say. "Lots of things happening right now."

Rudy shakes his head. "Ugliness for sure. I don't think it's goin' away anytime soon. Me, I see racial ugliness everyday. Two times this week, white people at the airport refused to ride with me, and I was the next cab up in the line. Said they wanted the next one, one with a white driver." He shrugs. "Happens so much, sometimes I don't give it a thought. Or maybe I do—in the back of my head."

Angela has been nodding. To me, she says, "You won't find any black folks who don't experience it at least once a week. It's the way it is and it isn't going to change."

"I would guess being a cop is like putting a cherry on top." I say.

"Uh huh," she says, sipping her latte.

"I got just a taste of it in Saigon. My girlfriend and I were at a tea café when a couple of guys first started in on me and then on her. She's mixed race, Caucasian and Vietnamese. It got nasty real quick."

Angela looks at me for a moment over the rim of her coffee. I don't think I've mentioned Mai to her.

Rudy laughs. "You Bruce Lee 'em?"

I smile and shrug. It was actually Mai who kicked their butts, but my ego prevents me from saying so.

Rudy finds a whole strawberry in his yogurt, saws it in half with his spoon, and pops it into his mouth. "The longest I ever went without experiencing anything was when I was in rehab."

"Rehab?" I say. "You?"

He nods. In nineteen ninety-two. My family dragged my ass into it. I fought 'em, but it was the best thing ever happened to me. Been clean and sober since."

"Good for you, Rudy," Angela says.

The big man nods. "Don't matter if you're white, black, gay, religious, poor, or rich, drugs and alcohol will bite your ass and take you down. We were all the same in there. All of us had reached rock bottom, we all wanted to get cleaned up, and each of us had to go through the same thing to get it." Rudy chuckles, remembering. "One time, I held a well-known TV anchorman as he cried his eyes out into my shoulder. An old homeless man comforted me when I couldn't stop shakin'.

"All of us were tryin' to get ourselves clean, get sane again. Because we all wanted the same thing and needed the same thing to live, it made us all the same. You follow me? Some might have come in with prejudices and hate, but when you're strugglin' up from the bottom, from the sewer, you unite with each other. You laid down your ignorance and fear of others outside of who you are, and you clung to those people. You clung because you knew you were all the damn same.

"I wasn't a hater, but I'll tell you the truth, sometimes a white man would do somethin', an Asian man would do somethin', a Jew, and I'd feel prejudice boilin' up inside me. It bothered me a lot, because I didn't understand it. It wasn't me. But it was, you follow? It *was* me."

He finishes his yogurt and pushes the dish to the center of the table. "But rehab changed me. Oh, I'm not no angel and I still get those feelin's sometimes, but not very often. When they do come up, I think about being at rock bottom with all those people. And how we were needin' each other and helpin' each other." Rudy sighs, leans back in his chair, and pats his belly. "It's simple, but if we all took the time to think about it, about needin' each other and helpin' each other, it would be a better world."

We sit without speaking. Bob Dylan has replaced Leonard Cohen.

"I'm glad I got in your cab the other day, Rudy," I say. Not to break the silence but because I want to say it.

He extends his hand. "Me too." He smiles. "I've been thinking about those martial arts lessons of yours." He looks at Angela. "Can you see me trim and movin' like Bruce Lee? 'Cept I'd be Rudy Lee."

Angela looks up at the ceiling as if trying to visualize it. Finally, she shakes her head. "I'm not seeing it."

"Say what, girl?" he says, laughing with his big belly. "You dissin' me after knowin' me for only forty-five minutes? Okay, I get it now." He extends his big fist toward Angela. She bumps it, grinning.

"What are you hearing on the street, Rudy?" I ask.

He shakes his head. "Folks are mad. Black folks and white. Mad and scared because they don't know what's goin' on. You got a policeman ... can't remember his name. He always talks to the news?"

"Anderson," Angela says. "He's the Public Information Officer."

"Yeah, that's him. He needs to be talkin' more. Telling people what's goin' on, what to look out for, what the police are doin' about it."

"Normally the PD does keep the public informed about high profile cases," Angela says. "But when it's a highly sensitive one, hate crimes in this case, information is less forthcoming. Believe me when I say there are meetings going on up the kazoo. I know of three this morning in the Chief's Office. I attended one earlier at the FBI's office. I know Sandy Rogers from Channel Two has been at some of them and Dennis Hing From Channel Eight News has attended at least one. These two are longtime friends with the PD, and we can trust them to hold some stories when we need them held."

"Good," Rudy says, nodding. "And I understand. But the police need to balance it more. Right now, there is not enough information and when people don't understand, they fill in the blanks." He jerks his head in the direction of Lonsdale. "And act stupid in the parks."

"What are they filling in the blanks with, Rudy?" I ask.

"The usual bullshit. 'The police don't care.' 'If the victims were white more would be done.' Same ol' thing. They're trying to get some big national black leaders to come to Portland."

"Oh, damn," Angela says.

*   *   *

We bid Rudy goodbye outside of Starbucks and head back down Main toward the park. The number of protestors has thinned to about fifty, some sitting on the sidewalk, others talking in groups. Those who ignored the command to clear the park have been arrested and whisked away. We're walking behind about twenty-five officers now, still in formation but standing more casually than before. Some have removed their helmets. A few who know us nod. Those officers who left are probably on standby at Central Precinct ready to return in a moment's notice.

As we cross Third, Angela asks, "So you have a girlfriend in Saigon?" the way women do when they are very interested in the answer but pretend not to be.

"I do," I say, retrieving my cell. "Her name is Mai. Long story how we met. I'll tell you some time."

Oh man, speaking of Mai, she called forty minutes ago. Three times. Damn. All the noise in the park must have covered the ring. I retrieve the last call and hold it up to my ear as Angela uses her keycard to let us in the back door of Central.

"Sam? Where are you? I am in Hong Kong now. I will get on the plane in thirty minutes and fly to San Francisco. I will be there at four o'clock in the morning, I think. Maybe six. My—what do you call—oh, itinerary is in my bag. When I get to San Francisco, I will call you and tell you exactly what time I will get to Portland." A few seconds of silence. "The funeral was beautiful. Very beautiful." Another pause. "I need to be with you." Pause. "See you soon, Sam. I love you."

"That her?" Angela asks, as I bend to drink from the hall fountain, more to collect myself than out of a need for water. When I straighten, Angela asks, "Are you tearing up? Something wrong?"

I shake my head. There is just too much to explain and I doubt she wants to hear it.

When we get off the elevator, I tell Angela I'll see her in the office and I head into the restroom. In the privacy of a stall, I listen to Mai's message again as well as the first two. In the first, she said our father had called Harry, his policeman friend, and asked him to help her through the red tape to get a fast flight out of Saigon. After the funeral, she and Father had talked at length about what would happen now that her mother had passed. They didn't come to any conclusions about the house and the jewelry stores, but for now, Father is going to remain in the house, though Mai said he would probably sleep in the servants' quarters where I stayed. She felt bad about leaving so soon but Father encouraged her, saying she needed to be away from all the chaos and confusion to better think about her future, her family, and to talk with me about it too.

Man, the thought of talking with Mai about it is at once exciting and a whole lot scary. She came into my life like gang-busters a little over two months ago and ever since our lives have been running Code Three. When she was here, we didn't have a second to rest, and while we had a few wonderful moments in Saigon, we were preoccupied with some violent craziness.

Am I ready to make a big life decision right now? No. My head might be on a lot tighter than it was a few weeks ago, but I still got a ways to go. I'll listen to Mai, but it's all I can do right now.

"Chuck?" Steve's voice echoing in the restroom. "Chuck Norris? You in here?"

"No."

"The Fat Dicks are here. The boss wants a meeting."

*　　*　　*

Everyone is gathered around the center desk, probably

because attempting to stuff the Fat Dicks in BJ's office would be straining the capacity limit and reducing the quality of the air. The two big men are eating from heaping plates of chiliburgers, the kind they sell in the self-serve cafeteria at the Federal Building next door where they charge by the pound. At five bucks a pound, these guys are working on at least a ten-dollar plate each.

When I was a trainee in the Traffic Division, I worked with a slender guy named Stiles who loved chiliburgers. One day after eating an especially large one for lunch, we got into a foot pursuit with a car thief. Stiles was a faster runner than I am, even with a pound of chili and soggy burger buns in his stomach, so when the thief fell in the middle of an intersection, my partner was there first to plop down on the kid's stomach and pin his arms to the pavement. Just as I ran up, I heard my perspiring and winded partner, go, "Uh oh." Then he power puked the chiliburger all over the suspect's face.

"Hey, Sam," Richard Cary says, with a wave of his fork. "Grab a chair. There's donuts back by the coffee."

"Hi, guys," I say. I nod at BJ and he smiles back, his face red. "No donuts for me." I pull my chair over next to Steve.

"Angela was just telling us about the demonstration in the park," BJ says to me. "Observations, Sam?" Hmm, is this newfound respect I'm seeing in his face? Will it last?

"Well, I worked a lot of them when I was in uniform. This one was typical. This time the primary reason for it was the two murders, but the focus quickly shifted to clashing with the police. Judging by what little we watched, it looked like there were people there who want answers about the hate crimes, others who wanted to wave signs about their particular cause, and a few just wanted to vandalize and fight the cops."

"Then sue the city," Angela notes over the brim of her coffee.

I nod. "If I had to guess, I'd say this protest was organized, at least enough to get people to come downtown, but it wasn't terribly intense. If there isn't a break in the case in a day or two, I think people will get more charged up and the organizers will be even more, well, organized."

"Thanks to Facebook, Tweets, and blogs," Steve says.

"Tell them what you've got, Steve," BJ says, as the Fat Dicks scrape the last bit of chili from their paper plates and drop them in a wastepaper basket. Richard Daniels heads back to get some donuts.

Steve tells us he's got a snitch inside EHWP, Every Human Wants Peace, an organization that fights for the rights of anyone they perceive is getting jerked around by the system. She said there is going to be a huge rally at City Hall in the next few days. They're not going to get a permit because they don't want to be restricted by rules, such as the masses overflowing into the streets, carrying wooden signs, using sound devices like megaphones, and so on. They're going to have speakers from the black community, the Muslim community, and the LGBT.

"Lesbian, gay, bisexual, and transsexual," Richard says, setting down two donuts in front of his partner and keeping two for himself. "No bestiality reps?"

"No doubt the anarchy crowd will be there too," Steve adds. "To get the rock throwing started."

"I'll see if the precincts know about it," BJ says. "What about your meeting with the Fee Bees, Angela?"

"Typical. The four of us gave them information and the FBI gave us nothing. Said a couple of agents from their hate Crime Unit will likely fly in Monday or Tuesday. It was basically a waste of time for the four of us to go over there."

"We were ordered by the Chief's Office," BJ says.

Angela shrugs. "Yup."

BJ says, "Okay, before Richard and Richard tell us of their findings, Sam, what do you think of those two characters we interviewed, if you want to call it an interview?"

I look at the Fat Dicks who have finished off their donuts. "Angela and I helped uniform capture a couple of street punks. We're pretty sure they were involved, caused, encouraged, forced, whatever, a confused drunk, a black man, to step into traffic at Third and Couch. Fatal. The case is being presented to the DA's office. Right now one of them is free and the other will likely be free later today."

"Here are the reports," Angela says, handing them to Richard Cary.

I continue. "The boss and I talked with them this morning." BJ sniffs, uncrosses and recrosses his legs. "The one with the nick of 'Puke' seems to be a pretty hardcore white supremacist. He's got some knowledge, at least bullet points on the issue, and he's quite angry and violent. I would guess we'll hear more from him. His buddy, Executioner, is a follower, a scared one. Of course, a blind follower can be dangerous, especially if he wants to impress his so-called leader. I gave him my card in the event he wants to chat."

BJ hands Angela the report on our interview. "Angela, as soon as we're done here, please call Northeast Precinct and give them everything we have on these two guys. Executioner lives on Northeast Fourteenth with his mother, and Puke has a North Dekum address. Ask the beat cars to watch their comings and goings. Let us know if either of them has a car and anything else pertinent. Make sure Central Precinct has their info too. They were hanging out in Old Town, maybe to score some dope. We want to know where else they are hanging out and with whom." Angela nods, jotting a note.

"Okay," BJ says, looking at the Fat Dicks. "Tell them about your find."

Richard Daniels scoots his big frame up higher in his chair. "Actually, we didn't find it. Sam and Angela located the video from Big Ed's. Good work you two." He looks at the TV at the back of the room. "Did our old VCR ever get fixed, Boss?"

"As hard as it is to believe, it did. Let's gather around back there."

Daniels slips in the video and pokes the fast forward button. On the screen, what looks to be the lobby of Big Ed's is empty. The timer in the lower right corner shows the rapidly advancing minutes.

"What we're interested in starts about one thirty a.m. Actually, let's begin riiiight here." He punches Play. "One-o-nine. That's the entrance to the apartment building. One-o-nine aaaand, one-ten. There see her?"

"The victim," Angela says, pointing at the screen. "Walking up to the door. Looks a little drunk."

"Yolanda Simpson," Richard Cary says. "We figure she's coming in from a night on the street. Her pimp said she'd been working. We didn't find any money in the room or in her purse, so we assume he got it, or maybe the killers took it. Okay, it's one eleven now, and going by the ME's time of death, she's got about twenty-five minutes to live at this point."

I've seen lots of homicide victims, but seeing one a few minutes before their murder is eerie. Seems like there ought to be a light on her face—some kind of dramatic effect. I want to shout, "Don't go in there."

The high-definition quality is excellent, even in min-imum-lighting conditions. She fumbles at the door for a moment, opens it, bangs it against her foot, which slams it shut again. Normally, it would be funny, but everyone knows where this is leading. She angrily hits the door with her palm, fumbles again with the handle, pulls it open, and stumbles through.

"Okay," Daniels says. "I'm going to bump it up to one twen-ty-five. Aaaand, twenty-three, twenty-four, here. Look at these two."

Two women are walking south toward the apartment, both in their late thirties, maybe early forties, wearing all black leather jackets, dark cargo pants, boots. Not dressed quite the same, but close. One has shaved the sides of her head and left the hair in back long. Can't see the other gal's hair. Both are stocky, thickly built, like beer drinking construction workers, or powerlifters who are more interested in how much weight they push than about building an aesthetic appearance. If they were male, I'd say they had prison builds.

They stop in front of the doors, look behind them and across the street toward Big Ed's and the hidden camera. Both have large, blocky heads with similar bone structure, and even from a distance, there is no mistaking the hardness in those faces. Angela's cousin at the steam bath place said he thought they might be twins. Maybe. I'd bet a kidney these women don't give a hoot about grandkids, baking pies, or cutting cou-pons. As Johnny Cash sang, they'd shoot 'a man in Reno just to watch him die,' then go get a burger with fries and extra ketchup.

Without saying a word or even looking at each other, they turn in unison and enter the building.

"Scary looking bitches," Angela says, shaking her head.

"Been pumping iron down at Oregon State Prison, I'd guess."

"Think you're right," Steve says.

Richard Daniels pushes the fast forward. "Fifteen minutes later, they come back out ... forty-three, forty-four, okay here."

The women exit the doors, stop for a moment, check the sidewalks to their left and right, glance across the street toward the camera—thank you very much for another face shot—and head back in the direction from which they came.

"Cold as ice, these two," Richard Cary says. He looks at Angela and me. "Good work on getting this. My money is on them. Now to find out who they are."

I say, "They looked right toward the camera twice. Can we get enlargements?"

"As we speak," Cary says. "Should have them within the hour."

"I like your hunch about prison, Angela," BJ says. "I'm friends with Al Love, second in command in the joint. I'll email a pic to him and see if he knows them."

"Hoping the enlargement shows blood splatter," Angela says.

"As long as we're hoping," Steve says. "I'm hoping the enlargement will show name tags, first and last."

"Anything on the perps who jumped Lieutenant Sanderson and his friend?" BJ asks.

Daniels says, "Installing video cameras down on the waterfront was okayed by the City about a year ago, but they still haven't done it. No witnesses, either. The place gets busier with concert and theater strollers later in the evening, but Mark and David were there in midafternoon, around three. Richard and I have talked with a few street people in the area, but no one knows anything. If you got any snitches who hang around there, please hit them up."

Angela says, "So we got Mark's assault, the two homicides, the cross burning, the Molotov cocktail chucked at the mosque, and the death of the ped in Old Town. The two turds are good for the ped, but the question remains can the DA make a case."

"I think so," Richard Cary says. "Peavy is helping Traffic with the interviews now."

"Maybe suggest to Peavy and Sergeant Bing to ask where they were when Mark and David were attacked," I say.

"Done did," Richard Cary says, making a note.

"If no one has anything else," BJ says, standing, "finish up what you got to do and head for home. If you get done an hour early, go ahead and take off. Good job, everyone."

"When is the last time you guys slept," I ask Daniels.

"Don't know. Wife said if I don't come home sometime soon, she was going to find herself a sailor boy, maybe two of 'em."

"Mine probably already has one," Richard Cary says. His cell rings. "You got Detective Cary in person. Yes. Okay, great, be right down." He lumbers to his feet. "Criminalistics have the blow-ups of the women."

*　　*　　*

The Fat Dicks and Angela and I are huddled in the hall outside of Criminalistics looking at the blow-ups. We each have a set of three pics pulled from the video before they entered and a set of four pulled when they were leaving. Close up, both women are even scarier. The one on the right has a shaved head and long mullet thing going on. The other wears her hair like a nineteen-fifties businessman: short, lots of Brylcreem, parted on the side, with a little wave in the front. Both are broad-shouldered, with stocky frames and tree-trunk legs.

Looks like they would have an easy time kicking my butt. Steve will be disappointed there are no nametags, but Angela is first to check for blood.

She says, "It's hard to tell because their clothing is so dark. And what's with the leather jackets? It didn't get below sixty degrees. Might they have been—Eureka! Look at the mullet's right pant leg, just above her boot."

"I don't see anything," I say. "The pants are so dark."

"I see it," Richard Daniels says. He looks at my photo. "You're looking at the shot before they went in. Look at the second set, when they came out."

I see it. "Looks like four spots between the top of the boot and the knee ... and look, something's on her boot top, the toe part. See how the streetlight reflects off it? Like it's wet. Her other boot and her partner's boots don't reflect a thing." I look up at three smiling faces. "Can I get an 'hoorah'?"

*　　*　　*

Back in the office, the Fat Dicks gather their things and head back to the Detective's Office, while Steve, Angela, and I make notes, send mug shots of Puke and Executioner to Central and Northeast Precincts, send the close-up shots of the two women to Central, and create files on all of them. At a little after four, BJ gives us a quick briefing before heading home. He tells us he sent pics of the women to his buddy at Oregon State Prison who had already left for the day, and he had given Deputy Chief Rodriguez a status update. Steve is next to go. "Have a good weekend you guys. My gut tells me I will single-handedly capture everyone involved in all of the crimes, but I couldn't do it without my helpers." He takes a bow, clicks his heels, executes a sharp salute, and leaves.

"Great guy," Angela says. "A geek, but funny and knows his stuff in the Intel biz."

I nod. "I'm enjoying working here. Pretty good deal considering three days ago I didn't know if I was going to come back to work." Whoops, said too much.

Angela looks at me, frowns. "What? What do you mean?"

"Nothing. Please forget what I said." I shuffle some papers and stick them in my desk drawer. "Guess I'm ready to roll too."

Angela's phone rings. "Detective Clemmons. Yes. Yes ..."

I stand, stretch, and pick up my briefcase. I start to wave goodbye when Angela holds up a finger for me to wait. She pokes the speakerphone.

"Could I have your name?"

"You recording me?" the female voice asks suspiciously. Youngish, early twenties.

"No, ma'am. Not without your permission."

Long pause. "Okay. I go by Hallgerd, you know, like in the Norse poem. Google it. Anyway, my boyfriend is the one who threw the firebomb at the temple place."

I retrieve my cell and punch up Google.

"The mosque on Northwest Twenty-fifth?" Angela asks.

"Yeah. He set the cross on fire too. The one in front of those niggers' house."

Angela doesn't react, at least on the outside. "In Northeast Portland, Stanton Street?"

"Yeah."

"How do you know?"

"Shit. How do you think?"

"You were with him," Angela suggests.

Pause, then, "Hey, you black or something?"

"Green. Where is your boyfriend now?"

"Said he had to work, but I just called him there and they said he had the day off."

There it is. More crooks get snitched off by disgruntled girlfriends and wives than anything else.

"Where does he work?" Angela asks.

"The Hilton. He's a cook. Shit."

I don't think the caller was ready to tell us that yet. Angela smiles at me.

"Where do you think he is?" Angela asks.

"I don't think, I know where he is and I will take care of her. You going to bust him or what?"

"I'd sure like to talk with him. What's his name?"

Pause, then, "I don't want to tell you right now."

"You're not giving me much here. How old is he?"

"Twenty-four."

"What does he look like?"

"You ask too many questions."

"Okay, you tell me how you want to play this."

"If it's like the last time he did this, he won't come home 'till late tonight. I'll call you tomorrow."

"Okay," Angela says. "The office is closed tomorrow, but you can still get a hold of me. Call the same number you just did, leave a message and your phone number, and I'll call you as soon as I check my messages. Okay?"

"Yeah. You'll bust his ass right?"

"Busting is what we do, uh, Hallgerd. Thank you for calling."

"Check this out," I say, holding up my cell. "From Google. It's from a site about Norse myths and religions. It says, 'Gunnar's home is attacked by enemies. Gunnar keeps them away with his bow, but then his bowstring breaks, and he asks his wife Hallgerd if he can get two locks of her hair to make a new bowstring. Hallgerd asks him if much depends on getting her hair. *My life* he answers. Hallgerd then says: *Now is the time to remind you of the slap you gave me in my face.* She refuses to give away her two locks, and Gunnar is killed."

"Hell hath no fury," Angela chuckles. "You available tomorrow should she call?"

Damn. "Uh, not really. Mai is flying in."

"Mai. Your Saigon girlfriend?" She asks in a voice straight from the grave.

"Yes."

"Serious?" she asks too casually.

"Very."

She nods, biting her lower lip. "Okay." She looks at me for a moment, then, "You know why I'm asking, right?"

"I think so but I'm not sure."

She shakes her head and laughs. It sounds half real and half forced. "Men are such bricks. Sam, I never tiptoe around anything. You might have noticed." She looks at her hands, then back at me. "I've had a crush on you for a couple of years or so, but I heard you had a girlfriend, an attorney or something."

"Yes. Tiff. She works for Children Protective Services."

"Heard you broke up a couple months ago. Didn't hear you had a new one."

"Look, Angela. You're very attractive but I—"

She waves me off. "Save it, Sam. You're safe. I don't mess with another woman's man, never have, never will. But now a question needs to be asked. Now that you know, can we still work together?"

"Uh, well, yes, I like how you work. Can you work with me?"

"Yes, I'm a big girl. So tell me about her."

I laugh. "Well, you two have the same in-your-face personality," I say. Then for the next ten minutes I give her a heavily edited version of how we met here in Portland, a little about our father, Samuel, and a little about my visit to Saigon. With all the violence and killing left out, the tale is actually quite nice.

"I'm happy for you, Sam, and I mean it," she says standing. Her eyes cancel out her smile. "I'm going home now. If I hear anything from our Nordic princess, and it sounds like I will, you sure you don't want me to call?"

I start to say I'm sure, but I suddenly feel fifteen years of the thrill of the hunt rush through my veins. "Call me and I'll see what's going on."

*　　*　　*

Outside the office, the elevator opens before I can push the button, and Clarence Sanders steps out nearly bumping into me. He's wearing sweatpants with Portland Police Training Division down his right pant leg and a blue T-shirt with the words Defensive Tactics Instructor over the pocket. Given his thin physique and horn-rimmed glasses and his black Woody Allen look, I've often wondered what his students think the first day of DT training. Whatever it is, I'm sure he makes a believer out of them within minutes.

"Sam!" he says, slapping my shoulder. "I was just on the way down to your office."

"Hey, Clarence. BJ let us skate out a little early today."

"Must be tough. Hey, I was going to see if you want to help me teach a DT class for about an hour. Great bunch of eager, young recruits."

"Sure, just let me know when."

"How about now?"

"Now? I'm not sure about the overtime issue."

"No sweat, man. My lieutenant will square it with BJ. Come on. Pleeeese."

I laugh. "Well, since you begged."

We get off the elevator on the twelfth floor and head down the long hall to the DT room. Along the way he says this is the third class for the eighteen recruits. I've taught a lot of classes here over the years, to recruits as well as veteran officers. I like the eagerness of new people. A few have joined my private school after they settled into the job and got a regular shift.

"On your butts, people," Clarence barks like an Army drill instructor to the recruits chatting in groups, all of them dressed in blue sweatpants and blue T-shirts. It always amazes me how Clarence can bring up a deep, guttural voice from his thin frame. Sometimes he does it to be funny and other times he's as serious as a heart attack. The problem for the recruits is they never know which. "Make a semicircle. Move people."

My quick perusal notes three females, two blacks, one Asian, and the rest white males, no one over thirty. It's a stringent process to get hired by Portland—written tests, psychological exams, physical fitness tests, a background check all the way to grade school, and an oral board. Most who try don't make it. The hiring age is twenty-one. I think it should be twenty-five or twenty-six. We get the occasional military veteran, men and women who are usually far more mature than those who have not served. This group looks to be fresh out of college. Their young eyes have no clue of the sights awaiting them.

Clarence centers himself on the class. He's got his command presence working for him, appearing taller and heavier than he did out in the hall. "We have a special treat today. This is Detective Sam Reeves, currently assigned to the Intelligence Unit."

A few people nod and exchange looks. I'm sure it's because they know about my shootings and court proceedings.

"Sam has taught defensive tactics all of his career, and he is a high-ranking martial artist with nearly thirty years of training under his tattered, multi-striped black belt. He's going to show you the palm-heel and a couple other things. Okay, Sam?"

"Of course," I say, moving to the center of the semicircle as Clarence moves out of it and around behind the group. "Excuse my street clothes. I didn't know I was going to be helping with the class until five minutes ago. You might have noticed Clarence can be quite persuasive."

"Moi?" Clarence says innocently. The class chuckles.

"You will hear some officers say defensive tactics training is b.s. With all due respect to these otherwise fine cops, they are categorically wrong. There are several reasons why they might say this, none flattering to them. The bottom line is they are wrong. You've got a world-class trainer in Clarence Sanders here—you can buy me lunch, Clarence—learn from him and train hard, so one day you can enjoy your retirement."

Clarence has moved behind a fleshy, overweight recruit with a blond buzz cut. Clarence nods, a signal he and I developed a few years ago to let the other know a particular student has a bad attitude, likes to hurt training partners, or tries to make the instructor look bad.

"May I demonstrate on you?" I ask the young man.

"No problem-o," the recruit says with a smirk as he lumbers to his feet. He checks to see if his T-shirt is covering his belly. I weigh two hundred and I'm guessing he goes two twenty-five at about six foot two. He looks strong, but he's carrying at least thirty pounds he doesn't need.

"Sam Reeves," I say, extending my palm.

"Markus Stone," he says, jutting his jaw and crushing my hand. There's one in every class, bullyish, over confident to a fault, or making up for a lack of it. My instincts tell me he has been pushing people around all his life, and getting away with it. I know Clarence and the other instructors will watch him carefully during his training months.

"Tell me, Marcus," I say. "Have you ever heard of the Japanese proverb 'The nail that sticks out gets hammered down'?"

He shakes his head as the meaning of my question sails over it. "Nope. Supposed to mean something?"

"Yes, sir, it does." I turn to the class. "I know Clarence has taught you how to strike with the palm heel. We always recommend not to strike a subject's head, but if it's all you got at the moment, and it's what you have to do to get control of a violent person, then you hit with the heel of your palm, right?" I point at a young woman with a blond ponytail to my left. "Why?"

"You never hit hard with soft." I hear a few snickers but I ignore them. She says, "I mean you never hit a bone with your fist." More snickers. My look stifles them. "If you got to hit a person's skull, hit with your palm heel," she says.

I nod. "Very good. Not all cops remember and they're easy to identify. They're the ones with a cast on their hands. But the palm heel can be used for other things too. Tell me, Marcus, has Clarence taught you how to do the shoulder twist to get behind a suspect? Where you pull one shoulder and push the other?"

"He has," Marcus says, as if he has doubts about the technique.

"Good," I say squaring myself on the big man. Instead of standing relaxed so I can demonstrate the technique, he deliberately tenses his upper body. When someone this size makes himself rigid, turning him is next to impossible—unless you got a trick.

"As you know, to execute the shoulder twist"—I pantomime in the air pushing his right shoulder with my left palm and pulling his left with my right—"you must do the technique quickly before he resists. Even someone smaller than Marcus is hard to turn when he balks."

I look at the class, then suddenly turn toward Marcus and smack my palm against his upper chest with a resounding boom. When he snaps his arms up in surprise, I slam a palm heel against his right shoulder and simultaneously yank his left one toward me, spinning him until his broad back is against my chest. The class roars with laughter and applause.

"But if you startle him for an instant, he's distracted by the sound and feel, which takes his mind off tensing his torso."

When Marcus, now red-faced, starts to spin on me, I squeeze his shoulders and whisper into his ear, "Stay." He does.

"How's your chest?" I ask him.

Marcus shrugs. "It doesn't hurt."

"Exactly," I say. "But the palm-heel slap made a loud noise, didn't it."

"Sounded like you hit a fifty-gallon drum barrel," a recruit cracks.

"Exactly, again," I say. "There are two good elements in this technique for police work. First, the palm-heel slap and the hollow-sounding boom produced a startle effect." Marcus doesn't say anything. "Even if he doesn't admit it." Chuckles around the room. "And the second element is it didn't hurt him. For a moment, he might have thought it hurt, given the noise and the suddenness of the move, but it didn't. In the end, we got results without hurting the suspect, which is always a good thing. Who needs a lawsuit, right?"

I move to Marcus's side, keeping my hand on his shoulder. "Clarence will be teaching you about balance in a future class, but allow me to give you a little tease. For someone to be off balance, they only need to be leaning about ten degrees in any direction. Marcus, please lean back just a little. Okay, stop. Good. Everyone agree this is about ten degrees?" The class nods. "From this position, it's much easier to force him the rest of the way over. For example, if I use my palm heel"—I smack it against his forehead, again startling him, and push him over a little—"he begins to fall backwards." I grab a wad of his shirt to hold him up. "Versatile tool, the palm heel, isn't it?"

Marcus glances my way then back toward the far wall. He tenses his body so as not to get caught off guard again.

"The beauty of unbalancing someone is it often takes very little force to topple them in the direction they're leaning."

I touch his chest with my right palm. When Marcus looks down, I quickly stick my left index under his nose so it looks a like a funny moustache. A half second later, and in one smooth move, I push it into his philtrum and upward, snapping his head back. His massive body falls backward and he lands with a thump and an *oomph* of exhaled air. The entire move took about two seconds.

Before he can get his breath, I push his head with my palm heel until the side of his face is on the mat looking away from me. Keeping my hand there to restrain him, I use my other hand to grind a knuckle into the sinus cavity under his chubby cheek. Again, as if rehearsed, he yelps and thrashes his feet about.

I pull my hands away. "Stay right there, Marcus," I say, patting his chest. To the class, "My point in this demo is to show you four critical elements in your defensive tactics training, elements you can expand on. The first is the versatility of the palm heel. You can use it to hit, push, and press. Second, is the element of surprise. Startle the brain, and the subject is yours for a second, maybe two. That gives you a critical advantage, even if it's for just a moment. Third, you saw the importance of unbalancing people in two ways. You saw how to unbalance someone's mind by startling them, such as when I slapped Marcus's chest and later when I distracted him by touching his chest with my palm. This allowed me to slip my finger under his nose to execute a takedown. You also saw how shifting someone's weight even as little as ten percent can weaken their balance. "Lastly," I look at Marcus and lift my finger, "you saw how the technique, even when applied with one lonesome digit, and combined with the other elements, can conquer size."

I help Marcus up into a sitting position. "You okay, sir?" I ask. He nods and I help him the rest of the way up.

"Understand this class, I'm not suggesting you use one finger to take a street crook down. But wouldn't it be cool?" They laugh. "What I'm saying is this: Technique, meaning knowledge, trumps size, most of the time. Listen to your instructor and learn what he has to offer you." I look over at Clarence. "I return them to your deadly, I mean, capable hands."

He winks at me as he moves to the front of the group. "On your feet, people," he says in his famous growl. "Pair up and let's work on the chest slap and shoulder twist. Marcus, you going to live?"

"Yes, sir." The big man turns to me and extends his hand. This time he doesn't squeeze the crap out of my hand and his eyes look different than they did earlier. "Thank you," he says, with a slight nod.

"Partner up with Andrews," Clarence says, slapping him on his back. After Marcus moves over to his partner, my friend looks at me, smirks, and says in a low voice, "See how good you are? You gave the kid lots to think about. He just might turn out all right."

* * *

I normally take the Banfield Freeway out to the Thirty-Third Street exit on the east side of town, but after crossing the Burnside Bridge I turn off and head to Water Street. Incredibly, I find one lone parking space, a rare item in this part of town, and it's only a few steps to the entrance to the Vera Katz Eastbank Esplanade. I follow the looping walkway down to the floating portion that extends some seventeen hundred feet along the Willamette River. I haven't been down here since Tiff, my old girlfriend, and I came down last summer and sipped wine from a brown paper bag. Seems like eons ago. The walkway arcs out into the river a ways from the embankment, giving one the sense of floating. There are railings on each side of the twenty-foot-wide walkway, semi-comfortable wooden benches every few yards, and seagulls watching me from thirty-foot-high metal pylons lining the walkway on the riverside. It's quite beautiful, really, though I doubt if Mark and David will ever think so again.

It's a mild, late afternoon with only a few clouds in the west waiting to create a magnificent sunset in about three hours. The water is smooth as a botoxed forehead, but beneath the surface the river moves north as it has forever; it's just not in a hurry right now. When I worked uniform, I had the displeasure of being dispatched to at least half-a-dozen victims of the Willamette River. Floaters, cops call them. There is never anything good about seeing a dead body, but there is nothing creepier than wrestling a two-week-old floater onto a dock and having a small crab unexpectedly crawl out of its frozen-open mouth.

Only a cop could turn such a magnificent view into something grim. I ought to give tours to grade school kids.

I sit on a bench at about what I'm guessing is the midway point on the long, curving walkway, a spot where I can see five of the bridges arcing across the Willamette. Some of those floaters entered the dark depths from high up on those bridges.

I retrieve my cell and punch in Mark's number.

"Sam," he answers, his voice as heavy as the bricks we once found in a floater's coat pockets. A Mafioso killing, the Homicide dicks thought. If I remember right, it turned out to be a love triangle between three Italians.

I say, "Hey, buddy, how are you?"

"Okay. Just got back from the hospital."

I ask how David is but I can guess judging by his lifeless voice.

"Still in a coma. Didn't talk to the doctor today but Kathy, she's one of the nurses I've gotten to know, told me more by what she didn't say about him. His progress, or lack thereof."

"Be careful about reading too much into these things, Mark. Easy to do given where your head is right now."

Long pause. "Yeah."

"I'm sitting on a bench on the walkway as we speak."

"The Eastbank Esplanade, you mean?"

In the ten minutes I've been on the walkway, I've had it all to myself. Now I see a lone man walking along, about fifty yards off. He looks down at the water, up at the seagulls, over to me, and back up at the seagulls.

"Same one. Where'd they jump you?"

"It makes me uncomfortable knowing you're there, Sam. By yourself?"

"Yes, but it's okay. It's a beautiful day here and should be a fantastic sunset. So where did it happen?"

"Not sure exactly. Close to where it ends at the Steele Bridge, I think. About three quarters of the way or so from the Hawthorne Bridge."

The man is about fifty feet off now looking across the river at the city. When he turns toward me, he smiles. Hmm. Slim guy, neatly combed blond hair, wearing a torso-hugging western style shirt, slim jeans, and white running shoes.

"I'd like to see you," Mark says. "You got weekends off?"

"I do, but there is a chance I might have to go in tomorrow. Some things coming together with all these hate crimes. Also, Mai is coming in tomorrow morning. Not sure when yet."

"Oh. Well some other—"

"No, no. Not what I meant ... How about now? I can swing by for a few minutes."

"Okay, I'd like that. I need to take some meds now. Pain coming on strong. I'll be okay when you get here."

"Okay, buddy. See you in a few." I stuff my phone in my pocket.

"Going to be a beautiful evening." The blond man has stopped a few feet away, as if unsure about me.

"Yes it is," I say, standing.

"Hi there," he says nervously, and with an unnecessary wave. "Beautiful, no? I like to come here a couple times a week. I like the quiet. It gets so busy at night. You must like the quiet too."

I don't say anything.

"There's lots of people here around sundown, but it's not my scene. You must not like it either?"

I look at him without saying anything, letting my silence work its magic.

He takes a tentative step toward me. "You have a beautiful physique. I can tell even with your coat on."

I don't respond.

He smiles. "I think you're shy. It's cute. I am too."

"Let's sit down," I say, gesturing to the bench.

"Yes!" he says, almost giddy. "Thank you very much. I will take you up on it." He doesn't sit as much as he sort of perches on the edge of the seat. He twists toward me, his knees together, his hands folded in his lap.

"How old are you?" I ask.

"Twenty-six." He smiles. "Born and raised here in Portland. How about you?"

"What's your name?" I ask.

"Clive. Yours?"

"Portland Police Detective Sam Reeves." I flash my badge.

"Ohmygod!" he says in a rush, his hands slapping the sides of his face like the *Home Alone* kid.

"Mellow out, Clive. You're not in trouble. I just want to ask you a couple of questions."

The guy's face is so intensely red he just might have a coronary. I caught him by surprise but his reaction seems a little extreme. "Oh my God," he says, shaking his head back and forth like a crazy person. At least he's spacing his words now. His hands grip the front edge of the bench seat, his knuckles white.

"You say you come down here a couple times a week?"

He nods slowly, his big, panicked eyes never leaving mine,

his Adam's apple moving rapidly up and down his throat.

"Did you hear about the assault on two gay men down here a few afternoons ago?"

The panic in his eyes intensifies. He looks out at a tug working its way up river.

"Did you?" I nudge.

He nods, folds his hands in his lap, and takes a deep breath.

"How did you find out about it? The paper?"

His eyebrows bunch together and then his entire face clenches tight as a fist. "I ... uh ... yes, the paper." His lower lip has a slight tremble.

"Listen, Clive, you didn't break the law, you're not in trouble, and I don't give a rip if you're gay. Okay?"

His nod is nearly imperceptible.

He knows something. Finding out I'm a cop is shocking but the intensity seemed a little over the top. I wonder ...

"You're married, right?"

His eyes widen even more. "How'd you know?"

I lift my palm. "As I just said, I don't care about any of those things. I just want to ask you a couple of questions." When his expression doesn't change, I say, "Okay?" He nods.

He looks at me for a moment and something passes across his eyes. "Hey, why are you down here? Are you playing out a scene, a fantasy, or something?"

I give him my "you've-got-to-be-kidding" look.

His face reddens. "Okay. I was just making sure."

"Listen, Clive. If you know something, I have to make a report. But I'll leave your name out. I'll list you as a CI, a confidential informant. No one will know but me where I got the information."

He swallows hard again. "I don't know. My wife can't know

about this. I mean, I got kids, a profession. I mean ..." He shrugs.

"I repeat, Clive. No one will know but me where I got the information."

He looks out at the river. "Okay," he says, snapping his head back to me. "I saw them. Those thugs. I'm sure it was them who beat up those two men."

"Where were you?"

"I was leaving. I came down here about thirty minutes earlier, hung out for a while, but not much was happening. So I was leaving. I've thought about it a lot since. I didn't see those thugs when I was down here because I only came this far on the walkway. Actually, a little ways farther."

"The assault happened almost at the end, near the Steele Bridge."

"Yes, that's what I thought. Because the walkway ... see where it arcs sort of to the left? All those pylons there would have blocked my view."

"You said you saw them."

A young man and woman about thirty yards down sit on a bench like ours. The woman rests her head on the man's shoulder.

"Yes. I was leaving and I heard running steps and laughing. When I turned, these four boys were practically on top of me. One of them pushed me really hard, and I like slammed into the railing with my hip. I have a big bruise."

I retrieve a small writing pad from my jacket pocket and a pen. "Tell me what they looked like. Start with the one who pushed you."

"I didn't see any of them very well. When I heard them and turned, they were practically on me. Then when I got pushed,

I was thinking about my hip and how I almost went over the railing and into the Willamette River. Told my wife I bumped into a desk at work really, really hard. But I did notice a couple things. The one who pushed me had like this cherry-colored hair. It looked awful. He was tall and very skinny."

"White? Black?"

"White. They were all white. One boy was way ahead of the other three so I can't describe him, not even his clothes. The two other boys turned and laughed when I practically went over the rail. They were both wearing black clothing, tops and bottoms. One had black, longish hair. Like real, real black. Dyed I'm sure. He was husky with muscles. Not as many as you but he had them. The other boy was slim to medium with this awful buttery-colored hair. Dyed too."

Oh man, there is a Buddha. "Did you notice lettering on anyone's clothes, jacket, sweatshirt, whatever?"

Clive shakes his head. "There could have been but I didn't have a chance to see. Usually, I do see those things but not this time."

"No problem, Clive. You've been most helpful. Think you'd recognize these guys again, at least the three of them?"

He thinks for a moment. "Their hair for sure. Faces?" He shrugs.

After getting his personal information for a report, I say, " Clive, you've given me some critical information. One of the victims is still in a coma, and the other was badly hurt. Like I said, my report won't have your name on it, but I can't guarantee we won't need you to ID these guys."

Clive swallows hard.

"Listen. Appreciate your cooperation. If you've been following the news, you know there's been an upswing in hate crimes in the city recently. I would imagine it's dangerous doing what you're doing, so take it from a guy whose been working these streets for a long time, watch your back. Okay?"

He closes his eyes and nods.

*　　*　　*

Mark looks like shit and shaking his hand is like holding a limp rag.

"Yeah, I know, I look like shit," he says in response to the look on my face. He steps aside to let me into the stylish Tudor-style home he and David share in Portland's Alameda district, an upscale neighborhood of old but expensive homes in the upper Northeast side. Several movie actors have lived in the Alameda area, some still do, preferring the quiet life style over Hollyweird, which is only a short hop away by plane.

"Right you are, Mark," I say with forced joviality. "How are all your owies?" Hope that wasn't too flippant considering he didn't get them falling out of the bathtub.

He gestures for me to sit on a plush beige loveseat. "My body is doing better. The meds cloak some of it."

He remains standing after I sit, looking first toward the kitchen, then toward a chair across from the sofa. He seems to have forgotten I'm here. His hair is greyer than it was three days ago and his normally ramrod posture is slumped in defeat.

"Mark?" He turns his head toward me, his face puzzled as if wondering when I came in. "Can I fix us some tea?" I've been here many times over the years for barbecues, small parties, and movies on their eighty-three inch television. Twice I've cooked for them here when they were both down with the flu.

"What? Oh ... no, no. I made it right after you called. It's in ... the kitchen. I'll get it."

223

"I'll come with you," I say. Mark looks like he would spill all the tea before he could make it back into the living room.

The kitchen is a mess: dirty dishes all over the place, cupboards open, and newspapers lying about. Mark picks up two steaming cups, looks down at them, and sets them back on the counter. "Forgot to put in the bags."

I pull out a kitchen chair. "Sit down, buddy. Let me get it." I scoot some dirty dishes aside to make room for our cups.

"No, I can ..." He opens the only closed cupboard.

I move over to him, take his arm, and guide him toward the kitchen chair. "Sit," I say. He does, shakily. "There. Good. I'll get the tea bags, which as I recall, are in this drawer." They are. "You, my friend," I say, dropping in the bags, "get the Tazo Calm tea; I get the green." I set them on the table and sit across from him.

"I look like shit and I feel like shit, Sam."

I let him talk.

He bobs his bag up and down in his cup. "David and I have always been active in the gay community, actually, the entire LGBT community. We've fought for specific legislation to help gays, we've been involved in court watch when others have been victimized, we've visited friends in the hospital who have been assaulted, we flew to New Mexico when a teenage boy down there was dragged to death behind a pickup."

"I remember you going down, three years ago, I think."

Mark nods. "We've done this for years. But all that time, I was oblivious as to what it actually feels like to be ... selected."

The trembling in his hands has stopped, but his face suddenly becomes distorted with anger, the skin around his eyes and mouth tight with it. But his eyes are full of helplessness.

"I feel so helpless, Sam," he says, stirring the tip of his finger in the hot tea. "Not for me, for David. He has always ensured I'm happy, content. I have tried to do the same for him and I've always wanted him to feel safe. Not just feel it, but really be safe."

"It's the cop in you."

He nods. "I failed him. I'm a cop I should have protected him. I wasn't even carrying my gun. Sometimes I carry it, sometimes I don't. If I'd known we were going down to the waterfront, I would have brought it. But it was a last-minute decision after having dinner. David wanted to go. It was such a beautiful day ..." He shakes his head as he squeezes the tea out of his bag harder than necessary. He drops it onto the table. "I should have discouraged it. Said no, because I didn't have my gun." He pauses, thinking. "If I'd had it, I would have shot all of those brain-dead monsters."

I hope Mark doesn't notice the guilt on my face. I haven't been carrying my gun on the job. I didn't have it the first day because I didn't know I was going to start immediately. The next day I forgot it. Today I knew I didn't have it when I left the house. I'm running out of excuses.

He takes a deep breath and eases it out. He looks up at me. "I feel very alone. It seems like the city, the country, the world doesn't care. Feeling this way makes the pain more intense. Understand?"

"I think so, Mark. But I don't agree. A lot of people care."

"Intellectually, I know that. I've got you on my side, which I'm so grateful for, our friends from the community have called expressing their concern and offering to do things for us. But in my head, my thumped head, I feel alone. David and I were attacked because of who we are. We hadn't hurt anyone or stolen anything. We were just sitting peacefully, enjoying each other's company when we were selected to be hurt. Maybe they wanted to kill us, but got scared off. I don't know. But in the end they did it only because of one part of who we are.

"Sam, now that you're working hate crimes, please keep this in mind. When someone is a target of a hate crime, remember it victimizes their family too, and their friends, and their community. Our gay friends are terrified right now, and I know there are thousands of others in Portland we don't know who are frightened. Remember, one cruel ignoramus can strike fear into thousands."

"I'll remember, Mark. Promise."

I tell him about going down to the waterfront earlier, my chat with Clive, and his description of three of the four assailants.

"Yes!" Mark says excitedly. "The yellow-haired one. I remember him or, uh, I have a sense of him, anyway. It was a weird colored hair, longish. I was down on the walkway, curled into a ball and covering my head with my arms, and I could see him, the blond guy. He was watching whoever was kicking me. I remember his awful hair."

Mark shivers. "And I will never forget his god-awful laugh."

*   *   *

Just as I walk into my house, my cell phone tinkles an email alert. It reads: Samuel Le. "Talk in twenty-five minutes on Skype."

I have just enough time to turn on my PC, make a protein shake and a cup of green tea, check my mail, and give Chien a serious belly rubbing.

"Father," I say, when his face appears on my monitor. "How are you?" The question is rhetorical. I know how he is. Ten days ago he lost his teacher; a man who was also my father's best friend—he died protecting my family. Adding to his already deep sorrow, my father just buried his beloved wife.

"At least I got my health," he says with a shrug. Same thing Mister Axelbrad from the antique store said a couple of days ago.

"Well, you look good. I'm so very, very sorry about Kim."

"Thank you." He didn't say it loud enough for me to hear, but I saw his mouth form the words. "The pain is almost more than I can bear, Son." This time I heard him.

I look down at the keyboard. I don't know what to say to him. I've only known him for two months, and I've only been calling him father for a week and a half. Our short relationship has been about him helping me to keep from going nuts and teaching me things about the martial arts that border on the bizarre. What can I give him? What can I give a man who has all the answers? What can I do to help a—

"Son."

I look up at the monitor. Into his eyes. I know he just picked up on my thoughts.

"Looking at you through this miracle of technology is more than enough. Knowing you are now part of my family is more than enough. Knowing you will take care of Mai is more than enough."

We look at each other for a long moment, both of us barely nodding. To anyone looking through the window, it probably looks weird but it's working for us. Father and son having a moment. Words not necessary.

I speak first. "Mai called this afternoon. She expects to land in San Francisco tomorrow morning. Saturday here, Saturday night for you, I think."

He nods. "She had to be there with you. She is worried

about me I know, but I have Linh and An and I knew she needed to be comforted within your embrace." He smiles, remembering. "I saw magic between you and Mai the first time I saw you together. I was concerned at first, but I saw it grow in the chaos of our week in Portland, and I saw it bloom during the craziness of your few days here in Saigon." Again he smiles and chuckles. "There is an old Irish saying. 'A son is a son till he takes him a wife, but a daughter is a daughter all of her life.' Thankfully for me, Mai is my stepdaughter, so I get to keep you both."

"How is it going there? How are Linh and An?"

"Your half sisters are managing. We will comfort each other and help each other through this. It is what families do, no?" I've heard him say this. Maybe it's his way to affirm after all these years that I am now part of his established family.

He knows I'm back at work so I fill him in on the hate crime activity.

"Are you carrying your gun?" he asks, though I think he already knows the answer.

I shake my head.

His eyes flash. He looks to the side then back at me, the anger in his face palpable.

"Son, it is time to suck it up."

"What?" Not what I was expecting to hear. What happened to the understanding and the compassion? No Buddha quotes?

"I understand what you went through after your last shooting, and I understand you not wanting to carry a weapon, but if you are going to go out there on the frontlines, your fellow officers and the public expect you to take with you all the tools necessary to protect them. And so does your new family. You accepted the responsibility, so live up to your promise."

I look into his unblinking eyes for a long moment then down at my keyboard. He's right, of course. Not carrying my gun is the most stupid thing I've ever done. Still, I'm not sure if I can.

"Do what needs to be done, Son," my father says softly. "And it is the nature of the beast that the thing needing to be done is tough."

"Yeah."

As quickly as his anger came on, his face softens and his eyes twinkle. His raised index finger appears on the screen as if he were about to make a proclamation in the Roman Senate. "The older you get, the tougher it is to lose weight, because by then your body and your fat are really good friends."

I sputter a laugh. "What the hell?"

He shrugs, a smile tugging up the ends of his mouth. "It is the only quote I could think of about doing tough things. I do not know who said it. A fat negative person, I would think."

I laugh again. This isn't the first time he has chewed my butt and made me laugh all within the same minute.

"How is your Afghanistan veteran doing?"

"Nate? I'm not sure yet. We've talked only a little. He's carrying some deep hurt. I'm trying to hook him up with some counseling."

"He is a good man?"

"My gut says he is."

"Then he is."

"Thank you. He's a good kenpo fighter, and very good with an Indian war club. And he's scared of his wife."

Father laughs. "Well, fear of a wife is a good thing." His smile fades quickly and he looks off to the side. When he looks back, his eyes are glistening. "I should go. Please tell Mai to email me so I know she is there safe. Let us talk again in two or three days."

"I will tell her and yes let's do." We look at each other for a moment.

"Goodbye, Son."

I shut off the Skype and the PC, scoop up Chien, and settle her into the crook of my arm.

"What do you think?" I ask her. She looks up at me and makes a weird sound between a purr and a meow. I head out the patio door and watch her alert on the hundred-member croaking frog chorus. I've heard them at night for all the years I've lived in this house but I've yet to see one. Maybe they're Ninja frogs, masters of disguise. "Ready, Chien?" When she nods, I take three more steps and on the third one, every last frog ceases croaking at the same time as if cued by the head Kermit. Just as all the other times I've shown this to Chien, she looks up at me with a puzzled look on her face. "Oh yes, I still have the power, my friend. And don't you forget it." No longer impressed, she burrows her head into my arm and within seconds, she's catnapping.

We head back into the house, lock the patio door, and head into the kitchen. I set Chien down. "You want a little snack before we hit the hay?" She flips her tail and moves over to her bowl. I open the bag and pour her a little. "Not too much, missy. You got to watch your figure." I get a cup of yogurt out of the fridge, grab a spoon, sit at the table, and wonder what the hell I'm going to do about carrying a gun.

CHAPTER NINE

A sliver of morning sun has found its way through my curtains, and the light falls across the floor, over my nightstand and mattress, and across my eyes. Chien sees I'm awake and snuggles herself across my throat.

"Hello! You're lying on my Adam's apple." I push her away with my chin, and she protests with an indignant meow, jumps down off the bed, and scampers off toward the kitchen, her not so subtle hint it's chow time.

Six thirty. Mai thought she might be landing in San Francisco around sixish. I stick my cell in my pocket and go about changing the sheets, tidying the bedroom and the bath. Chien comes in and yells at me because I have yet to feed her. I head into the kitchen, drop some food into her bowl, and make coffee. I just start wiping down the counters when my cell rings.

"Mai?"

Hard breathing. "Sam, I am in the U S of A. San Francisco. We were a little late so I am walking and running to my other plane, the one going to Portland."

"To me."

"Yes! To you, handsome boy. So comb your hair and put rouge on your cheeks."

I laugh. "You must have gotten some sleep on the flight. You're full of piss and vinegar."

"You said that all the time in Saigon, and I still do not know what it means. No, I did not sleep at all so I am crazy right now. Okay, here is my plane. I think I am the last to get on."

"I will be at the airport when you get here. It's about a nine-ty-minute flight. Call when you land."

"I cannot wait."

"Tell the pilot to step on it."

"Step on what, Sam?"

I finish cleaning the house, take a shower, and slip on a pair of jeans and a black polo shirt. Don't know why but I've always worn a lot of black.

"Chien, want to go for a ride?"

She runs toward the door and looks back at me.

My cell rings. I won't answer it. Mai wouldn't have landed yet. No, I'd better. Maybe her plane is having problems in San Francisco.

"Hello."

"Sam, Angela."

There is no damn way I'm going into work. No way, no how.

"The Nordic princess call?" I ask. "Hallgerd, wasn't it?"

"She did. Left a message at work and said her boyfriend didn't come home last night. She sounded seriously pissed. She asked what it takes for the cops to use deadly force on him. Anyway, apparently he hooked up with someone for the week-end. So the bad news is we can't get him today. The good news is Hallgerd will more than likely still want to help us."

"Sounds good. Let's hope we can do it Monday morning and wrap it before quitting time, just like on TV."

"Glad you're on board, Sam. Isn't, uh, I'm sorry, I forgot her name. Mary?"

Sure she's forgotten it. Those three letter names are tough to recall. "It's Mai. I'm actually heading to the airport now to pick her up."

Silence, then, "Okay, Sam. Have a good weekend."

I scoop up Chien and carry her to my pickup and a minute later we're on the way to the airport. Chien sits on the center console and drapes her tail across my driving arm. Her post is just high enough for her to see the freeway walls out the side windows and the overpasses out the windshield.

Angela. The agony of an unrequited crush. About five years ago, a thirty-year-old waitress at my coffee stop got one on Gordon, a partner I had for a brief time while working East Precinct. Gordon was a veteran cop, balding, packing an extra forty pounds around his belly, and had never taken advantage of the City's dental plan. But Cindy, who shared every one of Gordon's traits, and even looked like him a little, had a love-on for the guy, disregarding the fact he was married and a new grandfather. She even found out where he lived and went to his house. It was there at the front door she found out, Madge, Gordon's wife, still had a blazing love-on for the guy after twenty-six years of marriage. Old Madge chased Cindy across the lawn, armed with a Teflon-coated skillet. Cindy managed to outrun her and jumped into her beat-up nineteen seventy-five Plymouth Scamp and actually got the old car to lay a patch of rubber.

I don't think Angela is that way. But then I don't know her. Maybe I should start carrying a knife.

Thankfully, traffic is light so it's an easy drive to the airport. They've made a nice turnout about a mile away from the pick-up area where cars can wait until family or friends arrive. It's near a tarmac where there is a steady and deafening stream of arriving jets, their screaming engines shaking my truck, their tires screeching puffs of smoke.

I certainly didn't expect to see Mai so soon. When I left

Saigon last week, everything was up in the air as to whether I would return there or she would come to visit me. Either way, we didn't expect we'd be together in barely a week.

My father once said to me everything in life is impermanent; our jobs, cars, health, cities, our relationships, and the only thing permanent is the fact everything is impermanent. Damn right. In the last two months, my life has been all about change. My relationship with Tiff ended and within a week, Mai walked into my life. I had no father for thirty-four years, then one day I met my pop. I was enjoying being a cop until one five-second burst of gunfire changed everything.

After the shootings, I went from sort of happy, to depressed, to suicidal, back up to depressed again, then up to happy, then all the way up to joyous, which is where I am with Mai right now, joyous. The job? I'm not sure yet. My martial arts? I'm happy. I need to get back into a training regimen but I'm happy with it. Maybe I shouldn't think about it because Mister Funster, the Impermanence Overseer, will blow out my knee.

I check my watch. Mai is due in any time now. I know she is going to be hurting over her loss. I don't have anything planned for us to do because I'm assuming it's probably best to go with the flow. If she feels like going to a restaurant or a movie, we can do it. If she just wants to hang out at the house, we will.

Man, the tarmac is busy. I didn't ask Mai what airline she was taking so any of these could be carrying—

My cell beeps.

"I'm heeeere," Mai sings into the phone before I can get out a hello. "We had a wind or something and I got in ten minutes early. Okay, okay, there's my suitcase on the turn, uh, thing. Whatever it is called. It's blue. Not the turn thing, my suitcase. And I tied a ribbon around the handle so I can see it better.

Okay, I got it now. Sam? Are you there? Why don't you talk?"

I laugh. "Because you haven't stopped."

"Oh, okay. Where are you? You decide not to pick me up? You forget me already? Have another girlfriend? Boyfriend?"

"Mai?"

"Yes?"

"Mai, walk out onto the sidewalk, take a deep breath, then another, and I will be there. Black pickup, remember?"

She laughs, that fat opera singer laugh of hers I love. "I guess I am pretty, what do you call it? Oh. Weirded. No, not weirded. I am pretty wired up right now."

"Me too. Keep looking left and you will see me. When you do, don't look under my shirt."

"What? You crazy, Sam. Of course I will look under your shirt. Maybe not at the airport, but as soon as I can. Okay, okay, I see you. You are behind all those taxis. You see me?"

"You the little woman by the pillar wearing the black *burka*?"

"You are so funny, Sam. My ribs might break from laughing."

"Okay, I need to sign off so I can work my way to the curb. Byyyye."

I scoop up Chien before she knows what's happening and stuff her under my shirt. I push her up until her head and one paw protrudes from the top of my polo shirt. She could do a major job on my flesh if she were a cranky kitty. But instead she licks my neck.

There's Mai, and once again the sight of her takes my breath away. She stands near the curb like a tourist attraction, oblivious, as always, to everyone's blatant stares. One gawking man, fifty-ish, ponytail, wearing a pink dress shirt, clips a pillar with his shoulder, knocking him into a one-hundred-and-eighty-degree spin. Embarrassed, he collects himself, glances furtively in Mai's direction, and walks briskly away. She didn't notice.

I'm in the second lane over from the curb waiting for a yellow cab to move out of the way. I hold up my palm for her to stay where she is and she nods. Her cascading raven-black hair frames a face of such heart-stopping beauty even the words of a master poet could not describe it, nor could the grandest of painters, classic or modern, capture her exquisiteness on canvas, even if the palette were heaven sent. The perfection of those brown eyes with their suggestion of elongation, and the green specs in them, their very memory sends my heart rate into dangerous palpitation.

Over the top? Not even a little.

The cab is finally moving. I do the back and forth parking thing until I'm next to the curb. A few feet away, a female airport police officer is trying to untangle a cluster of cars.

I look back toward Mai. What the ...? I don't know where they came from but a half-dozen black men, all dressed in brilliant red sweats with the words Wack Funky Boy$ across their chests, have formed a semicircle around her.

*   *   *

I'm out of my truck in an instant and moving around it toward the sidewalk. They're all talking at once to her.

"You don't sing, girl? No problem."

"No, ma'am. No problem. We'll give you a tambourine."

"How 'bout this? We'll call you the Asian Pearl."

"No, Cleve. Jade Pearl sounds better."

I stop. These guys all look the same. Not just the sweats, their faces, physiques, all in their early twenties.

"Jade Pearl? Ivan, that don't make no sense. A jade and a

pearl is two different things."

"I know. It be the point."

Cleve looks over at me. Recognition. First him, then me. "Sensei!"

"Cleveland," I say, shaking his hand. "You guys trying to recruit my lady into your group?"

"Your lady? Oh no, oh no," he says, holding his palms up in front of him in mock fear. "We just playin' with her. But listen here. She would be the main attraction. She could ... Sensei, you know there's a cat under yo shirt?"

"Chien!" Mai cries, dashing over to me. She cups the little white head between her palms and kisses the top of her head. The cat touches Mai's chin with her paw and looks up at her lovingly.

"Aaaand me?"

Mai looks up at me, her eyes spinning my world. "Oh, sorry. I forgot about you." We embrace, being careful not to crush Chien. "*Em yeu anh*," she whispers in my ear. I know that one. It's I love you.

At the Saigon airport we couldn't embrace since a public display of affection is looked down upon, especially among the older people. Here we can kiss, but the moment isn't right, especially with the Wack Funky Boy$, one of the top Baptist singing groups in the country looking on.

Cleveland shakes his head. "We offer her fame and fortune and you offer her a cat under yo' shirt."

I laugh. "Mai, this is Cleveland Duvall, an off-and-on student. The tall one is Ivan and Roy in the back. They're triplets. Those three guys are their brothers ... sorry gents."

Cleveland says, pointing at each, "Michael, Ray-Ray, and Claud. They're triplets too. Two years younger than us."

Mai shakes hands with each. "Triplets! Three, right? Your mother have triplets two times?"

"And one set of twins," Ray-Ray says. "All boys."

"My goodness," Mai says. "Your poor mother."

"Not poor," Cleveland says. "Uh-uh. She rich in handsome boys."

From behind me. "If you're ready to go, please do so now."

I turn to see the female airport officer.

"Oh, sorry," I say. I look beyond her at the stack of cars waiting. I grab Mai's luggage and swing it into the bed of the truck.

"Nice meeting you, Mai, and God bless," Cleveland says, as I open the door for her. "Hope you didn't mind us playin' with you."

Mai smiles. "Nice meeting you too."

"We're off to San Diego, Sensei," Cleveland says. "Big doin's at the Calvary Baptist down there."

I shake his hand. "Miss you in class, Cleve."

He shakes his head. "You know. Family. Work."

"Make it when you can," I say, hurrying around the front of the truck.

"I will, I will. And don't forget you got a cat under yo' shirt."

Oh, right. I extract Chien and hand her to Mai. She cuddles the cat to her chest and rubs the cat's head with her chin. Not until I maneuver us out into a flow lane does she look over at me. "I am so happy to see you, Sam," she says, barely above a whisper. "I needed to be with you."

"I am so happy to see you too," I say. I don't ask her about her flight or if she's tired. Those things don't matter right now. All that does is she's here and we're together. "There's a place to park about half a mile up here."

I pull into the turnout where I parked earlier, and barely get the truck into park before Mai puts Chien on the seat between her and the door and slides into my arms, awkwardly because of the console between us, but in my arms nonetheless. She buries her face into my neck and begins to sob, harder and harder, her body shaking and convulsing, her tears soaking my neck. Her embrace is so tight I can barely breathe, the console edge digging into my ribs.

After what must be fifteen minutes, her crying subsides, stops. And now she sleeps. Behind her, Chien is spooning Mai's rear, her eyes slowly closing in the heat of the sun.

Time passes. According to my dash clock, we've been locked into this contorted position for twenty-two minutes now. It was at the nineteen-minute mark when I began to think the cartilage in my chest might shred like Hawaiian pulled pork. At twenty-three minutes, Mai stirs, kisses my neck, and leans back.

"Why are we sitting here, Sam?"

"Sorry, I just thought—"

Her sleepy eyes twinkle. "Just screwing with you." She smiles when I laugh. Her face does, anyway. Her eyes are filled with sorrow. "Thank you for being here for me."

I touch the side of her face. "I will always be here for you. Always."

We kiss, finally.

*　　*　　*

"In some ways it seems like only yesterday when I was in your house," Mai says, looking around the place. "But in other ways those two months seems like a long, long time ago."

I set down her suitcase. "Much has happened in the past weeks. The ol' house is the same, but we are different."

Mai slips her arms around my waist and puts the side of her head against my shoulder. "So much is changing," she says. "It makes me scared."

"Mm, change can be scary. But it can be exciting too. What would our father say about it?"

I can feel her face smile. "He would probably quote a movie and then say something like how there are always at least two ways. But when we are scared we are too concerned about what is happening to us, so it is hard for us to see another way."

"Wow, pretty good. You just make it up?"

"No, I have heard him say it before."

"Hungry?"

She shakes her head. "I just want to take a shower and sit with you on the sofa. Have some tea."

I pick up her luggage, and say while fighting a smirk, "The guest room doesn't have a bathroom so you'll have to use the hall bath."

"Sam."

I look at her innocently. "Yes?" She's doing her raised eyebrow thing. "What? You're not staying in the guest room?"

"That is a big fat no."

"My bedroom?"

"Do one-legged ducks swim in circles?"

I can hear Mai singing in the shower as I make tea. She not only has a bad singing voice, she sings quite loudly. I prepare the pot and cups, and slice up a couple of apples and some cheese. Chien loves cheese and keeps meowing and curling around my calf for more. "No more, little missy. You don't want to clog your system." She flips her tail at me and saunters out of the kitchen just as Mai walks in.

"Where you go, Chien?" Mai asks, toweling her hair. She's

wearing tight grey yoga pants and a powder blue tank top. If I weren't holding the teapot, I'd stick my knuckles into my mouth and chew on them. She looks that amazing.

She moves toward me, dropping her chin as her eyes—the green specs in them sparkle—look up at me. "You checking me out or just reading my shirt?"

I gulp. "There isn't anything written on your shirt."

"Then you were checking me out, my bad boy," she says, slipping into my arms, her body damp, warm, and our fit—perfect.

"Not really." She pinches my butt. "Oooow—" Her mouth covers mine, and a moment later I'm consumed.

*   *   *

"You think the tea is cool enough now to drink?" Mai asks into my bare chest.

"Probably evaporated," I say into such a tangled mess of raven-black hair I can't see her face. I prop myself on an elbow to see over her shoulder. "It's almost four. We came in here around ten thirty this morning."

"My jet lag feels better now."

"I feel like I have shaken baby syndrome."

"I do not know what that means."

"It was a compliment."

After the first time, Mai fell asleep and I laid here watching her. It was better than any movie, any concert, or any play I have ever seen. She is the most beautiful, wondrous, incredible woman I've ever had the good karma to know. I love her and she loves me back, which really works out great.

I had just started to fall asleep when she awakened, probably around noon. Her sobs awakened me, her face turned into her pillow, her entire body trembling.

"My mother is gone," she cried. "Mother is ... gone."

I pulled her into me and held her until she once again cried herself out and fell asleep. About twenty minutes later, she began to slowly and ever so sensuously move her body against mine. Neither of us fully awake, we floated in a shared dream of sumptuous pleasure until we exploded together in a shuddering release that brought Chien running into the bedroom to see what was going on. We fell the rest of the way asleep shortly after.

Sometime in the early afternoon, Mai's crying woke me again, and once more I held her until she quieted. She didn't sleep this time, but stayed snuggled against my body. When my muscles could no longer be still, I slowly straightened my legs and torso to a symphony of popping bones.

"It sounds like the Fourth of July in your body, Sam," she said into my neck.

"Sorry. Had to move. My circulation had stopped."

"Let me see," she said, worming her hand down to my home entertainment center. "Your circulation just fine, big guy." My creative memory might have added the "big guy" part.

We made love again and slept until awakening a moment ago.

"You hungry?" I ask.

"I could eat a water buffalo."

"Not too many of those around here. I can whip something up in the kitchen or we could go out somewhere."

"My goodness. You cook too?"

*   *   *

We fix a light dinner of stir-fried chicken and vegetables, with rice, and green tea. Afterwards, I teach her how to melt dark chocolate, and combine almonds, peanuts, and a big scoop of protein powder to make healthy peanut clusters. After we clean the kitchen, we move into the living room, put on some new age music, and snuggle ourselves into my black leather sofa.

We talk about Mai's mother. Even in the short time I spent with her, it was clear the beautiful woman was smart, savvy, funny, and highly protective of her family, traits I see in Mai. Telling Mai this makes her tear up and bow her head. "Thank you," she whispers. After a moment, Mai fills me in a little on her parent's history. Some of it I know, some I don't.

Kim's father had commanded a North Vietnamese prison during the war, the same prison where Samuel, our father, had been incarcerated as a POW. One day her father witnessed Samuel fight several Australian prisoners who were planning on killing the camp commander, an act that would have ultimately cost the Australians their lives and the lives of other prisoners. Intrigued over Samuel's phenomenal fighting skills, Kim's father ordered Samuel to teach him his martial art. In exchange he promised not to punish the Australians. Though unsettling at first, Samuel grew to like Kim's father, and her father to like Samuel, and their friendship developed. At first, it was based on their long discussions about books, film, classical music, and the martial arts. In time, it grew to a place where they could sit with each other, sip wine, and be comfortable in the silence.

One day when Samuel was rinsing off under an outdoor shower on the commander's property, Kim, who was visiting her father, walked around the corner and nearly bumped into the naked American prisoner. Two seconds later, Kim's father rounded the corner. In any other North Vietnamese prison,

Samuel would have been shot dead on the spot. But Kim's father laughed at the shocked and embarrassed looks on Kim and Samuel's faces, and then introduced them to each other.

Mai was a year old then, a product of a relationship between her mother and an American serviceman with whom she worked on an American base in the South. Kim's father served with the North and Kim worked with the Americans; a political split which struck me as peculiar, until I considered the American Civil war; families were often split by ideology, boundaries ...

Samuel remained with Kim's family after the war ended. He wasn't aware of my existence, and his mother and father had passed just before he went into the army, so he had no deep ties to his own homeland. He quickly fell in love with the country, the people, and the culture. The Green Berets had taught him the language and, as a result of his years in prison talking with guards, South Vietnamese prisoners, and Kim's father, his Vietnamese was by then flawless and virtually without accent. And, Samuel's mannerisms and slight physique helped him to blend into his adopted country. Mai said those who knew the difference gave him a hard time, and his phenomenal martial arts skills came in handy. I look forward to him telling me those stories.

Kim and Samuel married about two years after the war ended and spent the next three years living with Kim's parents. Linh and Anh were born a year apart to the newlyweds, and shortly thereafter Kim's father passed away and soon after, her mother. The young parents remained in the house for two more years, sold it, and used the money to buy the first of what would be eighteen jewelry stores. They moved every year or so until eventually buying a condo near the Tan Son Nhat Airport in Ho Chi Minh City, or Saigon as many people still call it.

Chien is fast asleep in the bend of Mai's leg where she and I are entangled on the sofa. I ask Mai to tell me two things her mother taught her. Her head is resting against my shoulder and I can feel the vibration of her words. "The first is to stick up for those who cannot do it for themselves. Family, friends, strangers, it does not matter. I remember one day, I was about ten, and she and I were walking back from the outdoor market when we saw this man kicking a dog. Mother yelled at the man to stop and he said something real bad to her and kicked the dog harder. Mother took a *bầu*, uh, zucchini, from our basket and beat the man's face with it. Other people had to pull her away from him."

When I laugh, Mai smiles. "He was a stray dog so we took him home and he lived with us until I was about fifteen. He died of old age but he had a wonderful life with us."

"I can see you doing the same thing," I say. "But with round-house kicks."

"Yes," Mai says with a smile. "The other thing she taught me was the most important part of the body. Do you know what it is?"

"Well, judging by the good time we had today—"

She slaps my chest. "You are a bad man. And I like it. But no, it is the shoulder. Mother says ... said ... everyone needs a shoulder to cry on. Your shoulder for your family and friends to cry on and their shoulder for you to cry on."

Mai doesn't say anything for a long moment, then, "Thank you for your shoulder, Sam."

CHAPTER TEN

"I'm back, Ari," the big woman called out over the roar coming from the shower stall.

"Get everything, Cork?" Arizona asked, shutting off the water. "Hand me the towel, will you, hon."

"Milk, soup, and eggs." Corky draped a white towel over the shower door. "Vegetables looked like they've been in the mini market since last week, which they probably have. Slim pickins at one a.m."

"Damn, it's one already? What happened to the night?"

"Well, I was working on a flier when you suddenly ravished me."

"I ravished you? Ravished?" Arizona pushed open the shower door, wrapped the towel around her thick waist. She smirked at Cork. "I don't think so. Like I've said before, the only time you say no is when I ask if you've had enough."

Arizona weighed around two fifteen at five feet ten. Her forearms, calves, and butt were the only parts of her big body without ink. Even her cow-like breasts were tattooed, a horizontal "WHITE" across her right one in blue lettering and a horizontal "POWER" across her left. Across her firm belly was "14 WORDS" the S dripping blue blood. Three Nazi swastikas decorated the front of each beefy thigh, and both of her thick upper arms were covered with a collage of bleeding skulls, Nordic crosses, and an assortment of Celtic warrior bands.

Corky unwrapped Arizona's towel, snuggled into the nakedness, and kissed her deeply. "Turn around, baby," she whispered. She began wiping the water droplets off Arizona's back. "It's too late to call Colonel White now."

"Maybe he's gone somewhere. He didn't answer all afternoon."

Corky gently pulled Arizona around and commenced to dry her shoulders. Water from Arizona's wet hair dripped down onto Corky's hand and rolled over the swastika tattoo on her wrist. "We'll try again in the morning."

"Okay," Arizona said, unzipping Corky's dark blue sweat-shirt. "You think Colonel White has heard about our strikes?"

Corky shrugged out of it and let it drop to the floor. She wore nothing underneath. Her thick body, heavy breasts, square face, thick jaw, and ocean-blue eyes were nearly identical to Arizona's, who was a year younger. Corky's only tattoos were the swastika on her right wrist, the "88" on her right shoulder, a symbol for the eighth letter of the alphabet and code for Heil Hitler, and the "14" on her left one, a code which refers to a white supremacy slogan.

"I'm sure he has," Corky said. "It's got to be national news."

Arizona wrapped her arms around Corky and leaned the side of her face against her shoulder. "It's all so scary. Exciting, but scary too. I'm always so grateful God gave me your shoulder to lean on."

"Haven't I always been here for you?" Corky whispered into her ear.

"Yeah," Arizona said, squirming herself tighter into the embrace.

After a moment, Corky leaned back and smirked. "Now I've got you all dried, you wanna take another shower?"

"With you?" Arizona asked flirtatiously. "But I'm not dirty anymore." She leaned into the stall to turn on the water. "You remember the poem mama always sang?"

"I do!" Corky laughed, naked now. She squished herself into the small stall behind Arizona. She squeezed a dollop of liquid soap into her palm, rubbed her hands together, and begun smearing it on Ari's shoulders.

"Wash your face and hands with soap," Corky sang. "Wash them every day. Keeping clean by using soap, will keep the germs away."

CHAPTER ELEVEN

In my ear: "Sam. Sam! Are you awake?"

"I'm meditating."

"On what?

I push my face deeper into the pillow. "Sleeping."

"No seriously. Are you asleep?"

I roll over and bite Mai's shoulder.

"Hey, you hungry or something?"

"Yes."

"You eat English muffin, not Vietnamese babe."

"I'm not going to touch that comment."

"What do you mean? How can you touch a comment?"

"Geeze." I stretch, yawn. "What time is it, anyway?" I ask, too groggy to scoot up and look over Mai's head to see the clock.

"Who knows?"

"The clock is right behind you on the dresser."

"I am too tired to roll over and look."

"Remember the first time we slept together?" I ask.

"Yes, because it was two weeks ago. If it was three weeks, I would forget."

"We both got beat up after."

"Yes we did," she says. "But we got ... how do you say it?"

"Hurt?"

"No, well, yes. But I was trying to say ... we delivered ... delivered some payback. That is how you say it?"

I chuckle. "We did, didn't we?"

"I am hungry."

I force myself to sit up and look at the clock. "Damn. It's twelve forty-five. We missed breakfast and lunch.

*   *   *

After lunch, Mai asks if we can train a little so she can work out the kinks from the long flight. We have never trained together, but we've fought together, once here in Portland and a couple of times in Saigon. Oh, and how could I forget, when we first met at my school, our father had her demonstrate a couple of things on me. She isn't as fast as he is—but then no one is—but her speed is nonetheless scary quick.

After warming up on the patio, we move out onto the lawn to practice what I call your turn/my turn, in which I throw a kick or punch, and she blocks and counters. Then she throws a kick or punch, and I block and counter. After, we do a little no-block sparring, a fun exercise where everything works because no one blocks the other person's attack or counter.

When not training, Mai's gestures and mannerisms are graceful and gentle, reminding me of a girl I knew in college who was a well-known ballerina in Portland before moving on to make her mark in New York. Her normal way of walking was so incredibly graceful and light, it seemed at any moment she could take flight. Mai moves similarly outside of training, as if she could walk on sand and not leave footprints.

But not so when fighting and training. Mai's grace is still present, but her movements are an intriguing blend of hard and soft. One moment she is like a petrified tree, especially when punching or shield blocking, and the next she is as lithe as a panther. One instant she is directly in front of me and in the next she is four feet over from where she was when I threw my technique. She knows precisely when to use her power, and when to use her speed and agility. I've been training for about twenty-eight years with a variety of experts, but I don't possess her ability to transition from a hard Japanese style to the lithe, whip-like movements of a fluid kung fu system.

"May I show you something I have been working on?" she asks when we pause to catch our breath.

"Out here or back in bed?"

"Cute. Okay, throw a roundhouse kick at me, at my tummy."

"Tummy?" I laugh. "Tough fighters don't say tummy."

"Oh, sorry. My English. What do you say?"

"Better to say tum-tum."

"Really? Okay. Thank you. So throw a roundhouse at my tum-tum. But do not hit me."

"Don't do what?" I ask, launching a lead-leg kick at her middle. I stop it short and leave it hanging there.

"Okay, if I try to stop your big powerful leg like this,"—she forms her arms into a shield with her forearms side by side—"your kick would break my arms. You said before you can break baseball bats." I nod. "So it would be crazy for me to try. I am just a fra, uh, fragile girl. Fragile, right?"

"Right word, wrong person," I say, putting my foot down. "So what are you working on?"

"Okay, you know, Father's style, Temple of Ten Thousand Fists, teaches to move fast, right?"

"There should be another word for speed when it comes to his moves, but yes I know."

Mai frowns as if she didn't follow. "Okay, so what I am working on is moving real fast so I do not get kicked. But I do not move back from the kick."

"You mean like if the kicker throws a right roundhouse kick

you move to their left, in the direction of the kick? Not exactly new, you know?"

She nods. "I know, but I am trying to do it different, er, differently. Moving where the kicker's roundhouse will go works when you know the kick is coming. You see the setup?"

"You see it coming." I suggest. "The kicker telegraphs his move."

"Yes, that is the word. The kicker lifts his leg, or makes his body lean to the side before he kicks. But what I am working on is moving into the kicker's body with mine close enough to touch him. Moving like when you jump because a noise scares you."

"A startle."

Mai nods. "You did not see the telegraph and suddenly the kick is almost hitting you. But instead of jumping in the same place ... no, I mean jumping in place when you become startle, startled, you move into the guy who kicks. Am I saying it right?"

"I think so. Your opponent might be real fast or you're distracted in some way, and you don't know the kick is coming until it's about to hit. It startles you."

"Yes, yes. Your English is very good, Sam. So if you know the roundhouse is coming, it is easy to step in the same direction so kick does not hit you so hard. But if you do not know and suddenly it almost hits you, instead of screaming *Trời ơi*!—it means like oh my! or oh shit!—you move into kicker."

"Interesting. You're talking about moving your whole body without blocking the kick? You do know some fighters can kick over sixty miles per hour?"

"Yes, my whole body and yes, I know some people can kick very fast. Let me show you. I am not good at it yet but I am better than I was a few months ago. Please kick at me again. A roundhouse at about half speed."

"Okay," I say, assuming a stance, and affecting a menacing expression. "Say hello to Buddha when you get to Heaven." I snap out a medium-speed kick.

Mai waits until my foot is halfway to her before exploding to my inside, her chest nearly touching mine. My kick hits only the air behind her.

"Wow! Amazing," I say. "You waited until my size eleven was nearly to you before you moved. Lots of people can duck their head fast, but you moved your entire body."

"Yes, I waited because I wanted to make it hard for me. Have you seen Father do this?"

I tell her about the first time I met him. It was in the park up the street, and he was trying to convince me he was my father. He was sitting on a bench, no more than a step away from me. He said something that angered me, and I lunged for him. Not only was he not there at the end of my lunge, he was suddenly standing behind me. I even banged my shins into the bench. For a moment I thought he had somehow disappeared and then reappeared. It was a whole lot eerie.

"Please try faster this time, Sam. Not all the way because you are too fast. Maybe seventy-five percent. Aim at my tum-tum again."

"How about eighty percent?"

"How about seventy-five?" She places her palms over her eyes. "This way I cannot see you telegraph. Please tell me when you snap the kick out."

This time I snap out my other leg.

"Kick!"

I barely see her jerk her hands from her eyes before she is

standing so close to me I can't see her clearly. And it doesn't help that her thumbs are pressing the skin just below my eyes.

"Pretty fast, huh?" she asks, kissing me.

"Fast? I mean, damn!"

"I could have put thumbs in your eyeballs but I like kissing better." She gives me another. "I am not ready for a real fast kick yet, but I hope to. My goal is to move all the way behind you before you finish a fast kick."

I laugh. "You sound like Father now. He does something beyond comprehension and then says he is working on making it better."

She shrugs. "It is what the martial arts is about, no? Pushing our ... lim ... limits."

"Yes. But some of the things Father does is so far beyond a normal person's limits it's not even a thought for anyone else, let alone a goal.

Mai smiles. "He is amazing. Sometime I forget how much so because I see him do these things all my life."

"If he lived here he would have a following greater than Bruce Lee. He'd be in the movies, be on every talk show, have his own reality show and—"

Mai shakes her head. "Of course, he would never do any of those things."

"I know."

"He would probably buy a cabin in a forest and live there, meditating and working to make things better."

We finish our workout with a hand drill where she again dazzles me with her speed. My hands are probably as fast as hers, but she is definitely faster with her kicking speed. And no way can I move my entire body as fast as she can.

When we stop, I ask, "Want to take a quick shower and

walk a couple blocks up the street to a coffee joint? It's where I first met Father. Actually, he met me before I met him since I was unconscious at the time."

"Coffee sounds good." She drops her chin and looks up at me in an X-rated sort of way. "Want to shower together and save water?"

I scratch my head like I'm really trying to decide, then, "Letmethinkyes."

In the kitchen, my cell is ringing and vibrating its way toward the edge of the kitchen counter.

*   *   *

"Sensei, it's Nate." Sounds worried. Music in the background. Laughter.

"What's up, Nate?"

Long pause, then, "I'm a loser." Another pause. "I'm at a bar."

"Oh man. Why?" I mouth to Mai that it's one of my students.

Nate exhales, long and loudly. "To get away from my wife. She won't let me have a beer at home."

"How many have you had, Nate?"

"Two."

"Nate."

"Two, I swear."

"So what's going on? You need a ride home? I'll call you a cab."

"I'm at Tall Cool Ones, Thirtieth and Tillamook. Hole in the wall." Long pause. "I don't need a taxi. It's just ..."

"What is it, Nate?"

More laughter in the background. Willie Nelson on the

sound system. "To all the girls I've loved before."

"Nate?"

Whispering: "I didn't stop it, Sam. I knew ... but I let it happen. I let them kill those ..."

"Wait there. I'll come get you." I give an apologetic look at Mai and she nods it's okay. "Ten minutes, Nate. Don't leave and don't drive. Okay?"

"Sam ... I'm sorry. I shouldn't have called. I ..."

"Ten minutes."

I click off the cell. "Sorry about this. It's the vet I told you about. He's at a bar and he doesn't sound good." I look down at my sweatpants and T-shirt. "Going to slip on jeans and a dry T-shirt."

"Me too," Mai says.

Three minutes later we're changed and Chien is waiting at the front door like a dog about to take a car trip.

"Can Chien go with us? Pleeeease?"

I roll my eyes like I'm put out by the idea.

In the truck, Chien takes her place on the center console and we shoot toward Tillamook Street. "I barely know Nate," I say, "but it seems he's been put into my life for some reason. Or I've been put into his."

"Now you sound like Father," Mai says, rubbing Chien's neck.

I smile, nod. "I've been able to share my pain about the shooting with you, Father, Mark, and my psychologist and it's really helped me. It's said pain shared is pain divided, but in Nate's case, he allowed a crime, an atrocity, to happen. It's a tough one to share with people. I can only assume he's told only a few, if any—maybe his wife. If he can't share it, he has to carry the burden alone, and it's heavy."

Mai kisses the top of Chien's head. "I think you are right, Sam. Nate is in your life for a reason. Father has a quote about this. He taught it to me when I was little. It is Chinese. 'If you want happiness for an hour, take a nap. If you want happiness for a day, go fishing. If you want happiness for a year, inherit a fortune. If you want happiness for a lifetime, help somebody.'"

I laugh. "I like it, but I'm always amazed at how you and Father can remember so many of those things."

She shrugs. "We are supersmart, I think. Father loves to quote movies and—" She leans toward the windshield. "Are those men going to attack the other man?"

"Yes," I say, goosing my truck toward three men circling Nate on the sidewalk outside of Tall Cool Ones. "The other man is my student."

The three men sport big beer bellies and fleshy red faces, and two of them are wearing their baseball hats backwards. The one without a hat has a heavy beard and looks like he might be Middle Eastern. As I slide to a stop at the curb, the one without a hat launches a haymaker. I push my door open as Nate easily deflects the wild punch. He grabs a wad of the man's size triple-x T-shirt with one hand and a handful of his curly black hair with his other, and yanks him down onto the sidewalk next to his athletic bag. That thing seems to go everywhere he does. I approach silently from his nine o'clock so as not to distract him.

One of the backward baseball hat guys looks at me and then at Mai behind me. He smiles. Everyone smiles when they see her.

Mai calls out, "Sam!"

Arms circle my legs and something slams against my butt, sending me on a fast descent to the concrete. I snap my head to the side so as not to chip the cement with my nose, and slap my forearms down to save the rest of my head.

My arms don't shatter, which is good, but whoever tackled me begins crawling up my back. Heavy dude. A big-ass drinker, I'm guessing. I turtle my head to keep him from choking me and push up hard with my right arm. He's suddenly off me but I know it's not from what I did.

I jump to my feet to find Mai kneeling behind the guy, her arm wrapped around his neck, his eyes fluttering closed. "Sorry, Sam," she says, squeezing the man's face purple. "I did not see him until he bumped into me when he run to get you."

"No problem. I just—"

Hands on my ankle. It's the bearded guy Nate dumped a moment ago. Damn, he's a big one. I use my other foot to stomp down on his wrist, specifically the radial nerve just above his thumb. He yelps and involuntarily releases his grip. When he starts to push himself up with his other hand, I chamber my knee high. "Stay—" I slam the heel of my shoe down on at least three of his fingers—"down!"

Nate falls to the cement at my feet. He looks up. "Hi, Sensei." Doesn't seem as depressed as he did on the phone. The man who knocked Nate down grabs his leg and drags him across the sidewalk. I start to go after the guy, but I'm suddenly spun around. Man, I need to work on my awareness skills.

Someone new. Where are they coming from? And why are they all so fat? He draws back his fist, not all the way to New Hampshire, but to Ohio, Cincinnati, the burbs. Not waiting for it to come West, I slam the arch of my foot into his shin. There isn't a lot of padding over the sensitive nerves on the shinbone, even among the obese. His face contorts in pain and his punching arm hesitates. I slap his kisser.

As an off-duty cop defending myself, I have to try not to

take it too personal when complete strangers try to hurt me, and I have to keep in mind whatever I do is going to be scrutinized up the kazoo by my PD. The cop shop discourages officers from taking action off duty. And should the media find out I've been involved in a bar brawl, it would be like Christmas for them. All this and I have Mai and Nate to worry about. It's not easy being me sometimes.

Which is why I slapped the guy as opposed to ripping out his larynx. Still, I slapped him really, really hard.

The blow spins the man all the way around. When I see his face again, his eyes are rolling like wheels in a slot machine. I slap him again for good measure. Guess that's all the nerves in his face can handle because the last one made his knees buckle. I grab his collar so his head doesn't hit the sidewalk.

Mai has rolled her sleeping guy over onto his stomach and is restraining him with an arm lock. She looks at me, her eyes going wide at whatever is going on behind me.

Thinking I'm about to get attacked from my rear again, I step away, shield my head with my arms and spin about. There is no one there, but ten feet over, Nate is facing a new man—two of his attackers are sprawled on the sidewalk. The new guy is slashing the air between them with a long knife. The man looks untrained but his blade looks deadly sharp. He's got a buddy standing a few feet away. No visible weapons on him.

"Take it easy," Nate tells him, holding his open palms up as if he were being robbed. He sidesteps over to his bag. "Just let us leave and no one will get hurt."

I move up so I'm in alignment with Nate but about a dozen feet over to split the man's attention. I circle to his right to split it more.

"Hurt?" Knife Man says, maneuvering so he can watch both

of us. "Meaning you two."

"Yes, sir," Nate says. I've always taught rookies about the power in saying sir and ma'am. "And you will be hurt, as well," Nate adds calmly. He bends toward his bag.

The man fakes a chuckle. "Me?" He looks over at his buddy who smirks like a Hollywood villain. Farther over, the guy whose fingers I stomped has scooted his whimpering self over the wall of the bar, where he sits looking at his crushed fingers and probably thinking he will have to hold his beer mug with his left for a long while. Off to my right, Mai still holds her man in an arm lock but he's awake now and starting to squirm around in protest. Should I go to her or stay with—

"Unless you haven't noticed, Tonto," Knife Man says, bringing my attention back to him, "I got the knife."

Out of the corner of my eye, I see—what on Earth? Mai launches her lower half into the air, as if attempting a handstand while still jamming her prone man's arm behind his back. She lands hard on top of him, driving her knee between his legs, smashing his groin and his coccyx bone. His scream is primal.

The cry draws Knife Man's attention for only a fraction of a second, but it's long enough to give Nate a chance to reach into his bag of tricks. "Knife? That's not a knife," Nate says, now holding his war club in front of him. "*This* is a knife. Sorta."

A *Crocodile Dundee* reference. Father would be impressed.

Knife Man's eyes widen for a moment before he laughs. "You gotta be shittin' me."

His friend touches Knife Man's shoulder. "Jim, I think we oughta just leave."

Jim jerks his shoulder away. "I think you need to man up and take care of this big asshole and let me and Cochise have some fun."

"Nate, back up toward the truck," I tell him. The situation has moved into a deadly realm and we have got to get out of here. "Mai, let your man go and move toward the truck."

Knife Man lunges, and surprisingly fast for someone his size. Suddenly manning up, his friend charges me. Time to end this now. I wait for him to close, aaaand *bopbop … bop*, two fast palm-heel strikes to his forehead, and one to his jaw hinge, just below his ear. I catch him before his head slams the concrete.

Knife Man's blade skitters across the concrete and bumps against my shoe. I look up to see the big man cupping his blood-pumping nose with one hand and laboriously hopping from one leg to the other, as a squatting Nate uses the club end of his antique weapon to smash each foot as it touches down on the sidewalk.

"Ow ow ow ow," Knife Man yelps, looking like an out of shape River Dancer.

The door to the bar opens and people begin streaming out.

"Nate," I say. "We got to go."

"Check, Sensei," he says, then whacks Knife Man's kneecap, sending the yelping man to the sidewalk, yelping even louder. It's hard to say if it's his knee or his feet no longer supporting him.

"N-uh-r-t-uh-n-ah," Nate says proudly, standing and looking down at his handy work. "Makes others dance." He drops his war club into his gym bag and backs toward me. Mai joins us, leaving her man curled into the fetal position, his hands between his legs.

A dozen or so bar patrons stand on the other side of the fallen fat men, no one moving to assist them. Maybe the patrons are glad the bullies finally got their comeuppance.

"Watch everyone in all directions," I say, backing toward

the truck.

"I'm so sorry about all this, Sensei," Nate says out of the corner of his mouth. "About getting you and your friend involved in my shit. It will be the last time, I promise."

"We can talk after we get out of here."

We back all the way to the truck. Mai scoops up Chien who yawns, no doubt sleeping through our ordeal, and scoots over next to me, sitting on the console. Nate drops his bag on the floor and slips in next to Mai. I goose the throttle, and we leave the crowd and the injured behind us.

"My name is Mai Nguyen," Mai says calmly, as if she had been shopping instead of choking out a guy and pile driving his privates into his throat.

"Mine's Nate. I'm so sorry about all this, Mai. I hope you were not hurt. Sam, are you hurt?"

I tap in a number on my cell. "Nate, I want to know what the fight was about after I finish this call."

"Is he pissed?" Nate whispers to Mai.

She nods. "Pretty pissed, yes."

"This is Detective Sam Reeves. Please hook me up with a supervisor." I glance at Nate. "I'm trying to keep you out of jail right now, but I also have to cover my butt. You understand, Nate?"

He looks down at his folded hands.

"Hi, Bernie. Detective Reeves, Intelligence. Off duty. Have you received a call from Tall Cool Ones at Thirtieth and Northeast Tillamook? Fight call? Yes, please look." I look at Nate. "Nine-one-one supervisor is checking the computer. "Yeah, Bernie. Nothing. Good. Listen, if you get a call, my friends and I were involved. Attacked. We've left the scene because it's dangerous for us to be there." I give Bernie my cell number and home address. "We'll be there if the officers need to talk to us. And I'll write a Special Report tomorrow at the office. Yes. Okay, thanks, Bernie."

I make a right. "Unbelievable. No one called the police. My guess is the bar owner runs a tight ship there, and everyone knows not to call the cops. Still, I can't believe a passersby didn't call."

Nate doesn't look up. "I'm so—"

"Sorry," I finish for him. "I know. Tell me what happened."

Nate takes a deep breath. "I had just called you and was waiting. I was thinking about how I was messing up my life and how I had to get a grip on myself before I screwed up everything good I have." He glances shyly at Mai who is looking down at Chien. To me he says, "I started to, you know." He looks back to Mai who is still tending to Chien. Though she is between us, she is letting us talk as if she wasn't here. Nate looks at me and traces a finger down his cheek and makes a face like he's crying. I nod that I understand. "I guess the Middle Easterner saw me, and he says, "Trouble in the teepee, Tonto? Find out your papoose isn't yours?"

"What a jerk," I say.

"That's what I said. Actually, I said, 'What did you say, Taliban, asshole?'"

I sputter out a laugh. "Uh, not a diffusing technique, Nate."

"I agree, Sensei. But after what he said to me, and the tone he used. It was like Indians are a joke. And him being a raghead, people I am trying not to hate. I just lost it."

"The man with hair here?" Mai asks, touching her face.

Nate nods. "The bearded guy against the wall. You do something to him, Sensei?"

"He's not going to text for a while."

"Taliban are people in Iraq and Baghdad, right?" Mai asks.

And other places," Nate says. "He was some kind of a Middle Easterner. I just called him a Taliban to get to him."

Mai shakes her head in confusion. "When I go to Portland State, I have two friends from Mexico. They speak Spanish a lot and they teach me a little. The man by the wall with a bad hand, he speak Spanish, I am sure. He cry about his *mano*. Word mean hand in Mexico, uh Spanish. And he cry about his *la cabeza*. It mean head."

"He was Mexican?" Nate asks incredulously.

Mai shrugs. "I think so, Nate."

* * *

"Please turn there, Sensei," Nate says, with a slight tremble in his voice. "Third house on the left."

"The wife going to be mad?" I ask innocently. "What's her name, by the way?"

"Liluye. Mad is an understatement."

"Pretty name," Mai says. "Does it have meaning?"

"'Chicken hawk singing when soaring.'"

"Pretty," Mai says, as I bite the insides of my cheeks.

"One last thing," I say, as I pull up to the curb. "The law doesn't look too favorably on someone carrying around a war club. Carrying it to and from training is one thing, but taking it to a bar is a whole other issue. I've had three defense attorneys as students over the years and all three said they would never take on a client who defended himself with a knife. Said juries hate knives, no matter how justified the defense. And here you are carrying around a freakin' war club tomahawk. I'm not telling you how to live your life, Nate ... well, maybe I am when it comes to this. Please don't carry the thing into bars, shopping malls, public swimming pools, daycare centers—"

"Lord save me," Nate says scooting down in the seat.

"I'm just trying to keep you out of trouble."

"No, not that, Sensei." He points toward his house. "It's Liluye, and she's on the warpath."

I look toward the house. What the—Liluye is a dwarf? A little person?

"Naaaate!" she bellows from the porch. She's wearing jeans and a white blouse, her head just slightly higher than the door-knob. Even at thirty yards away it's obvious she's very pretty with long black hair down her back. She stomps toward us like she's mad enough to eat a two-by-four spiked with nails.

"She already see you, Nate," Mai says. "Your goose is screwed."

Nate shoots Mai a confused look. "You mean my goose is cooked?"

"Yes, that one," Mai says as I get out of the truck.

"You guys stay in here," I whisper.

"Nate, where have you been?" Liluye shouts, moving across the lawn. "And who is the woman?"

I must admit it doesn't look good with Mai and Nate sitting scooched down side by side in the truck.

"Hello, Mrs. Whitehorse. I'm Sam Reeves, Nate's martial arts teacher." She glances at me and then back to the truck "The woman is Mai. She's with me. Mrs. Whitehorse, can I speak with you for a moment? Over here by the tree." She looks up at me but doesn't move. "Please. In the shade, please. Hot one today, huh?"

She hesitates for a moment, looks back up at the truck window where Nate is still sitting low in the seat, then back to me.

"Please," I say once more, gesturing toward the tree.

"I'm Sam," I tell her again, as she joins me under the big tree. I feel a little awkward, not knowing if I should bend over, stand at my full height, or drop to one knee. She's actually, a little taller than I initially thought. About four feet, maybe four feet one. The only other time I've talked with someone this short was when I arrested a man for stealing a motor scooter. He crashed it after a short chase and fought like a wildcat when I tackled him at the entrance of a shopping mall. It wasn't good public relations for a six-foot, two-hundred-pound weight-lifter to scrap with a little person in front of a hundred holiday shoppers. But he was tough. And I'm betting Liluye is too.

She shakes my hand. She really is quite pretty. Big brown eyes, high cheekbones, full mouth.

"Mrs. Whitehouse, besides being your husband's teacher, I'm a Portland Police detective."

She nods. "You're the policeman who shot—"

"I am, yes." When she doesn't react or say anything, I go on. "He told me about what happened in Afghanistan, and I'm sure you're aware he is suffering a lot."

In the minute or two we've been under the tree, Mrs. Whitehorse has been agitated and fidgety. But after what I just said, she abruptly stills.

"Mrs. Whitehorse, I don't know your husband well, but as a cop having dealt with thousands of folks in all kinds of situations, I've developed a pretty good ability to read people. My take on Nate is he's a good man. He's suffering greatly for standing by and allowing injustices to take place in Afghanistan. If he weren't a good man, he wouldn't be suffering at all. You see?"

She nods slowly.

"Is he a different man now than the one who left for

Afghanistan?"

"Yes," she says softly. "He's angry, confused, he won't talk to me about it. He wants to drink but his body doesn't handle it."

"Is the Army helping?" I ask.

"No."

"Listen, I saw a psychologist for a while after my shooting. She mostly works with cops but she sees other people too. She's good. Not a touchy feely person but an ass kicker, if you pardon my French. She trims all the fat and psycho mumbo jumbo, and gets right to the problem. From the first session, she gives the patient something to do and think about. And it really helps. Cops don't like the idea of going to her, but all those I know who have think she's great and swear by her. I do."

"She sounds perfect for him," she says, looking over at the truck. Nate is sitting so low I can just barely see the top of his head. She probably can't see him at all. Mai smiles at us.

"I think Doctor Kari Stephens would be a good fit for him. Okay, what do you think of this plan? We'll get him to promise not to go drinking again." I laugh. "He's not much of a drinker anyway, right?"

"Two beers and he falls apart."

I laugh. "Anyway, he'll promise me not to drink again. I'll tell him to sit down and talk with you about what he's going through."

"He won't do it."

"Mrs. Whitehorse, I've only been his teacher for a week but he's been training for a long time. He understands the teacher-student relationship, and I think he respects me as a martial artist and my history with the PD. Plus, he's called me twice now when he's gotten into trouble. I think he'll listen."

Nate's wife covers her face with her hands and her shoulders begin shaking.

I soften my voice. "If I may suggest, Mrs. Whitehorse, please go easy on him. I know all this is going to pass and he'll be fine. I understand he's about to be hired by the fire department. I think he will make a good fire fighter. Of course, his tomahawk is useless against a fire."

Her hands are still over her face and her sobbing abruptly changes to laughter, which makes her cough. I gently pull her hands down.

"What do you think?" I ask.

"You are a wise man," she says. "Thank you so much."

"No problem. Nate's a good man who just needs a lot of adult supervision right now. But with a gentle touch. Tomorrow, I'll call Doctor Stevens and get it going."

She touches my arm, smiles, nods. "I'm glad Nate found you. When I read about you in the paper two months ago and saw you on the news, I remember thinking it was so sad for the family and so sad for the officer. I saw something in your eyes and I knew you were a good man too."

"Thank you. I appreciate it. Lets the four of us have dinner soon. We'll make Nate pay."

She laughs. "Can I get him now?"

"Of course. But no butt kicking."

"Darn," she says with a wink.

A few minutes later, Nate and Liluye are in their home, and Mai and I are on our way.

"Remember when I say Nate was put into your life for a reason?" Mai asks, her hand resting on my leg. Chien is sitting on the console again watching the road. When I nod, she says, "I am pretty smart, eh?"

I smile. "Humble too."

"I thought the small woman was going to beat up your friend. But after you talk to her, she cry and then hug Nate for a long time, then they walk into their house. You think they make love right now?"

I laugh. "Hope so."

She kisses my cheek and then rubs Chien's head. "You show your girlfriend a pretty exciting time, Sam."

"I'm so ..." I was going to apologize for getting her involved in the brawl, but I think she enjoyed herself. "Are you hurt, anywhere?"

"Hurt? No." She looks at me with those same dreamy eyes she had when were in bed. "You were a very gentle lover."

*　　*　　*

We returned to the house so I could change my shirt. It got slimed when I was tackled to the sidewalk. My forearms are a little sore after slapping the concrete to break my fall but there are no skin abrasions. Mai has a small scrape on her knee from slamming home her awesome knee drop. I slip on a black polo and we head out the door.

"It's about dinner time," I say, as we cut across my lawn. "Why don't we save the coffee joint for another time and get something to eat. There's a deli a couple of doors down from the coffee place where we can get a sandwich and take it over to the park. Whatdoyuhsay? Whatdoyuhsay, huh?"

She punches my shoulder and I overreact to the blow. "You are so weird. I think food in the park sounds wonderful. And it's going to be a beautiful evening for a walk."

Two blocks up the street I point out the coffee place where I got sucker punched to the cement. I say, "When I was lying between those tables floating in and out of consciousness, I was only partially aware of a mysterious stranger wearing red Converse shoes and kicking the dog snot out of my attacker. I eventually passed out, and the next thing I knew I was lying on a park bench on which sat an odd man wearing red Converse and teasing me about getting sucker punched. Then he told me he was my pop." Mai laughs, though Father and I have told her the story five times.

We get a couple of roast turkey sandwiches on sourdough, a big cup of mixed fruit and yogurt, and a bottle of orange juice, and head over to the park. It's beautiful here, as always, especially in early evening when the giant fir trees are silhouetted against pink cotton ball clouds, and a balmy breeze is pushing away the day's heat. About a hundred yards across the park, a group of children are playing. There's a slide, a merry-go-round, and some kind of modern version of the old monkey bars. The sprawling lawn is dotted with people lying about on blankets, groups playing badminton, joggers, and the obligatory black Labrador retriever leaping to catch a Frisbee.

"I think this is the actual bench Father carried me to," I say, as we sit. "I weigh two hundred or so, he tips the scale at one sixty, plus he's sixty-five years old. How the hell did he carry me? I was unconscious."

Mai unwraps a sandwich and hands it to me. "How does he do many of the things he does?" she asks rhetorically. "Before I met you, I just thought these things are what Father does because I see him do them all my life. I mean, I know, er, I knew they are special things, but I just did not see them as so special because I see him do them all the time." She shakes her head. "I do not think I make sense."

"No, not too much sense." I laugh, and snap my shoulder away quickly from her punch. "But I understand. For me it was all new, having him pick up on my thoughts, feeling the pain of his punch from the other side of his three-hundred-pound bag, seeing him move so fast it defies logic, seeing him heal people, and hearing him talk about the Fourth Level where, for crying out loud, he wills a technique without physically doing it—freakin' eerie."

She nods. "I think you are right."

"Will we ever be as good?"

"No."

"No?"

"Father's life has been different than ours. He have many special teachers: very old Chinese masters who live in mountains, very special Buddhist monks, people who have ... I do not know how to say."

"Reached the eerie level?"

She spoons fruit into her mouth, nods. "I like it. Yes." She swallows her fruit, and says, her eyes taking on a mischievous look, "Can I show you something I am working on?"

About fifty yards off to the right, the Frisbee dog runs onto a blanket where a young couple are curled together. The young woman lets out a squeal as the man angrily pushes the dog's head away. The dog's owner, a tall, skinny bearded man in his twenties yells at the young man. We're too far away to hear any specifics, but I'm guessing the hippy-looking dog owner thinks it's his right to let his dog run off leash and terrorize other people. After an indistinct but clearly angry sounding exchange, the hippy walks off with his dog scampering far ahead of him.

"Like father like daughter," I say. "Always working on something. Sure, love to see it."

"Cool," she says with a schoolgirl giggle. She extracts a note pad from her purse, writes something on it, and sets it face down on the bench. "Okay, stand in front of me and make a stance." I do. "Okay. Now I will give you an, uh, op ... option. An option of a technique to do. When I give you the option, you think it. Do not do it. Only think it, okay?"

"I think I understand."

She sighs dramatically. "Sam, it is not hard."

"Okay, okay. Give me the option. I will only think of my choice."

"Yes, very good. And think it quick. Okaaaay—kick.

I think of my muay Thai roundhouse—it's my favorite. I once used it to break a baseball bat.

"Roundhouse," she says.

I must have a shocked look on my mug because Mai cracks up.

I sputter, "How in the hell ..."

"We can do another," she says, giddy with victory. Our father gets just as exuberant when he demonstrates something. "Okay, be ready in your stance. Reeeady—hand technique."

Backfist.

"Backfist."

"No damn way!" I practically shout. How in the ...

Mai laughs again.

"Okay, one more. You can sit down. This time, think of three numbers between one and one thousand but all the numbers have to be the same."

"Do what? Think of three numbers all the same ..."

"Between one and one thousand.

Three hundred thirty-three.

I nod when she asks if I've chosen. She picks up her pad, covers the bottom section with her hand and shows me the top.

333

Whoa. "No. Damn. Way."

Laughing like a fat opera singer, Mai says, "Okay, think of a color."

Blue.

"Got one?"

When I nod, she moves her hand from the bottom section of her writing pad.

Red.

I lift my eyebrows.

She frowns. "Not red? You think of wrong color, Sam."

"Oh, so it was me?"

Mai laughs. "I told you I am still working on it. But three out of four not too damn bad, no?"

I shake my head in disbelief. "I'm floored. I really am. Are you picking up my thoughts like Father does? I mean, wow."

She nods sagely, then laughs. "No. It is just an old magician's trick. I just figured out how to do it with martial artists. Most people choose three hundred thirty-three. And most people pick red, except you because you are a crazy boy. Most martial artists think roundhouse kick and backfist. People who do not do martial artists think jab and front kick. It is all—what you call, averages."

I shake my head and chuckle. "So it's all math and odds. You had me thinking you had superpowers."

She drops her chin and looks up at me in a way that ought to have a For Mature Audiences Only sign hanging on it. "You do not think I have superpowers?"

I bob my eyebrows. "Ooooh yea. You got super-superpowers."

She smiles evilly and stuffs the last of her sandwich into her smiling mouth.

I say, "Well, even if it was just math, it was pretty cool. But there is no trickery to Father's skills."

"No trickery to his. He can do things ... Sam?" She points at something behind me. "The black dog ..."

It's the black Frisbee dog again, this time barking up a storm at several people sitting around a picnic table. The hippy dude is at least fifty yards away, walking toward the table. Actually, it's more of a stroll, no hurry to retrieve his annoying dog.

There is a baby stroller parked in the shade a few feet away from the table. I can barely see a little hand moving about in the air. Two of the men are trying to shoo the dog away, but the animal appears to be getting more aggressive as it circles the table, and the tone of its bark is changing from excited to angry.

Even over the barking, I can hear the infant start to cry. One of the women, is already moving toward the stroller just as the dog rounds the far end of the table. It stops, and watches her. The dog lowers his head. Oh no. I spring off the bench.

The dog charges, leaps, and slams his front legs into her butt, knocking her forward and into the carriage, tipping it over onto its side. The toddler spills out onto the grass.

I've never been much of a runner, but I'm willing myself to speed, waving my arms and shouting "No! No! No!" in hopes of distracting the dog. But it's focused on the wailing child: its snout low to the ground, the hair on the back of its neck bristled. My yelling doesn't penetrate its brain. Everyone at the table is yelling too, and trying to untangle themselves from the fixed bench seats.

The woman ignores the creeping dog, sacrificing herself to snatch up the toddler. Before she can stand all the way upright, the dog clomps onto her lower leg. I'm almost there, and I can't tell if the animal has her actual leg or just her jeans. Judging by the screams, it's the leg.

One of the men kicks the dog in the side, but the animal only sidesteps without giving up its "kill."

"Wait!" I shout from a dozen feet away. "Don't kick it again." If the dog has a mouthful of her leg, kicking it away just might inadvertently tear off a chunk of meat. "Lady, don't move. Don't move."

Coming up along side the dog, at least an eighty pounder, I simultaneously grab a handful of the scruff on the side of its big black head and reach around its thick neck with my other hand.

The dog tries to fight against the hand that's got its scruff, but I'm blocking it with the side of my chest. "Eeeeasy boy," I say, digging my fingers of my other hand into its throat. "Eeee-asy now." I find the windpipe, and pinch it between my thumb and index finger.

"Hey! Hey!"

I'm guessing it's the hippy. "Mai," I call out. "Hold him back."

The dog's struggle lessens. Stops. His mouth releases the woman's leg and someone pulls her away. The dog's front legs buckle, then its back ones. He plops onto his side.

"What are you doing to my dog, man?" the hippy shouts. Mai is pushing against his chest to keep him back.

I keep hold of the dog's scruff and pin its head against the ground with my knee as I move my pinching hand around to get a better grip on its windpipe. I don't apply pressure this time so the unconscious dog can breathe, but I'm in position should he awaken cranky. "Anyone call nine-one-one?" I ask, looking up at the astonished faces.

"I called the police," a male voice says. I hear sirens now.

Another woman has taken the toddler and is scurrying across the lawn toward the parking lot. A man is helping the bitten woman to lie down. She's grimacing and I can see a widening bloodstain on the outside of her calf.

"You don't have the right to keep me from my dog," I hear the hippy shout. I look over just as he knocks away Mai's hands. She goes with the flow and one hand moves to his forehead and the other to the small of his back. She presses against his head, pushes on his lower back, pivots, and dumps him onto the grass. Nice move. He starts to get up.

"Look at me!" I say loudly. He does. "I'm a police officer. You stay seated or I'll file an additional charge on you."

"Additional?"

"Additional."

The dog's eyes flutter open and his legs begin digging at the ground as if running. "Nighty night, Fido," I say gently, as I again pinch his windpipe. The thrashing slows and his body goes limp. He's out again.

Across the lawn, two police cars speed our way.

*   *   *

Mai is laughing.

"I know what you're thinking, Laughing Woman," I say, bumping her shoulder. It's twilight now and we're heading back to the house. "You're thinking once again what a fun date I am. Thrills and chills and attacking dogs."

"A little. But I was also remembering how the man's face looked when you said you were a policeman and you said about the additional charge."

"He was an irresponsible jerk. I hope the woman and her husband sue the tie-dyed shirt off his back. His dog took a big chunk out of her leg."

"The dog might have eaten the baby."

"Animal Control got there fast, thankfully."

"Will they shoot the dog?"

"No. They'll check it for rabies and then a judge will decide what will happen to it. He will also decide what will happen to the hippy man. Maybe a heavy fine, maybe jail. It's all up to the courts now."

"Where did you learn to make dog pass out?"

"I had a student once who trained dogs. He brought it up when we were working on carotid constriction techniques, which you did very well earlier, I forgot to mention."

"I think maybe karma brought you and me together to make people and dogs pass out."

"A match made in heaven, that's us."

Happily, the rest of the evening is uneventful. We watch TV, eat popcorn, and talk a little about Mai's mother and what might happen now with the family business. When I ask if she would like to live here, she says of course she would, but the wise thing to do is not make a decision on anything right away. Even in despair she is a wise and wonderful woman.

While I'm at work tomorrow, Mai has a list of activities: she is going to visit a couple of girlfriends she met when she was going to Portland State, and she wants to work in my yard. Wednesday, she plans to clean my entire house. Mostly, she wants to stay busy while she absorbs the sorrow of her mother's passing, think about the family business in Saigon, and think about where her life will lead her.

She falls asleep first and I watch her for a while wondering how I got so incredibly lucky.

*   *   *

"Hey, detective," the acne-splattered face of the tweaker says, leaning out from behind a tree. His voice sounds like someone took a coarse file to his vocal cords. "What's happenin'?" He's bleeding from a hole just under his nose, right smack where I shot him.

"Sweeeet biiiitch," the skinny naked man says in his syrupy tone as he leans out from the other side of the tree. I don't see Mai but I know he's talking about her. He's got a bleeding hole in his face too. "Sweeeet sweeeet by-iiiiitch. You gonna shoooot her, toooo?"

"Don't shoot my dog, pleeeease?" little Jimmy whines from behind me. I turn to see him struggling to hold onto a leash attached to the Frisbee dog. Blood oozes from a hole in the boy's upper chest. Jimmy's face turns ugly, mean, his pointing finger both an accusation and a command to the dog. "Get him, boy! Get him good."

"Yessss!" the naked man hisses. "Get him gooood Fiiiido. Detectiiiive Reeves, he ain't got no guuuun this time."

Crying. I hear crying. It's Mai, I think. Where is ... Mai?

"Sam."

Mai's face is just inches from mine, her head buried into her pillow, tears streaming from the one eye not scrunched into the down. I think she's still asleep. Her shoulders tremble.

"Mai," I whisper. "It's okay. I'm right here." I force the tweaker, the naked man, Jimmy, and the dog out of my head. They leave without a fight.

Mai's eye opens a little, then squeezes shut against the tears, which sends more rolling over her nose. I wipe them away with the sheet.

"You were crying in your sleep."

"My mother is gone, Sam. I need her. Need to talk to her."

I kiss her cheek, touch her forehead with mine, and leave

it there.

"Do you talk to your mother?" she asks. "I mean, like in your head?"

"I do, all the time. I thank her for teaching me, for putting up with me when I was a jerk, for encouraging me in the martial arts, and for letting me have such a wonderful relationship with my grandfather, her dad."

"You think she hears you?"

"Yes. Your mother will hear you too."

Mai snuggles in closer and buries her face into my neck.

* * *

"Your gun?" Mai says, lying on the bed and watching me slip on my jacket. Warm rays slip through the slits of the window blinds, which mean another hot day.

As a detective, I have to conceal my weapon under a jacket. Not a biggee in the winter, but in the summer when it's hot, wearing a coat can be miserable. Thing is, I've been wearing a coat every day since I've been back to conceal I haven't been carrying one.

"Father tell me to make sure you carry it."

I exhale dramatically. "I will, I will, nagging woman." I pull open the bottom drawer and dig under my socks for my holstered Glock Nine. I pick it up and shut the drawer quickly so Mai can't see the full magazine sticking out from under a pair of white Nike socks. I stand and make a big deal out of slipping my belt through the holster.

"There," I say, patting the flap of my jacket, "you ol' fish wife."

She slides out of bed, all breathtaking and heart stopping five-feet-eleven gorgeousness in matching red panties and tank top, and slips her arms around me. "I do not know 'fish wife,' but if it means your family wants you to be safe, then it is okay." She kisses me.

When we finally stop, I groan, "Oh man. Maybe I'll call in sick today."

She kisses me quickly and says, "Go to work my police boy. I have things to do, people to see."

I whine, "Okaaaay. I'll call when I can and see you about four thirty. It's okay to wear this red outfit again."

Driving away from the house is about the hardest thing I've ever done. But then seeing her off at the airport when she and Father flew back to Saigon was gut-wrenching agony. Actually, it might have been even harder to wave goodbye to her at the Saigon airport last week, gut-wrenching multiplied to the power of ... whatever. I'm not good at math. And clearly I'm not good at goodbye.

I have fallen so hard for Mai. I'm giddy with it, silly with it, and it ... hurts? Yes, I feel a sort of pain. Leaving her just now hurts my chest. Thinking about her going back to Vietnam—it's almost hard to breathe. Got to get my mind off it. I pick up my cell.

"Mark, it's Sam. How are you doing? And David?"

"Hi, Sam." He sounds a little down. "I'm doin', you know. David is the same. You?

"Heading to work. I'll let you know what's up with the two suspects I told you about yesterday."

"Thanks, Sam ... for everything."

"No charge, my friend. Listen, I'm downtown and traffic is crazy. I better get off the cell. Call you later."

I park in the lot across from the Justice Center and hold my head down as I approach the fifty or so protesters outside the front doors. I don't see Jesse Jackson or Al Sharpton anywhere, but I'm sure they're on their way. There is at least one news station parked out front. A van pulls up to the curb and then another. Several more people get out with signs and banners. There will be lots more.

I excuse myself several times as I make my way through the crowd, keeping my head down and scratching my forehead to cover my face with my palm. Several people ask if I'm a cop but I don't answer. I get to the double glass doors that lead from the sidewalk into the building's large foyer but a big man blocks the way. He's black with a shaved head, dangling earring, and protruding veins in his forehead. Intellectually, I know protruding forehead veins don't mean anything, but in my imagination they have always given me pause, even more than face tattoos. It's silly to be intimidated by a blood vein and ink, but what can I say? Hey, some people freak out at clowns.

"Excuse me," I say. He doesn't move. "I said excuse me."

"You work here?" he asks, folding his arms. He's got big ones, like a doorman at a trendy nightclub. The sleeves of his burgundy sweatshirt are cut to prove something.

"I work on a farm collecting eggs. You going to move?" Saying stupid things is how I deal with not being intimidated over those veins.

"Cop," he spits like it's the dirtiest word he's ever uttered. "Smart mouth, muthafucker. You all by yourself."

I look behind me at the protesters waving their signs at passing cars. Someone with a megaphone tries to get a chant going but only a couple of people pick up on it. Not the most organized group. I see only one person looking our way, a middle-aged white woman with long grey hair falling down her back. A sixties flower child still fighting for the oppressed.

I look back at the big vein. "Well, there is just one of you between me and the door. It's your decision whether you want to stay out here to chant and walk in circles or go downstairs and get booked for obstructing a public building. You got five seconds."

He leans back against where the two doors meet, unfolds his arms, and says, "Is that right? What if I say—"

I grab his upper arm, which gives me more control than if I grab his forearm, and shove it against his big torso. When he resists my push, just as I thought he would, I yield to his energy, using it to spin his big self around and into the glass door. I use both hands to jam his arm up his back, into a hammerlock. Most muscular guys don't have a lot of range and I don't have to go too far before I feel him tense with the pain. He's not going to give me the pleasure of hearing him yelp, but he's standing on his tiptoes in a desperate but ultimately futile attempt to escape the pain. It's good he's not making noise because I can move him into the lobby without alerting any of his fifty-plus friends.

I maintain the hold with one hand and use my other to pull open the heavy, pressurized door. Drawing on all my strength, I drive with my legs to force him through the opening. It's about twenty feet across the lobby to another set of double glass doors that lead to Central Precinct on the main floor and to a bank of elevators. A passing uniformed cop on the other side of the second set of double glass doors looks my way.

"What do you got?" he says, pushing through the doors.

"Protester didn't want to move. Let's put him in Central's holding room."

"Cuff him?" he asks. He snaps his head toward a burst of noise behind me. "Uh oh."

"Let's get him in the back first," I shout. "There a riot squad anywhere?"

"Just heard someone call for them on the PA a moment ago," the officer says, gripping the man's other arm. The big guy, who hasn't uttered a peep since I grabbed him, isn't exactly resisting. It's more like he's stalling by making himself heavy. The officer fumbles with the heavy door while trying to pull the man as I push him. This time the man leans his hugeness back into me and turns his head just enough for me to see his smirk—and his freakin' vein. A second later, hands grab me from behind and yank me backwards.

It happens so abruptly I inadvertently pull my prisoner's arm away from his back, stretching his shoulder tendons. He bellows loudly over the shouting crowd. He's a jerk not a felon, so I let go of his arm so as not to cause him serious injury. I'm pushed forward and up against the side of the left glass door. Just as I think I'm going to be crushed by the weight of the mob, I hear a deep, guttural command voice.

"Get back! Do it now! Get back! Do it now!"

With my face squished against the glass, I can just barely make out helmeted black shapes streaming through the doors.

I'm free. I spin around to see our Star Wars officers, their shields in front of them, forming a shoulder-to-shoulder line across the lobby, cutting off the mob from gaining entry into Central Precinct. The officers step forward as one, and the people, many of them screaming epithets, begin backing toward the doors.

My prisoner! Where is he? The uniformed officer who had been helping me lays sprawled on the floor on the other side of the glass doors.

"You okay?" I ask, helping him to his feet. His shirttail is out and his hair is disheveled.

He shakes his head. "Well, what a fun time. I haven't been knocked on my ass by a mob since, well, never. Where's your prisoner?"

"Looks like he beat feet out of here. One more charge when we get him. Do me a favor and put out his description and say he escaped from custody."

"Name?"

I shrug. "Didn't get it. I'll recognize him if I see him again. You see those veins in his forehead?"

As the officer broadcasts the man's description, I look across the lobby where a couple of riot officers are restraining an obese woman down on the marble floor, her screams amplified by the echo-producing lobby.

"I'm Dusty Hamilton," the uniformed officer says. "Nights Central. You're Sam Reeves, aren't you?"

I nod. "Thanks for the help. It's not just a little embarrassing to lose one."

He laughs. "Sixty against two isn't in our best interest. You work yesterday?"

"Sunday? No."

"We had a similar situation in here at noon. Officer Davidson from day shift got hurt. He was shoved into the edge of the glass door. Riot guys did some payback with their batons and made thirteen arrests."

I shake my head. "Don't think all this is going away anytime quick. In fact, it's likely to get worse. I'll write up a report on my guy when I get upstairs and write you in."

"Okay. Nice meeting you. By the way, I'm a supporter."

I know he's talking about my shooting. "Thanks, Dusty. Stay low, eh?"

Amazingly, my ride up in the elevator is without incident. Why does it seem of late my presence anywhere turns everything to crud? I can't walk into work, enjoy a picnic with Mai in the park, pick up a friend at a bar, or take a taxi ride from the airport without drama. Okay, cosmos, choose someone else for a while.

"Chuck? Chuck Norris?" Steve says looking up from his PC.

"Funnier every time you say it," I say, smiling. "Hi, Angela. Have a good weekend?"

She nods. "And you? Your woman get in okay?" I'm not sure how to read her tone. Kind of a cross between conversational and I hope your woman's plane went down in the sea.

"She did. Good to see her." I hope that didn't come across as *neener-neener*, but I don't intend to play games with her.

"Good," she says. Disingenuously? I'm not sure.

Oh man, one more thing.

"You heard from ... Hallgerd, wasn't it?" I take off my jacket for the first time in the office. I adjust my gun on my hip and sit behind my desk. Got to remember to keep the butt end away from people so they don't notice the gun doesn't have a magazine in it.

"Not yet," she says. "Hopefully, they haven't made up. I'd like to get this cross burner."

"Understood," I say.

"You ready for some bad news, Chuck?" Steve asks.

"No."

"Your buddy Jason Tibbitts, AKA Puke, got a Get Out of Jail card yesterday at noon."

"Oh man. This city! What about knocking an elderly woman down?"

Steve nods. "Not enough. Assault a judge and see what you get. Or get nailed for not paying your taxes." He shrugs. "It's the system. Speaking of, you ready for some more bad news?"

"No."

"The Fat Dicks didn't get a chance to interview him before his release."

"Great," I say, wadding a Post-it note and tossing it hard into the can.

"Morning," BJ says, coming out of his office carrying a coffee cup and a manila folder. "Gather at my feet my children."

Geeze.

He sits at the desk next to me and we all turn our chairs to face him. He takes a swig from his coffee mug, which depicts an image of Jesus on the cross with the words: "Jesus Hates Capital Punishment."

"Captain Love called me from the Oregon State Prison this morning. Remember, I called him Friday about the women on the video? All we got is a swastika tat on one of them, their stevedore physiques, and those hairstyles. I didn't think Love would be able to help much since so many of the ladies at OSP look like them, but I think we hit pay dirt. He knew exactly who I was talking about."

"Excellent," Steve says.

BJ smiles. "You guys ready for a surprise?" I can tell the lieutenant is one of those guys who likes the power of having information no one else does. Likes to drip it out slowly because once he's spilled it all, he's got nothing.

"Yes," I say, nodding and looking at Angela. "I think I'm ready for a surprise. Angela? Steve?"

Steve nods and winks at me when BJ looks down at his folder. Sucking in his breath through his teeth, he says, "I'm ready, damn-it."

Angela grips the arms of her chair. "I'm so ready it hurts."

"Okay," BJ says, looking up from his folder, oblivious to the teasing. "These two women, you know what's really special about them?"

This is so annoying.

"What?" Angela asks, giving BJ his satisfaction.

"They're sisters," BJ announces, holding up two eight-by-tens.

We all scoot closer to look at the photos. BJ lays them on the desk and turns them around so we can get a good look. The pics capture the women from head to mid thigh. Both are wearing white T-shirts and tan khaki pants, common OSP prison attire. They're posing against a cyclone fence.

"Do you think they're twins?" BJ asks.

One has shaved the sides of her head, the auburn hair in the back long and bunched around her thick shoulders. The other has a little boy going to Sunday school haircut. But they do look enough alike to be twins.

"Not sure," Steve says to satisfy BJ.

The boss smiles. "They aren't but they could pass as twins, right? They're the Potter sisters, Corky and Arizona. Captain Love says they are freaky weird and a whole lot scary." He taps the pic on the left. "This is Arizona. Her sister calls her Ari. She's the youngest at thirty-seven. The one with the mullet is Corky, or Cork, as Arizona calls her. She's thirty-eight."

"They're carrying some extra weight on their guts and butts," I say, "but it's obvious they've been hoisting weights in the joint. Look at their massive shoulders and upper arms."

"Uh-huh, uh-huh," BJ says. "That's what Love says. Said last year Corky, this pic here, picked up a black woman in the mess hall and threw her completely over two dining tables. They were four feet square with about three feet between them. The black woman cleared both without touching them. It means this Corky woman threw her over ten feet through the air."

"Shit!" Steve says. BJ frowns at him. "Sorry, boss."

"Corky is the leader," BJ continues. "According to their records, which goes back to when they were twelve and thirteen, Corky has always been the leader."

"What kind of crimes?" Angela asks, her face grim as she touches the image of the swastika on Corky's wrist.

BJ picks up the printout his friend faxed him. "If I may summarize, the girls lived in Oakland, their first eleven years in a number of foster homes, some of them in the black community there. Both girls were raped before they were ten. Somehow they ended up in Portland in yet another foster home where Corky was raped and Arizona was forced to watch.

"When they were twelve and thirteen, they stole their foster parents' car and before they crashed it on North Williams, they tied a black kid, a Crip gangbanger, to the bumper and dragged him a couple of blocks. The Crip survived and the girls were sent to MacLaren Youth Correctional Facility for four years. And it was a rough experience for them. During their stay, they accrued several assault charges, in which most of the victims were a minority of some kind. Mostly black kids, a few Asian, and even a Sikh.

"Corky got out first when she turned eighteen and lived on the street and in crash houses until her sister was released a year later. This was around nineteen ninety-four when the white supremacist and skinhead movement started losing momentum. At least the number of charges for assaults and killings went down.

"The Potters were arrested for assault in the midnineties but didn't do any time. Then they disappeared for a few years. They're not in the system, anyway. Love says they might have been living in Idaho. But in nineteen ninety-nine, they were arrested for trying to buy an assault weapon in Salem from an undercover ATF agent. They fought the arresting cops and hurt two of them badly. One cop got a concussion and the other got his arm broken so badly he was forced to retire. Arizona gave the officer the concussion and Corky destroyed the other one's arm. Actually, she broke the arm repeatedly. It doesn't say how she did it."

"When did they get out this time?" Angela asks.

"Uh ..." BJ flips the pages. "Oh, here. Arizona got out first just before last Christmas. Apparently she lived with an acquaintance in Eugene until Corky got out in March. All they know about Arizona's acquaintance is she had been in the joint and was a member of the Aryan Brotherhood."

The Aryan Brotherhood is a white supremacist organization found in many if not all prisons. The AB, as it's often called, makes up less than one percent of the prison population but is responsible for about one in five murders in the federal system alone. I arrested one about four years ago. Had Aryan Brotherhood tattooed across his chest and AB tattooed on both sides of his neck. Resisted hard, but I finally got him under control with a knee lock that nearly broke his leg. He never showed pain, not even a furrowed brow. Just mumbled, "I give up."

I ask, "Did Love have information on this acquaintance?"

BJ shuffles his pages. "Karen Blackman. There is some irony for you. Did four years for attempted murder of a black grocery clerk. Don't know the story behind it, though. OSP intelligence says she has some kind of a connection with a man by the name of Colonel Benjamin White. His name used to be Parker but he legally changed it a few years ago. Has ties to a militia group in Montana and runs a small organization based on white power."

"I know about Benjamin White," Steve says. "He's a big man in the white supremacy movement. My money is on the sisters as the do-ers of Qasim Al-Sabti and Yolanda Simpson."

I say, "They certainly look strong enough to hang a man from a lamppost, and we got them coming out of Yolanda Simpson's apartment building."

"Guess what I just found?" BJ says, looking at the last page in his folder.

I want to say "A dinosaur egg?" but I refrain.

"What?" Angela asks, and winks at me.

"I'm looking at a list of the Potter sisters' friends in the joint. One is a Betty Tibbitts."

"Jason Tibbitts' sister?" I ask. "Mother?"

"Born in seventy-one," BJ says, looking at me. "Got to be my friend Puke's mother."

*   *   *

"Who is it?" Raspy voice, slurred, maybe drunk.

"Missus Findorff?" I say from the side of the front door. Angela stands on the other side.

No response. I knock again, harder.

"Who is it, Cranky Knocker?" This is followed by an awful hacking. Sounds like she's trapped in a smoking chimney.

"My name is Detective Reeves, Missus Findorff. We want to talk to you about Execu—er, Carl. He is your son, correct?"

We tried Puke's address a while ago but it turned out to

be a Seven Eleven. The Custody Report for Executioner, Carl Findorff, said he lived with his mother at this address.

Silence. Now shuffling feet approaching and fumbling at the door locks. The door opens a couple of inches and an awful face peers out, followed by enough cigarette smoke to make me wonder if I should call for a fire truck. I remember a partner, a guy who owned a few horses, describing a street person's face once as looking like they'd been "rode hard and put away wet." Missus Findorff's looks worse. Dead stringy grey hair, a face draped in flaky dry skin, eyes that look like they've been rolling on a sandy beach. They look me up and down.

"What?" she says in a voice rubbed raw with nicotine. "What do you want with Carl?"

I wait until she stops coughing, a dry, painful sounding hack. "We want to talk to him about a case," I say, noting even a serious washing wouldn't help her stained and cigarette burned bathrobe.

"You know where he is?" Angela asks.

"Who' there?" Missus Findorff snaps with a frown. "Who said that?" She opens the door wider but not as wide as her red eyes open when she sees Angela. "Who the gulldamn are you?" she spits. She looks at me. "She with you, cop?"

"This is Detective Clemmons, Missus Findorff. My partner."

"The hell you say," the old woman sneers, which makes her even more ugly. Her hard glare makes her face muscles twitch as if smelling something bad, something even worse than the stench coming out of her house. "I don't give a sugar damn who she is, she can just detect her black ass off my porch. I don't like colored people on my property. In fact, I don't like no colored people, no how."

Angela steps toward her and I quickly step between them, my back to my partner. "Where can we find Carl, Missus Findorff?" I ask.

"Listen you old hag," Angela says peering around my shoulder. "When I was born I was born black and now I'm grown up I'm still black. When I'm sick I'm black and when I go in the sun I'm black and when I'm cold I'm black. And when I die I'll still be black."

"What's she saying to me?" The old woman snarls, straining to stand on her tiptoes to see over my shoulder. I come up on mine to block her.

"But you, lady," Angela says, nudging me aside with her hand, "you were born pink. When you grew up you were white." The old woman's drooping eyes burn with hatred. "When you're sick you're green, when you go out in the sun you're red, when you're cold you're blue, and when you die you will turn purple. So who are you calling colored?"

The old woman backs up a step. "What is she sayin'? She don't make any sense."

"I'm not sure, Missus Findorff. But about your son." She looks at me, the hatred in her eyes almost tangible. "Is Carl here?

"He went to take a shit," she says, backing through her doorway. "And the hogs 'et him." She jerks her head toward Angela. "Now get that ... that ... off my gulldamn porch. And you too, cop." She slams the door in my face.

I turn to face Angela, raise my eyebrows, and exhale air from my puffed cheeks. "Wonder where Executioner got his beliefs? You think maybe his sweet mother laid the seed and people like Puke added the fertilizer?"

She steps off the porch. "AKA, spreading the shit." She

slides her radio off her belt. "Four Four Four, tell Seven Thir-ty-Two to clear the back."

"Seven Thirty-Two, we copy."

Almost to the car, Angela says, "Maybe someday I'll hear this kind of crap and I won't feel like ripping the person's face off." She shrugs. "But today isn't the day."

"Thanks, guys," I call to the two uniformed officers who were watching the back. They wave back and head for their car. To Angela, "You just make up the color speech?" I don't get the smile I was shooting for. I slip into the passenger seat and Angela gets behind the wheel.

"Nah, I read it somewhere. I just tweaked it a little."

"It was good, but you know it went right over her head."

"With people like her, it usually does." She pulls away from the curb. "You want to get a burger or something?"

"Sure. You buy."

"Me?"

"Yes. Whichever partner catches the most crap from a citi-zen should have to buy."

"This is logical to you?"

We get a couple of Whoppers and find a shady place to park by the Glendoveer Golf Course. I like these June days when the temperature is in the seventies and there is a light breeze fluttering the new leaves. About fifty feet away and under a tree, a brown and white rabbit munches on his lunch. There is a two-mile walking path around the outside of the park and it's a favorite strolling place for families, especially kids who love the bunnies. Glendoveer is full of wild rabbits.

I remove the buns and chomp into the meat and tomato.

"You don't eat the buns, huh?"

"Sometimes. But I don't need white bread dough clogging

my arteries." I wipe my mouth with a napkin. "Mind if I ask you a personal question, Angela?"

She looks down at her chest. "Yes, they're real."

"Wha ... what?" I sputter. "No, no, I wasn't going to—"

Angela laughs into her burger.

"Oh man."

Smirking, she chomps into her burger. "Go ahead. Ask your question."

I take a small bite and look at her. "Okay. I can only imagine comments and reactions like old lady Findorff's has been part of your career. How does it make you ... uh ..."

"Feel?" she asks tightly, looking out the windshield at the rabbit.

"Yeah, feel. I mean, I haven't known you long, but for me it's like who cares if you're black and I'm white? Like with my other black partners, I don't even see you as black. I just see you as a good detective who's good at intelligence work."

Angela chews her bite a little longer than necessary, her eyes looking straight ahead. She sips from her cup of cola and rolls an ice cube around in her mouth.

"That supposed to move me to tears?" she asks, still watching the rabbit.

"Is what supposed to?"

"What I mean is," she says, twisting toward me, her eyes sad—not mad, but sad. "Is it supposed to be some kind of a compliment you don't see me as black? It's like you're saying, 'Golly, Angela, I don't think of you as a black woman. I think of you as something better.' Well, take a long hard look because I *am* black."

"No, no, no. All I meant was—"

"What you meant was I fit so well into your white world

you don't see what I really am. You're not the first to say the 'I-don't-see-you-as-black' line, and you won't be the last ignorant white person to say it."

"Hold on. I'm not stupid. I just—"

"Didn't say you were stupid. Said you were ignorant. It's the only explanation for you saying what you did."

I drop the rest of my burger into the paper bag. "Angela ..." I look out the windshield, not sure what I'm going to say. Another white and brown rabbit appears from the brush, sniffs where the first rabbit is munching, and joins him in the feast.

"May I tell you something about me, Sam," Angela asks, her tone softer.

"Please," I say.

Her eyes mist into thought as she stuffs in the last bite of burger and washes it down with a swig of cola. She wipes her hands clean on a napkin and drops her garbage in the sack. She looks up at me.

"I'm thirty-seven years old. Until I was about twenty-six or –seven, I was confused about who I was, and the bad part, the weird part, is I didn't know I was confused. Kind of like you not knowing you're ignorant."

"Now wait—"

"If you're going to interrupt me all the time, this is going to take awhile."

I gesture for her to continue.

"I grew up "white" in Salt Lake City, Utah. There weren't any blacks in Salt Lake when I was younger so all my friends were white—all my parents' friends too. I lived there until I went to the University of Portland when I turned nineteen. There, my friends were white and I lived in a white community. I joined the PD when I was twenty-five, one of just a few black officers. My friends on and off the job were white.

"When I got my permanent patrol assignment, I worked Eight Seventy, an all white, upscale neighborhood. I did fall in love with a black man, but Darrin had grown up the same way I had. All his friends were white too, and all the guys he worked construction with were white. All our married friends were white. White, white, white.

"Before I married, I dated a couple of white guys, and after my divorce, I dated a few more. Slept with a few of them." She laughs. "Close your mouth, Sam. I know this is TMI, too much information, but if we're going to work together, I want you to know this about me."

I nod.

"But here's what struck me later when I thought back on all this. For all those years, it was like I was grey. Not black, definitely not white. It hit me like a bolt of lightening about eight years ago, a couple of years after my divorce.

"As stupid as it sounds, it struck me I needed to be black because I am. Black. It's like I looked at my hand for the first time, and went, 'Girl, you a black woman.' Understanding this wasn't going to change the world, certainly not the white world, but it definitely changed how I perceived things. Most importantly, how I perceived me.

"I know some cops see me as some radical bitch." She shrugs. "That's their perception. Personally, I don't think I am. Oh, I can be a bitch. But radical, like in a racial way? No. Sure, sometimes I like to wear African style clothing, which might intimidate some people, especially the ignorant ones. But I don't give a rip because I'm no longer trying to fit into their world so they are comfortable.

"I'm no longer grey, like I was for twenty-eight years. I'm

black and I'm still getting used to it. Sometimes it's like I'm standing outside myself, like I'm standing on the high tree limb above those rabbits, looking down and watching how I'm fitting in. Or not fitting in."

Angela looks at me for a long moment, as if trying to read how I'm taking everything she's saying. She looks back out the window.

"You asked me how does it make me feel when dumb shits say dumb shit things. I'd be lying if I said it doesn't bother me, but you might be surprised to know it doesn't bother me very much. Mostly I think how sadly ignorant they are. How some of them, like these white supremacist and, to be fair, some of the black supremacists, too, are so preoccupied with hatred. It bothers me they are wasting their lives and hurting other people because of their stupid-ass beliefs. It bothers me so much, I want to kick in their faces and give them a good reason to hate me."

I smile. "I think I understand," I say when she doesn't say anything else, "at least as much as a non-black person can. There's no way I can ever understand the black experience, and I certainly won't insult you by saying I do. But I'm glad you told me this. I think it will make us better partners."

She nods. "I think so too."

No longing, romantic overtones. Good.

She studies my face. "And while I'm 'sharing,' here, I want to clear the air about one more thing. I was woman enough to admit I had a crush on you. *Crush*, by the way. Not love. I know the difference. Since I told you, I've been going out of my way to let you know it's okay to talk about your woman, but every time I do, you act like I'm—like I'm jealous or something. You need to get over yourself, Sam. Really!"

I sputter a laugh, partly out of surprise she would accuse of me of such a thing and partly because, well, maybe I have been doing what she says.

"Okay, I hear what you're saying. Maybe I was a little bit of a jerk, but maybe you were just a little bit jealous of some other woman getting all this?"

"Shiiiit," she says, turning to look out the window, though I can see by the side of her face she's smiling. When she looks back, her face is serious. "So are we cool?"

"I'm cool," I say. "You cool?"

"I'm cool. We understand each other?"

"I do. Do you?"

"Always did," she shrugs.

"Shiiiit."

She retrieves her cell. "Let me call my phone in the office and see if our gal left a message."

A white rabbit is munching now where the two brown and white rabbits were. If this was a movie on the Oprah network, this moment would end with a black rabbit hopping into the scene to share the meal.

Angela slaps my arm and points at her cell. "Hallgerd left a message." She listens. "Sounds pissed," she says as she continues to listen to the rest of the message. Smiles. "He's there, at their apartment. Sleeping." She starts the car. "Fifty-three-o-four, Northeast Beasley. Ask dispatch for a uniform car to meet us one block south on Beasley."

"Can do," I say, picking up the mic. As I make arrangements with dispatch, Angela calls Steve on her cell.

"Hey, Steve," she says as I hang up the mic. "Yeah? Well call me Missus Norris one more time and I'll decap one of your knees. Listen, we're following a lead." She gives Steve the

address. "Two suspects. White male, first name Aaron, probably two A's. Unknown last name. I'm guessing in his early
twenties. Active white supremacist. Runs with a female who
goes by 'Hallgerd,' also early twenties." She gives Steve the
address. "That's all I got. I'll hold."

To me she says, "Hallgerd slipped and said 'Aaron.' I don't
know what it is about the name but I got about three in my
white supremacist files."

"Triple Seven will meet us a block south," I say.

"Good. Then we'll—Yes, I'm here, Steve. Super." Angela
gestures for me to write. I pull my pen and pocket notebook
from my coat. "Putting you on speaker so Sam can write it
down."

"Ready when you are, Steve," I say.

"Hey, Chuck. Okay, here we go. I'm reading this off the
screen. Last name Baker, common spelling. Born six, twenty-five, eighty-nine. Wowsa. Good thing you're going Chuck.
Get this, dude is six-foot seven, two hundred and thirty-two
pounds. No warrants. Uniform has had one contact with him
in January of this year at a mini market at Beasley and Thirty-Second. Loud argument call—female half was gone by the
time officers arrived. Baker was cooperative with officers. It's
all I got. Be safe, you guys."

"So no warrants," I say.

"Time to pull out our b.s. skills. At the least, we'll get some
good intelligence on him and this chick, Hallgerd. At the most
he'll admit to the firebombing and cross burning. Okay, there's
the uniform car." Angela pulls in behind it.

A black officer named Lawrence Kingston gets out and
steps up to Angela's window. I've heard he played football at
the University of Oregon. Looks to have gotten soft. We greet

one another and Angela fills him in. Lawrence tells us he saw Baker waiting at a bus stop up the street a couple of weeks ago but never talked to him.

"He gave me the stink eye when I was cruising by so I just figured he didn't like the po-lice. So he's like a KKK or something?"

"We think so," Angela says. In a heavy accent, she adds, "Da boy sho will be none too happy to see our black asses."

Kingston laughs. "Which apartment?"

"Fourteen C," Angela says. "You familiar with the building?"

"Very. Been there lots. It used to be a no-tell motel but someone turned it into cheap apartments. Never been to Fourteen C but I know it's on the corner of the third level. On the backside, there's a bathroom with a window a midget couldn't get through."

Angela nods. "Okay. That makes it easier. The three of us will go up and knock-n-talk. The girlfriend's snitching him off so she might be friendly. He's got no priors and no warrants. I'd like to smooth talk him into coming down to the office, but if he refuses ..." She shrugs. "We're back to square one."

"Let's do it," I say.

We quickly walk the half block to the common parking area. The lot is littered with trash, old beater cars, parts of bicycles, and battered couches and chairs. A paint chipped railing meagerly protects people on each level from toppling down to the concrete.

"Look up at the third landing," Kingston says without pointing. "Fourteen C is to the right, last apartment." An old truck is parked just below it, oxidized white, with the faded words, Jake's Laundry, on its side.

Angela leads the way across the lot to stairs covered with fast food wrappers, cups, and dented beer cans. We move quickly to the third floor, hang a left, and head down the walkway past several apartments, some with their curtains open. Occupants rush to their windows to see what is going on. Lawrence and I move to the far side of Fourteen C and Angela leans against the doorframe next to the doorknob. She raps on the door.

Silence ... footsteps ... a brush of cloth on the door. Probably someone peering out the peephole. Fumbling with the lock now ... the door opens.

"Hallgerd?" Angela asks, leaning around the door facing.

"Detective Clemmons? Oh, shit. You're black."

"Is Aaron here?"

"Yeah, but he ain't gonna like this."

Next to me, Lawrence shifts his weight from one leg to the other, making his duty belt creak. Hallgerd leans out of the doorway. Early twenties, five feet four inches, stocky, black Harley Davidson T-shirt, black work jeans, black motorcycle-type boots. She sputters a nervous laugh when she sees Lawrence.

"No white cops workin' today?"

I raise my hand. "Here."

"Where is he, Hallgerd?" Angela demands.

"Sleeping it off. He's a grizzly when he's hung over."

"He got any weapons?" I ask.

"He does. Got himself a samurai sword. A short one. Watusi, wakazuzu, some damn thing."

Wakizashi. Samurai short sword.

"Where is it now?" Angela asks.

"On the floor at the side of the bed. You wanna shoot his cheatin' ass? Go right ahead."

"We just want to talk to him," Angela says. "Ask him to

come out. With nothing in his hands."

"No offense," Hallgerd says, smirking. "If he knows your kind are out here, he ain't comin' or at least he ain't comin' out all happy like."

Angela glances at me, her face tight, eyes narrowed. She raises her eyebrows, as if to ask me how I want to play it.

"Can we come in?" I ask the young woman.

She looks at Angela. "You should of told me you was a—"

"Hallie!" Muffled voice, coming from another room. Hallgerd turns worriedly and looks into the apartment. "Who the hell you talkin' to out there?"

She nods for us to come in. Angela slips by her, smiling sweetly at the woman's hard face and scrunched nose. Lawrence gets the same look as we enter but he doesn't smile. Executioner's Mother of the Year did the same thing with her nose. It's a white supremacist thing, I guess.

The curtains are closed and only one small lamp reveals the clutter. Their decorator must be the same person who did the parking lot and stairs. Instead of a cheap painting of a lake on the wall, the young lovers have tacked up a huge red flag with a black swastika. Along side it are several framed photos. One is of Hitler addressing the troops, two are aerial shots of World War II German war planes, and a large one shows a formation of young, blond boys and girls wearing white shirts, ties, and dark pants. Hitler's Youth.

Angela decides not to depend on Hallgerd to call out her man. "Aaron," she says. "I'm Detective Clemmons. I'd like to talk with you, please."

"Who the hell are you," the voice booms, like a cannon.

"Just told you, Aaron. Detective Clemmons, Portland Police. Come out here, please. And leave your sword on the floor."

Angela pulls her coat flap back exposing her holstered Glock Nine and wraps her hand around the grip. Lawrence moves over to the side of the door, his hand on his weapon. Mine is empty so there's not much point in gripping it.

"Aaron," Hallgerd says, stepping toward the door. "There's niggers out here and they want to shoot you."

Smooth. Hallgerd just did the ol' switch-a-roo. It's classic, the female calls the police and when the police start to take action, she takes sides with her man.

"Stay back," Angela says, gripping her arm and pulling the woman away from the door.

Hallgerd slaps Angela's hand away. "Take-your-stinking-hands-off-me!" she shouts, sounding a little like Charlton Heston in *Planet of the Apes*. Now I'm coming up with movie references—maybe it's a family thing.

"That's assault," I say. "She's going with us."

"What the hell!" the voice booms a hair of a second before the door rips open.

My mouth drops as Aaron's big head barely clears the top of the door facing.

*   *   *

My first thought is if this monster is a cook at the Hilton, he must tower well over seven feet tall with his chef's hat on. And what's up with all the big people I've had to deal with since I've been back? Don't little people commit crimes anymore? Like Hallgerd, he's wearing a black Harley Davidson T-shirt and those black and white checkered pants cooks wear. Big head, hair buzzed close to his scalp, shoulders like the hood of a Dodge truck, massive gut, and legs the size of courthouse pillars. He's holding his left hand behind his back.

"Show us your hand!" I bark.

He ignores me and eyes Lawrence. "You gotta be shittin' me!" he says. "Why the hell are you stinkin' up my apartment, Neeee-groid?"

Lawrence is crouching, his hand tightening on his still-holstered Glock. "Show us your hand!" he commands.

Out of the corner of my eye, I see Angela has pushed Hallgerd against a wall and forced her arm behind her back. Aaron looks over at them dumbly, as if still not all the way awake and trying to get his brain to compute.

"Halli? What the hell? You let these niggers into our house?"

"Last time, Aaron," I say. "Show us your hand." Even if I had bullets in my gun, Lawrence is in my line of fire.

From my left, Hallgerd pushes herself away from the wall and spins on Angela. To my right, Aaron shows his hand, and the *wakizashi* he's gripping. I sense more than see Lawrence draw his weapon.

I snap the top of my foot between the big man's legs. Aaron blinks. I was hoping for more of a reaction.

"Drop the sword," Lawrence screams, aiming his gun at Aaron.

Aaron stands dumbly. He isn't pointing the blade at me or at Lawrence but rather holding it stiffly as if he isn't sure what to do next. I do, though.

Lawrence is on Aaron's left side so I step diagonally to his right, hoping the officer doesn't shoot, and drive a hard left hook into Iron Ball's lower right ribs, shoveling it deeply into his liver. It takes him a second to react, and when he does, he bends sharply to his right. Determining he's human after all,

I grab his weapon arm with both hands, yank it out straight, and slam it down against my rising knee. The tree branch-like cracking sound of his elbow joint is loud and sickening. The *wakizashi* clanks to the floor and his arm drops dead at his side.

Aaron just looks at me, his face neutral. He's probably too stupid to know a trashed elbow hurts. Or maybe he's trying to remember his favorite color. I quickly kick the weapon back into the bedroom.

Grunting and scuffling noises behind me. Before I can turn, I'm bumped hard from behind and knocked forward a few steps. I manage to stay upright and turn to see it's Hallgerd who fell against me as Angela struggles to get control of the woman's flailing arms.

Aaron is growling. I turn just in time to see him bend down to wrap his good arm around Lawrence's hips and hoist him up into the air, like a big Scot in a caber toss—except those guys use both arms. At some point, Lawrence had holstered his weapon. I start to move toward them, but again the woman slams me from behind. Annoyed now, I spin around and sweep her closest foot out from under her, palm her face, and slam her to the floor. She hits the carpet hard enough one of the framed photos of Hitler drops onto a table and scatters a deck of playing cards all over the floor.

I growl at Angela. "Keep her under control."

Lawrence, still being held upright, his feet about a foot off the floor, is yelling now and slamming his fists onto the top of the big man's head. Ignoring the blows, Aaron heads toward the open door at a half run, still looking like a big one-armed, log-throwing Scot.

Lawrence's head hits the top of the door and the officer's upper body drapes limply over the big man's shoulders. Aaron turns sharply, maybe to see where I am, a move that slams the officer's head into the door. If Lawrence wasn't knocked silly from hitting the top door facing, the second blow surely did the deed.

Aaron moves quickly out onto the walkway. "No, no, no," I shout, as the big man crosses the yard-wide walkway and launches Lawrence over the railing.

Silence. Then a hollow *whump*!

I burst out the door and commence to go nuts.

Since the big ape apparently doesn't feel pain, I work on debilitating targets. I start with a thrusting sidekick into Aaron's kneecap. When his upper body dips toward his buckling leg, I whip my world famous roundhouse shin kick into the femoral artery on the inside of his thigh. That leans him farther to the side but still he doesn't go down. Instead, he begins lurching toward me, dragging his dead leg, with his dead arm hanging from his shoulder, and making growling noises. Now I know why he hasn't gone down, he's a zombie.

I lunge toward his injured side and sweep his crippled leg just as he tentatively puts his weight on it. He falls hard, the impact sending a ripple of vibration along the suspended walkway. I take advantage of the moment to peer over the railing.

"Lawrence!" The officer has landed on the top of the old white laundry truck, about a ten-foot drop. If the vehicle hadn't been there, it would have been another ten feet or so to the pavement. He's sprawled on his back with one of his arms behind him. He squints up at me, teeth bared.

Sirens off in the distance.

"I think my arm's broke," he groans. "You get the son-of-a-bitch?"

"Gimme a sec, Lawrence. Be right back. Don't try to climb

down."

"O ..." soft groan, "kay."

I hear scuffling inside the apartment, but the sun is too bright out here, making the apartment too dark to see what's happening. Aaron is moving again, scooting on his side toward me. Man, he must be burning hate for energy. He reaches with his good arm. I push away the thought of breaking it too. That would be mean.

"Lay all the way on your belly, Aaron," I say, moving to the side of his injured arm, "and stretch your good arm out to the side."

Surprise, surprise, he doesn't do it. Instead, he reaches toward me, doing his zombie thing. I step just beyond his reach.

Sirens getting closer now.

"Come on, man. It's over." I reach down and grab his wrist with a plan to apply a joint lock but in a surprising burst of speed, he twists his arm in such a way he's able to secure my wrist and pull me toward him. He's too strong to resist so I go with his pull and drop my knee hard into his floating rib, a vulnerable spot that hates it when a two- hundred-pound guy drops all his weight into it.

Aaron lets out a loud gush of air and jackknifes his torso upward and right into my palm-heel nose strike. I don't retract my hand, but instead push his injured nose until the back of his head whacks the concrete. I lean on his face.

"You ready to cooperate, Aaron?" I ask.

He grabs my wrist with his good hand but he is too weak to push it away. "Jew mutha—"

Another twenty pounds of pressure on his damaged nose quiets him.

"I want you to roll over onto your belly. You understand?"

"He says something that sounds like a yes with groans. "I'm going to remove my hand from your nose now, but if you do anything I don't like, I will break your other elbow. Understand?"

"Yeaff."

"Roll over now." I step back and he rolls over with a lot of groaning and grimacing. Guess all his owies are starting to kick in now.

I slap a cuff on his good arm and attach the other cuff to one of the railing bars. Department rules say we can't handcuff a person to a fixed object, but the author of the rulebook isn't here trying to secure a zombie.

An ambulance and two police cars turn into the parking lot and kill their sirens.

"Up here!" I shout at the medics and officers getting out of their vehicles. "On top of the truck. It's Officer Kingston. Lawrence Kingston. He was thrown from up here. Needs a gurney." One of the ambulance guys waves an acknowledgement and opens the back of his rig to get out his equipment. "And we need a couple of officers up here."

Not wanting to barge blindly into the room, I move over to the side of the apartment door and peek in, allowing my eyes to adjust to the semidarkness.

Hallgerd is lying face down on the floor, just below the swastika flag, her wrists cuffed behind her. Angela is sitting on the young woman's big butt, sidesaddle, her elbows resting on her knees and breathing like a rhino with asthma.

"You okay?" I ask, trying to stifle a laugh. Her shirt is hanging out and her jacket is torn at the shoulder.

Angela looks up at me, blood trickling from one of her nostrils. She nods. "Lawrence?"

"Truck broke his fall but it was still quite a drop. Might

have landed on his arm too. Is your girlfriend there okay?"

Angela looks down at the back of Hallgerd's head. "You okay, bitch?"

"Fuck you, nigger Jew."

Angela looks at me. "She's fine, but she might piss blood for a while." She smiles innocently. "I don't know why."

We get Hallgerd to her feet and Angela warns her if she resists, she and I are going to rain a badass storm all over her fat butt. I like cool threats.

We apply wristlocks on her cuffed hands and walk her out the door. I tighten mine a little in anticipation of an angry outburst when she sees her man cuffed to the railing. She has one, but it's directed at him.

"Hope you get a cell with a limp-wristed faggot named Bruce, you cheatin' asshole," she shouts, punctuating it with a solid kick to his ribs with her big-biker boot.

Aaron twists hard and yanks at the railing bar he's attached to. "You called them, didn't you? You Nazi bitch!" His grimace reminds me I didn't double lock the cuff. Now each time he yanks on it, the steal gouges deeper into his flesh. Whoops.

Two uniforms I don't know step out from the stairwell and hurry toward us.

"I want the bitch arrested for kicking me," Aaron screams.

"When?" I ask. "You need a witness and I didn't see her kick you in the ribs just now. Did you, Angela?"

"With her right boot into his floating rib?" Angela asks. "Nope, didn't see it."

"Hi, guys," I say to the uniforms. "Thanks for helping. The male here might have a broken elbow, but be careful he might not know it's over. Would you run him down to Detectives? We'll meet you there. He's wearing my handcuffs, by the way."

Angela and I walk a now-compliant Hallgerd down to one of the two uniform cars and sit her in the back of one. We barely get the door closed before she lunges across the seat and slams her head into the far window. Angela jerks the door open.

"Listen, lady," she says. "Bang the door again and we'll pull you out, hogtie your feet to your handcuffs, and put you back in on your belly."

Hallgerd lowers her head. She takes a deep breath, then, just louder than a whisper, "Sorry. I'm just pissed. I can't believe how stupid I am. I've wasted so much time and love on his sorry ass."

Angela stands by the open door looking at her for a few seconds. I don't know what she sees but she gives me a 'give us a moment' gesture with her finger.

"I'm going to check on Aaron," I say, and move off to the other uniform car. When I look back, Angela is kneeling at the door opening and talking in earnest with the young woman.

I find big Aaron sitting quietly in the backseat as the two officers watch one of the medics check his elbow. "Okay," the medic says. "Make sure jail intake knows about your arm. I'm pretty sure it's broken."

"Shit," Aaron growls. He looks over the medic's shoulder at me. "Hey, he's the asshole who did it!"

"It was an accident," I say.

A white unmarked car pulls into the lot with BJ on the passenger side and a uniformed lieutenant named O'Connell driving. O'Connell has worked Southeast Precinct forever. Lawrence is one of his people.

"You and Angela get into a fight?" BJ asks through his rolled down window. Is he going to pounce on me? Lieutenant O'Connell looks at me, his face expressionless. I hate that look. Give me anger, disgust, or glee. Just don't give me expressionless.

I say, "Pretty much, BJ." I look over at O'Connell. "Lawrence Kingston is hurt pretty bad."

"Where is he?" O'Connell asks, opening his door.

I nod toward the white truck. Two medics are on their knees next to the officer, and all we can see from here is Lawrence's bent knee.

BJ lifts his eyebrows. "Better tell me what happened."

*   *   *

"You and Hallgerd going to have a little confab over a latte at Starbucks when she gets out of jail?" I ask Angela on the elevator ride up to our office. She's rubbing her shoulder. "The pain going away yet?"

"A little, just like you said it would."

"I've been around fight injuries for a long time. Like I said earlier, I think it's just a strain. Not unusual when you have to wrestle someone without benefit of a warm-up. Free tip: next time, tell the perp to wait so you can warm up before you thrash around with a biker mama. And wear sweats and a T-shirt. It's more comfy."

The elevator dings open and we step out. She turns to me. "I got more information out of Hallgerd. Her real name is Gloria Davidson. Been hanging with Aaron for about six months, more or less playing the role of a hater."

"Playing the role?"

Angela shrugs. "After you went over to check on Aaron in the other car, we just looked at each other. She was sitting there in the backseat, blood coming out of her nose, her face glazed with sweat, and her hands cuffed behind her, and me kneeling down in the doorway, my jacket sleeve torn, and me perspiring up a storm too. I don't know what it was about the moment but I saw her visibly sag into herself. It was as if a big weight had been lifted off of her."

"What do you think it was?"

"Don't know. She doesn't have an arrest record, but her parents filed fourteen runaway reports on her when she was in her teens. Lots of issues growing up, looks like. She was twenty-two when she fell in love with Aaron and became what he wanted her to be. A neo-Nazi. But getting arrested, fighting with me, seeing how close Aaron came to getting shot before you stepped in ... I think she might have had an epiphany."

"Just like that? You believed it," I say.

Angela shrugs and looks down at the floor before nodding. "Yeah," she says looking up at me, still nodding. "Maybe she's a master bullshitter but I don't think so. Something happened in the backseat just then. I could see it and feel it." She shrugs again. "Think I'm being naïve?"

"I don't think you're naïve at all. You were there. I wasn't, so I don't know. It was a great opportunity for her to rip into you, but she didn't."

"She asked how Lawrence was. If Aaron hurt him badly."

"Interesting. Maybe it's the ol' 'it's all fun and games until someone loses an eye' thing. It was fun playing the white supremacist role until reality came a calling."

"Maybe." She digs into her hip pocket and retrieves her cardkey. "I talked with an Intelligence officer in San Francisco PD a couple of weeks ago. He said out of every ten white supremacists there are two just in it for the ride, for the excitement. They either don't care about the philosophy or they're too stupid to understand it. I don't think Gloria is stupid and

I don't think she's a hard-core believer. By the way, she said she would talk to me anytime I wanted."

"Good source and a good job by you."

Angela slips the cardkey in and out of the slot. "At the risk of sounding corny and maybe even more naïve, maybe, just maybe, there's a chance to make a difference here."

"Yeah," I say, grinning and lightly punching her shoulder.

"Ow! My injured arm."

"Yipes! Look at you guys. If you two aren't Mister and Missus Norris then I don't know who is"

"Can it, Steve," Angela and I say almost simultaneously.

Steve chuckles. "You guys alright? Angela, your sleeve—"

"I know," she says, plopping down into her chair. "The city is going to get billed for my jacket."

I call down to the jail and ask how Aaron is doing. A Sergeant Baxter says the duty nurse determined Aaron had a broken arm and arrangements were being made to take him to Emanuel Hospital to have it set and casted. Baxter said there were plenty of beds in the jail today so he will likely be held, but since the victim of the Attempt Murder is a lowly police officer and it happened in Portland, he can't say for sure. It will likely be reduced to Assault on a Police Officer, but at least he will be held long enough for us to talk to him about the cross burning and whatever else he has been up to. I fill in Angela and Steve.

Angela says, "They probably won't hold Gloria long on her assault on me. But she's got to answer to her role with Aaron in the cross burning and throwing the firebomb. If she follows through with wanting to talk to me, I'd like to arrange it to happen at their apartment. We can look at all of Aaron's white supremacy paraphernalia when he's not around. If she moves out as promised, she won't care what we see."

The door buzzes and BJ walks in carrying a brown paper-wrapped package, big enough to hold a basketball.

"How are you two?" he asks.

"My big toe doesn't hurt," Angela says. "But I'll probably stub it later."

"Lieutenant O'Connell and I talked with Officer Lawrence Kingston," BJ says, setting the box down on Angela's desk. When he doesn't continue, I ask how the officer is doing. "He's got a broken arm, his left one, and a minor concussion and possibly some broken ribs. Said you disarmed the suspect just before he was going to shoot him. Good job."

When Steve starts to say something, probably a Chuck Norris comment, BJ stops him with a raised palm. He looks at Angela and then to me. "I must say I don't care for all the violence you two have been involved in, but I also understand these people are a different breed. I just pray we won't have anymore."

Well, at least he doesn't yell at us for fighting this time.

"Oh," he says, patting the package and looking at Angela. "The desk officer down at Central Precinct said a courier dropped this off a couple hours ago. Your name's on it."

"No stamps," Steve notes. "I'm thinking it's a bomb. A big one." He looks at his watch. "Oh, look, it's time for me to go downstairs, go out the front doors, and go to a Starbucks five miles away, and get a latte."

Angela stands as I move over to check the package. A courier delivered it so there's no need for stamps. It's addressed to "Angela Clemmons Police Department" in red felt pen. No street numbers or city and state. No return either.

I ask the boss, "Desk officer say if the courier mentioned a sender?"

BJ shakes his head. "Said he was on the phone so he just waved at the courier. Didn't even notice what company the kid worked for."

"Think we ought to call the bomb techs?" I ask BJ. "There's one in Dicks. Tony Merrill."

"I think it's okay," Angela says, retrieving scissors from her drawer. "I haven't pissed anyone off enough to warrant them blowing me up."

"Ooookaaaay," Steve half sings.

Angela cuts the tape from the sides of the box and pulls the brown paper away, revealing a blue and red Nike shoebox, a big one, like boots come in. She drops the paper into the trashcan at the side of her desk and begins snipping at the duct tape around the top of the box. She removes the lid, revealing several wadded clumps of newspaper stuffed tightly inside. She begins carefully removing them.

Steve says from his desk, "I never get presents. How come Angela—"

"Oh my God!" Angela shouts, snapping her hands up reflexively, flinging wads of paper into the air. She stares down into the box, her face contorted in horror.

"What?" I ask, stepping closer.

"What is ..." BJ asks. "Oh, shit!" he bellows, backing away. "Holy shit!"

Angela squeezes her clasped hands together under her chin and backs away numbly.

The black and white, shaggy haired Cocker Spaniel's head has been placed in a clear, supermarket vegetable bag and secured with a green twist. The head sits on its severed neck. Blood has pooled at the bottom of the bag. A fuzzy ear drapes over one eye, the other one is partially open, and looks up at us through the plastic.

The room is silent, except I swear I can hear everyone's heart beat. One beat, two beats, three beats.

"There's a note." Steve's voice makes us all jump. "There, next to its ear."

No one moves to pick up it up.

Finally, Angela steps forward. She turns her head to the side to look at the box with one eye, as if to see only the note and not the head. She carefully slips her hand into the box and, using just the nails of her index and middle fingers, lifts the sheet out and drops it quickly onto the desk.

Something, written on the other side in red ink shows through, the same felt pen used to address the package. Unable to do anything more, Angela steps back again, resuming her hands clasped tightly and pressed under her chin posture, her head shaking slowly, side to side.

BJ doesn't move nor does Steve. So I pick up the scissors and slip the pointy ends under the paper and flip it over.

At the top of the page, a carefully drawn swastika. Below it, and written across the center of the paper in blood-red ink and poor spelling, the words:

YOUR DOG MEAT NIGGER

CHAPTER TWELVE

Female voice. "Who is it?"

"It's me, Puke. Can I come in?"

"Were you followed?"

"No. I did like you said and then some. I zig-zagged all over the place. No one followed me."

"Remain."

Puke made sure his hood was covering his dyed hair and folded his arms. He walked to the end of the porch, peered over the side, and moved back to the door. Nice old house. Across the street, two elderly women strolled along the sidewalk, both walking wiener dogs.

God, I hate old people, Puke thought. Especially old people with little shit dogs. Worthless, all of them. Ought to be shot. A bullet cost a dime or so, right? Forty cents would eliminate all four.

The door opened behind him. Looking through the screen he didn't know if it was Corky or Arizona. He only met them a couple of times down at OSP. Twins. Dykes. Goofy hair. Their names were bullshit too.

"Come in." The woman held the door open as Puke slipped past her. "Been about a half year, right?"

"Yeah. About right." Who in the hell wears a mullet these days?

"Ari will be out in a minute."

Then this is Corky, Puke thought. She's in the blue T-shirt. Gotta remember. He looked around. Do they live here? No furniture. Nothing but a couple of big rolled-up carpets in the center of the room.

"How's your mother?" She gestured for Puke to follow her into the kitchen.

"Pissed as usual. Some nigger got in her face, but ma had to eat it 'cause she didn't want to do any more time in the hole." He chuckled. "Been in there three times in the last eighteen months. She says in one way it's a bad place but also a good place 'cause she don't have to share no space with no mud people."

Corky handed him a can of soda. "The hole sucks. Did two months in there. The ghosts and demons of all the other sad mutherfuckers who done time in it come out at night."

Puke shivered thinking what it must be like. The idea of going to prison freaked him out. Doing time in the hole would send him over the top.

"Sup, Puke?" Arizona said coming into the kitchen. Wearing a black T-shirt, Puke noted.

"Hey. Fourteen words."

"Fourteen words back at yuh," Arizona said.

All three chanted, "We must secure the existence of our people and a future for white children."

"Fourteen more," Corky said.

The two sisters chanted, "Because the beauty of the white Aryan women must not perish from the Earth."

It was all Puke could do to not laugh at these two homely bitches chanting about the beauty of white women. "Don't know that one," he lied.

"Learn it," Corky snapped. "Without white mothers the white race would soon perish. Illegals popping out five point six brown babies but whites having only two per family."

He nodded, and quipped, "And there's nothing more confusing than Father's Day over in jig town." He laughed.

"What have you been doin'?" Arizona asked, getting a soda out of the refrigerator. She ripped off the tab, drank.

Puke took a sip from his can. Room temperature. Corky picked it up off the counter. This supposed to be some kind of brain fuck or something?

"Me and Executioner thumped a couple of fags down by the river and screwed with an old nigger wino in Old Town. Cops nabbed us for the wino but they can't prove nothin'."

Corky frowned, pulled out a kitchen chair, and nodded for Puke to sit. Arizona leaned against the kitchen counter, her arms folded across her great breasts, her top hand positioned so she can sip from her can. Corky remained standing too, towering over him.

They got ugly down solid, Puke thought, but big breasts on twins can excuse a lot of faults. I wonder if there is any chance I could—

"Pull your goddamn hood off your head," Corky snapped.

What the hell? Puke thought. He started to give her a hard look but hers stopped him. He pulled off his hood, his yellowish hair bright under the bare-hanging bulb.

"You read the paper?" Arizona asked.

Puke shrugged.

Corky bent down to him. "The fags you thumped, one was a cop—a detective lieutenant."

"Oh, shit," Puke said, slumping back in the chair. "Shitshitshit."

"And you stepped in it," Corky said. "We expect heat from our activities but by hitting a cop, you have brought it down on us hot and heavy."

"You're the ones who said to do some shock and awe," Puke said defensively. "So me and Executioner did some. There was no way to tell those fags was the law. They was wearing regular clothes." He shook his head. "I didn't know cops could be queers, anyway."

Arizona's eyes narrowed and blinked several times. She glanced over at her sister then pushed away from the counter to make a wide arc around the table. Puke watched her nervously.

"You and your friend firebomb the Muslim temple?" Corky asked. Puke turned back to her.

He didn't know what she was talking about but it sounded like something he should have done. "We did," he said, nodding his head rapidly. "Got it good."

"Did you now?" Arizona asked, from behind him, her mouth close to his ear. Puke startled and turned part way around. "You guys do the cross burning too?"

"Yeah, yeah," he said quickly. "Like I said, shock and awe."

"You see the news this afternoon?" Corky asked. When Puke turned back toward her, he was startled again at how close her face was to his. "TV news? The Jew media? You see it?"

"No. I was trying to find this house." He noticed for the first time there was only the table and chairs and a refrigerator. None of the usual things found in a kitchen. "You guys live here?"

"Too bad," Corky said, as she trailed her fingers down his chest, over his belly, and between his legs. She cupped him.

Puke looked down at her hand and back up into her eyes. *What is she doing? Damn, she's scary looking. But hey, maybe they want to do something.*

"Because," Corky said, her voice just above a whisper, her

lips inches from his, her hand gently kneading, "they had one of those teasers on the TV a while ago when I was at the Seven-Eleven. You know, they give you a little and then say, 'story at five.' Want to guess what the story was?"

Puke's face was flushed, as his eyes moved from her hand up to those breasts straining her T-shirt, back down to her hand. "I ... don't know," he gulped. This was going to be awesome, so damn hot.

Arizona's hand grabbed deep into his hair roots just above his forehead and yanked his head back so his face looked wide-eyed straight up into the hanging light bulb. Before he could choke out a grunt and wonder if his neck was broken, Corky snapped her hand closed over his privates like a sprung bear trap crushing everything he held dear and near.

"Damn!" Corky laughed at how loudly the boy screamed. Still crushing his crotch, she stepped to his side to avoid getting kicked by his flailing legs. "Put your hands down on the side of the chair seat," she shouted when he reached desperately for her wrists. "Grab the seat and do not let go of it unless you want a whole lot more pain." When he did as she commanded, she mentally counted to five before relaxing her hand.

When his screams finally diminished and turned to heavy sobs, she returned to lightly kneading and petting his now aching crotch. Tears trailed down his cheeks and when he tried to look down, Arizona yanked his head back up by his dark roots.

Corky said, "You really should stay up on current affairs." Her face again close to his. "Want to know why?" She lightly tickled him now with her fingertips and brushed her breasts across his thin chest. "Because they said the police have the person in custody who is responsible for the cross burning and firebombing of the temple." She lightly kneaded him again.

"So you see, you lied to me."

"I ... I just meant—" Arizona twisted his hair in her fist and tightened down on the roots. "Owowowow. Shit! Okay."

"Sorry," Arizona said, dragging her ponderous breasts across his upturned face. "Is this better?"

Puke tried to speak but it comes out, "Mmmnuordd."

Corky's sudden crushing grip ripped him from his moment. He screamed so frantically he choked on his own spit.

"Keep holding his head back, Ari," Corky snapped at her when she nearly let go of his hair.

She did as she was told, which made Puke hack and gag, spraying spittle upward toward the harsh light. He writhed and bucked in the chair.

"Release him," Corky commanded. When Arizona obeyed, Corky simultaneously let go of his crotch. Without hesitation, the boy bent forward and vomited between his legs and onto the floor. "Oh my god," he wheezed, reaching for his groin.

"Do not let go of the seat of the chair," Corky said into his ear. "Sit back."

"Oh, oh, oh," he groaned, and tears and snot ran down his face. He started to wipe his face on his shoulder but Corky pressed her index finger under his eye.

"Sit. Still." Her whisper was like cold fog. "Look at me, Puke." When he did, she said, "You with me? You're listening now?"

He exhaled a big breath, blinked the tears out of his eyes, and nodded.

"My sister and I argued about you earlier," Corky said conversationally. "I wanted to kill you and she wanted to give you another chance."

"What?" the boy said dumbly, his mouth hanging open, his

eyes huge. Neither of the women said anything. "Why? I mean, we fucked up with the queer cop but I made it right."

"You made it right," Corky repeats.

"Yes," Puke said, looking at her and trying to twist to see Arizona. Like a child trying to please an angry parent, he said, "There's this nigger cop, a woman. She and a bunch of other cops caught me and Executioner after the wino deal. She like hurt me after I was handcuffed. The bitch." He didn't want to say she had crushed his balls too. Didn't want Corky to do it again. Why are all these chicks killing my balls, anyway? he wondered.

Corky raised her eyebrows.

"Well, she really pissed me off, you know. When they released me from jail, I seen her name on the report. Angela Clemmons. So I called the police station, asked where she worked. The Jew cop tells me she works at the big station downtown. I'm thinkin', okay cool. What was really cool is there's this neighbor by Executioner's house, an old man and he raises dogs. They're always yapping in his backyard. So I snatch one, not full grown and not a puppy. We kill it, you know, and I pack the head in a box and have one of those delivery douchebags take it to the police station." He forced a laugh.

Corky straightened. "Really? For real?"

"I did!" he practically shouted. "Put a note in too. 'You're dog meat nigger.'" He laughed again, this one more fake than the last. He looked from one sister's face to the other.

"There a way they can trace the package?" Arizona asked, massaging the back of his neck with one hand.

"No. The delivery guy didn't see me good. Had my hood up and I kept looking down. Gave him forty bucks so he didn't ask nothin'. Wore gloves when we packed the head and wrote the note. It's all good."

Arizona moved around and stood next to her sister. "Not bad. Not bad at all." She looked at Corky. "This make up for bashing the queer cop?" Her acting needed some work but it was good enough to fool Puke.

"Might have been a fluke," Corky said, as if she still wanted to kill him. "You need to do something more to show us you've got it together."

"Like what?" Puke asked, thinking these women were scarier than he didn't know what. Kinda hot, though, the way they fill out those T-shirts but still a lot scary too. Hot, scary, and nuts. Yeah, a whole lot nuts.

"Something with more bang for the buck than just pissing off a cop," Cory said. "Something to affect a lot of people. We want to terrorize the community, let them know white people aren't going to take it anymore."

"Like what?" Puke said again.

"Lot of illegals in Portland," Arizona said. "Taking all the jobs, getting welfare, even getting social security. We know an old white woman who can't get any social security but a goddamn Pedro can."

Puke nodded. He had heard about this but he can't remember what exactly. But he knew there was a lot of Mexicans all over town. He didn't like how they looked and how they all had a horde of kids hanging off them. He heard they were taking over outer Northeast.

"We need to shock and awe the Mexican community," Corky said, wrapping her arm around her sister's waist. "You follow what I'm saying? We want to show the beaners they aren't wanted here."

Puked frowned, not understanding.

"Hurt just one of them," Arizona said, stepping close to the boy, her breasts eye level, just inches from his face, "and you hurt thousands." She looked at Corky. "Right, Cork?"

"Comprendo, mi amigo?" Corky asked Puke, trailing a finger up his thigh.

"Hurt one," Puke said, his eyes moving from Arizona's jugs to Corky's finger.

"Hurt," Arizona said softly, bumping her hip against his shoulder, "with extreme prejudice." She looked at her sister.

Corky's eyes flashed. "Very good, Ari. Got it, Puke?"

* * *

"That is so horrible and sad about the dog and your partner," Mai says, as I back us out of my driveway. "She must be so angry."

I wave at my neighbor, but Bill looks away quickly, trying to look as if he didn't see me. "She freaked," I say. "Actually, we all freaked, but she was the target so she nearly went into shock. The message wasn't about the job. It was personal. Horribly, horribly personal."

"Will the police catch the person who did it?"

"Yes," I say, tight-lipped. "We think it might be two guys, both white supremacists, who Angela and I had previous dealings with."

"Where is she now?"

"Steve, a guy in the office, took her home. She'll be okay. She's tough and no stranger to racist stupidity. I think she just needs time to get her head in a better place. Might take awhile, I don't know."

"When I go to Portland State University, I saw a sign. It say 'End discrimination. Hate everybody.'"

I smile.

Mai watches some skateboarders slide on a hand railing, before saying, "When I was a teenager, about fourteen, I did not like a Korean girl who went to my school. I only talk to her maybe two times but I did not like her. Everyone hate her. People said Korean people were a, what is word, oh, cross, yes a cross between Japanese people and chimpanzee. They said a long time ago, Japanese people take a boat to Korea where there were only monkeys. They mate and make birth to Korean people."

I slow to let a truck make a wide turn at a corner. "That's awful," I say.

Mai nods. "Yes, most awful. But when you are a child you sometimes go along with your friends without thinking"

"What happened between you and the Korean girl?"

"Father hear me talk about her one time with a friend. When my friend go home, he took me to a tea cafe. When he ask why I hate this girl so much, I could not tell him why. Only she was Korean. I think he already know it was my only reason."

I chuckle. "I'm sure he did. Not much of your teenage stuff got by him, I would guess."

Mai smiles, remembering. "No, no stuff get by him. Anyway, he tell me we hate people because we do not know them, and we will never know them because of our hate for them."

"Very good."

"Yes, good as usual. Anyway, he tell, told, me to make an effort to know her. Then if I do not like her as a person, I can decide not to be around her."

"Did you make the effort?"

Mai nods. "And she became my best friend for two years before her father's business transfer the family back to Korea. We still email."

I turn into the church parking lot. "That's a great story, Mai. Sadly, hardcore racism and hate, the very things going on right now, can't be so easily settled."

"I think Father would say easy is the only way it can be settled." She shrugs sadly. "People can be stupid, no?"

"Yup. On the PD we call it job security." I turn off the key. "You ready for a workout?"

"I am! I am excited to meet your students."

"Great. Tonight, the seven o'clock class is my black belt class—my Dirty Dozen. There's Nate's car, which makes it thirteen, and with you, there'll be fourteen of us this evening."

"Dirty Fourteen," Mai laughs.

*   *   *

My students are stumbling all over themselves around Mai. All twelve of them, ten guys and two women, are greeting her warmly and shaking her hand, most of the guys holding it longer than necessary. Nate waves and smiles from the far corner where he's been shadow sparring with his war club. Everyone is wearing uniforms and belts except for Mai who is dressed in the traditional Vietnamese black satin pants and white top I saw so often in Saigon. No one wore it so well as Mai.

"This is Todd," I say to her when the big man shakes her hand. "He was Chien's babysitter while I was visiting you."

"Oh," she says with a charming tilt of her head. "Thank you so much. Chien very special cat. She want to come to class tonight but Sam say she should stay home." She looks at me pretending to be disappointed. "Maybe you can fix up a bed for her in the corner."

"Yes, Sensei," Todd says with a smirk. "I think it's a super idea."

"Good to see you again, Mai," Nate says, shaking her hand. To me, "Sensei."

"How are you, Nate?"

"Whatever you said to Liluye, well, everything has been great. Thank you."

"Glad to hear it. She struck me as a wonderful woman. Don't mess it up."

"I won't. Promise."

I call the class to order and everyone falls into three rows. The lowest-ranked student is a second-degree black. They have been with me through a myriad of ups and downs, theirs and mine, for many years. Tough, all of them, with intense fighting spirits, and several have street experience as well as full-contact fights in the ring. I wouldn't hesitate for a moment to take any one of them into the darkest of places.

I lead them through a warm-up of arm rotations, hips circles, and light leg stretching. Then, with a proud gleam in my eye, I ask, "Mai, would you like to teach something?" She's standing in the back row. "Sorry for putting you on the spot." Some of the black belts look back at her. I haven't told them of her skills.

"Oh," she says. "Yes, of course."

I gesture for her to come up front. "People, Mai studies a style called Temple of Ten Thousand Fists. It's a blending of many arts: hard karate, soft kung fu, the dynamic kicks of tae kwon do, and the grappling arts of jujitsu, and Vietnam's own style, *vovinam.*"

"Whoa," Tom says. "She's got skills too?"

"Mai," I say, gesturing Tom to come forward. "Tom just volunteered to be your victim, er, demonstration partner." Several of the other guys look disappointed.

Mai bows her head slightly, smiles. "Thank you, Tom." She looks at the class. "Temple of Ten Thousand Fists is my father's style he learn from Master Shen Lang Rui. My father teach me since I was a child. He is very excellent. I am not. The style is about, uh, it is based on speed. You know already there are many kinds of speed, like how fast you move, how fast you see, reflex speed, things like that. I will show you movement speed. I think you know this already, but I will show you how I do it. Maybe it is the same, maybe different. Tom, you attack, okay?"

"With what?" Tom says assuming an on-guard stance, feet staggered, fists on each side of his head.

Mai stands casually. "It does not matter," she says with a shrug, drawing some chuckles.

"Ooookaaaay," he says, circling his arm as if he's about to pitch a ball. He launches a medium-speed sidekick at Mai's midsection. She doesn't move as he stops it just short of hitting her.

"I'm sorry," she says gently. "Please hit as fast as you can and do not stop your blow from hitting me."

I smile to myself.

"Seriously?" Tom asks. "Same technique?"

Mai shrugs. "Something different. Sidekick is too easy."

Tom lunges in with a snapping backfist, one of his best and fastest moves. But Mai is no longer where she was when he struck. First she is beside him and then behind him, her controlled hand strikes a blur, the sound of her clothing like a flag whipping in a powerful wind. She stops abruptly, smiles at Tom's shocked look, and then pulls his foot out from under him with hers. He hits the floor so fast he's unable to slap the mat. He grunts loudly.

Gasps all around. "Shut the kitchen door!" Beth shouts

from the second row. Nate applauds. I've seen Mai move before, but I'm stunned by what she just did.

Mai helps Tom to his feet. His face is flushed and he is still a little shook. "I am sorry," she says, touching his arm. "You are okay, no?"

"Uh," Tom says, checking himself over. The class laughs. "I'm glad you controlled whatever it was you did."

"Me too," Mai says. "I do not need a homicide rap." She looks at me and tilts her head. "That how you say it, Sam?"

When the class stops laughing, Mai says, "Okay. When going fast, it is still important to be accurate. Many fighters are fast—"

"Not like you're fast," Eric says.

Mai smiles and continues, "But sometimes being too fast makes fighters not accurate. Fast and accurate is best. Tom did a backfist, a very fast one." He beams. "He is strong and fast so I do not want to try to block him because he would hurt my little girl arms." The class laughs when she bats her eyes.

Mai lifts Tom's fist up next to her head as if he's just thrown the backfist. "So I step to his side fast like this so I do not have to block, and he hit only the air. At the same time I touch his eyebrows with my fingers like this. You feel when I did it, Tom?" He nods. "To pretend a poke in his eyes. Then I fold, folded, my same arm like this, to hit his neck here with my elbow point." She touches his brachial plexus at the side of his neck. "If I do hard he would get dizzy and feel much pain. Then I unfold my elbow and scratch across his eyes when I bring my hand back to my chest. Then for fun I hook his close ankle with my foot like this, and he goes down to mat."

"It was like you hit me just once," Tom says. "But now I can feel all the places."

"Yes," Mai says, with the same enthusiasm as our father exhibits when he is teaching. "And if I use my other arm too, I can hit three more times. When you do fast, you hit six times the same as when someone else hit just once. But it is important to hit every time to a target which hurts very bad. It makes the speed more effective."

Some of the students are nodding, others are shaking their heads.

"Okay, people," I say. "Let's work on Mai's combination. Mai would you be so kind as to walk around and help them?"

Ninety minutes later I form up Sam's Dirty Dozen plus two. "Special thanks to Mai for showing us her speed concepts and to Nate for not hacking Davis to death when he demonstrated his war-club moves."

"I concur, sir," Davis says, getting a laugh.

"Lots of good ground work tonight," I say. "Adam, how's the neck after Benny's hard takedown?"

"Sorry," Benny says, meaning it.

"I'm okay, Sensei. I might have to turn my head like a robot for a couple days but I'm good to go."

"Good," I say. "Beth, the nose? Looks like it stopped bleeding."

"I'm fine, thank you. Breathing is overrated, anyway."

I shake my head a little as I walk from one end of the front row to the other. "I've said it before and I'll say it again. I couldn't ask for a better group of students. Nate, Mai, you two fit in perfectly." They smile and nod.

"Ready!" I call out. Everyone snaps to attention. "Salute!"

"Thank you for teaching us," they say in unison.

"Thanks everyone for teaching me."

From my workout bag in the corner comes the shrill call of

my cell phone.

*   *   *

"Hey, Chuck, it's Steve. Sorry to bother you at home."

Steve calling me after work can't be good. "No problem. I'm just finishing a class. What's up?"

"You gotta call Carl Findorff."

"Findorff? Who is ...? Executioner? What did he want? How did you ...?"

"I was at the office with BJ. I forgot my glasses and ... doesn't matter. What matters is I retrieved a call from Findorff and he sounded really scared. Wanted you to call him right away at this number."

He gives it to me and I type it into my cell. "Did you call Angela?"

"She's waiting for your call. When I couldn't get you, I called her. She was out getting groceries. Said she'd wait for you to call before going home. I've been trying you off and on since."

"Thanks, Steve. The boss still there?"

"Gone home. I'm in my car and heading to a restaurant to meet my wife. If you need to go out, BJ will authorize it."

"High protein, low fat, Steve."

"Thanks, Chuck."

"Everything okay, Sam?" Mai asks. She's changed back into her jeans and blue polo shirt. I'm still wearing my uniform. The last of the students wave as they head up the stairs, leaving only Nate.

"There's a possibility I might have to work a little tonight. I'm sorry."

Mai touches my arm. "I watch police shows with Father

sometimes. I know your job is crazy."

I smile and tap in Executioner's number.

"Detective Reeves?"

Ragged breathing.

"Carl? What's going on?"

"Detective." I hear hacking coughs. "Detective, I think Puke might have … I don't know … like hurt someone really bad."

"Where are you?"

"Uh, Thirty-Eighth and Belmont, I think." More coughing, hard breathing. "I'm hiding in someone's shed."

"Where is Puke now?"

"Don't know. We were in the big brick restroom at Laurelhurst Park. He … hit … when I saw what he did, I panicked. I ran."

"Hold on." I look over at Nate. "You got your cell?" I look back at mine. "Wait a minute. I think I can do this on my phone. Still learning about this thing. Carl, putting you on hold. Don't go anywhere."

Coughs. "Okay."

I go to my history and connect to Angela's number.

"Angela. Sam here."

"Did Steve call you?"

"Listen. I got Carl Findorff, Executioner, on my cell. He and Puke did something tonight in Laurelhurst Park. I don't know what yet, but Executioner ran off and is hiding somewhere around Thirty-Eighth and Belmont. Where are you?"

"Sitting at the Safeway at Thirty-Ninth and Powell. Luck have it, I got my radio. Left the office in such a state I forgot to take it off my belt. Okay it's on now."

"Listen, I'm at my school about ten minutes away. Why don't you start heading toward Belmont but don't go up against

Executioner. The good news is he called me. The bad is he's
really scared and confused right now, so who knows what he
might do. When I'm close I'll let you know and we can coordi-
nate meeting on Belmont. Ask for a uniform car to meet us at
Thirty-Seventh."

"Agreed. I'll get it going."

"Good." I pause for a moment, then, "You okay, Angela?"

"Yup," she says without hesitating. "More pissed about
what they did to the little dog."

"Okay. Call you in a few."

I get Carl back. "Carl?"

"I'm really scared, Detective Reeves. I don't know what
to—"

"What happened? Let me put you on speaker for a second."
I hand the phone to Mai, and strip off my wet T-shirt and slip
on a dry one. Might as well keep on my black uniform pants.
"Carl, you there?" I say bending toward the phone. I slip on
my shoes and gesture for Mai and Nate to lead the way up the
stairs. "Carl?"

"I ... the guy. I mean ... shit. I think Puke killed him."

I gesture for Mai to give me the phone back as we head out
into the parking lot. I take him off the speaker. It's nearly dark
now.

"What the hell happened, Carl?" I shake hands with Nate
and mouth, "Sorry, I'll see you later." Mai and I head to my
truck. "Wait a sec, Carl." I put the cell against my chest and call
over to Nate. "Can you take Mai to my house?"

"No," she says quickly. "I will go with you." The look on her
face destroys my protest.

"Okay, but you got to stay in the truck if I get out.
Understood?"

"Yes, Master."

"Mai."

"Yes, I will."

I wave at Nate, and Mai and I get into the truck. "Go ahead, Carl," I say, driving off the lot.

For a second I think he hung up, but his heavy breathing gives him away. A second later he's spitting out verbiage like a machine gun. "Puke came to my house this afternoon. Said we had to, in his words, 'fuck up a mud real bad.' He said 'do him with extreme prejudice.' I wasn't sure what he meant until I saw his baseball bat, one of those big fat ones, all wood and heavy as hell. He even brought a ball in case the cops saw us. I said I didn't want to go and he got real mad and jammed the bat in my stomach."

"Carl," I say. "You got fifty pounds on him."

"The guy was crazy. He was swinging a frigging bat. I mean, shit!"

"Sam, look out," Mai says, as I streak through a stop sign. A white Mazda blares angrily at me.

"Hold on a second, Carl." I put him on hold. "Sorry," I say to Mai as I connect with Angela. "Hey, I'm about five or six minutes away. What kind of a car you got?"

"Red Camry. I asked dispatch to have a uniform check the Laurelhurst Park and another to meet us in the lot at the medical marijuana clinic on Thirty-Seventh. Heard a car volunteer for the park but they haven't radioed arrival. I'm approaching Hawthorne now." Hawthorne is about five blocks from Belmont.

"I got a black Dodge pickup. Mai is with me. Ask the uniform car to check the north side restroom first. Okay, putting you back on hold." I get Carl back. "Carl, so you went to

Laurelhurst Park, then what?"

Mai is nodding her head. She's smart enough to pick-up on the seriousness of the situation and her martial senses are on alert. I got to admit it's kind of cool having her watch me in action. I poke the speaker again so she can hear.

"We waited under this big tree. They got trees where the limbs sort of hang all the way to the ground. Puke wanted to hide in there and wait for someone."

"For who?"

"Anyone not white would do but he wanted a Mexican. And he got one, like after only ten minutes of waiting." He pauses, before asking in a quiet, worried voice, "Am I in trouble, Detective Reeves?"

"What happened next?"

"The guy went into a brick restroom. The one on the north side. Puke made sure no one was around, then we went in. The guy ... he was taking a piss and ... damn ... I thought Puke ..." Carl's voice begins to crack, "I don't know. I thought he was just going to scare him with the bat, you know. Maybe hit his knee or something." He's sobbing now.

"What happened, Carl?" I'm on Thirty-Ninth now, a few blocks north of Belmont. "Carl? You there? Carl!"

"Yeah."

"What happened next?" Mai is chewing a nail.

Nearly inaudible, "Puke bashed him in the back of his head. Goddamn. Blood exploded ... all over the wall. I just ... I panicked," Carl says. "I split and started running. At first I didn't know what direction I was going, then I saw the service station at the corner of Thirty-Ninth and Belmont. I ran down Belmont and saw this shed down this long driveway."

"Standby, Carl," I bring up Angela. "Hey, where are you?"

"Wreck at Thirty-Ninth and Hawthorne jammed me up. I'm around it now."

"Executioner said Puke used a bat to whack a man in the head in the restroom in Laurelhurst. Don't know if he's alive or dead. Executioner was there so we need to grab him too. Have you heard any of the uniform cars arrive?"

"Yes. Six-Forty is waiting for us at the marijuana place, and Six-Fifty just arrived at the park and will check the restroom. I just turned down Belmont."

"We're at Belmont too. Okay, I see you two cars ahead in front of me."

Angela says, "Sam, Six-Fifty just came on. I'm holding the radio up to my cell so you can hear."

"Dispatch: Six-Fifty go ahead."

"Car Six-Fifty. We got a Fifty-Five in the restroom here."

"A murder," I say to Mai. She remains calm.

"It's a mess. My god. We need ... send a supervisor, detectives, Criminalistics, and at least two more cars to help us tape off the area."

I switch back to Carl. "You still in the same place, Carl?"

No response

*　　*　　*

The Reverend Billy Souls wore his usual black suit, white shirt, and red tie. With his ample midsection he looked a little like a black Santa, if Santa's white beard had a ring of yellow tobacco stain around the mouth. He had developed a powerful voice over his years as a preacher and a religious leader in the black community, and tonight it boomed throughout the Martin Luther King Center, sometimes so loudly it distorted the wall-mounted speakers. That wasn't unusual and folks often laughed when it happened, but tonight no one in the jammed-packed room was in the mood to smile, let alone laugh.

"Things are no different now than they were thirty years ago," he said into the handheld microphone, leaning over the edge of the stage and gesturing like a rapper. "No different than they used to be in places like Selma and Little Rock."

Throughout the stuffy, jammed recreation room, fliers fanned perspiring black faces and a sprinkling of white ones.

"Amen, Reverend," a splattering of voices agreed.

"Whites are still killin' black folks," boomed the reverend.

"That's right, Reverend."

Billy Souls pointed his finger at no one in particular. "I didn't know Qasim Al-Sabti ..."

"He was a good man," called a voice from the back.

"... the one whose friends called him, Ocnod. But I did know Yolanda Simpson, a proud, new mother. I counseled her many times over the years. Oh, she was a confused woman." The reverend shook his head vigorously. "Confused. A woman who made some bad choices. A beautiful black woman trying to get herself together. They are both dead—murdered. Murdered for daring to be black."

He leaned so far off the stage it looked like he might fall. "We are well into the new millennium and we shouldn't be tolerating this. When is it gonna stop? When, I ask you?" He wiped a white handkerchief across his wet forehead.

An elderly, heavyset woman sitting in the third row said in a voice trembling with rage, "Who says we toleratin'?" She stood laboriously. "I never ever tolerated having disrespect put on me, and I ain't gonna tolerate any bullshit now."

"That's right," a voice encouraged.

"Uh huh," someone standing along the right side of the

room called out. "Say it how it is, Millie."

"I agree one hundred percent," boomed a tall, middle-aged man, standing along the left side. He wore a bushy afro and a long brown overcoat. "It's time we take it to the streets and show the white devils we aren't going to take it any more."

"No," Reverend Bill Souls said raising his palms toward the crowd and vigorously shaking his head. "No fighting in the streets." He was a peaceful man, and he had organized the meeting to bring people together for strength and to have a place to talk about positive things they could do as a group. And, to prevent exactly this—violence. Too many of his people would be hurt or killed if violence erupted. "We did it twenty-five years ago. But not now."

A young mother stood, a baby sleeping in the crook of her arm. She radiated a calm strength, a dignity that quieted the room. "Then what is the way, Reverend? Will we continue bowing and scraping to the white man while he kills us off? Who will die next? My baby? Will she be the next victim?"

"My name is Sara Jean Moore," said a white woman near the front, standing and facing the crowd. "Until six months ago, I was Mrs. Lamar Moore, married to a fine black man who many of you knew." She cleared her throat and continued. "I say 'knew' because he was stabbed to death six months ago as he walked through Unthank Park. Stabbed to death by a black man who was never caught. My heart goes out to the families of Yolanda Simpson and the Middle Eastern man, but what about Lamar? Why haven't the cops caught his killer? Why wasn't there a meeting like this when he was killed?"

"I'll tell you what," a man in the third row from the front said without getting up, his arms folded across his chest. "They aren't doing anything because Lamar was black. Just another dead nigga, is how the police figure it. Wait and see what happens with these newest ones. There isn't a damn thing going to happen, it's the truth."

Half-a-dozen black gang members stood by the back door on the right side of the room. They didn't wear distinctive colors as did the generation before them, but many in the room knew of their affiliation and feared them. A short and stocky young man with the bearing of a leader spoke out. "They be harassin' us, that's what they doin'. Every damn time I turn around some po-lice be jackin' us up, searchin' us, makin' us lie on the ground, and callin' us bangers."

Four opposing gang members, also dressed nondescriptly, leaned against the opposite wall next to the other exit. The tallest one called out loudly, "'Cause you are a banger, muthafucker."

A boy next to him made an exaggerated gesture of reaching inside his jacket.

"Oh my God!" a female voice cried out.

"Gun!" A man in the front row shouted, "He's going for a gun!"

Chairs scraped, toppled over. Shouts. A scream. A dozen people scrambled toward the stage; others sat on the edge of their seats, looking about in confusion.

"All right, all right," The Reverend Billy Souls bellowed, waving his arms. "Let's everybody calm down, now. We don't want no violence." He looked around anxiously, pulling nervously at his beard. "Is Pamela Clark from Gang Mediators here?"

"Right here, Reverend," A woman waved from the back.

"Pamela, are any of your folks here?"

She nodded and pointed toward several people wearing

green windbreakers moving toward each side of the cafeteria.

"Good, good. It's important we pull together as a community," the reverend pleaded, looking pointedly at the two gangs, now engaged in animated discussion with the mediators. "Folks, we need to send a message saying we will not stand for racial violence in our city. It's important we—"

"We gonna meet up with you muthafuckers later," the short stocky leader on the right side called out to the gangbangers across the room. He and his people headed for the side door, stopped, and in unison turned to pantomime shooting a gun at the rival gang.

After they left, the other gang members snorted and forced fake laughs, and resumed talking quietly with the mediators. Tension in the room eased and worried faces returned to the reverend.

"Prejudice depends on ignorance," Billy Souls said, visibly more relaxed. "Like mushrooms, it grows and spreads quickly in the dark. It shows itself not just among the obvious, like these white supremacists, but in the white corporate world, in politics, and in housing."

"If they don't want to be around us," a middle-aged portly man said angrily from his seat. "I sure as hell don't want to be around them. I'm just sick of it."

Heads nodded.

The reverend raised his hand. "I appreciate your thoughts, Mr. Strong, but I think we need to address the specifics of what has happened over the past few days. Police Chief William Bates was supposed to be here tonight, but apparently other duties have kept him away."

"Amaaaazing surprise," a male voice said. Laughter. Heads nodding.

Reverend Billy Souls raised his hand for order. "Since no representative from the police department showed up, let us review what we know about the murders and—"

"I'm here!" Chief Bates called from the back of the room. "I'm here."

* * *

A streak blurs the corner of my right eye.

"Sam!" Mai shouts.

I hammer the brakes and my big Dodge screeches to a stop a hair width from a pedestrian who slaps his hands defensively on the hood of my truck. Our eyes meet. Recognition. He dashes off.

"Carl," I say, goosing my truck to the curb. "Which way is he going?"

"He run between those two buildings," Mai says, pointing south.

I push open my door and scoot out. "You stay here, Mai. Don't leave the truck. If you see a police car wave at them and tell them I've—"

"Sam!" Angela shouts running toward me, waving her portable radio. "Uniform is chasing a kid armed with a bat. A neighbor pulled into their garage and saw him in there hiding. Covered with blood."

"Where?"

Angela points north. "Next block over on Morrison. Same hundred block, Thirty-Seventh."

Never rains but it pours. "Have the uniform car waiting for us come here and look for Executioner. White male, twenty-one, black hoody, heading southbound—"

"They're over on Morrison looking for Puke. Must be ten

cars over there."

"Sam," Mai calls, from where she's now standing on the passenger side of the hood. "Man you tell me about before have yellow long hair, right?"

"Mai, I'll talk to you in a bit, okay? Right now I have—"

"Man who look the same, do like this." She thrusts her head forward and looks left and right. "Behind corner of building there," she says, pointing to the north side of the street. "He have something in his hand, a bat, I think. He saw you, and he go back behind the building."

"Let's go," Angela says. She turns and races toward the building.

"Stay here, Mai. Tell the officers Carl ran south." I dash off after Angela.

*   *   *

The Reverend Billy Souls stood off to the side so Chief William Bates could have center stage. The Chief had been greeted with hard glares from the audience moments earlier as he walked up the center aisle. Two television crews followed him in and quickly set up their cameras and lights along one wall, flooding the stage with brightness. Radio news reporters crouched below on the floor, arms extending tape recorders toward him.

Bates took a moment to gather his thoughts. When he began, he spoke clearly and slowly, using short, open-handed politician gestures. "I'm glad to have this opportunity to address the Black community." He paused for a moment, realizing it wasn't the best opening. He went on, "I, like you, have been saddened and angered by the tragic events of the past few days, and I—"

A female voice called out, "I want to know why you allow white supremacists to be in our city?"

"I'll tell you why," a male voice boomed from the back, "It's all part of the white man's plot to keep the niggers down."

"That's right!" chorused several people around the room.

"A ridiculous notion," Chief Bates said, his face flushing. He shrugged his shoulders slightly to unstick his shirt collar from his damp neck. "We have people working around the clock on these cases, and I can assure you the person or persons responsible will be arrested in short order."

"We don't trust the police to do the job," a man said from the front row. Heads nodded throughout the room. "They're out in our neighborhood everyday, harassing us, putting us down, whipping on us with their clubs. They're no different than Nazis."

Chief Bates tightened his lips. Before making chief two years ago, he had spent his entire career working in Southeast Portland, a large, sprawling, and primarily white community. It wasn't that he didn't like black people; it was he had never gotten comfortable speaking to a room full of them. Especially when they were angry.

"Does anyone have questions regarding the investigation?"

The Reverend Billy Souls took a step toward the chief, asking, "Chief Bates, we're wondering if there are any black officers or detectives working on the case?"

The chief brightened. "Yes, of course. In fact, one of the chief investigators on these cases is a fine, hard-working black."

*   *   *

We're in a passageway between two brick buildings, our

backs to a graffiti-covered wall, Angela in the lead. She maintains a cautious advance while giving dispatch our location and telling them we have Jason Tibbitts.

There's only about four feet between each building. The wet cement walkway is garbage strewn, dank, and smells like a blend of urine, rat dung, and sweaty bricks. It's twilight and what little sun is left does little to light the spaces between the looming walls. Above our heads a single light bulb protrudes high up on the wall. It's too weak to read the small graffiti but bright enough to expose us. Angela has pushed her jacket flap aside and is resting her hand on the grip of her Nine. My empty Glock is sitting in my dresser drawer at home. I should have it with me, but I rarely carry it off duty—yeah, sure, that's the reason.

"Is there someone's backyard on the other side of the bushes?" I whisper, looking at a six-foot high hedge at the end of the passageway about twenty feet from us.

Angela nods. "This is my old beat. Most of these businesses have these mini alleyways between them and behind them too. Homes on Morrison have grown large hedges so they don't have to look at the backs of the buildings."

"Can Puke get through them?"

"There's a lot of ways through those hedges. You thinking he's gone back through?"

A faint clunking sound from the end of the passageway.

We reflexively crouch. "Which direction?" I whisper.

"Behind this building."

I look down the passageway toward Belmont as a big truck passes by.

Angela whispers, "He might have run into a dead end. In some places, the hedges have grown between the buildings, blocking the passageway. I've seen some holly with big-ass thorns."

I say, "Ask radio to get someone to find any holes in the hedge. Tell them to look behind Coffee and Chat, I think that's what the sign out front said. Approach from Morrison and—"

A brushing noise. Cloth on brick? Angela starts to advance. I touch her shoulder and whisper, "He's got a bat. Distance is our friend." She nods.

There is no rush right now. Let Puke's brain freak him out. Even he should be able to figure out the hopelessness of his situation. He's trapped. He's got a baseball bat. We've got a gun. Cops all around.

We wait, our eyes on the hedge. One minute, two. A motorcycle passes by the opening on the Belmont end. Then another and another—the roar reverberates off the brick walls in our narrow passageway.

Blond hair at the edge of our building, orangish under this light. Now it's gone. A minute passes. Another. There's the hair again, more of it this time, the funneled air in the passageway making it dance. A bit of forehead follows, an eye. It widens in alarm.

"Freeze, asshole," Angela shouts, clearing her weapon from its holster in one smooth move. "Let's see those hands. Do it now, Puke."

The head disappears.

"Listen, Puke," I call out. "There are police officers all over. You're blocked whichever way you turn. Throw the bat out where we can see it and step out with your fingers interlaced behind your head."

Silence. One minute. Two.

Then, "Did Executioner call you?" Puke's voice is defiant,

bordering on hysteria. "Did he?"

"It's over, Puke" I say.

"Did he?"

"No," I lie. "Your bad luck. Somebody saw you. Come on. There's no need to get hurt. Drop the bat and come out."

"Executioner hit the beaner. I just went along but I didn't know he was going to do it."

"Thanks for telling us, son. This is good info. Right now, we need you to step out where we can see you. Without the bat."

Silence, then, "I picked it up. The bat I mean. After he hit him I picked it up."

"Understood. Come on out now."

"You don't believe me. I can tell."

Angela lifts her radio to her ear. The volume is on low but in the last few seconds the chatter has been heavy.

"Something going on out front," Angela says, looking back at me. "I heard 'Thirty-Seven and Belmont. One in custody.'"

"Executioner," I say. "They got him."

Over her shoulder I see a blood-splattered Puke step into the opening.

*　　*　　*

"My officers are pulling out all stops to get these despicable racists off our streets," Chief Bates told the crowd once they had calmed after his 'one of the investigators is a fine, hard-working black' comment. "They are as dedicated as I am to eradicating racial violence."

"Shiiiit!" someone hissed. "You better start with your own department."

"I have to get going. I want to thank you all for coming,"

Chief Bates said, forgetting they had invited him.

There were more questions as the chief moved quickly toward the stairs at the side of the stage, but he raised his palm and flashed a big smile. "Sorry, but I've got to get back to the station to make sure the investigation is moving along," he said, feeling like a naked man moving through a crowd of critics. As he neared the back, he stepped up his pace and passed quickly out the door without looking back.

"May I have your attention please," Reverend Billy Souls called from the stage. "Before we dismiss, let's make sure we're clear on what's happening with our march to City Hall."

"Before you get into it, Reverend Souls," a man near the front said, rising to his feet. He turned around to face the crowd. "I want to tell you all one thing, although it should be pretty obvious by all the bullshit Bates just shoveled at us. The police aren't going to bust their asses over these murders. They're as scared of these white supremacists, as the supremacists are of us. The police are sitting back right now doing absolutely nothing about this. I guarantee it."

* * *

The sickening yellow hue from the lone light bulb falls on Puke's blood-spotted face, an eerie mix of light and shadow. His head is tilted downward so his flashing, crazy eyes and toothy smile are just barely visible from under the ridge of his forehead. The black hoody and his black pants are covered with dark, wet splotches. In his right hand he's gripping the baseball bat, a particularly fat one, wooden, and smeared with blood.

"Drop the bat, Puke!" Angela barks, her gun thrust toward the young man. "Do it now!"

A thick strand of Puke's hair, wet with blood, moves stiffly in the funneled breeze. His body doesn't move and his face remains frozen in a chilling, I've-made-up-my-mind smile. Made up his mind to do what?

"Angela. Lower your weapon," I whisper from behind her shoulder. "I'll disarm him. Let me in front of you."

"What?" she says, out of the corner of her mouth, her eyes not leaving Puke. "This guy is nuts, Sam."

"I can disarm him. Lower your weapon."

"Sam, I don't think—"

"Nigger."

The ugly word whispered, though Puke's posture and facial expression don't change.

"Woof woof, nigger," he whispers.

The dog's head. It was Puke. I see the cords in Angela's neck tighten.

"I'm moving in front of you now," I say, lightly touching her back.

But before I complete my step, Puke lifts the big bat straight up over his head. But he doesn't move. His body is perfectly still except for a stiff strand of red and bleached-blond hair moving about in the breeze. A small trickle of blood rolls off the bat and over Puke's hands.

"Put it down, Puke!" Angela shouts. "Put the bat down!"

Angela's shooting arm is trembling so badly now I'm not about to step in front of her. I sidestep over to the other wall to divide his attention.

"Listen, Puke," I say. "Put the bat down. No one needs to get hurt." I take two steps forward, my shoulder brushing the brick wall, so I'm almost diagonal to him. "Don't make this worse. Lower the bat."

Puke's arms begin quivering, his chest heaving. He says

something but I can't make it out.

"Fourteen words?" Angela asks.

"Fourteen words," he growls, all teeth and flashing eyes. "We must secure the existence of our people and a future for white children." He charges toward Angela.

"Freeze, asshole!" Angela shouts, scooting backwards on the wet cement, her Glock arm extended. "Freeee—" Her feet go out from under her and she falls hard on her rear. Her gun, still in her hand, smacks against the slippery concrete. Amazingly, her finger doesn't reflexively yank the trigger.

I lunge forward to launch a kick, but my support leg slips out from under me and I go down on my right side. Dumb move trying to kick on a slippery surface. But now I'm down, and I can get some leverage. I thrust my foot forward into the side of Puke's knee just as he brings the bat down onto Angela's hip.

The impact from my kick diffuses most of the bat's energy, but it still hits her hard enough that I swear I can hear bone crack. Her Glock goes skittering along the cement, stopping a few inches from her foot. Puke is knocked into the brick wall, hitting it hard with his shoulder. He groans, and his injured knee buckles and he curls down onto his rear. He's still thinking, though, and quickly snatches Angela's gun by its barrel before she can retrieve it.

He starts to grip the weapon properly, but I quickly crabwalk the gap between us and drive my size eleven into the side of his head. He bounces off the wall again, unfortunately impacting it with his shoulder rather than with his skull as I'd hoped. Angela is fast this time and snatches the gun from his hand as if she'd practiced it a thousand times.

"Sam!" Mai's voice. I look toward the entry to the

passageway. She's running toward us. "Are you okay? Why are you lying down?"

"Stay back," I shout. "Get out of this alley, Mai."

I look back just as Puke gets to his feet, his weight on his good leg. He's bleeding profusely from where I hit him under his left eye. He lifts the bat over his head.

"Freeze, ass wipe!" A voice from the hedge-end of the building. I see a hand gripping a gun and a blue uniform-covered arm protruding around the corner. The officer enunciates, "Put. The. Bat. Down. Son."

Puke slashes the bat through the air, missing Angela only because she dropped fast onto her belly. She doesn't shoot nor does the uniformed officer. Too much danger of crossfire. Puke raises the bat again, his effort shaky.

Not enough time for me to get up, so I dive across the short space between us and grab his crotch in a vice grip developed from twenty-five years of lifting weights. I'm sprawled on my front so I can't see his face, but judging by his piercing scream I know he's feeling it.

I twist onto my side without letting off on my crushing grip to see Puke—miraculously, incredibly—eating the pain of my debilitating groin crush to hoist his bat. He's too weak and racked with pain to lift it over his head, but he still manages to get it high enough to generate deadly force.

His eyes—those evil, flashing eyes—meet mine. He's going to bash my head. I reach for his closest ankle with my other hand to yank his foot out from under—

Boom!

Time slows.

Red sprays from Puke's eye. His right one.

His head snaps back.

Falling.
Head slams onto the concrete with a nauseating thump.
Boots dance on the cement.
They stop.
The bat rests, perfectly balanced, across his chest.

CHAPTER THIRTEEN

The night is giving way to the grey of morning. I remember my father telling me a few days ago—could it be only a few days ago I was in Saigon?— how twilight was always the most dangerous time in the war—evening and morning. It was still dark enough not to see well but light enough that supplemental lighting didn't help. The streetlights on Woodstock Boulevard aren't helping much right now, and neither are the neon signs adorning the businesses along this stretch. I'm feeling a strange sense of peace. Not sure why other than maybe all the adrenaline has drained from my body.

I'm guiding my pickup along Woodstock with Mai pressed against the console and Angela thigh to thigh with her on the other side. BJ told Angela he didn't want her to drive home so I volunteered to take her. She is my partner, plus, I thought spending a little time together might be a way to come down from the shooting—a debrief might help her. But it's been a quiet ride except when I asked for her address. She spoke so low I had to ask her twice to repeat it.

In the hours after my first shooting, I didn't shut up until I fell asleep eight hours later. I spat out a sort of stream of consciousness patter, pausing just long enough to suck in some air. After my second shooting, I barely spoke at all. Well, I did have a screaming fight with my girlfriend whose idea of support was shouting, "How could you have killed him?" After she walked out on me, I mostly stared out my bedroom window. Oh, and I kicked my kitchen cabinets and smashed my wall phone. Doc

Kari my shrink says any kind of reaction to an abnormal event is considered normal. I might have pushed the boundaries of the definition just a bit.

"You have someone coming over, Angela?" I ask, my voice sounding unwelcome in the silence.

"Myrrr ..." She clears the frog out of her throat. "My friend Diane is going to take the day off work. I told her I would probably just sleep but she insisted."

"Good friend," Mai says. Out of the corner of my eye, I see Angela nod.

We ride another block and Angela asks Mai, "Someone told me you and—I forgot his name—caught the other suspect— damn, I forgot his name too."

"Executioner," I say. I try to frown at Mai to show her I don't like her having risked her safety but there's probably more pride in my face than displeasure.

"Yes," Mai says sadly. "Nate and I got him. But we lose him."

Angela squints at her trying to focus. "We?"

I say, "Apparently Nate, one of my students, had been behind us since we left the school. He saw me almost run over Executioner and then he saw me follow you between the buildings. He hooked up with Mai and the two of them went after the guy."

"He was strong and big," Mai says, but my kick make him crash into a ... what do you call ... oh, dumpster. He fall against a dumpster. When he tried to get up, Nate hit his knee with his hammer thing."

"Nate hit Executioner with his war club?" I told him not to carry that thing around.

Mai nods. "War club. Yes. When Sam and me helped Nate fight those guys at a bar, Nate hit a man's feet and knee with it and he said it 'makes others dance.' This time he hit Executioner real hard in his knee, and Nate say, 'Make man never dance again.'"

I glance over at Angela. Thankfully, she is in too much shock right now to comprehend anything Mai just said.

"When Nate hit knee, Executioner fell back against the door. It was a door to a nightclub, a bar. Later, I heard a policeman call it an 'asshole bar.' I think I know what it means. Anyway, the door was a little bit open already and Executioner fall inside. There were people there and they block us from going in to get him. I think they thought we were the police even though they look funny at Nate's Indian club. We could have kicked their asses, but we think maybe not a good idea. Sorry, I think we messed up."

I shake my head. "No, you didn't mess up at all. You made the right choice. You told the police where he went, right?"

Mai nods. "They went into the asshole club but the man was gone by then. They arrest two assholes while they look for him."

"You did fine," Angela says quietly. "Thanks for your help. You and—Nate?—you two slowed him down. The police will get Executioner. Turn left at the next block, Sam."

"Did Duvall and Miller treat you okay?" I ask, pulling to the curb in front of a large Colonial home with well-manicured shrubs and lawn.

Angela nods. "Yeah. They want me to get some sleep so my recall improves. They want to talk again, probably tomorrow. I think I remembered everything but sleep sounds so good right now."

"You'll remember more after a day or two," I say. We look at each other. "You did everything right. You saved me from getting a big dent in my head."

"Are you okay where he hit you?" Mai asks.

Angela lightly touches her hip, looks up at Mai, and nods. "He hit me twice in the same spot. It will bruise but I'm okay." She pats Mai's hand and nods her head at me. "You got yourself a good one here, Sam." Mai smiles. "But do me a favor, Mai. Don't chase down any more bad guys. It's dangerous."

"You want us to come in with you?" I ask. "Make you some soup or something?"

"I'm good, thanks. Just want to sleep. Can I call you later?"

"Of course. Call me anytime. Don't come back to work until you're ready. And don't dread your sessions with Doc Kari. She's tough but good. She'll screw your head back on right, so listen to what she says." She thanks me and opens the truck door. "Angela." She looks back at me. "Thanks again for saving my head."

* * *

"I am glad you are okay, Son," my father says, his tired eyes looking at me through my monitor. You too, Mai."

"I'm sorry Mai got involved in this," I say.

"Son, we've had this conversation before. Mai is an adult, well trained, very experienced. I trust her judgment as to when and when not to act. The samurai have a saying, 'Take arrows in your forehead, but never in your back.'"

Sometimes talking to Father is sort of like talking to the Wizard of Oz. Whoops, I got to be careful what I think because he might pick up on it.

"Too late," he says. His eyes—tired, sad, wise—study me for a few seconds before he says, "So once again you found yourself in the dragon's lair."

I wait for him to say more, maybe ask how I'm doing or what I'm thinking. Instead, he just looks at me, without expression, forcing me, as he has many times, to think.

In Saigon, we talked about the warrior life, how it chose our family and immediate friends. No one has to accept the charge, of course, but if we do, we must deal with whatever comes with the territory. I chose to be a cop and all that goes with it. The job put me into a place to save a life by taking one. A couple of months later, I took two more lives. I was doing my job but that time, I failed, and an innocent died.

A line from *Fiddler on the Roof* pops into my mind. Tevye was lamenting how his family and all the Jews in his village were struggling to scratch out a living. At one point he looked to the heavens and said to God, "Sometimes I wonder, when it gets quiet up there, if You are thinking, 'What kind of mischief can I play on my friend Tevye?'" Then later Tevye says to God, "I know, I know. We are Your chosen people. But once in a while, can't You choose someone else?"

Samuel nods. Did he just pick up on what I was thinking?

"He chose you," he says. Oh man. His ESP, or whatever it is, is turned up high tonight. "It chose you, Son. You chose it. It just happened. Whatever the case, do what you got to do to get through this most recent event and do it quickly. Things are about to turn worse there."

"What?" I say. "What do you mean?"

* * *

"Tired?"

Mai forks a big chunk of scrambled egg into her mouth. "Why do you ask, Sam? Because we have been awake all night?"

"Yes."

"Okay, then yes, I am tired."

I refill her glass with orange juice and scoot the bowl of grapes closer to her. Chien is sitting in a kitchen chair, her eyes even with the top of the table. She watches us. She doesn't meow or beg. She sits with an imperious expectation that we will share our breakfast. I give her a small piece of egg. She takes it without nipping my fingers.

I say, "I'm still wired. It's only nine a.m."

Mai sips her juice. "Would you like to meditate a little and then lie down for a while?"

I nod. "The PD will probably leave me alone this morning but they'll no doubt be calling this afternoon. They'll grill me a bit but they will zero-in on Angela. When a police officer kills someone in the line of duty, the Homicide Unit investigates it just as if it's a homicide committed by a citizen, and some."

"What does 'and some' mean?"

"Police departments, at least it's that way with Portland PD, over investigate cases where police are involved. They don't want anyone saying a shooting got whitewashed. They look at every minute detail."

"This is good, right?"

"Yes, but it's hard on the participants."

Mai sips from her glass again, looking at me over the rim. "I have to tell you something." I raise my eyebrows. "I saw it happen."

Chien looks at me. "You saw what?" Chien looks back at Mai.

"I saw you fighting the awful man. And I saw Angela shoot him."

I reach for her hand. "Oh no." Chien nuzzles our hands.

She shrugs. "I know you told me to leave the alley, and I

did. But then I peeked around the wall."

"Where were the officers who talked with you and Nate?"

"The police with uniforms talked to me first and then when they talked to Nate, I went to look for you. You told me to leave and I did, but for only a second. I was too worried. When I look again, I see the man lift the bat, and I run into the alley. Then Angela shoot and I dropped down to my knees. The police in uniforms came running in and told me to leave. When I saw you were okay, I did."

"I'm so sorry you saw it happen, Mai. I've been so selfish talking about my experience and here you witnessed the young man getting shot."

She envelops my hand in both of hers. "It was shocking but I think it was the only way. The man was evil and he was trying to bash your brains out. He was not just shoving you like a bully on a schoolyard. He was trying to do same thing to your head Gallagher does to watermelons."

I laugh, a release of nervous tension, a flash of exploding watermelons.

"He is very popular in Vietnam," she adds with a shrug.

"I think we have lots to talk about, Mai. But unless you want to do it right now, I suggest we sit first. There are several small pillows in the spare bedroom."

She leans across the table and kisses me. "Sounds like a plan, Stan. It is how you say?"

"Close. You know what the Zen policeman said to the bad guy?"

"No."

"You have the right to be silent."

"Not so funny," Mai says, standing. "I have to use the bathroom first."

"Confucius say, 'House without toilet is uncanny.'"

"Sam, stop while you are behind. Besides, I do not understand that one."

I give her one long kiss as we walk down the hallway. She branches off to the bathroom, and I head to the spare room to arrange our cushions, side by side. Chien snuggles down between them.

Silly, forced levity is better than allowing gloom to dominate our feelings. We've both been through a lot these last couple of months—shootings, fights, the deaths of friends and family—and while I hope I never get used to it ... I'm not sure how to finish my thought. I guess while watching the life ebb out of someone's eyes never gets easier, it does lose its newness. Does losing the newness make it less shocking? Maybe. Is this a good thing? It is for a cop.

My first dead-body call was a fifty-year-old, three-hundred-pound man dead on the toilet. I've read since it's not an uncommon place to die, though it's certainly an undignified one: The pants bunched around the ankles and the face scrunched up. One has to wonder if the person had only eaten more roughage.

Okay, I really need to get control of my mind. Too tired to think straight, too wired to sleep, and too philosophical for my own good, if you call my line of thought philosophical. I sit on a cushion and cross my legs, squirm my rear a little to get comfortable, and place my palms on my knees.

My next dead-body call was a man who had been eating dinner with his wife and three kids when he just keeled over face first onto his plate. My next one was a suicide, the ol' garden hose from the exhaust pipe into the car-window trick. The guy was a TV reporter on one of the local channels. After this the dead bodies just sort of stack up in my memory, so to speak. There were probably at least a hundred, maybe closer to a hundred and a quarter. Every cop gets them but my beat seemed to get the most. So did I get used to them? Yeah, I guess I did, or maybe I just got better at turning off my feelings about them.

Every violent death I've seen I remember clearly. My first was a shotgun killing—a sixteen-year-old stepson did his mother's boyfriend. The guy had been beating the boy's mother with a glass ashtray, and it wasn't the first beating. The kid retrieved the weapon and pumped a big slug through the man's heart. It stands out because it was my first homicide and when I asked one of the ambulance crew what the red thing was stuck to the bottom of my shoe, he said with a nonchalant shrug, "An aorta." I guess loose aortas no longer impressed him, or he, too, was shutting "it" off.

In the last fifteen years, I've seen violent deaths at traffic accidents, family fights, street gang drive-bys, and armed robberies. The blood and guts part of it doesn't bother me much other than to remind me how quickly the human body can be destroyed.

What bothers me the most is the tragic waste of life. A nice young woman is driving home from work and one error, by her or by another motorist, and she's gone. A snap of the fingers. An old man is sitting on his porch enjoying the evening when a half a block away, a gangbanger shoots several rounds at another gangbanger for looking at him wrong. A stray bullet travels down the street, across two lawns, past a mailbox and an oak tree, and punches right through the old man's face. Another snap of the fingers. Most homicides are a result of bad choices by everyone concerned. But cases involving the innocent always penetrate my wall.

The last two months have been the worse. Deaths executed by me, by my father, by his teacher, by my new friends in Saigon, and now by my partner. Have I gotten conditioned to them? No. Each one has taken a chunk out of me, out my heart, my mind, and my soul.

I remember this teacher I had when I was in the academy, an old detective—at least I initially thought he was old. I don't remember what class it was but I remember him. He was a nice looking guy but his face was etched with deep lines around his eyes and his mouth. I remember thinking they didn't look like age lines but something else. One day he said, "Look at my face, people." He paused while we all looked at him intently trying to appear like we were making some intelligent assessment. "I'm forty-two years old. This is what fifteen years working homicide does to you." It really threw me. Would the job cut into me the way it had cut into him? In seven years, would my face show the same traumas?

Still, here I am back on the job. Where did that come from, anyway? My mother? As a single mother she certainly did what needed to be done raising me, sticking with me even when I was an obnoxious teen. My grandfather? He was there for me—a lot, kicking my butt when it needed kicking, taking me to karate lessons three times a week, and teaching me to make thoughtful choices. When I was about fourteen or fifteen and it became obvious I was going to be above average in height and my weight lifting was beginning to show results, he said I had to decide what kind of a big guy I was going to be. Would I be a big, stupid bully, or a big, smart man who helps others? It was an easy choice. I remember thinking I would say those words to my son someday. Thank you grandfather.

Chien lifts her head to look up at the doorway. I follow

her gaze to where Mai is leaning against the door facing, arms crossed, and looking down at me. If that's not love in her eyes then I don't know what is. Am I the luckiest SOB ever? Yup-a-roo.

"This is a good space, Sam. You could put a little table here next to the wall, with a small light on it or a candle. You could add a vase with a flower or a small statue of Buddha or Jesus, or both. Make it a simple place, your place, where you begin to feel calm when you come and sit, even before you begin to meditate. I could make it for you if you like."

"I'd love it," I say, taking her hand as she sits next to me.

"Turn toward me, Sam and I will turn toward you. Knees to knees." Chien gets up and moves slightly behind Mai, her tail twitching with displeasure at being forced to move. "Put your hands on your knees, your palms up. Now reach across with your right hand and feel my pulse on my wrist with your fingers. And I will reach with my right hand to your left and find your pulse. Okay, I found it. Wow, yours is really fast, Sam."

"Gee, I wonder why?"

"Stay focused, my boy. Do you feel mine or not?" I nod. "Good. Now silently count about five of my heartbeats and I will do the same with yours. Okay, I counted. You?" I nod. "Now take a deep breath. Quietly, Sam. Do not breathe like a water buffalo. Breathe in slowly, quietly, and let it out slowly, quietly. Repeat. Good, much better. Now, this time, when you breathe in, silently count my heartbeats until you are full of air. You will probably count to seven or eight. If it is six it is okay and if it is ten, it is okay too. Hold it in for about five heartbeats, and then let your air out slowly as you count my heartbeats for another six or eight or ten. Just stop counting when all the air is out. Okay, let's try it one time without me talking.

Close your eyes, please."

I close them and straighten my back as my father taught me. I can't sit in lotus yet so I sit cross-legged. In the past even this position has cramped my legs after a few minutes, but it is different this time because our hands and knees are touching. I got to say there is something a whole lot erotic about the position. Got to stay focused, though. Got to stay focused.

After a few minutes, our breathing pattern is in sync—in, hold, out, hold. It's like I'm part of Mai, a rider on her heartbeat. But I need to stop thinking about it and just ride, ride, riiiide ... Riiii ...

"You feel relaxed now," Mai's gentle voice says on my in-breath. Then as I slowly exhale, "Your body feels loose, rested, good. Your mind is calm, as peaceful as a still, blue lake. Keep this wonderful feeling with you as we open our eyes."

Opening my eyes is a struggle at first. I just want to stay floating on my lake, drifting about as if every bone in my body were gone, taking with them all my disjointed, random, and goofy thoughts. Mai's face is the first thing I see, those incredible brown, green-specked, almond-shaped eyes smiling into mine.

"Of all the times we have sat together, this is the longest you have gone."

"Really?" I say, looking over at the nightstand and the red numbers on the digital clock. "Ten thirty? What time did we come in here?" Chien meows once from where she's moved onto the bed.

"Nine thirty-five. How do you feel?"

"Fifty-five minutes! I can't believe it. Uh, I feel good, rested."

"Still want to lie down?"

"I think so. I want to call Mark in a little while and tell him about Puke. If you'd like, we can stretch a little now, hit the shower, and then see if we need to sleep." I shake my head in disbelief. "Incredible how meditation makes me feel."

Mai and I stretch for about half an hour. I show her some of my favorites, and she shows me a few yoga poses to release my hips and lower back, places I seem to carry most of my tension. Mai's lithe, long muscles are at once breathtakingly beautiful, erotic, mesmerizing, powerful, and dangerous.

"Here is an advanced move, Sam. You can try it with me but I think it will break your spine in half if you try."

I plop onto the carpet and cross my legs. "Not an incentive for me. So let's see it, crazy woman."

Mai kills me with her smile and squats down Asian style, her butt resting against her heels.

"Wow," I say. "You're right, I can't do it, but a few days ago I saw about a ten million Vietnamese in Saigon doing it. So I'll hold my applause."

"Tough audience," she says as she leans a little to her right, lifts her left foot until only her toes are touching the floor, and extends her leg slowly out to her side until it is straight and lying on the carpet, her foot flat on the floor, toes forward in the classic sidekick position.

"Good lord!" I say. "How ... are you double jointed?"

"Do not applaud yet," she says, wiggling her hips a little to adjust herself. She presses her fingers into the carpet and gives herself a little starter push to—stand? No way. If I weren't seeing this ...

Starting at the bottom of the one-legged, deep squat, and with her other leg extended out to her side and lying on the floor, Mai begins to ascend. Her facial muscles quiver as her locked-out leg lifts a foot off the floor. Two feet. Three. She's halfway up now, her extended leg straight as an arrow. Good Lord, now she is standing all the way up, her left leg still completely extended and horizontal with the floor.

"You can applaud now," she says with only a hint of strain in her voice. She contracts her leg and sets her foot down.

In comparison, I probably look like a ninety-year-old man getting up. "I got to tell you, Mai. If you lived here and taught, you would make a killing. Hollywood would snatch you up in a quick hurry and you'd be a star."

"Brad Pitt," she says, grabbing my shirtfront and pulling me into her. "I want to make a movie with Brad Pitt. And I want him to wear a toga and to carry a spear."

*   *   *

After I push Mai down on the bed and make her forget all about Brad, we hit the shower, and lay down in my bedroom, this time to sleep. I awaken first, a little after two, and tiptoe out into the living room. I call Mark and update him on what's happening and tell him I'll let him know when Executioner is caught.

When I called him, he had been sitting at David's bedside reading his favorite Tom Clancy novel to him. I tell him I know David is listening. We say the words. We know they don't mean anything but we say the words.

While I'm thinking about it, I call Doc Kari and tell her about Nate and ask her if she could work him in and send me the bill. She said she would be happy to see him and in appreciation of his service, her's would be pro bono. Great woman. She had read about the shooting in the morning paper and asked how I was doing. I told her so far so good but I'd like to see her when this case was wrapped.

I call the Fat Dicks and find them at lunch. Richard Cary says he talked with Duvall and Miller, the two dicks who caught Angela's shooting. Miller doesn't think there will be a problem with the Grand Jury, meaning the shooting will be declared self-defense. Executioner is still on the lamb but they didn't think it would be for long since every beat car had a picture of him.

"Oh," Cary says. "FYI and a heads up. Charles Little from IA was in Detectives talking to Miller and Duvall. Don't know what about but you and Angela should make sure your story is airtight."

"No need," I snap. "It went down as we told it last night."

"Hey, Sam. Don't kill the messenger. I'm just saying, okay."

"Yeah, okay. Sorry. Let me know if you get Executioner, will you?"

"You got it, pal."

Internal Affairs. Wonderful.

*　　*　　*

"You people got a fucking snitch in your midst"

Corky knew it wasn't wise to make the colonel unhappy. Rumor has it those who have are buried somewhere on his one hundred acres up in northern Montana. Probably b.s. but even if it's only half true, it's not good.

"The only excuse we have, sir," Corky said, her voice cracking, "is the two young men proved to be unreliable. We shouldn't have trusted them. We should have done the job ourselves."

Corky and Arizona had never met Colonel Benjamin White. They learned about him in the Oregon State Prison from other white supremacists. They were told he was the top of the umbrella that covered other smaller organizations and groups. Colonel White was a wealthy man; some of his money collected from bank and armored truck robberies, and some from donations from people who wanted something done about the deplorable state of affairs in this country. One inmate told them she had worked for Colonel White for two years back in the mid-nineties, and ARM, Aryan Resistance Movement, received donations from all kinds of sources, including politicians, and some Hollywood elite. Contributions from big names were done through third-party representatives to hide their identities, but she had seen a list.

The sisters were also told Colonel White put hits on people in the joint, smuggles in white supremacist literature, and has paid for the legal defense of select prisoners. Supposedly, he paid a small stipend to prisoners who were serving time for crimes against minorities, and in return he used their names in his monthly newsletter called *ARMED Truth*. He referred to them as white victims, political prisoners condemned by the Jew media and incarcerated by a so-called legal system that placated black, Hispanic, and Southeast Asian watchdog groups.

About two years ago, Corky called in a favor from a guard and got her to mail a letter to Colonel White. In it she told him about their history—the foster homes, the sexual assaults, the attacks by blacks and Mexicans—and how when they were just teenagers, they administered some payback by dragging a black gangbanger behind their car.

A couple of weeks later, an inmate who worked in the prison's office told the sisters she overheard a discussion about a letter inquiring after the two sisters. She caught a quick look at the envelope on the desk and the return address was somewhere in Montana, from an employment service. She couldn't remember the name of the service, though she would definitely remember if it had been from the famous Colonel Benjamin White.

It had to be, Corky figured. Who else? They had never been in Montana and Colonel White was the only person they knew there. No doubt he was discreetly checking to see if the info in her letter was true. Two weeks later they received a letter from him. He said he liked the idea of two strong women in the movement. He suggested they continue their correspondence and he would send them literature about ARM.

A couple of months and around a half-dozen letters later, Benjamin White told them if they wanted to be Third Stage members they would have to prove their loyalty. He said this wasn't about raising their right hands and taking a little Girl Scout oath. It was about them demonstrating their true desires to be Valkyries for ARM.

Corky was thrilled, though she wasn't quite sure what he meant by "demonstrating." So every day out in the yard, Corky talked to Arizona about what they should do. Snapping out stiff-armed Nazi salutes wouldn't impress him, nor would drawing swastikas on their cell walls. Spreading the word about ARM to new inmates might be a way, but that wasn't much of a demonstration either. Eventually, Corky decided the best way to show their loyalty as well as their understanding of the movement would be to shank a Filipino bitch who had been giving them a lot of grief.

It went down two weeks later and a lot easier than anticipated. When two guards in the laundry room went to break up a fight between two black sluts at the far end of the huge room, Arizona, as she had been instructed, clamped one hand over the Filipino's eyes from behind and the other over her mouth. Corky drove her big fist into the small woman's solar plexus to soften her and make it easier to drag her behind one of the large washers.

With one hand still covering the Filipino's eyes, Arizona removed her hand from the gasping woman's mouth just long enough for Corky to fill it with powdered laundry detergent. As Arizona covered the bitch's mouth again so she couldn't spit it out, Corky rammed a number two pencil between the choking woman's ribs. They left her face down on the floor and quickly joined the others to watch the guards struggle with the two combative women.

The Filipino woman spent eight days in the infirmary. The sisters didn't tell anyone they were the culprits, but the investigators knew the sisters hated the woman. They were questioned twice but to no end. As with many unsolved attacks in the joint, the case worked its way to the bottom of a pile as fresher assaults came in daily.

Colonel White, through inside sources, heard about the hit and the rumor the sisters did the dirty deed. An exchange of cryptically written letters provided him with enough details to convince him of their culpability. Their next letter from him was an acceptance into ARM as Third Stage members.

Since the sisters had each spent time in the hole, six times for Corky, Colonel White was unable to influence their early release. So the women spent the last year and a half learning about white supremacy, teaching what they had learned, and talking about doing what they had to do to get to Second Stage in ARM.

"I must say I am disappointed in you two," the colonel said. "I had big plans for you."

After all they'd been through to get the Colonel's attention, this was not what Corky wanted to hear. Unconsciously she worried her forehead with her knuckles. "Please give us another chance, sir. We want desperately to prove ourselves. We've turned Portland upside down with our first two acts and we've spawned some copycats, graffiti artists, arsonists, cross burners." Her forehead was bright red under her abrasive, desperate knuckles. "We are anxious to do more."

Arizona, who had been leaning against a door facing and listening, walked over to her big sister and slipped an arm around her waist. She knew instinctively when Corky was stressed. She lifted her eyebrows to which Corky shrugged and mouthed, "He's not saying anything." Arizona frowned and buried her head into Corky's neck.

Arizona didn't have her sister's brains or a clear understanding as to what a good position in ARM meant, but she knew it was important to Corky. All their life, her big sister had guided her, kept her safe, and loved her unconditionally. Corky had always watched out for her on the streets and she watched out for her every time they did a stretch in the joint. She loved Corky in every definition of the word. She would die for her. Shit, she'd kill for her.

"I don't like the press coverage these two guys are getting," Colonel White said. "Law enforcement is looking likes heroes for killing the one named Jason 'Puke' Tibbitts. At least that kid had some guts—he bashed that spik's brains out with a bat but the other one, the one that got away—what the hell was his ... oh, yeah, news outlet called him something like Executioner. Said he was with this Puke character when he bashed the man, but didn't like what was happening and called the cops on his buddy. That makes him a traitor." The colonel's voice had been getting increasingly agitated. "There's nothing worse than a goddamn traitor. It can bring an organization down faster than nothin' else. His real name was Carl something. Here it is, Carl Findorff, aka Executioner. Has the son-of-a-bitch contacted you?"

"No, he hasn't tried to contact us," Corky said. "We've only met him twice, both times he was with Puke. Puke was the leader—he's the one we worked with. The other kid, Executioner, he was just a follower."

"Well, if he's a follower, he might very well get a hold of you." Benjamin paused, maybe to let the thought sink in. "The other one, 'Puke,'—crazy damn kids and their names—every major online newspaper is talking about what this character did, and how he died. But they're making him out to be a crazy person and that's not good. And this Executioner, the talking heads and blogs are making him out as some kind of a goddamn hero instead of the snitch that he is. Goddamn traitor turned in his own buddy. No telling who else he'll drag into this."

"I heard some of it this morning on the news," Corky said. "Sorry, sir. I didn't mean to interrupt—"

"Okay, listen up. I want you to find this character, this Executioner, do it today or do it tonight, and this is what I want you to do ..."

*   *   *

Mai and I spent all afternoon sitting on my patio, our two lounge chairs side by side, drinking tea, eating fruit, and talking. We swapped funny childhood stories, told edited versions of past romantic relationships, talked about our martial arts training, and about our feelings toward each other. The looming question is what are we going to do about our relationship.

Will Mai move here? Me to Vietnam? Neither of those options is easy to do. Not impossible, just not easy.

We talked about Mai's mother, Kim, and about our father. Mai left Saigon a day after the funeral. Thankfully, the chain of jewelry stores will run themselves for a while; their managers are well-trusted employees and friends. But decisions will have to be made about the businesses, where Samuel is going to live, and a number of other issues.

Mai looks at her watch. "It is five o'clock. We have sat here all afternoon."

"It's been great," I say.

"We have meditated, stretched, made love, slept, and chatted. Yes, I would have to say it is a great day. But now I want wine."

I laugh. "I didn't know you were a wine drinker."

"Of course. In Vietnam we have snake wine. It is some scary shit. That is how you say it, right?" I nod and laugh. "A whole snake, usually a killer cobra, is put in the bottle with rice wine. Another way is to put the, uh, what do you call it? Okay, body fluids. They put the snake's body fluids into the already-made rice wine and you drink it right away. I think these kinds were first made in China. People think they cure lots of health problems and give you energy. I think they just make you forget health problems because the wine makes you drunk."

"I hate snakes," I say. "I don't think the words 'wine' and 'snakes' should be used in the same sentence."

Mai shrugs in phony resignation. "Such a sissy boy. But we have rice wine too. Most is made in people's homes. It is sad but sometimes homemade rice wine kill people or make them blind."

"I got a bottle of California wine in the fridge. It probably sounds boring to you. No snakes in it."

"I think it sounds wonderful. And some cheese, please. I will wait here for you to bring it."

"Oh man," I say, getting up. "What I won't do for a pretty face."

"Well said, big boy." This time I didn't imagine "big."

We spend the rest of the evening doing the same thing we did all afternoon. Around eight, we both begin sinking, a result of the lost night of sleep and the Zinfandel, the first bottle and half of another. As we walk on wobbly legs down the hall to the bedroom, I'm thinking we should consummate the day. But by the time we lie down, and snuggle into a tight spoon, we're content to just enjoy the warmth of each other's body. After I shut off the lamp, we lay quietly for a several minutes before Mai says, barely loud enough for me to hear, "My mother is gone." Then sleep carries her away.

I close my eyes looking for sleep but end up watching the shooting replay on the inside of my eyelids.

Blood spraying from Puke's eye.

Head snapping back.

Falling.

Boots dancing on the cement.

The bat perfectly balanced on his chest.

CHAPTER FOURTEEN

"Who is it?" The voice sounded more drunk than sleepy. "You know what time it is, Mr. or Mrs. Cranky Knocker?"

Corky leaned close to the door and affected a polite, little girl voice. "Sorry. It's kind of an emergency. I'm looking for Ex ... uh, Carl. I know it's late. But I heard he might be here."

The door opened just enough for a face to peer out, a face of an old woman with dead, grey hair, flaking skin, and eyes that looked as if every blood vessel had been broken. The eyes moved up and down Corky. "Who ... What do you want with Carl, Miss Cranky Knocker?"

Corky put on a worried face as she looked at Mrs. Hall from under the pretty pink scarf covering her strange hairstyle. A shabby sports coat over a white T-shirt and baggy work jeans completed her ensemble.

"I'm sorry to bother you, ma'am. A friend of Carl's has been hurt and I wanted to tell him." She batted her eyes at Mrs. Hall, thinking this would be easy with this dried-up old drunk. "Could I speak with him? I'm really sorry it's so late."

The old woman jerked forward into a chest-rattling cough. If she had had any suspicions about Corky, they were quickly forgotten as she hacked phlegm into her palm.

"Got a cold or somethin'?" Corky asked, struggling to contain a laugh.

Mrs. Hall nodded, coughing even harder. She jerked her thumb toward the side of the house, sputtering, "The little shit sleeps in the garage." She pushed the door shut. They could still hear her hacking on the other side.

Corky grinned. "Fuck you very much, you dying old hag," she mumbled.

"You oughta get an academy award, Cork," Arizona whispered, as she stepped out from around the corner. She held a six-foot-long wooden plank.

"Hear what she said, Ari?" Corky pulled off her scarf and jumped down from the porch. "He's in the garage."

"The perfect caper, huh Cork?" Arizona asked, leading the way around the corner of the house. "The old frog is so out of it she'll never remember you and she never saw me."

Inside the one-car garage, a hanging light bulb flickered and cast a gloomy light over stacks of old papers, magazines, boxes, bottles, paint cans, and other unidentifiable junk. Executioner lay on an old mattress in a corner, shivering in spite of the warm night and the three soiled blankets covering him. A burning cigarette leaned against the side of an overflowing ashtray.

He was scared shitless. He couldn't get the image of the Mexican's exploding head out of his mind and the look on Puke's face as he cocked the bat back to bash the man again. The guy had to be dead. He just had to be. There was so much blood all over the wall. He didn't wait to find out. He split before the bat hit its target again.

He shivered again and pulled the blankets over his head. The police would be looking for them, and he'd be accused of murder along with Puke. Especially since he got away from the cops behind the nightclub. "I should have given myself up. I'm not a murderer," Executioner said into his blankets. The image of the exploding head flashed across his mind again. He shook his head. "What have I got myself into?"

He heard the familiar squeak of the little garage door. "Ma?" he said, pulling the blankets off his face. "Ma, are you ... Oh noooo ..."

"Hi, Judas," Corky said, as she and her sister stomped quickly toward him. "Ready for some pain?"

Executioner rose up on one elbow. His long black hair stuck out every which way. "Wait. What are you two doing—?"

Corky stomped her big oxblood boot onto his stomach.

"Ooooh!" he bellowed, jackknifing so hard he sat all the way up. Then Arizona kicked his ribs, knocking him onto his side.

"MyGodmyGodmyGod," he groaned curling into a ball and covering his head with one hand and trying to protect his ribs with his other. "Please," he managed to grunt, but the kicks came like a rainstorm, starting with a few heavy drops, and then a thunderous downpour.

Corky smiled as she watched her beautiful baby sister kick Executioner's chest, legs, arms, and neck. After a moment, Corky's lips parted a little and her breathing became ragged.

*   *   *

It's three a.m. and I'm looking out the bedroom window, my forehead against the cool pane. Looks like fog creeping under the streetlight and around the porch light on the house across the street. Unusual for summer.

I finally stopped seeing the movie on the insides of my eyelids but still sleep wouldn't come. I even sat on the edge of the bed and meditated. It relaxed me but it didn't help me fall asleep. I saw an interview on the tube a while back with a doctor who specialized in sleep issues. When asked why we need to sleep at all, he said science is still trying to figure it out. As illogical as it sounds, he said, the only reason the boys and girls in lab coats can determine we need sleep is because—we get sleepy. They probably got a ten-million-dollar federal grant to come to such an insightful conclusion.

I sigh, which fogs the window for a moment. Fog outside and now fog inside. I close my eyes and like a movie on super-fast forward, all the violence of the last few months plays on my mental screen: the second shooting in the bedroom; the sniper at Portland State; the fight on the skywalk; Mai's fight in the Saigon tea café; the horrific fight in the warehouse; the claustrophobic fight in the dirt tunnel; and the crazy blur of a fight in the alley outside of my father's house. I keep thinking all that violence is behind me but it keeps coming.

I remember Father talking in Saigon about a quiet fishing village along the coast where he and Kim planned to move when they retired. It was a beautiful place, he said, peaceful in spirit, and with good food and good people. I wonder if he will go there now without Kim?

"I'd like to go there." Whoops, I said it out loud.

"Where?" Mai says, scooting across the bed. I turn and she slips into my arms, her lithe body warm, comforting. She wiggles her face into my neck, kisses it, and settles in as if she plans to sleep there. "Where do you want to go, my love?"

"The fishing village Father and your mother wanted to retire to. I don't remember its name."

"*Châu Đốc.*" She hugs me tightly. "Oh, Sam."

I know she is thinking about her mother. I hold her until her shaking body stills. Eventually, she leans back and looks at me.

"Why are you standing here? It is in the middle of the night."

I shrug and smile a little. I turn her to the dark window. "I do my best thinking looking out this window." I shrug again. "I do my worst too."

"It is a good place," she says, wiping her hand on the glass, only to discover the fog is outside. After a long moment, she asks, "Do you think it is over? This ugly violence?"

I shake my head, unclear to myself if I mean no or I don't know. "All we got is one stupid young man. His friend is still out there. And there are the people, maybe two sisters, who killed a man and a woman." I blow a little hot air onto the glass and draw a heart in the fog. It gets the reaction I hoped it would. Mai kisses me. " For now, let's just say it's over."

"Okay," she says.

I move us toward the bed. "I think I can sleep now. Your hug relaxed me."

I spoon into the warmth and contours of her back, my arm draped over her waist, and my mind slips into sleep.

*   *   *

Rain or shine, Edna and Malcolm Washington always took their mile walk at 6:30 in the morning. They would get up, dress for the weather, and head out the door. They had followed the routine for the last eighteen years since Malcolm had retired.

Thirty-five years ago, they were the first black family to move into the Southeast Portland neighborhood, but now there were lots of black folks there. It wouldn't have made much difference to them if the neighborhood had remained all white because they liked people no matter what their color. "Life's just too short to worry about the small stuff," Malcolm always said. And racism was just being small.

When they would reach the library on Cesar Chavez Boulevard, they would turn around and walk back down to Thirty-Seventh past the school. Two blocks short of their home, they always stopped at the Mini Mart to buy a newspaper, two cups of hot chocolate, and one pastry to share while they stood outside at the corner of the store to watch the interesting people walk by.

"I love this fog, Eddie," Malcolm said squinting over the hot chocolate's steam as he sipped. It was nearly summertime, but a weather front had brought fall fog the last few mornings. In fact, it almost felt like October, and the two were bundled in heavy wool overcoats, Edna with a pink stocking cap pulled over her head, Malcolm with a blue one.

"I know you do, I know you do," Edna said with mock disgust. She hated the cool weather. "I hope you're getting your fill." She took a bite of the pastry.

Malcolm chuckled at her, and nodded a greeting to a beer delivery man pushing a hand truck stacked high with cases of empty beer bottles out the front door. "It's the romantic side of me, Eddie," Malcolm said, and chuckled again as she shook her head with feigned disgust and waved him off with a gloved hand. They watched the beer man stack the cases of bottles in the back of his truck, then climb into his cab, grind the gears, and accelerate noisily away.

For the first time since they had been standing outside the store, the parking lot was empty. At the same time, the traffic signal a quarter block away held back a string of early commuters for a moment, and it was so quiet Edna and Malcolm could hear themselves sip their chocolate.

Then they heard something else.

"What was that?" Malcolm asked, lifting his head from his cup.

"I heard it too, Malcolm," she said, looking toward the corner of the market. "It sounded like it came from around the corner or out back, maybe."

He stepped off the sidewalk and looked down the side of the store, seeing the usual stack of empty cardboard boxes and a graffiti-covered green dumpster.

Edna peered nervously around her husband. "It sounded like something in pain, an animal or ... Oh sweet Lord. You don't think ...?"

"Hush up, Eddie. I can't hear." Malcolm began moving slowly along the side of the building. He still held his newspaper in one hand, his hot chocolate in his other. "There ... there it is again."

"I heard it too," Edna said, her voice quivering. She stayed right on her husband's heels, one hand on his shoulder, the other sloshing her drink. They crept with soft steps past the boxes and past the dumpster.

"There," Edna whispered. "Sweet Lord! It sounds like a person hurt, Malcolm."

He peered cautiously around the corner, seeing another dumpster, more boxes and an old, rusted yellow Ford, its trunk open and full of bottles. He took a breath for courage and stepped away from the corner, feeling exposed and a whole lot vulnerable. With Edna still holding onto him from behind, he moved along the backside of the market, partially bent, setting each step carefully in front of the other.

"Oh!" he exhaled, dropping his newspaper and slopping hot chocolate onto his fingers. "There! Do you see it, Eddie?" he whispered, ignoring the burning liquid.

"What? Oh sweet Lord! Oh my. Oh my."

It was a bare foot, human, toes up, sticking out from the far side of the dumpster.

The big toe moved.

There was the sound again, louder now, and clearly a moan. Crouched even lower, Malcolm took a careful step forward, his face scrunched in concentration. A second foot revealed itself to them, wet from the fog, white as chalk. Not just Caucasian white, Malcolm thought. Bloodless white.

He dropped his cup and moved quickly toward the dumpster; Edna stood fast. "What is it, Malcolm?" she asked. "Malcolm? What is it?"

He didn't answer.

"Malcolm?"

He inched around the corner of the dumpster. He saw the shins now, white thighs covered with goosebumps, the penis, the stomach. There was blood on the chest, and the chest, so muscular, was moving, breathing.

Malcolm's own chest heaved. He couldn't see the man's head because of a big bucket in the way. He stepped to the side.

It was a young man's face, swollen, bloody. A purple knot the size of a golf ball covered one eye socket. Coagulated blood pooled below one ear. The man's head rested on a plank of wood, his long black hair matted with blood and spread out on the asphalt. His arms—they were big arms, muscular, and they were stretched out, right and left on the plank.

It took a moment for Malcolm's brain to register what his eyes were sending, a sight so horrible, so ...

Nails. Long black nails penetrated through the hands and into the board.

"Sweet Holy Mother," Malcolm choked out, barely audible. Then louder, "What have they done to you, son? What have they done?"

Edna, still frozen in place behind the dumpster, dropped her chocolate at the sound of her husband's exclamation. "What is it, Malcolm? What is it?"

CHAPTER FIFTEEN

"Hi, Sam," Charles Little says, his mouth smiling but his eyes as serious as a heart attack. He is in his forties, chubby, fleshy faced, thinning blond hair, wearing a blue pinstriped power suit, no doubt on purpose, something they learn in interrogation school.

I nod, and open the front door wider to let him in. He called around nine this morning and asked if he could swing by for a few minutes. "Nothing formal," he said. "Just a chat," repeating the infamous three-word Internal Affairs' calling card. There is never a "just" when it comes to IA. "This is my friend Mai." I say.

Little extends his hand, smiles. "Nice to meet you, Mai." For once a male doesn't eye her up and down.

"Nice to meet you," she says.

"Oh, what a charming accent," Little says. "Southeast Asian, I'm guessing. Thailand? Vietnam? Cambodia?"

"Very good. Vietnam."

"My favorite. I've been to all three. Vietnam is so beautiful. Hard to believe the Vietnam War ever happened."

Mai nods. "We call it the American War."

"Oh," Little says, starting to smile but then stopping, not sure if Mai is joking. "Of course. So glad those dark years are over."

Mai sits on the end of the sofa. "For some it is still not over, eh? For some Americans and for some Vietnamese."

Little nods thoughtfully. "Mm, right, right." He looks at

me. "May we have a brief chat? Mai, no problem if you'd like to sit in."

I gesture toward the leather loveseat. When he turns away to sit, Mai winks at me. Her comment about the war just took his power away for a moment and made him uncomfortable. My woman is so smart. And I'm not offering him tea or coffee, either. I sit next to her.

Little sits formally, opens the attaché case between his legs, and extracts a yellow legal pad. "The Chief's Office has asked our office to look at the elements surrounding the shooting at Southeast Thirty-Seventh and Belmont, in which you and Detective Angela Clemmons pursued one Jason Tibbitts between two buildings, subsequently confronting him at which time he presented a bat and attempted to strike one or both of you."

"Did strike, Little," I correct. "He *did* strike Angela with it twice and was about to strike me."

Little clears his throat, jotting a note. "Of course. Did strike. Sorry. To continue, at which point Detective Clemmons unholstered her sidearm and fatally shot Mister Tibbitts."

I don't nod or say anything. I shouldn't be rude to Little since he is just doing his job. Few detectives want to work Internal Affairs, which is why it's a mandatory rotation. Some get off on the power while most hate the twelve months or longer assignment. I don't know Charles Little well, but he seems like a decent guy, though a little button-downed, like he should be wearing a bowtie with his white shirt. He's okay; I just resent what he represents.

Little continues. "My understanding is both you and Detective Clemmons were off duty at the time of the incident."

"We were," I say, deciding not to be so hard on him.

"I wonder if you might tell me of the circumstances leading up to the shooting? How you learned of the whereabouts of Mister Tibbitts and of one Carl Findorff. Mai, I believe you had contact with Mister Findorff."

She looks at me, not sure if she should say anything.

I interrupt and tell Little of Angela's and my first contact with Puke and Executioner on Burnside Street, the clash BJ and I had with Puke in the Detective's holding room, my assessment of Executioner and my giving him my card, and about how he called me after fleeing the restroom in Laurelhurst Park. I explain to Little that Mai and I were at my martial arts school, and I contacted Angela and told her Executioner had just called and told me he was with Puke when he struck a man in the head with the bat. Angela and I decided to meet Executioner where he was hiding behind a building on Southeast Belmont. Then I explained with a little more detail than Little had presented as to how the shooting went down.

"Thank you, Sam," he says, scribbling madly for a moment. "Now did either of you call for uniform support?"

"Yes, Angela asked for a uniform car to meet us at Thirty-Seventh. Then shortly before we got there, Puke, er, Jason Tibbitts, was seen in the area by a citizen, and shortly thereafter, the blocks, especially Morrison, were saturated with uniform cars."

"Very good," Little says, making a note. "One more thing. According to your reports, there was a time lag of a few minutes as you waited in the passageway. You knew Mister Tibbitts was just around the corner of a building and you ordered him to step out, which he subsequently did, which led to the shooting."

I'm not sure where he's going with this so I don't say anything.

"There are no records at Dispatch indicating either of you called for backup while in the passageway. Did anyone ask for it?"

Little has done his homework. "I don't believe so," I say. "The situation was quite tense and I don't remember if dispatch was advised once we got into the passageway."

"I see. Might Detective Clemmons have asked for backup without you knowing? I believe she was the only one with a radio."

"If she did, I don't recall. Like I said, the scene was quite tense."

I honestly don't remember, though I'm thinking she didn't. Actually, I didn't give it a thought at the time.

"Did at anytime you two discuss or mention there were uniformed officers in the backyard of a residence in your line of fire?"

Shit. "Uh, I don't recall if we did. Like I said, the situation was tense."

"There is no mention of you drawing your weapon, Sam."

"I didn't have it with me. I was at my school when my informant called me." There is no rule saying off-duty officers have to pack their weapons. Of course, I haven't been carrying one on duty either.

Little doesn't say anything as he writes quickly. "Now, why did you take Mai with you on a police matter?"

Double shit. "Time seemed of the essence," I say, feebly. "Of course, I didn't know the situation was going to deteriorate as it did."

He writes. Then, "Mai, may I ask you a question?"

She looks at me and I give her a yes with my eyes. "Yes," she says.

"Thank you. Just one. Had you and this Nate ... I'm sorry. I can't begin to pronounce his name." When I don't help him, he asks, "Did you and Nate plan ahead to attempt to capture this Carl Findorff?"

Mai shakes her head. "Sam and I did not know Nate was behind us. When I saw Nate go after the young man, I go to help."

"I see. Well, thank you for jumping in. But understand we always caution citizens not to get involved in situations where there is a potential for violence. I'm glad neither of you were hurt."

"Thank you," she says.

Little scribbles something and looks up. "Thanks so much, Sam, Mai. These are all the preliminary questions I have. I won't take anymore of your time."

I know he can't tell me anything but I ask anyway. "So are we going to be shot at sunup?"

He smiles. "It's up to the Chief's Office, Sam." He looks at me for a moment. I can almost hear his brain: Should I?— Shouldn't I? "May I speak in confidence?"

"Of course." This is weird. It's not like we're friends. I've never worked around him and I've barely spoken to him.

"Thank you. I've always admired you, Sam. I did some tae-kwondo when I was younger and many pounds lighter, and I have more or less followed the sport, though I don't prac-tice anymore. I followed your competition years and saw you fight once, a Korean guy, forgot his name. You owned him," he laughs. "I also liked how you taught defensive tactics when I was a recruit. You probably don't remember me, but I really respected your humane approach to dealing with combat-ive people. I hate the macho attitude some instructors have.

Also, I hated how the media treated you after your shooting in the hostage situation. Anyway, between you and me, I don't think you and Detective Clemmons are in too much hot water. Maybe a letter of reprimand in your file about violating policy."

Okay, now I feel like pond scum for how I've been treating him. "Thanks, Charles, for your kind words and for your thoughts."

"Sure," he says with a smile. "Plus, according to the paper this morning, the public is applauding what happened to this Tibbitts character. He was a white supremacist, and in light of the series of racial murders we've been having, you and Detective Clemmons might get statues of yourselves over in dark town."

Ouch. I'm not about to comment.

After we see him off at the door, Mai says, "Wow, I think he have a man crush on you."

My cell rings.

"Hey, Sam. Rudy here. Just wanted to check to see how you're doin'."

My cabbie friend's voice always cheers me up. "Doing okay. Seems crap has a way of flowing in my direction."

"For sure, brother. But unless I misread you, and I never misread anyone, you can handle it."

"Thanks for the confidence. How's the diet?"

"Four pounds.

"Excellent, Rudy."

"Not really. I put four pounds on. The wife is madder than a kicked chicken."

I laugh hard. "My gal is here from Saigon. Like you to meet her before she goes back."

"I'd be honored. Maybe in a couple days when you've chilled

some? Hey, you know what? How 'bout you two come to my house for dinner. Meet my biscuit burner."

"Sounds great, Rudy. Thanks for calling and, well, cheering me up."

"Take care, my friend. Call you in a couple of days to set it up."

I walk into the kitchen where Mai has made us some tea. "We got a dinner invitation. Don't know exactly when yet but probably this weekend."

"Fun," Mai says.

"I met him at the airport last week. We clicked right away. He's one of those guys who makes you feel good about being alive."

"He sounds nice."

"The magic of friendship, huh? I saw this poster the other day and it kind of describes Rudy. It was something like, 'People rarely remember what was said, but they always remember how you made them feel.' Fits Rudy perfectly."

"I like it," Mai says, setting our steaming cups on the table. "I think that about you. I cannot remember anything you say but I like how you make me feel. You are a good, uh, feeler."

"Cool. It works out because I like feeling you and—"

My cell rings.

"Sam. BJ here. How are you?" Subdued tone and faux concern.

"Hi, boss. Doing okay. I'm just worried about Angela. You talk with her?"

"I have. It's starting to hit her, I think. She knows it was a good shoot, though you two did a lot of things wrong. IA call you?"

Did a lot of things wrong. Now for the real reason he's calling.

"Came by actually. Took a statement from me and asked Mai a couple questions." I'm not going to mention IA thinks the investigation won't go too far.

"I see." Still not getting a read on his expressionless voice. "Well, Sam. You should know I asked IA to investigate."

"You what?" There is no way I just heard what I just heard.

"There were a lot of wrongs. I want this investigated by IA so the Chief's Office has all the facts."

"Do you think Angela and I were lying, BJ?"

"I didn't say that."

My face flushes hot. "I hear you're good at being an administrator," I snap, "and I understand you don't have a lot of street experience. But you do know police work outside of an office cubicle is often chaotic, don't you BJ? Shit happens on the street, shit there is no way to plan for or train for."

"I'd appreciate it if you didn't curse," BJ says.

My free hand clenches. "You what? Listen BJ, I'm a grown man and I don't need to be told how to talk. I understand you're easily offended and I respect that. But I'm not eight years old and you're not my parent. Let's keep our discussion on topic."

"Okay." His voice is calm but there is a slight quiver in it. Nervous? Angry? I can't tell. "Since you've been in the unit you have been in fights and you have involved Angela. Last night you were off duty, and you and Angela got in over your heads. Maybe Angela went along because she looks up to you. I don't know yet. Right now I can't decide if you're a good officer or a loose cannon. And since I can't decide, I generated an IA investigation."

Temper. Got to hold my temper. Breathe, one, two, three.

"Okay, BJ, you got to do what you got to do. I also have to say this. If you were really initiating an IA investigation to get all the facts, I would be fine with it. It's good for the public, good for the media, good for the PD, and especially good for Angela and me. Thing is, I don't think getting the facts is your primary motivation. I think you want to hang me."

"Listen, Sam—"

"No, you listen, BJ. I'm at home. I'm not on the clock. You want to talk more about this, you need to call me in on the City's dime, and I will have my union representative present to record your statements. Goodbye."

Mai lifts her eyebrows. "Wooo-eeee. BJ is your boss, right?" I nod, knowing what she's going to say. "Is it okay to talk to your boss like you did?"

I shrug. "Probably not."

Mai touches my forearm. "Are you angry?"

"Yes, I am. Frustrated too. Because things ought to be different."

Mai steps behind me and massages my shoulders. It immediately melts me. She says, "When I was younger and could not decide the best way to do something, Father would tell me to take a leap and build my wings on the way down."

"Pretty good," I say. "I think I just leaped. I just hope I can build my wings in time."

My cell rings. I ought to turn the thing off. Uh oh, it's a PD number.

"Sam Reeves."

"Sam, Karen at the Chief's Office. How are you?"

"Doing okay, Karen. Is there a poo storm on the Fifteenth floor?"

She chuckles. "Not like last time. Sorry, Sam. Didn't mean to be insensitive."

"Stuff happens, right. What's up?"

"Deputy Chief Rodriguez wants to talk to you. Hold and I'll connect you."

You got to be kidding me. Who's next? The president? Mai raises her eyebrows. "Bigger boss," I mouth.

"Sam? Rodriguez. How you doing?"

He actually sounds cheery. What the hell?

"Doing okay, Chief. Worried about Angela."

"For sure, Sam. But I'm sure you know by now she's one tough cookie. Talked to her thirty minutes ago. I told her to take all the time she needs and then get back to work. I'm confident she'll be good to go."

"Yes, sir."

"How about you? You ready to hit the bricks?"

Ooookay, not what I was expecting. I was ready to hear the ol' 'turn in your badge, boy.'

"Uh."

"Well said, Sam. You can take some time if you want or if you're good to go, we need you. The Fat Dicks need you. I understand there are two sisters on the loose who are good for Yolanda Simpson and Qasim Al-Sabti. And there is going to be a huge protest at City Hall. I need people on the street who know what the hell's going on."

"BJ just called and said—"

"He's a good man, Sam. Never doubt it. Can I trust you with something?"

What the ... ? "Sure. I guess so."

"Let me put it this way, Sam. I like you. I think you're a good cop. But if you repeat what I'm going to tell you, I'll fuck with your life."

Damn. "Yes, sir."

Rodriguez laughs. "Listen, between you and me, BJ is out of

his element here. He's good at what he does but this just might be over his head. He's going to work up here in the Chief's Office for a while. A temporary basis thing. I'm sending over Lieutenant Foskey to boss you guys around. Know him?"

Rob Foskey and I partnered at North Precinct for a few months. Good cop and I've heard he's a good lieutenant at the Southeast Precinct. "I do, Chief. I like him."

"Great. And he said the same about you. I'm also looking for someone to fill in for Angela, someone who has worked Intel before. I wish I could get someone before the demonstration, but I don't think I can make it happen so quickly. So it's up to you, Foskey, and Steve to hump the Intel and help the Fat Dicks and the precincts with the protest."

"Understood," I manage, still in shock.

"Good. Think you can come back to work tomorrow?"

"Uh, yes."

"How about today? It's still early."

I laugh. Don't know why. It just comes out.

"Sam?"

"Sorry, Chief. Been some crazy phone calls today."

"Try working up here sometime. Oh, and Sam?"

"Chief?"

"Don't worry about IA."

Damn.

* * *

From where she leaned her shoulder against the bathroom door facing, Corky watched her naked sister in front of the sink scrubbing madly at the bloodstains on her hands and arms. Arizona straightened and glared at Corky in the mirror. "There's hardly no water pressure in this goddamn place and the hot water isn't for shit." She angrily swiped a strand of hair from her eyes, leaving a smear of blood across her nose and forehead. "Damn!" she blurted. She began splashing water from the weak trickle onto her face. "Damn! Damn! Damn!"

Corky, still wearing her bloody T-shirt and jeans, moved toward her sister. She placed her palm on Arizona's bare back and lightly patted it. "What has gotten into you, Ari? You hardly helped at all with Executioner, you threw up all over the car, you've been snapping at me, and when you aren't talking pissy, you're ignoring me."

Arizona scrubbed her face hard enough with a sponge to remove a layer of skin. "I-can't-get-this-blood-off, Cork. I think it's gone, then it like comes back."

"You're clean, Ari. It's your imagination working on you. Get in the shower and soap up all over and you will be fine. I'll give you a massage after I get cleaned up and we'll sleep. Okay?"

"Arizona turned to face her sister, her face and arms dripping water. "This is so crazy. What we did to the boy. I know he called the cops but damn, I mean, what we did to him. I mean, how is it helping our cause?" Corky reached out and tried to grip her arms, but Arizona stepped back from her. "I'm not as smart as you, Cork. I mean, I understand punishing him, but ... damn."

"Listen, Ari," Corky said taking a step toward her.

"No," Arizona said, shaking her head. "No. I know what you have to say, but you listen to me."

"Okay," Corky said, folding her arms. "Talk."

Arizona picked up her bunched jeans and covered herself with them. Normally, she liked it when Corky looked at her naked but it somehow felt strange right now. Everything was changing.and there was so much she didn't get. This whole white-power thing was hard to understand and she didn't know why Corky was so intense about it. Yes, they had some hard times growing up, their time in juvies and in the joint, but they'd paid back most of the niggers and beaners, and some. She understood revenge was important and she felt good dishing it back at them, but to hurt people they didn't know, like the one they strung up and the raghead hooker. They hadn't done nothing to Cork and her.

Arizona saw something in Executioner the first time he and Puke came to see them. It was the way he spoke, like he wasn't as smart as Puke, and he didn't understand everything going on. She also noticed he didn't seem to have the same enthusiasm for white power Puke had. He seemed like a follower and the more she thought about it, she began to see just how much she was too.

"The boy was so scared last night, Cork. Not just after we started beatin' on him, but before. I think I heard him crying when we first went into the garage. I think maybe he was confused too. Like he didn't know what he had gotten himself into."

Corky bunched her eyebrows. "Confused 'too?' Too. You confused about something?"

"No ... well, yeah. I mean ... Goddamn-it, Cork. You shoved a pipe wrench up his ass. What the hell? What does that have to do fighting for white people's rights?"

"We were sending a message, Sister," Corky said, moving toward her. She touched her arm. "I've explained it to you a dozen times, two dozen. If whites don't resist what's happening in this country, we're going to be stomped into the dirt. We're a minority now. Beaners popping out dirty brown babies like there's no tomorrow. Five or six a family on average. Blacks? They don't even know 'cause their men are knocking up black bitches all over town. The average unmarried black ho has four kids with four different fathers and she don't know or remember who the fathers are. White people have only one or two white babies. You think it's bad now, just wait fifteen or twenty years and see how much we're outnumbered."

"But killing these people. And puttin' nails in Executioner's hands. I know I carried the board and everything but I just don't see—"

Corky's slap knocked Arizona against the sink, sending a glass and a bar of soap to the floor. Arizona dropped her pants and covered the side of her head with her arm, but Corky anticipated her sister's move and slapped the other side of her head instead. Arizona dropped to her knees and began crying hysterically.

"I will not have a sister who is just another goddamn sheep standing by as the black and brown wolves tear this country down. Now stand the hell up," she said, grabbing a wad of Arizona's hair and yanking her to her feet. "Stand the fuck up and look at me. Take your hands away from your face. See what you made me do? I didn't want to hit you but you made me. You understand? Do you?"

Arizona nodded as tears rivered down her face. "I'm sorry. I just don't think—"

"You don't have to, Ari. Thinking is my job. Haven't I always taken care of things? Taken care of you?"

Arizona nodded, her head down. "Yes," she whimpered.

Corky wrapped her arms around her sister's naked body and kissed where she had slapped her. "And I always will, my sweet. I always will." Arizona snuggled her face into Corky's neck and allowed herself to be rocked gently from side to side. "Let's shower together and lie down. It's been a busy day."

* * *

While Mai piddles around in the kitchen, I take a shower, dress in blue jeans, a black polo shirt, and my cord jacket. I retrieve my Glock from the dresser and slip it into my belt holster. I start to bump the drawer closed with my hip when I see the loaded clip sticking out from under a pair of dark socks.

Once again I wonder if I've lost my mind carrying an empty weapon. I've never done anything this stupid in my career—in my life. It's irresponsible, it's dangerous, it's negligent on every level of police work. If another officer got hurt or killed because I couldn't do my job, I'd be fired, maybe even sued by the officer's family, I'd get death threats from other cops, I'd have to leave the city. I could never look in the mirror.

I move my socks out of the way to reveal the entire magazine, a six-inch black rectangular container holding a cache of fourteen copper-tipped nine-millimeter bullets. It looks ominous just lying there. But if someone were to pick it up and slap it firmly into the handle of a weapon, the gun is still incapable of firing because there isn't a projectile in the chamber. Not until the slide is yanked back does a bullet slip into the compartment to wait quietly, patiently for the slightest pressure of an index finger.

I'm still looking down into the drawer. All I got to do is pick up the clip. I've done it a thousand times before, more, probably. But this time I don't seem to be able to. I mentally will my hand. I command my hand. Nada. Just as I start to think I'll have do a *Doctor Strangelove* and grab my right wrist with my left and force my hand into the drawer, it reaches in on its own.

My fingertips touch the clip first, feeling the cool surface. I trail the pads of my fingers from its base, along its side, to the top. I tentatively touch the top bullet; its surface is cooler than the clip, and harder. There are thirteen more rounds under it, all lined up. Ready to go.

One of my first coaches told me of a shooting he was involved in back when every cop carried revolvers. When asked by an outraged, pious-ass reporter why he shot the holdup man six times in the chest, my coach smiled sweetly, and said, "'Cause that's all the bullets my gun held, ma'am."

Without me commanding my hand, it wraps around the mag and lifts it an inch or two off the bottom of the drawer. Has it always felt this heavy? It feels so solid, so substantial. So deadly. I look at the holes in the back. Fourteen of them but ... oh my God. Oh my God! Somehow I don't drop the mag. I should because it's so vile, so abhorrent, so ...

Fourteen holes in the back but three of them are—empty.

They are the three missing rounds I fired into a revolting abomination of a human being as well as a—God forgive me—a sweet, young innocent child.

Still holding the damnable mag, I take a long deep breath, hold it in, slowly release it, and hold empty for a few seconds. I repeat the pattern three more times until I'm once again breathing normally, or close to it, and my heart isn't pounding against my Adam's apple.

I'm still holding the mag.

Do what needs to be done, my father has said. No argument there. But am I a warrior, as he so often describes our family? Oh man, I'm not going to get into the whole yes I am and no I'm not thing now. I got to go to work. I'm needed there. Rodriguez told me so on the phone and after I hung up, Mai said as much too. I know my father would tell me, if not with his words, his eyes, to man up and do what needs to be done.

I flip my jacket flap out of the way, rip my Glock from its holster, and slap the mag into the butt of the weapon. Ha. I just rammed it right up the Glock's butt pretty as you please. I head toward the door.

But I'm not putting a round in the chamber. I don't care what bureau policy is.

* * *

"How are you doing?"

"What, no Chuck Norris digs?"

"Giving you the day off. Talked with Angela a little while ago." Steve scoots his chair over to my desk as I plop heavily onto my chair.

"I tried earlier but she didn't pick up. How is she?"

"Sounded tired and pissed because IA came by. She was worried about you."

"I'll call her later. And I'm doing fine, thanks, Steve. Rodriguez was adamant I get back to work."

Steve stands. "I'm going to top off my mug. You want a cup?" I nod and follow him back to the pot. "Lot's happening on the front. BJ is out for at least a while. We got Rob Foskey now. He's a good lou so no problems there. The other big news is we have Carl Findorff, your old buddy Executioner."

I stop my cup in mid sip. "Really. Where is he?" "Emanuel Hospital. Get this, he was found behind the Mini Mart off Cesar Chavez Boulevard. Naked as hell with a concussion and with big ass nails hammered through his palms and into a big board. And here's another 'get this.' The white supremacist was found by an elderly black couple."

"Oh man. Fat Dicks on it?"

"Yes, they're up there now. Speaking of, here's another 'get this.' What's that three of 'em? Anyway, last night sometime, Executioner wakes up and since the uniformed cop is outside in the hall, the kid thinks he can do a getaway. But he's all doped up and doesn't realize he's got a catheter in his dick. So he leaps out of bed, takes a running step toward the door, and gets jerked back like a charging dog at the end of a leash."

Just as we both reflexively put protective hands over our respective crotches, Lieutenant Foskey walks in. Rob is about forty-five, about my height, out of shape, fleshy face, beer gut, big feet, and big hands.

He nods, his face grim. "Sam, how are yuh?" Before I can answer, he says, "Bad news guys. Just got a call from the Fat Dicks. Carl Findorff died about thirty minutes ago. They were trying to interview him when he stroked out. One minute he's groggy but talking somewhat coherently and the next he goes into a spasm or something. Everyone comes running, but he flat lines and they can't bring him back."

"Damn!" Steve and I say at the same time.

"He was just a dumb follower," I say. "He could have been turned."

"The Fat Dicks get anything out of him?" Steve asks.

Rob nods. "Said they did. Should be here any minute. Let's go into my office. Sorry, Sam," he says, slapping my shoulder as we head into BJ's old space. "How are things?" He smiles. "Deputy Chief Rodriguez said you were anxious to come back."

"He can be persuasive but I'm glad he was." BJ's Bose, bible, cross of nails, and small lamp are gone. Rob has added a couple framed pics of himself with two teen girls. He sees me looking at them.

"My daughters. You can stop looking at them now." He looks at both Steve and me as we sit. "Sorry about BJ. He's a good man." He shrugs. "Fifteenth floor wanted a change."

"We're fine with it, Rob," Steve says. "Hopefully, you are."

"I'm glad to be here. I'm new, so treat me as such. Don't assume I know a lot about this white supremacy stuff. How about you guys catch me up while we're waiting."

For the next fifteen minutes, Steve and I tell our new boss about Qasim Al-Sabti and Yolanda Simpson's homicides, the video of the two sisters entering and leaving Yolanda's apartment building, the cross burning and firebombing attempt of the Muslim temple and the arrest of the suspect, Executioner's and Puke's involvement in the death of a wino, the confrontation with Puke in Detectives, the more peaceful interview with Executioner, the baseball bat beating death of the Mexican man, Angela and my confrontation with Puke, and the attempted capture of Executioner, which led to his beating and torture and, we just learned, his untimely and unfortunate death.

Learning Carl Findorff just died makes me feel ill. He was a big, scared, and dumb kid who I'm convinced could have been turned. I would have at least liked to have tried.

"I'm most impressed," Rob says. "You two and Angela have done some outstanding work. Let me know if there's anything you need."

"Thanks, Rob. Glad you're on board." We hear the door buzzing open out in the work area. "Sounds like the Fat Dicks are here."

"In here," Rob calls out.

A moment later, Richard Cary and Richard Daniels squeeze through the door like two great ships moving through the Erie

Canal. If Angela were here, there wouldn't have been enough room for all of us. Daniels is wearing a blue pinstriped suit and Cary a dark grey one. Both are sweating, both are wearing grim expressions. Not a good sign. Cary is carrying a greasy white paper bag, the kind bakeries use. The lieutenant gestures at the two remaining chairs.

"Fellas," Richard Cary says. He looks at Steve and me. "The lieutenant filled you in, right? Such a waste of a young life, hurting people and dying for something so terribly stupid. Live by the sword, die by the sword." He sets the bag down on the floor next to his briefcase. I'm guessing it's a pastry of some kind, but this is one of those rare moments when the boys have lost their appetite.

"Did he say much before he passed?" Steve asked.

"Quite a bit, actually," Richard Daniels says.

"The two sisters did him," Cary says. "Snatched him out of his bed but not before doing a boot party on him. The doc said he'd been hit over four-dozen times. Some marks were clearly made with boots and others with objects of some kind."

I think about the knee hit Nate did to him with his war club.

"Probably the board he was nailed to," Daniels says, "judging by the blood on the corners of it. It was a plank, about two inches by twelve inches, and six feet long. Heavy as hell. These women got to be strong to not only carry the plank but to carry it with Carl Findorff nailed to it. Unless they nailed him to it behind the store."

"What killed him?" I ask. "Head kicks?"

Carry nods. "Those too. And he spent the night naked in this cold fog we've been having, and he was in shock from his beating and the nails and the rape."

"Loss of blood," Daniels says. "The hand wounds, one eye socket, both ears, and his anus. Lots of internal bleeding too."

"Anus? Then you did say rape." I say. "Thought I misheard."

Cary nods slowly, the corner of his lip curled. "They violated him with something. Doc said he thought there was rust on him back there, so maybe a rusty pipe, an old crowbar, something similar. The boy said he was sleeping in a garage when they found him so who knows what was lying around. Anyway, it tore him up pretty good."

I can see why the Richards aren't eating.

"I want these women." I'm surprised when Steve and Cary look at me because I didn't realize I said it aloud. "Warrants in the works?"

"Made the calls on the way over here," Daniels says.

"What else did you get out of him?" I ask.

Daniels scoots himself about in the chair trying to get comfortable. His massive bulk and that ergonomic chair are not a good fit. "Said he had seen the women two times about a year back, down at the prison when he and Puke were visiting Puke's mother. But he said Puke recently met with them at a house on Southeast Tenth, near Taylor. Puke told him it was a big white house and there wasn't much in it. Nothing in the living room except some crap piled up on the floor and a table in the kitchen along with the appliances. Puke told him he thought they were just using the place and didn't really live there.

"Executioner said when he saw the sisters down in the joint, they sort of looked alike and acted like they were dykes for each other. Said they touched each other a lot and even got reprimanded for it by a guard in the visiting area. Executioner said they were strange in a scary kind of way."

Richard Cary leans forward. "The boy said he overheard

the sisters mention a man they called The Colonel, and caught a mention of Montana."

"Benjamin White," Steve says. "Army light colonel in Vietnam. Has a farm and a church outside of Butte.

"A church?" Rob asks.

Steve nods. "He's a reverend and preaches a theology structured to support his hateful beliefs about race. He believes Jews are the children of Satan or, as he calls it, 'the spawn of Satan,' and all races but Caucasians are the result of a mistake God made when he was creating the world."

"Idiots!" Richard Cary says.

"Idiotic beliefs," Steve corrects. "Some of them are incredibly intelligent, brilliant, even. But they got some twisted ways of thinking."

I look at the two Richards. "So did Executioner express a sense of the sisters' relationship with this colonel?"

"He did," Cary says. "Corky, who Executioner thought was the leader, commented a couple of times they wanted to get a position in his Montana organization. But they had to prove themselves first. Executioner took it to mean they had to do some big crimes to shock Portland when they got out. Executioner said his buddy Puke wanted to get into the organization too."

"The boy said he didn't know for sure why he was going along with Puke," Daniels says. "Said he didn't like blacks but it didn't mean he wanted to kill them. Same with Mexicans. When I asked him about the wino who got hit by a car, he couldn't look me in the eye."

A phone chirps and Cary, Steve, and Rob all reach for their cells. Mine, out on my desk, has been ringing nonstop since I've come in here.

"Mine," Cary says. "This is Cary. Yeah. Yeah. Both sides. Okay. Thanks, man. Coffee is on Daniels next time." He clicks off his cell. "We had Gary Rhodes who patrols the lower east side check out Tenth Avenue. Said there is one big white house on the south side of Tenth off Taylor and two on the north side. The one on the south side is for sale and looks empty. One of the two on the north side has a bunch of toys and a little girl's bike in the yard. The other white house is two houses down."

"Okay," Rob says. "What do you think of this idea? Cary will watch the For Sale house on the south side of Tenth. Daniels, you sit on the one without the toys in the yard on the north side. Sam and Steve, you guys take any pics we got of these women and show them at all the fast food joints in the area. Sam, double check if Gary Rhodes has for sure passed on what he learned to the other uniform cars in the area. In fact, why don't you call Southeast Precinct and make sure the sergeants on all three shifts have the sisters' pictures. Also tell them to ask the marked cars to stay off Tenth if at all possible. We want the women to be free to return to the house or leave it."

"We're on it, Rob," Daniels says. Steve and I share a look. BJ would have kept us in the office and had uniform do these things.

The lieutenant pats a stack of reports in front of him. "Anything you guys need let me know. I'm going to pour through all your reports from the last few days to catch up. Steve, why don't you stay in here and fill me in on anything the reports don't say.

My phone rings again. "Rob, if you don't mind, I'd like to catch my phone. Someone's been calling nonstop. Must not know how to leave a message."

"Of course," he says. "Everyone, please keep me posted on

anything and everything. Deputy Chief Rodriguez was adamant I keep him updated so he can keep Chief Bates informed.
I'm told everyone from the media, to the mayor, to the gov-
ernor, to every black watchdog organization in the country is
ringing the Chief's phone."

"Check, Boss," Daniels says.

"And one other thing, fellas, "Rob says, making eye contact
with each of us. "So we're all on the same page here, understand I might be a lieutenant but I'm a damn street cop first.
You all got desks and PCs and wear civvies, but I expect you
to be out on the streets serving and protecting while gathering
intelligence."

I instantly feel the energy rise in the room.

I walk the Fat Dicks to the door and give them my cell
number. I tell them to let me know if the sisters are spotted no
matter what time of night it is.

The message light isn't flashing on my phone, so either
six people called and didn't leave a message or one person
called six times and didn't. I scrounge through my papers for
the report Angela wrote on our interview with her cousin or
second cousin who works at the gay bathhouse in Northwest.
Here it is. Oh yes, Rose City Steam.

"Rose City Steam and Cream, this is Teddy."

"Teddy," I say, remembering his pierced nipples and athletic
supporter. "Detective Sam Reeves. I was in the other day with
Angela—"

"Gorgeous! I remember yoooou. No need to remind me.
You *coming* in for a steam?"

"Thanks Teddy, but no. I would like to talk with Terrance."

Teddy laughs. "Just playing with you, Detective. But if you
change your mind ... Hope, hope, hope."

"I won't, Teddy. Terrance?"

"Daaaamn. Okay, hold a sec."

"Detective Reeves," Terrance says. How you doin'?' How you doin'? Heard about my cousin, Angela. So scary what happened. You was with her, right? Right?"

"I was, Terrance. She did a fine job. She protected herself and me. She's a good cop."

"Yes sir, yes sir. I know this for sure. What can I do for you?"

"I was wondering if you'd seen those two sisters again, the ones you told Angela and me about?"

"The two dykes? No, sir. I asked too, I did. Two people said they'd seen them but it was the same day I saw them. Maybe they left town. You think?"

"No, we're pretty sure they're still around. Okay thanks, sir. Sorry about Angela. Please tell the family she did a good job."

"I will, yes, sir. Yes, I will."

Steve leans out the lieutenant's door and says it will be about another twenty minutes before we can hit the street with the sisters' photos. I call Southeast Precinct to fill in the day-shift lieutenant on the sisters' hideout and ask him to tell the district units to stay out of the area, but to be on alert. The Fat Dicks will probably need backup. The lieutenant says the pics of the sisters we sent out a couple days ago are tacked on the bulletin board, and he will have someone make copies for every officer.

I write descriptions of the women on the bottom of the photos we have and run thirty copies. Over the next ten minutes, I take three calls on my desk phone. The first one is a screaming man accusing Angela of acting like a judge, jury, and hangman. I try to reason with him, but he's so over the top enraged he won't let me speak and I can barely understand what he's saying. So I put him on hold and get myself another coffee. The second call is from what sounds like a black woman wanting to congratulate Angela for her kill. She claims God guided Angela's gun hand to rid the Earth of the Satan-possessed man. The third was a man in support of the shooting. I couldn't detect his race, though he used the term "white devils" several times. My first caller is still on hold. Even the flashing red light looks pissed.

Richard Cary calls and says he's sitting down the street from the white house that's for sale and Daniels is watching the other one. Cary is sitting in an old Ford pickup and Daniels is in a crumpled tan Honda, vehicles they borrowed from Drugs and Vice.

I call Nate and ask how he's doing.

"Doing fine, Sensei. But I feel bad the kid got away from me and Mai."

"It was smart of you not to pursue into the bar," I say. "You guys probably wouldn't have gotten hurt but you would have likely hurt someone. You don't need a record and Mai is a visitor here and doesn't need the hassle."

"Gotcha, Sensei. But I feel bad the guy is still on the lamb."

"You haven't seen the news, I take it?"

"No. Why?"

I update him.

"Damn," he says softly. "I mean, damn. He was crucified? And the people who did it were women?"

"Sisters. We're on it. Hoping to get them in the next few hours."

"I need to listen to the news more. I did hear about the march on City Hall. Wife and I were thinking about going to it. Not to protest the police but to show our support for the fight against racism."

"Just keep your eyes open, Nate. There could be problems. If there are, get away from it. Don't get involved. And leave your war club at home."

"Hear you loud and clear, Sensei. You be safe."

I call Mai. "I miss you."

"I might miss you too, but I do not know who this is."

"You're cute."

"Oh, hi, Sam. I like driving your truck. Every time I stop and every time I go, the tires make a loud screech noise and there is lots of smoke."

"Remind me to laugh later."

"Okay, Sam. I will."

"I'm calling to tell you I will be late tonight. We have a lead on the bad guys, bad women in this case, and we'll be working it for a while. It could be an hour but more likely it will be longer. Sorry."

"Okay. Don't worry, I'll be alright," she says.

"Are you at International Gifts?" She dropped me off at the station so she could go shopping for my spare room. Her license is still good from when she went to Portland State University and she knows her way around.

"I am. So far I have some cushions, incense, candles, a vase for a flower, and a small statue of a wooden Buddha, and it was carved in Vietnam. I will fix it nice in your room. We can sit there when you get off work. It will be a very peaceful place and a good place for you to, uh, get wound."

"Wind down?"

"Oh yes. Sorry. Get wind down after crazy day."

* * *

"Outstanding work, Corky. Outstanding."

"Thank you, sir." Corky smiled at Arizona who was sitting at the kitchen table. Arizona tentatively smiled back.

"Just saw it on the news," Colonel Benjamin White said, his tone almost giddy. "All kinds of hell going on there. The shooting, the crucifixion. I mean, shit. When I said to nail him to a cross I meant it figuratively. But you actually done it. Ha ha ha. And the little shit died. Jesus Christ, girl. I'm mighty proud to have you in ARM. I don't think you and Arizona will be in Third Stage for long. You keep doing work like this and you will be in one of the top slots quicker than a nigger can dodge work."

"Thank you, Colonel White. This is our goal, our dream." Corky gestures excitedly for her sister to come over to her.

"What?" Arizona whispers, slowly rising. Although she and Corky had sort of made up, Arizona was still uncertain about what they were doing. She told Corky what she wanted to hear—how she was one hundred percent with her sister— but the truth was she wasn't. The two of them had enjoyed a soapy shower together and then fallen asleep after making love. That usually soothed Arizona into a feeling of security but this time it hadn't done anything to make her less confused.

Corky slipped her arm around her waist, pulled her in tight, and mouthed, "He likes what we did."

Arizona lifted her eyebrows and gave her sister a weak smile. Corky leaned in and kissed her deeply.

"You there?" Colonel White asked.

"Yes, sir. Sorry," Corky said, frowning at Arizona. She didn't like that Arizona hadn't returned her kiss with feeling. She grabbed Arizona's wrist and pushed her sister's hand under her white T-shirt. "Feel me." Corky mouthed. Arizona kneaded her sister's breast, glaring hard into her eyes. "We are so pleased, sir," Corky said, returning the hard look.

"I have one more job for you and upon its completion, I'd like you two to come here to Montana, to ARM, so we can talk about your future. Sound good?"

"It sounds outstanding, sir. Anything you want us to do, we're ready."

"Good girl," Benjamin said.

Girl? Corky stiffened a little at the offensive word. She jerked Arizona's hand out from under her shirt, and turned away from her.

The colonel said, "This Reverend Billy Souls seems to be some kind of mover and shaker there in your jig town."

"Yes, he is." She turned back to Arizona who was starting to move back to the table. Corky wrapped her arm around her and pulled her into her side, like a mother would a rambunctious child. "He's all over the media here and has been for years. He's got a march planned on city hall tomorrow. Supposed to be a big sign-waving rally or something."

"I know about it. And an even bigger mover is coming to speak. Calls himself Reverend Doctor Rothman Sterling. He thinks of himself as someone big and important—kind of like that blowhard Jessie Jackson." He laughs at his own little joke. "Well, I've set some things in motion that's going to put Portland on the map. Holly-Jew-Wood will probably make a movie about it."

"Really? What?"

"It's a need-to-know operation. But I have an important job for you two. It's easy and it's safe. First, you will need to buy a couple of throwaway cell phones ..."

*   *   *

Steve doesn't break free from the lieutenant's office until three forty-five.

"We just bonded," Steve whispers, holding up his crossed fingers. "We're like this now. We're talking about shipping you to graveyard shift."

"Great," I say, shoving the pics and the radios into his arms. "You can carry these then. And you can drive." I tell him the Fat Dicks are set up on the houses and two out of the three calls I got were supportive of Angela shooting Puke.

"Mine were like fifty-fifty," he says, as we head for the door. "Between yesterday and before you came in today, I probably fielded about a hundred calls. Some of those against were angry a black woman killed a white man. Hey, no one would have known her race if KGW TV hadn't run a picture of her side by side with the prick."

Five minutes later we're heading out of the garage in a grey unmarked on our way to Southeast Tenth. We ride in silence for a few minutes, but at an especially long red light, Steve asks, with concern in his voice, "You okay after this most recent?"

"I am, thanks. I keep waiting for the ball to drop. You know, waiting for my head to catch up with what went down in the alley. But so far, I'm good. I'm just concerned about Angela."

My shrink explained where your head is just before you get involved in something traumatic can make all the difference in how you deal with it. If your sergeant just ripped into you or you just had a fight with your spouse before you left for work, you might have a harder time dealing. This time I was pretty squared with the big stuff in my life. I got Mai in my life, and an amazing father, and I'm almost certain that police work is what I want to do, and I am coping better this time. Guess she was right.

"I'm glad, Sam. Let's hope Angela comes out of it okay."

"I think she—" My cell rings. "No way," I say, looking at my caller ID. "Angela! Your ears burning? Steve and I were just talking about you."

"Steve? Is he at your house?" Her tone is emotionless, flat, as if all the energy has been sucked out of her.

"I'm at work. Rodriguez called and twisted my arm to come back. So I came in around one this afternoon. Looks to be a long day."

"Why, what's going on?" That came out with more energy.

"We think we got the house where the sisters have been staying narrowed down to two. The Fat Dicks are sitting on them now, and Steve and I are going to cruise the surrounding streets and flash their picture around. How are you doing?"

"I want to come in."

"Yeah, I wish you could. But I think right now you need rest and—"

"I'm coming in, Sam."

"I'm not sure coming in is a good—"

"I'm not going to miss out arresting those two. I'll go into the office and get a radio and meet you guys out there."

"Angela, you haven't been released to ... Angela? Angela, are you there?"

"What?" Steve asks, turning onto Belmont.

"Angela said she was coming in. Wants to be involved."

"But she's not cleared."

I shrug. "What are we going to do? Should we tell Rob?"

"I don't know. No. She's a grownup and a veteran officer. I'm not going to tattle on her. Besides, we don't know she hasn't been cleared."

I shake my head. "Ooookay. I know nothing, I saw nothing." Steve finishes the cop ditty with me. "I wasn't even there."

I point at a Seven-Eleven. "Let's show the clerk a pic. We're about five blocks from the houses."

Steve guides us onto the lot and parks on the side of the store since all the spots in front are occupied. We get out and move up on the walkway in front of the store and head toward the door.

"Dudes."

Steve and I turn to see a kid, eighteen or nineteen, big like a football player, disheveled, red sweatshirt, dirty blue jeans, drunken eyes glassed over. "Dudes!" he says again.

After a while in police work, you get instant feelings about something or someone. They wouldn't hold up in court, but when one cop says to another "I got this feeling," other cops know right off what he's talking about. Same with the word "asshole." Tell another cop "I stopped this asshole," and instantly everyone's on the same page.

"You already said dudes," Steve says, clearly having the same feeling about this asshole.

The kid frowns, his body tenses, and he squints at Steve, probably trying to make the two images of my partner merge into one. "Already shaid ... whats?"

"Dudes," Steve answers. He looks at me. "Can you believe we're having to deal with this right now?"

"Who shaid whats?" the kid says, trying to put his closed fists on his hips but both slide off. His second attempt is a charm.

"Okay," I say. "We're done here. You need to go away."

The kid slowly turns toward me. "Buy me shome beers, dude," he slurs. He digs his right hand into his jeans pocket, actually finding it the first time. "I'll gives yous ten bucks."

"No," I say. "You need to take a hike and do it now. We're the po—"

The kid throws a big looping sucker punch.

I might have had a feeling about the kid, but I didn't expect a punch at this early juncture. Still, I duck just enough it passes through my hair. The kid actually looks at his fist with surprise.

With my palm, I push his face to his left as I quickly step around his right shoulder. He mumbles something, probably, "Where'd he go?" Before he figures out I'm behind him, I plunge my hands under his sweatshirt, grab big wads of his love handles, and squeeze like I'm wringing a washrag dry. His squeal reaches a high octave quickly. Then I rotate my fists forward an inch to convince him I'm ripping off a couple of oh-so-sensitive chunks of flesh, which launches him forward on his tiptoes. I drive him along the front of the store window and around the corner to our car.

"Cuff him, Steve," I say, bending him over the trunk and jamming his arm behind his back. I push the kid's little finger back to give him an extra shot of agony.

"Chuck!" Steve says excitedly, pulling his cuffs off his pants belt. "Amazing! You didn't do the jumping back kick like Chuck Norris always does, but I've never seen him make people squeal like a farm animal." He slaps on the cuffs.

I hold onto the kid while Steve calls for a uniform car to transport our prisoner. He's eighteen, too young to buy beer but old enough to go to the big boy jail for attempted assault and public intoxication. I try to talk to him, maybe offer him a little fatherly advice, but he won't have any of it. Claims he was at home all afternoon so it wasn't him who tried to punch me, and he's never had a drink in his life. Oh well. Like my first coach used to say, "We can't save everyone."

We stuff the kid into the back of a uniform car and apologize to the officers for sticking them with the transport. Back on track, we head into the store to show the tank top-wearing tattooed woman a photo of the sisters. She refuses to tell us anything, though she does ream us for causing a scene in front of the store. I start to comment on her choice of hair color—bright blue—especially since she's in her midforties, but I decide to keep my mouth zipped.

Next we head up two blocks to Save n Take grocery and show the picture to nearly a dozen employees. Two men immediately alert on them and tell us the sisters were in a couple of days ago. One man, powerful looking, says he's been hauling three-hundred-pound slabs of beef and pig for fifteen years but he thinks "these two bulls could kick my butt."

The shaved-bald bartender at Ace Tavern on Thirteenth and Belmont says they had been in there a few times but not for a week or so. They would each down half-a-dozen beers and not even look buzzed. The last time they were in, one of them started chewing on the other. He didn't know what it was about but he could tell it was getting tense. "I told them to chill or take it outside," he says. "I got to tell yuh, if those two would have gone at each other, they would have leveled the place."

On our way back out to the car, my cell rings.

"My sweet Sam, this is Efrem, Efrem Axelbrad."

"Mister Axelbrad, how are you?"

"I am fine, my boy. I wanted to tell you I saw that *nafka* I told you about, the whore, I saw her today."

"Where?"

"By Whittle's Funeral Home at Tenth and Taylor. About six this morning. Do you know it?"

"I do," I say. I patrolled the area back when I was a rookie. Got a call one morning when Mister Whittle discovered a break-in and tampering with one of the bodies. We couldn't tell for sure if there had been an act of necrophilia perpetrated by the burglar but judging by the way the body was positioned, he had at least thought about it.

"Bill Whittle is a longtime friend of mine," Mister Axelbrad says. "His wife died a few months ago, and he hasn't been much on working at his business. He hasn't closed it officially, but he's been in Prague the last few weeks. Has a brother there."

"What was the woman doing on the funeral home property?" I ask.

"She and another woman were just sitting there in their car, talking I guess. I couldn't see real clear, but they looked like they might be related. Sisters."

"What kind of car, Mister Axelbrad?"

"An old Ford sedan, nineteen eighty-nine, beat up. I know the year because I've sold two through my secondhand shop. It was a dull blue, damaged front right fender. Got masking tape around the headlight."

"Excellent attention to detail."

"Well, I know cars. Sold a lot over the years. But I was mostly concerned they were on my friend's business property. He never did get an alarm, see. When I pulled into the lot to check the place, they pulled out in a quick hurry. I looked around. The place hadn't been tampered with."

"You did real good, Mister Axelbrad. Is there anything else?"

"No. Are the authorities interested in both of them? Are they ones who killed Ocnod and the poor woman?"

"We don't know yet, but we want to talk to them."

"Persons of interest? Like they say on TV?"

"That's it, Mister Axelbrad. Please call me again should you see them. But stay away from them."

"I will, Sam my boy. Stop in at the shop anytime. I'll make us some tea. You're a lovely man."

"I will, sir. I promise."

Steve is heading south on Twelfth toward Hawthorne. "What's up?" he asks.

"Mister Axelbrad, the secondhand store owner who was getting robbed when I … stopped it. Anyway Angela and I dropped in to talk with him a few days ago and it seems one of the sisters had stopped in his shop in Old Town. He just called to tell me he saw both sisters this morning on his way to his Southeast shop. They were parked in Whittle's Funeral Home at Tenth and Taylor."

"Why park there?"

"Beats me," I say with a shrug. "Maybe they were working their way back home after dumping Executioner behind the Mini Market. But if they're staying in a house a couple blocks away, it doesn't make sense to stop there. Let's head to the Mini Mart." I look at my notebook and give him the address. "It's about twenty blocks away from the funeral home, eighteen from where they are supposedly staying."

The Mini Mart is a bust because this afternoon's crew wasn't on during graveyard shift. The educated guess is Executioner was dumped behind the store between midnight and six, probably closer to six, since the suspects were spotted only a mile and a half away at six. The middle-aged black woman behind the counter is scared to death, so Steve and I do our best to comfort her. Before we leave we have her laughing and feeling a lot better. She says she will make sure her relief gets the pics and the description of the Ford.

I call the Fat Dicks, and poke the speaker so Steve can hear. I fill in Cary and tell him about the sighting at the Save n Take and about Mister Axelbrad's sighting. Then I call Daniels to tell him. Before I can tell him about the suspect car, he asks, "Anything about a beater four-door sedan? Blue I think."

"Yes, a Ford. You got it at the house that's for sale?"

"No. Cary's sitting on it. I'm on the north side of Taylor. Got a beater here, Front damage, right side. Too far to see for sure, but it looks like it's been taped. Parked in the driveway at the north side of the house."

"That's the car! Any lights on in your house?" There is still a couple hours left of daylight.

"Can't tell for sure," Daniels says. "Could be the low sun reflecting off the windows. But it could be a lamp too."

"How do you want to play it?" I ask.

I hear a plastic bag rustling, probably Hershey's Kisses. "Cary has a call into Records to see if we can find out the owner of both of the houses we're watching. There's not much street traffic and no kids out, which is good. I've got a good spot three houses north of the white one, under a weeping willow tree. I'll stay here and watch. I'll get Cary to move from his house and set up on mine. Where are you?"

"We're on Hawthorne, about Thirteenth. We'll find a place to park on Hawthorne near Tenth and wait for whatever happens." We're in an unmarked sedan, a ride every crook in the world knows is a police car, even without the markings, so we don't want to get too close

"Good plan," Daniels says. "Stay in touch and listen up if we come on the air shouting. If there's a foot chase, I'm good for about nine, maybe ten seconds. Then I tag Cary and he takes it for the next four or five. I keep telling him he needs to work on his cardio."

Steve runs into the Burger King at Eleventh and Hawthorne and gets us coffee and Whoppers with cheese. When I first joined the PPD I was stuck in the middle of the drive-through line when I got an armed robbery call. I quit using the drive-through after that—at least when I'm on the job. We definitely can't get tied up now. Anything can go down during a stakeout, and it could happen five minutes after setting up or twelve hours later.

Steve pulls into an empty church parking lot so we can down the junk food. To kill time, I ask him about his years on the PD, and he tells me most of his years in uniform were spent working graveyard at North Precinct. An old PPD joke is if you get into trouble on the job, you get transferred to graveyard shift North, but in Steve's case, he says he never got into trouble; he just liked the action out there.

We eat in silence for a few minutes before Steve says, "You mind if I ask you a question about your shooting?"

I tell Steve to fire away.

He finishes chewing his mouthful, and asks, "You have trouble eating after?"

Didn't expect that question. "I lost my appetite for a while."

He nods thoughtfully at my answer, but I'm sensing he meant something else. Our eyes lock. There is something in his and I'm not sure ... Wait ... Steve, the funny guy in the office, the musician with the Oregon Symphony, the one quick with a Chuck Norris quip—all of it just falls into place.

"You've been there, haven't you?" I ask softly.

He studies my face for a long moment before looking out the side window at four skateboarders rolling down the middle of the street. They make us the instant they see us and all four cant their bodies toward the curb, leap it, and continue their journey on the sidewalk. The one in back salutes us before they surf out of sight rounding the corner of an apartment building.

"December twenty-fourth, twenty-one years ago."

"Twenty-one? I thought you've been on for only eighteen or nineteen."

"I was on Sacramento PD for three years before I moved up here." He takes a deep breath, lets it out. "My partner, Jim Gach, and I were chasing a gangbanger, a Blood, who had popped some caps at another police car a block away on a street called Smith Avenue, smack in the middle of black-gang territory. We were chasing him on foot when he went up onto the big porch in front of an old house and ran through the open front door. There were three or four elderly people sitting on the porch, and one old timer points to the door, and says, 'He went in there. Go get the punk.'

"This is before cops had to call in SWAT for every damn thing, so Jim and I ran into the place. Our instincts told us to go up the stairs and we were right. We found him hiding in a bedroom closet, crying like a baby. No gun on him. So we cuff his wrists and walked him down the stairs and out onto the porch. A couple more police cars had pulled up at the curb, and neighbors across the street were screaming all kinds of profanities at us about being slave masters and all.

"The old timers on the porch, old black guys and an elderly black woman, were laughing up a storm because we got the banger. Well, the men were. The old woman just stood there, looking off into space kind of confused. She was wearing an old dress and an apron, the kind with a big pocket in front. We start to move our prisoner down the stairs when suddenly behind us there was a lot of chair scraping and shouting. When I turned around, here was the old woman holding a gun, a Smith and Wesson Thirty-Eight revolver. The old guys were trying to get some distance from her. The people across the street couldn't see what's going on, but they were still ranting and cursing us for arresting the kid, while all the cops were yelling at the woman to drop the gun. It was mass confusion until she quieted everybody by popping a round into the porch.

· "Those old guys hadn't moved so fast in years. They bailed over the railing and all the cops were drawing their weapons, taking cover behind trees and car fenders, and shouting at her to drop it. Jim pushed our prisoner down so hard I lost my grip on his arm. That's when the old woman fired another round, one into the lawn about fifteen feet over from where I was. When I looked up, she was swinging the gun toward me.

"Three images burned into my mind right then and they still visit me at night now and then. First was the strange look of confusion on the old woman's face; it was a little out of focus because I was concentrating on the second thing, the ultra clear, yawning opening of the Thirty-Eight Caliber gun barrel. The third thing was how my bullet hit her between her breasts and slammed her back against the wall. She fired another round into the porch as she fell."

Steve hasn't touched his burger since he's been talking. He looks down at it as if surprised it's in his hand, and stuffs the second half into the bag, along with his napkins and soda cup. He wads the bag up and drops it on the floor between his feet. He looks out the windshield.

"We put it all together after. The gangbanger dropped the gun into the old woman's apron pouch as he ran by her into the house. He did it so fast none of the men saw it happen.

The old woman, slow to react, didn't pull it out for four or five minutes, not until we moved past her and we were going down the steps."

"I don't understand, Steve. I get it the men didn't see what the kid did but the woman must have. Why didn't she say anything? Why did she pull the gun and pop those rounds?"

Steve continues staring out the window, his breathing shallow. He turns slowly toward me. "Because the old woman was senile and completely blind."

*   *   *

As twilight begins to fall and businesses turn on their exterior lights, Steve and I sit slumped low and talking quietly. He tells me all hell broke loose for him and his agency, and he nearly lost his job. Rather than return to work where forever he would be known as the cop who shot and killed a blind, helpless elderly black woman, he resigned and moved his family to Portland where only a handful of people knew of the incident.

He had asked if I could eat after my shootings because he had trouble eating for months after his. It wasn't because of a loss of appetite, though there was that for a couple of weeks, but it was because he felt guilty eating. He had killed an innocent person, and he didn't feel worthy of taking in sustenance. He had a daily struggle for weeks justifying why he should be allowed to eat when he had deprived an old, confused woman of her remaining years.

Portland PD almost didn't hire him because by the time he applied here, he was down to one hundred fifty pounds. Too light for a guy six feet tall. In fact, he flunked the physical the first time. He put on twenty pounds and retried three months later, passing it, but barely. After an extensive going over by our shrinks who knew about the Sacramento shooting, he was given the green light to get sworn in.

I don't have to tell him that his story is safe with me. Instead, I tell him a little about my post-shooting days, how for one brief moment in my kitchen I considered eating my gun. I'd known cops who had and I thought, hey, how hard could it be? I didn't, and I went on to be stronger than ever, at least most of the time.

We sit quietly for a while, me wondering if we should have shared such intimate details and then feeling glad we did. We both understand the horror, the guilt, the haunting night-mares. Doc Kari is right. It does help to talk with someone who has gone through the same terrors.

"The Fat Dicks?" Steve asks, looking down at the car radio. "Four Ninety and Four Ninety-One, right?"

We're using a net used exclusively for stakeouts and other kinds of missions. We each have a portable radio. There is no dispatcher but if things get confused, we can ask for one to control communications.

"Four Ninety or Four Ninety-One. That you?" I ask into my radio.

"Four Ninety-One, I need backup. The suspects just got into the car, a blue Ford, old beater. The house is Eighteen thirty-three. I'm going to block the driveway with my car."

"We're coming," I say, as Steve floors it across the lot and out onto the street. A motorcycle rider leans on his little horn and lays a patch of rubber behind us. He shouts something.

Richard Cary's excited voice: "I'm there in ten seconds, pard."

Radio silence as Steve rockets us down Tenth.

Daniels: "I've blocked the car. The occupants are ... One of them ..."

Cary shouting: "Can't get my car started. I'm going in on foot."

I brace my hands on the dash. "Look out for the truck backing out." Steve breaks hard and cuts the wheel to the left, putting us into a rubber-burning slide. We rock to a stop a couple of feet from the right rear corner of the truck bed, which is now blocking the narrow residential street. The driver leans a long blast onto his horn before leaping from his cab. He's shouting but I can't make it out over the radio chatter.

Hard breathing on the radio, then, *"I'm ... she grupmmm."*

I hold my badge out the window at the truck driver who is about three paces from my door. "Portland police. Get back in your truck, pal, and get it out of our way."

He stops in his tracks, a big sneer on his mug. "You assholes got no right to—"

"Move your truck now or we'll arrest you and tow it."

Hard breathing, then Cary's voice: "Something's going on. I'm almost there but I don't see Daniels. His car is blocking the Ford but ..."

"Move the truck!" Steve shouts. I push open my door to get out.

The man sneers even more, waves me off as if I'm an annoying gnat, and slowly gets back into his truck. But he doesn't move it. My temper flares and I leap out of the car. I take two stomping steps toward the truck when the guy floors his throttle and burns a patch back up into his driveway.

"Come on, Sam," Steve shouts. "Just heard a bunch of radio static from one of the guys."

Angela's voice: "Four Twenty-One, I'm about there."

Lieutenant Foskey's voice: "Car Four Hundred. Anyone at

426

the scene yet?"

"We're two blocks away," I say, into my radio. I wonder if he knows Angela's voice?

Foskey: "Check, Sam. I'm requesting we get a dispatcher over here until we know what's going on."

"The boss is on the job," I say.

"Yeah, and so is Angela," Steve says nearly clipping a parked VW. "Hope she knows what she's doing." He glances up at the rearview mirror. "Hell-o. Your pickup driving buddy is following us."

"You got to be kidding," I say, twisting around. "Must want to go to jail."

Cary's voice, winded, high pitched, *"Daniels ... Daniels ... he's down."*

"Shit!" Steve blares, goosing through the last intersection.

"Up there on the left," I shout over the roar of the engine. "Oh no."

Daniels is lying partly on the lawn and partly on the sidewalk. A two-story white house sets back a short ways. Unlike the other well-maintained yards on this street, the lawn hasn't been mowed in a couple of months, there are pinecones all over the place, and a pile of newspapers on the walkway and steps leading up to a long porch. The suspects' car is still in the driveway.

"Order an ambulance!" Cary shouts as Steve and I bail out. He's on his knees stripping off his suit jacket. "He's been cut bad on his face and neck."

"We can haul him," I say.

Cary shakes his head hard. "I don't know how deep the neck cut is. We could damage his spine. Paramedics should do it."

"Where are the suspects?" I ask, while Steve orders an

ambulance and additional police units on his portable radio.

"They—"

"Hey, pal. I'm going to need you to move your car."

I spin around and nearly bump into Pickup Man. He's about thirty years old, an inch taller than me, medium build. "Are you kidding me?" I say. "Get out of here before I pop you for interfering with the police."

Police sirens wailing our way.

"Shiiiit," he sneers. He peers around me, deliberately bumping my shoulder as he moves toward Daniels. "What happened to the fat guy?"

Every once in a while I run into one of these people. They aren't from the suicide-by-cop crowd, but they are definitely martyrs. They want to go to jail, and they bait the police into hurting them along the way. Some just had a fight with their spouse and they want the cops to thump them to get sympathy from their wives. Some want to provoke a situation because they want to file an excessive force charge against the police. They're whack jobs whatever their motivation and I don't have time to deal with it. We've got to get into the house.

"Move back," I tell him.

He turns toward me. "What? You haven't moved your car out of the way yet?"

I grab his arm and Steve latches onto his other.

"Let go of me," Pickup Man demands before emitting a forced laugh. "You guys are looking at such a big lawsuit. My attorney will suck the City dry for manhandling me." Okay, there it is. He wants to sue the cops.

"Sixty-one," I say to Steve; he nods. Ten sixty-one is the police code for taking a person into custody. The guy must watch *COPS* because he suddenly stiffens his muscles and begins twisting about. He's either baiting us to up the force or he's suddenly changed his mind about getting arrested. "Down on your belly," I say.

Behind us I hear a wailing police car squeal around the corner, then another from the other direction. They cut their sirens.

"I want both your names," the guy manages before his chest hits the sidewalk.

"You can get them off the arrest report," I tell him. "Where are the women?" I ask Cary.

He shakes his head. "House maybe. I never saw them."

I look up as a young female officer runs up.

"He the doer?" she asks, looking first at Pickup Man and then worriedly at Daniels. Cary is still on his knees holding his wadded suit jacket against the side of his partner's face. He's whispering something to him. Daniels looks too dazed to understand.

"No," I say loudly to the officer over Pickup Man's cursing. His words are muffled because his lips are pressed against the cement. "But we're taking him for interfering and resisting. Let me use your cuffs, and you and your pard can book him for us. Fill out a Custody Report and I'll hack out a Crime Report later to connect to it."

"No problem," she says, watching me cuff him.

Steve directs two other uniformed officers to take up positions cattycorner to each other so they can each watch two sides, and monitor the whole structure. A third car rolls up. Steve shouts for the officer to drive his car over the curb and position it between all of us and the house. Good move. The women, if they're inside, could be armed with something other than knives.

"I'm suing you two, too," Pickup Man says, glaring at the female officer as she and her partner lead him away. "What the hell, shouldn't you be in high school little girl? Studying for the big test." She must have cranked the pain on his wrist joint because he suddenly yelps and dances on his tiptoes. "I'm suing all of you assholes!" he shouts into the night.

"We got to check the house." Steve says. "He's going to be okay, right Cary?"

Finally, the distinctive wail of an ambulance over on Hawthorne. A grey unmarked rocks to a stop at the curb. Angela gets out quickly and heads our way.

"Yes, he will," the big man snaps, his eyes glistening, his mouth agape. He looks back at the house, and I notice for the first time how the side of the structure looks like a face: two smallish windows on the second level and one longish one on the lower. Very *Amityville*. Cary looks back at us. "When I pulled up, Richard was staggering across the lawn coming from this closest side of the house. I never saw the women and he couldn't talk. He just fell. We shouldn't have been in separate cars. Partners should stay together ..." He looks back down at Daniels whose eyes seemed fixed on me.

"Richard," Angela says gently as she lowers herself to her knees. She touches Cary's shoulder and puts her other hand on Daniels' chest. "An ambulance is coming," she says motherly. "They'll take care of him." Cary visibly relaxes.

While he tells Angela what happened and the young female officer and her partner stuff Pickup Man into their backseat, I flip my radio over to the Southeast Portland channel and give dispatch a description of the sisters, their bizarre hair cuts, race, age, height, weight, unknown clothing. Armed and dangerous. Dispatch assigns cars to cruise the surrounding streets.

"How do you want to play it?" Steve asks. Angela stands and steps over to us.

"You sure?" I ask her. She nods, her defiant eyes conveying the conversation is over. "Okay then. I don't want to wait for SWAT. I want to check the house now."

"Let's do it," Angela says. Steve nods.

The ambulance kills its siren a block away, but with twilight upon us, its flashing lights continue to whip against the sides of houses and cars as it pulls up to the curb. A marked unit stops behind it and an officer by the name of Tad Elmore gets out. He is an old timer with about twenty plus years on. Good reputation.

"Tad," I say. "We're going to search this house. We'd like a uniform with us."

"Let me at 'em," he says, hitching his gun belt and nodding to Steve and Angela. He looks down at Daniels as the medics surround him.

As Steve tells dispatch we're going in, I give Tad a quick rundown of the sisters' descriptions. "And at least one has a knife."

Lieutenant Foskey's voice blares in quadrasonic on our four radios: "I'm still ten minutes away. Can we get SWAT out to do the house?"

Foskey is right, of course. We got the house contained so we should go by the book and wait for SWAT. Or at least try to order them out with a car's PA system. I look at Steve, Angela, and Tad and lift my eyebrows.

Angela looks down at the ambulance people tending to Daniels, and says with grinding teeth, "I want these bitches." Steve and Tad nod.

"We need to go in now, Boss," I say into my portable. "We

got plenty of people." That isn't much of a reason. Actually, it's not a reason at all.

Foskey: "Okay, I trust your judgment, Sam."

I stuff the radio into my jacket pocket, and say, "This has to go down smoothly, folks, or we'll all be washing cars out at North Precinct."

"I'm familiar with the house," Tad says. "Been here a half-dozen times on family beefs. Hauled the male half to jail twice and the female once. They're gone now and the bank owns the house. No basement, but as you can see, two stories. I think it's mostly empty. Three bedrooms and a bath upstairs, and the same downstairs, along with a living room and kitchen. The stairs to the second floor are right inside the front door to the left. Empty space under the stairs. Living room to the right. Short hallway on the left side leading through a dining room and into a kitchen. Another short hallway on the right side of the living room leading to a bathroom and the bedrooms."

I say, "Okay, we'll knock and announce and kick the door in. Tad, you take up a post at the bottom of the stairs and watch the second floor and the ground floor hallway to the kitchen. The rest of us will stream right and move around the perimeter of the living room and down the hall to the bathroom and bed-rooms. Don't know about guns but they did cut Daniels, and they've killed at least twice before. And they're crazy enough to nail a man to a board."

Angela and I look at each other, both of us thinking the same thing. *Please don't let this be a repeat of the alley.*

The uniform at the front right corner of the house gives us a thumbs up, pointing at his portable to indicate he and his partner behind the house heard us tell radio we're going inside. The officer in the back has either the worst post or the best.

One time I was posted at the back corner of a house as our narcotics people crashed through the front door and did the usual shouting and screaming. A window opened above me, and an instant later I was showered with white powder and dozens of hypodermic needles.

We move up to the front door.

*   *   *

"A cop, Cork? What were you thinking? Stabbing a cop!"

"Keep your damn voice down," Corky whispered, peering with one eye through the slanted window blinds. The room was mostly dark except for diffused red and blue lights strobing through the living room window. "I got to think for a second."

"The old nigger and the raghead bitch I sorta understood, but shit Cork, you stabbed a cop"

Corky spun away from the window and shoved her sister in the chest, knocking her back against a bare wall, her head hitting the plaster with a thump. Corky slapped her palm over Arizona's mouth and leaned in so close their noses were touching. "I said keep your voice down. Yeah, I stabbed him. Excuse me all to hell if I didn't want to go to jail. You want to go back?"

Arizona's "no" was muffled.

"Now at least we got a fighting chance," she hissed, her spittle making Arizona blink.

Arizona pried her sister's hand off her mouth. "A chance for what?" she snapped. "There's cops all over the damn place out there. I know if you hurt a cop they do a whole lot of payback."

"Haven't you learned anything, Ari?" Corky hissed into her sister's face. "What does a white warrior do when surrounded, huh? What do you do when outnumbered and surrounded by kikes, niggers, wetbacks, slopes, and motherfucking white sympathizers?"

Arizona looked at the sweat streaming down Corky's big face. Filtered, multicolored light reflected off its sheen. There was something in her eyes ... something ... insane. Was it new or had it been there all along? Corky punched the wall next to Arizona's head. "Answer. What do you do, Ari? Can your simple head remember?"

Arizona scrunched her eyes shut against her sister's intensity. "Kill 'em," she said weakly. "Kill 'em."

Corky nodded for a long moment. "'Kill 'em.' Damn straight sister."

Arizona tried to sidestep away but Corky cupped her shoulders and squeezed them hard. She was looking at Arizona, but the older sister's eyes were looking into some far off place.

After a moment, her eyes blinked back into focus and she gently touched the side of Arizona's face. "We're going to finish the job Colonel White assigned us to do. After tomorrow we're going to be such hot property in ARM we'll be in charge of people and telling them what to do. We'll be heroes, warriors." Her eyes suddenly flashed, though the light wasn't from the strobing police cars. "This is what we've been working for, fighting for. If we don't do it, the mud people and the Jew government, they're going to wipe out the white race."

"The hell with it now," Arizona said irritably, knocking Corky's hand away from her face. "It don't mean a damn thing now because you stabbed a cop. They're going to shoot us even if we give up."

Corky's eyes flamed again and she slapped Arizona's face hard, slamming her back into the wall.

Her head still turned away and her arm up to shield herself from another strike, Arizona hissed, "That's the last time I will let you hit me." She turned to face her sister, tears streaking down her cheeks. She lowered her arms like a bullfighter lowers his cape before a bull. "I've loved you forever, but you've gone crazy."

Corky reached for her and Arizona cocked back her fist. "No, no," Corky said, holding up her palm and shaking her head. "No more, Ari. I'm sorry. But you have to trust me. I'm going to get us out of this just like I've gotten us out of other bad situations."

"Listen, Cork," Arizona said tilting her head toward the window, her eyes wide with panic. "They're coming for us."

Corky grabbed Arizona's arm and pulled her toward the door. "You heard of hiding in plain sight, Ari?" she whispered. "'Cause we're going to do. It's the last thing the Jew puppets expect. You got to trust me now."

* * *

"I'll take the lead," Tad whispers. He and Angela are standing by the left side of the front door. Steve and I are on the right.

It's best to have a uniform up front so later the suspects can't say they didn't know it was the police coming in, even though they announced it. I know of three cases where suspects got away with shooting cops because their attorneys argued their clients thought they were being robbed by other crooks and were only defending themselves. Justice—got to love it.

"Yes," I whisper. "You and Angela go left. Steve and I will go right. Tad, you stay at the foot of the stairs while the three of us do the living room and check the other rooms. If we don't find them downstairs, the three of us will move to the second floor. Again, Tad, you stay on the ground floor by the stairs."

No one likes to watch the stairs but I don't give him time to protest. I want a visible uniform where the sisters can see him from upstairs and downstairs. Plus he's a veteran street cop. Steve is good but his street skills might be rusty.

"Ready?" Nods all around.

I turn my back on the door and look over my shoulder at a spot about six inches from the handle and lock. I raise a finger in the air, two fingers, three, and shout, "Police! Open up!" and, as fast as I can, I cross step and back kick the spot.

The door slams open with a spray of wood chips, hits the wall with an echoed bang, and bounces back. Tad shoulders it back open and moves to the left to the bottom of the beige-carpeted stairs, bent in a crouch, moving his Glock 9 from the top of the stairs over to the living room, and back to the stairs. Angela is right behind him, her gun extended. Steve goes right with me on his heels. We all do a quick scan before Angela moves over and takes the lead in front of Steve and me. We begin moving along the front wall, both of them holding their Glocks in a two-handed grip and looking over their sights. My weapon is holstered but I got my hand on it.

The room is illuminated by streetlights and strobing emergency vehicle lights seeping through the partially closed window blinds and broken doorway. The beige-carpeted room is virtually empty, save for a couple of old carpets bunched up in a pile in the center of the room, along with a couple of bulging green trash bags and an overturned armoire.

Because there isn't any furniture to check behind or under, we sweep around the room quickly, move toward the bedroom hallway, and post on each side of its entrance. I look over at Tad. The veteran cop is totally focused on peering over his weapon, sweeping it from the top of the dark stairs down to the hallway entrance to the dining room and kitchen, and back to the top of the stairs again. Good man.

Angela looks at me and I give her a nod to proceed. She treads lightly down the hall preserving the proverbial eggshells. The hall is partially lit by a light coming from a room at the end. She stops before a partly open door on the left. I'm guessing it's the bathroom, judging by a few inches of floor tile I can see in the dark room. While Steve keeps his gun trained on the lit bedroom, Angela kicks the door the rest of the way open, sending it slamming into a wall, followed by the sound of breaking glass tinkling down onto the floor. Isn't a broken mirror supposed to mean bad luck? The room is empty and we proceed to the first bedroom. The door is open.

Angela crouches, reaches a hand around the door facing and snaps on the light. She and I stream in and Steve watches the doors of the remaining rooms. Empty, except for several fast food wrappers on the floor.

Back in the hall, Angela resumes the lead. Steve looks at me, points at my hand on my holstered weapon and makes a question mark with his eyebrows. I point to him and Angela, to indicate they would be in my line of fire. He nods with a frown. Hope he bought it.

We repeat the procedure with the last unlit room. It, too, is empty. The last one, the one with the lights on, contains a pile about twice the size of the one in the living room, this one made up of garbage bags, a broken floor lamp, and a bicycle frame. Back out in the hall, Angela inflates her cheeks and blows out some stress. "Next hall," she says, and leads us toward the living room.

It strikes me, well, it doesn't actually strike me. I've been thinking this since Angela said she was coming out. For four years, Steve has been shuffling files, tapping a keyboard, and talking with snitches. Not exactly preparation for carrying out a SWAT mission. Angela's adrenaline is boiling over after shooting Puke and her anger about Richard Daniels has to be affecting her thinking. Then there is my gun issue. Still, here I am, kicking in doors and poking around in dark rooms with my gun in its holster and without a bullet in the chamber.

What a team we make.

I watch Angela peek around the corner to the living room and wave to Tad that we're coming out. Without looking back, she gestures for us to follow.

*　*　*

Corky's and Arizona's breasts and thighs were pressed tightly against each other. Corky was embracing her sister's trembling body, partly because she had no choice and partly to keep Arizona from moving.

"Don't move, baby," Corky said below a whisper into her ear.

Arizona had never been so scared in her life. Even with her big sister's body pressed against hers, which had always made her feel good and safe, and even with Cork's warm breath against the side of her neck, which always led to some glorious love making, Arizona wanted to run. Run like crazy and scream her guts out.

The part making her want to pee her pants was lying here in this dark, cramped hard place and listening to them. Their footsteps ... so near ... the rustle of their clothes. Sounded like three, maybe four of them. One of them was breathing really loud.

Oh God ... so close ...

*　*　*

We snake around the corner and move along the back wall toward the other hall. Tad, holding his Glock 9 in a two-handed grip is focusing his attention solely on the top of the stairs now. Angela stops at the door facing leading into the dining room. Tad said the first room was a dining area and the kitchen was on the other side. Angela must be able to see all of the dining room because, without turning toward us, she gives us a thumb up to follow her.

We curl around the door facing and scoot along the dining room wall toward the kitchen doorway. There isn't a dining room table in the dark room, but I can just barely make out several pieces of clothing on the floor and a scattering of blankets. After sleeping on hard prison beds for several years, sleeping on a wall-to-wall carpet under a thin blanket must seem like a luxury to the women.

The kitchen would be completely dark if it weren't for the ambient emergency vehicle lights coming through the living room blinds and the smashed-open door, seeping down the hallway, and into the kitchen to reflect off the chrome refrigerator. It's not much, but it's enough to see the sisters aren't in the kitchen. There are bags of food scraps, coats draped over the kitchen chairs, and a dozen or more soda cans and food stuffs setting about.

I open the back door and quick-peek around the door facing. I give the uniformed cop watching the corner a wave and point upward to indicate we're about to go upstairs. She nods.

Angela points up and I nod yes. She leads the way across the kitchen, through the doorway into the dining room, and—

Thump

The three of us freeze and look up trying in vain to see through the ceiling. I recognize the sound.

When I was a boy and living with my mom on Southeast Gladstone, the house we lived in was a ranch style with four large pine trees on the property, the biggest, about sixty feet high, its limbs a high roof over the house. During late summer and early fall, pine cones would fall from the tree and land on our roof with a thumping sound. In fact, when I go bald, I'm going to have a visible scar where one nearly knocked me out when I was out raking up pine needles. Other times of the year, squirrels chasing each other through the branches would dislodge them. It's not late summer yet, but I bet just now a nocturnal squirrel did exactly that. I did notice pine cones scattered about the front yard.

Or maybe it was the sound of a two-hundred-pound, weight-trained, murdering female moving around up there.

In a slight crouch, Angela steps over to the doorway and peers out to check on Tad; I look over her shoulder. He's gone. Looking over the barrel of her gun, she rotates left to quick-scan the living room and then swings her weapon back in the vicinity of the broken front door. Outside, flashing colored lights bounce off the trunk of one of the pine trees and off the paint gloss on the front door.

Angela quickly leads us toward the stairs. She snakes around the handrail and moves up a couple of steps. She points at the top of the stairs just as Tad's uniformed leg disappears into the dark. Not a good move on his part to do a John Wayne and charge into the unknown by himself. I can see the frustration on Angela's face as she looks back at me. She points at my feet, points at her eyes with two fingers, and gestures at the living room. I nod. I'll man the post down here. Angela and Steve move up the stairs and disappear into the dark.

So here I am watching the room now. I hate to admit it, but

I'm grateful I don't have to move up another set of stairs. The last time I did it, I entered hell through a bedroom door.

Doors. What was the old game show where the overly enthusiastic host would ask, "Will you choose door number one, door number two, or door number three?" If I were on the show, I'd say, "Well Monty, since the door into Mister Axelbrad's store a few months ago ended in a death, and the door into the boy's bedroom two months ago ended in death, and the double doors into the warehouse in Bien Hoa ended in death, and so did the trapdoor into the dirt tunnel in Saigon, well darn-it Monty, I ain't gonna choose none of 'em."

I look at the living room, the pile of carpets and other junk in the center of the room and at the far hallway we checked. Those doors were okay. A little nerve wracking, but they turned out okay. I can hear the troops moving around, moving through doors. Thing is, if I can hear them, so can the sisters.

How many houses and buildings have I searched as a cop? Couple of hundred at least, usually with negative results. Sometimes with funny results. Like the guy we found stuck in a heat vent in an adult movie theater. He'd been stuck for two days, dripping sweat, while the overcoat and hand-lotion crowd complained to the management about how cold it was.

There was this guy hiding under a bed in a house off Foster. The cop had written off the space as too small to hide anyone and was about to leave the room without checking. The burglar got spooked and shot the cop in the calf, the only target he could see from his cramped place.

Then there was the guy hiding in the fifty-gallon barrel of old motor oil in an auto shop down on Grand. We had fifteen cops searching the place when one of the guys just happened to see a nose sticking out of the black soup. The cop shouted at him to come up, hands first. The submerged kid was trembling so much the oil was rippling like the glass of water in the iconic scene in *Jurassic Park*. The kid finally surfaced, hands first, then his arms, and finally his head, all dripping black goop. The whites of the kid's eyes got big as saucers when he saw a dozen guns pointing at him. He sputtered out some of the dark gunk, and said, "Lemme ex-splain."

"Searching a room is simple when done right," my friend Clarence always tells the recruits in the academy. "But too many times cops make the same two mistakes. The first one is lots of coppers fail to look up when searching a yard. They look behind a tree and inside the tool shed, but they forget to look up into the branches or on top of the roof. When searching inside of a building, too many times they search the sides of a room but miss things in the center of it. Even SWAT guys make these mistakes occasionally."

The center of the room.

I spin around toward the pile of carpets and the broken armoire just as a holiday ham-sized fist slams into my forehead, lifting me off my feet and sending me back into the wall.

A skull-cracking pain in the back of my head replaces the skull-jarring pain in my forehead. I have a fleeting picture of Wylie Coyote tricked by the Road Runner to run full steam into the side of a rock cliff. As Wylie begins his comic slide down the wall, I descend into a world of dizzy nausea. The two-hundred-twenty-pound Road Runner drives her massive shoulder into my midsection, forcing out any remaining oxygen from my body, sounding like air brakes on a big truck. A second later, she stands upright with me draped over the same bulky shoulder, my legs extending out in front of her, my torso and head resting against her middle back.

Angela, Steve, Tad?

First I realize I only shouted those names in my head instead of out my mouth, and then I realize Road Runner is carrying me past the carpets—now flung aside—and into the dining room. The jostling isn't helping the fog in my head.

"What are we ..." Words. I hear words in the fog. ". . . doing with him? Cops ... around house." The words aren't coming from Road Runner. Not from me, either.

Okay, okay, I see boots, brown, big ones, running behind us. Man, it hurts to be draped over someone's thick shoulder while they run. Every jarring step knocks a little wind out of me, and my aching forehead keeps hitting the woman's larger than life rear end.

Hard to generate a lot of power from here, but I hammerfist her left kidney anyway, once, twice, three times. She stumbles to the side and my head hits something chrome. The refrigerator. It really didn't hurt much, at least not compared to the forehead punch a minute ago and when the back of my head banged off the wall.

I recognize the tile floor. It's the small mudroom or whatever it's called that leads to the back door where I saw the female officer out in the yard.

"Door, Ari!"

I lift my body enough to see the other person squeezing by us, the other—it's the sisters! Okay, I'm all the way awake now.

I punch Arizona in one of her big boobs. Not the best target, or my hardest blow given my awkward position, but it still knocks her against a pantry shelf.

The one carrying me is wearing a white T-shirt under a blue windbreaker. I snake my hand under the bottom of her jacket and under her T-shirt to grab some skin. She's a big woman, but she isn't fat. No love handles like the drunk teenager at the Mini Mart. I grab what flesh I can into my tight fist and rip it back and forth.

She yelps and reflexively flips me off her shoulder and right into the doorpost. Something crunches as the right side of my back, from my shoulder to my hipbone, hits the edge of the hardwood so hard the wall trembles. The crunch was either a rib or my cell phone. At least the ride's over.

"Freeze, assholes!" A female voice.

I look toward the yard to see the officer I waved to a few minutes ago, her gun pointing toward Arizona who must have jumped down the three steps before realizing a cop was standing a few feet away. "Don't kill us," Arizona pleads, raising her hands. "Please. Don't shoot us." She is as rattled as her sister is calm.

Deciding it's better to get out of the line of fire than to stay here and wonder if my head hurts more than my back, I push myself off the door facing and start to take a wobbly step down.

Big arms bear hug me from behind and lift me. Best laid plans. Okay, this is getting old. I get it now why little people get so mad about people lifting them up.

"Put him down!" the female officer shouts, making this even more embarrassing. Just as I start to kick back at whatever I can hit, my hugger, it's got to be Corky, leaps off the porch at the officer with me still in her tight embrace.

The quick thinking cop manages to lower her weapon and blade her body just as our combined weight of four hundred and twenty-odd pounds crashes into her sending the three of us to the ground in a thrashing pile of arms, legs, and lots of cursing.

The big arms crushing the wind out of me relax for an

instant, allowing me to drive a hard elbow into her side. Corky grunts, but before I can launch a second technique, a large hand slaps onto my face and pushes me so hard I roll a couple of revolutions across the grass. I manage to stop and I get up as quickly as I can, which is actually not that quick. My dizzy brain, aching back, hurting head, and general disorientation don't contribute to a graceful recovery.

By the time I'm all the way standing, the female officer, up on one knee, pops two rounds from her Glock at the escaping sisters. One of them yelps just before their feet disappear around a large hedge at the back of the yard.

"Think I got one," she says. She keeps her gun trained on the hedge. "Blew my knee out, though. Can't pursue."

I shake the fuzzies out of my head, most of them anyway. I grab at my radio. Gone. My portable must have fallen out when I fell against the wall. I pat my side and feel my gun. If I had my druthers, I would prefer to have lost my weapon rather than my communication. "Update radio and tell them which direction they're heading." She nods and I head off across the lawn, calling over my shoulder, "When the others come out, tell them where I've gone."

"Shouldn't you wait for backup?" she shouts. I slip around the side of the hedge to find myself on a graveled alley.

I swear I've been in more alleys the last three months than I have in the last fifteen years. This one is partially lit by random back porch lights and a couple of tall streetlights out on Tenth Avenue and Eleventh. Still, the shadows are deep and the hiding places are many. I move into one on the left side. It's dark and it conceals me, unless the sisters are here in the shadows too.

No, there they are at the end of the alley, crouched in the

shadow of a garage on the right side, their heads silhouetted against the streetlights on Southeast Taylor just ahead of them. They're looking in all directions; I'm sure they can't see me. They dart across Taylor. Corky is running fine. Arizona has a pronounced limp and is pressing her right hand against her right back cheek.

She's been ass shot.

I stay on the left side of the alley moving quickly from deep shadow to deep shadow, trying to keep pace with their silhouettes. Just before Taylor, I cross over to the right side of the alley and crouch in the same garage shadow the sisters had hunkered in moments ago. A marked police unit zips by. I reach for my cell. Damn. I'm no techie, but I'm pretty sure a phone shouldn't rattle when you pull it from your pocket. Must have been the crunch I heard when I hit the doorpost.

I step out onto the sidewalk only to see the police car round the corner and head north. The sisters are moving south.

I move across the street and into the next alley. For an instant I think I lost them but when I squat down, I can see two heads silhouetted against ambient light coming from somewhere. The one on the left is moving steadily while the other bobs to the right on every step.

To my right, a deep voice in the dark. "What are you doin' back here?"

I jump out of my skin and snap my hands up into a fighting stance. I can barely see that the figure in the deep shadow of the tree is a man and he's got something in his hand.

"Asked you a question, mate. If I don't like your answer I'm using this crowbar on your face. Tired of you shitbirds break-ing into my garage."

"I'm a cop in pursuit. I don't have any communication.

Need you to call nine-one-one and tell dispatch Detective Reeves is pursuing the two sisters south from Southeast Taylor in the alley between Tenth and Eleventh."

The man let's loose a smoker's laugh, then, "Well now, ain't this rich. You guys never found my car last year and two weeks ago a cop told me on the phone to report my stolen tools to my insurance company because they didn't have no cop to send out here. But they got 'em to chase little girls down an alley. No copper, I ain't calling."

"Listen pal, these are the women responsible—"

"Ain't my problem," the man grunts and heads back toward his house.

I look down the alley. I don't see them. I take off at a sprint, though not much of one considering I can't see the ground and my hip hurts. My head too. I slow near the end of the alley, step into a deep shadow, and listen.

There ... crunching brush in the backyard of a house behind me—sounds as if it's coming from the corner house on Main and Tenth. The sound is fading so they got to be moving toward the front of the house, toward Tenth. Why would they chance exposing themselves on the street?

Okay, there's why. No alley across Main Street.

I advance to the last deep shadow before Main. Listen ... nothing. I move just slightly out of the shadow onto the side-walk. The corner streetlight is out, making it hard for them to see me and hard for me to see them. I move forward along the sidewalk a few feet until I'm in the shadow of two big trees on the side yard of the corner house. Where are the damn police cars cruising the streets? Cops—they're never around when you need them.

Sound of movement at ten o'clock between the house and

a big tree, a weeping willow, its leaf-heavy branches forming an umbrella over the sidewalk. About fifteen feet in front of me, a limb moves aside and Corky, the one who likes to pick me up, peeks out, looking first toward Tenth and then back toward me. Her eyes widen.

I flip my jacket back and grip my gun, leaving it in the holster. "On the ground!" I shout. "Do it now!"

I can't remember the name of the program I was watching but there were these two hunters tiptoeing around in the brush, listening for sounds, and gesturing to each other. At one point, one of the great hunters whispered to his buddy, "I don't think it's here any—" He never finished his sentence because a giant boar, as big as a cow, exploded out of the brush and nailed the guy right in the gut.

The cow charging through the limbs at my nine o'clock is as big as a bull and runs pretty fast for one with a bullet in its flank. I sidestep her charge and drive my palm into her jaw hinge just below her ear as she passes. She staggers and stumbles over her own feet but manages to stay up. Corky is moving quickly toward me, her fist up on each side of her head. It's like she knows I'm not going to pull my gun.

I weigh two hundred and these two must weigh two fifteen, two twenty-five each, and it's not all prison food and McDonald's. BJ's friend down at the joint said they spent a lot of time pumping iron out in the yard. They will never win a body beautiful contest but they will win for most scary.

I throw a palm at Corky to keep her hands up and follow with a scoop kick with the inside edge of my shoe into her shinbone. She yelps and hops back. She reflexively reaches for her upraised leg, but quickly puts her foot back down and raises her fists again. Tough woman: eats the pain and is streetwise.

She begins limping in a circle to my left. Her sister, one hand rubbing the side of her jaw and also favoring a limb, circles to my right.

I lift my open palms near my shoulders and blade my body. I call this the I-don't-want-to-fight stance, one I teach to cops and citizens because it's nonthreatening and will sometimes calm a volatile person. Thing is, I want to fight them. I want to hurt them for Ocnod and Yolanda, for Mark and David, and even for Puke and Executioner.

How bizarre the sisters look. One has buzz cut hair on the sides and a mullet in the back and the other has slicked back hair like a salesman on *Mad Men*. Both have heads and torsos as blocky as Sponge Bob's, massive, blue jeans-covered columns for legs, herculean shoulders and arms, and breasts the size of Jersey cow utters. I point to the one who likes to lift me.

"You'd be Corky, right?" I try not to smile at how her eyes flicker. I look at the other one, who needs to take one more step to be in my sidekick range. "So that makes you Arizona." Her eyes widen but with more fear than surprise.

"Cork?" she says worriedly, looking over at her sister. I cross step with all the speed I can muster and ram my size eleven into the softness about six inches below Arizona's belt. She bellows, her upper body snaps forward and at the same time she flies backwards as if yanked from behind.

A dark grey, unmarked police sedan slides to the curb. If it had been one second sooner, its right front headlight would have nailed Arizona. Instead her rear hits the fender hard and she falls back onto the hood. BJ gets out.

Wait. BJ gets out? What is he doing here?

He moves quickly around the front of the car looking worriedly at Arizona. When he sees me, his expression does a one eighty. "Why did you kick her?" Slow learner this guy.

Arizona bends forward looking like she's about to vomit. A hard blow to the bladder will conjure puking, pissing, or crapping the pants—sometimes all three. BJ touches her arm and looks into her grimacing face with concern.

Apparently forgetting about me, Corky turns toward BJ, and shouts, "Get your damn hands off her," and charges him like a locomotive with a mullet. I grab at her arm but she jerks away from me before I can get a solid grip on her slick jacket.

As fast as any of my senior students, she grabs BJ by the throat with one hand and by his crotch with her other. I kick behind her knee twice to force her to buckle and get her head low enough for me to apply a sleeper hold, but her body is so rigid with BJ's additional weight her leg doesn't bend. As she cleans my old boss to her chest, I drive three hard-hook punches into her right kidney, the same one I hit three times with a hammer fist in the kitchen. She bellows in pain and sags a little. I grab at BJ's arms, but the woman recuperates in a nanosecond and presses the naive lieutenant over her head before flipping him end over end onto the windshield of the police car.

BJ's body lands so hard I'm amazed it doesn't break the glass. His back takes most of the impact, but his head connects pretty hard too. He's laying very still now, his eyes closed.

I reach for Corky's shoulder and she spins on me. I shield block her wild swing and start to drive a punch into her body, though it hasn't done much thus far, but I slip on something, probably weeping willow leaves slick with humidity. I don't fall but my right foot drops off the curb. It lands on its side and for a second I wonder if I blew my ankle, but just as quickly I realize it doesn't hurt at all.

All that took about five seconds, long enough for Corky

to drape her sister's arm over her shoulder and for the two of them to start stumble-limping across the street toward the shadows of another backyard. I automatically begin to pursue but a moan from BJ stops me.

"BJ?" I say, touching his shoulder. The back of his head is on the driver's side of the windshield and the rest of his body is stretched along the passenger side. "Where does it hurt?"

"Don't ... know," he says, grimacing and breathing laboriously. "Don't feel ... anything."

"Don't move," I say pointlessly. I start to go around the door to radio for an ambulance but I stop when a marked car careens around the corner and anchors it in the middle of the street. Stone Blackman gets out.

"Order an ambulance, Stone. Don't try to move him. And ask for the units in the area to block off the streets between Tenth and Eleventh, Main to Hawthorne. The two sisters are moving southbound through backyards. One has been shot in the hip but both are extremely dangerous."

"And tell Steve and Angela which way I've gone, will you?"

"Yeah, but what are you going to do?"

* * *

It's been ten minutes now and I'm still trudging through people's backyards, at least a half dozen of them, not one with a back porch light on. I can't think of any yard paraphernalia I haven't tripped over: sprinklers, tricycles, lawn chairs, and barbeque pits. Stepping into the pit sent me down onto all fours. The good news is I haven't fallen into a *koi* pond. Been there, done that.

Angela, Steve, and Tad haven't caught up with me yet. Even if they called out, I wouldn't answer, not when I'm so close to the sisters. I'm hoping the women think I stayed with BJ. Man-oh-man, Corky lifted him as if he were a child. The guy is at least one eighty.

The sisters are doing a good job of staying ahead of me. Sometimes I hear them and they sound only a backyard away, then all is quiet. Just when I think I might have passed them in the dark, or they've circled back, I hear them ahead of me again. The only thing I can figure is every couple of houses or so, they move down a side yard toward Tenth, wait until the coast is clear, dash down the sidewalk a ways, and cut back between houses to resume moving through backyards. Sounds crazy but desperate people do desperate things.

This has to be one the few blocks in the city where homes don't have fences between them. Each yard blends into the next with the occasional row of low shrubs to designate property lines and to send me stumbling.

There should be only about three more houses left before Hawthorne Boulevard. In fact, the last house is behind the funeral parlor Mister Axelbrad mentioned. If I had a radio I could have a couple units waiting for them there with open arms. They might be there anyway if they've sealed off the blocks. I've seen two police cars pass by on Tenth, but the cars were heading away from the funeral home. If it wasn't so dark, I'd try to get ahead of the sisters and greet them with a "Surprise!" But it's so dark—

Whoooosh ... Whump!

I'm stumbling backward from whatever slammed my chest but manage to stay upright. I got a one-second warning as I half heard and half sensed something cutting through the thin branches of a Japanese maple tree. I look down on the ground and can just barely see ... a hoe. Those bitches made me and threw a garden hoe. Okay, now I'm ticked off.

I raise my arms to shield my face against any other incoming and move farther to the rear of the backyard. I'm a little deeper in the shadows here, hopefully out of sight so they won't thrc a Honda riding mower at me next. When I can see the sisters' heads, they are always close to the back of homes, no doubt taking advantage of some of the interior lights leaking out into the yard. I pick up my pace. One more backyard to go.

It looks like a wall, maybe six feet high, separating the last house from the backside of the funeral home property. There is probably a driveway back there they use to bring in the recently deceased.

There, two dark figures slipping over the wall. I'm guessing that's Corky helping Arizona over before she pulls herself up and rolls over the top like a Hollywood stuntwoman. I approach the wall about thirty feet to the right of where they went over, which looks to be the back corner of the funeral business. I pull myself up enough to peek over and see Corky front kick a small door next to a loading ramp. It slams open and the two slip in and close it behind them. I recall Mister Axelbrad said the home isn't alarmed.

*   *   *

I quick-peek around the broken doorpost, slip in, and take cover behind a stack of cardboard boxes. I'm in a dimly lit hallway about thirty feet long, ending at what appears to be a room on the Hawthorne Street side where the public would enter. There is a door on the right side of the hall about half-way down and I move quickly toward it on quiet feet. Locked. I sidestep, though I'm not any less exposed, all the way to the end of the hall. I was right. It does flow into a large sitting room, also dimly lit by invisible ceiling lights. Must be on a timer.

Man, it's not just quiet in here but it's quiet-quiet, as if the place were hermetically sealed. The thick burgundy carpet, the beige marble walls and white pillars, the heavy window drapes, and the many plush chairs and sofas eat the sound. There is a fireplace on the wall to my left, though I can't tell if it's real, and an open room to my right with a placard over the door. OFFICE.

I look back at the large room, at how it seems to stretch on forever, with at least a dozen chairs and sofas set along both walls. There is a set of double doors near the far end on the left side, probably the chapel, and a couple of doors on the far back wall. No clue where they lead.

Man, this quiet is eerie. Not because I'm in a funeral home ... actually, it's probably some of it, but there is an uncomfortable sense of being in a vacuum. Or in a coffin. The sweet smell I detected when I first stepped into the hallway from outside infuses this room. Is embalming fluid sweet smelling? Don't know. Or maybe it's from the zillions of flowers brought into the building over the years. Or maybe they put some kind of deodorizer in the room to cloak the unremitting smell of death. Maybe it's just my imagination working overtime. No, the place definitely smells. Mister Axelbrad said the owner has been in Europe so it hasn't been aired out in a while.

It wouldn't be a good tactical move to stroll down the center of this room since the women might be hiding behind any of the many large pieces of furniture. I should stand fast and wait for a cop to notice the broken door and come in to check it out. They are probably surrounding this place right now.

There is only one big Victorian-style chair between the office and me, and happily I can see there isn't a big beefy woman waiting behind it to spring out. But what about in the office itself? Maybe the sisters are waiting for me in there.

Man, it's so freaky quiet. It's as if—

Thump!

I snap my head to the left. It's Arizona and she's hobbling fast toward a door at the end of the room, an overturned Victorian chair in her wake. Corky must have already gone through it.

CHANK chink, CHANK chink "Purple haze ... all in my brain ..."

I drop to one knee, my hand on my holstered gun. Jimi Hendrix's steel guitar and voice are so loud it just might burst my skull. Where in the ...?

CHANK chink, CHANK chink ... "Scuse me while I kiss the sky."

I stand laboriously, my hands over my ears, pushing myself through the almost overpowering weight of the god-awful sound. Every speaker in this building must be about to crack. Where is the source? And why is there Jimi Hendrix music in a funeral home, anyway? A customer's favorite tune? Nighttime janitorial staff music? If the sisters are doing this to psyche me, it's working.

CHANK chink, CHANK chink ...

I'm going after Arizona. I look down the long room and note all the chairs on this side are set a couple of feet away from the wall. I can easily see behind them, and the other furniture on this side don't offer much concealment. The only place Corky could hide is behind the far end of one of the sofas.

CHANK chink, CHANK chink "No, help me aw yeah! Oh no no, oh, help me ..."

Wilting under the crushing sound, I feel like I'm moving

through thick syrup down the left side of the wall. Across the room, the sofa and chairs are set up like mirror images of those on this side: two chairs across from each other, two low tables with lamps, two sofas, three more chairs, and two more sofas. I move quickly on the assumption Corky isn't in this room. Never assume, says the police maxim. I'm doing it anyway because I think I'm right. I assume I'm right.

I slip behind the first big chair and the second one. Now the first sofa.

Jimi's song ends. The sudden and grave-deep quiet sends tingles creeping up my spine.

Using both hands, I push against my end of the sofa to scoot it a couple of feet. No one jumps up and no one falls over. I walk quickly along the front of it, all the while watching the sofa across the way. No one is behind it either.

I continue moving behind chairs and tables, stopping to nudge sofas, all the while monitoring the furniture across the way, and looking for surprises behind me. I hate surprises, especially in funeral homes.

I've reached the double doors on the left. Locked. Sign reads **CHAPEL**. Were they locked before or did Corky lock them behind her? I'm ass-uming again because I think the sisters would stick together. I move over to the door Arizona went through. It reads: **EMPLOYEES ONLY**.

I can open it a crack and peek in or I can jerk it open and charge in like a SWAT elephant. Both are bad ideas. I should wait for other officers. But I'm committed now. I'll do the crack and peek.

I grasp the door handle, count to three, and jerk it open enough for me to do a quick-peek. I start to reflexively press myself back against the wall but stop because the short tile-floored hallway is empty. I slip around the doorpost and ease the door closed behind me. If anyone comes through it, the sound will give me an extra moment to react.

The hallway is about twenty feet long, ending with a set of double doors. Must be where they bring in the deceased. A length of chain has been wound through the two vertical handles for additional security. I scan for an escape route. Halfway down the hall on the right there is another set of double doors, the right one ajar. Across the hall—a single door.

I walk softly along the left wall and stop diagonal to the door that is ajar. I listen for a moment. Nothing. Not even Jimi Hendrix.

I cross over to the wall and put my back to it. The doors swing inward, which is a good thing because it's easier to see what is inside. I look through the crack and see a space about five feet square and another set of double doors. I ease myself in and position myself on the right wall opposite the doors. My gut is telling me the cat and mouse game ends on the other side of them. *Other side: A funeral home pun.*

So how am I going to enter this time? A flashbang would be nice. I've been on a lot of entries where SWAT tossed a flashbang into a room to discombobulate the inhabitants. Discombobulate and make them whizz their pants. Well, I don't have a banger at my disposal but I do have a loud *kiai*. I read once about an old karate master in Japan who could yell so loud it stopped the hearts of deer and stripped bark from trees. Silly folklore, of course, but legend is to strive for.

Open the door a crack and peek? Or do the SWAT elephant thing and charge in fast and wing it from there? I'm going with the latter because the chance of the sisters being inside is one hundred and one percent.

*　*　*

"We're trapped, Cork," Arizona whispered, her voice barely under control, her eyes wide and her jaw trembling. "I wanted to hide in one of those yards until they gave up looking for us, but you said we gotta keep going. I didn't understand why and I still don't. I got a damn bullet in my hip and the cop busted your shin."

Corky, perched on the end of one of two embalming tables, listened patiently until her sister took a breath. "You done, Ari?" Her whispering was controlled, her body relaxed.

Arizona was standing, bent over a second embalming table and resting on her elbows. She had tried sitting on the white plastic chair over by the counter but it hurt her butt too much. "I got lots more."

"Well, save it," Corky snapped. "First, you don't have a bullet 'in' your body. If it had gone in, you wouldn't have a four-inch gouge across your upper hip. You'd have a hole instead. You just got grazed. It stings, yes, but you're still mobile. Your mind is making you limp."

"Okay, okay," Arizona said, looking around the brightly lit room. Her sister turned on the overhead light when they entered. She looked at the wall of chrome drawers big enough to slide in a body, a long counter with small drawers where they probably kept their instruments for cutting, draining, and sewing. Against the other wall, a small bookcase, its shelves loaded with three-ring binders, CD cases, and containers of every shape. "Creepy place," Arizona mused before looking back at Corky. "But there's only the door we came in and no windows. There's no way outta here."

Corky smiled motherly. "Just chill, baby. We're going to go out the same way we came in."

Frustrated at her sister's annoying confidence, Arizona slapped her hand on the metal table, the sound like a gunshot in the room. "How? The goddamn cop is right out there somewhere. Maybe right outside these doors."

Corky smiled and Arizona knew it's meaning. It wasn't her we're-going-get-pizza smile or her I-got-a-new-sex-trick smile, but one she always got before she hurt somebody.

Corky whispered, "You need to trust me, baby. Just. Keep. Trusting. Me."

Arizona shook her head. "I just don't see how—"

Corky held up her palm and smiled the smile again. "Didn't you recognize the cop? He's famous."

*   *   *

Doors, doors, doors. Now one more.

A loud bang from within the room startles me. Loud whispering. Time to saddle up the elephant.

I slam my shoulder against the right door and let loose an eardrum shattering *kiai* from deep within my chest. But instead of the door bursting open and crashing against the wall, it's so heavy it opens only a foot and half, just wide enough for me to slither around it and enter the room in a crouch, my hand on the butt of my holstered Glock.

"Well, that was anticlimactic, Boss," Corky says, sitting casually on a chrome table, her legs crossed, hands on her knee. Arizona is standing next to a counter, her elbow resting on what look like a large kitchen blender. It's an embalming machine, and it looks full.

"Both of you," I say. "Interlace your fingers behind your head and turn around. Get off the table, Corky."

Corky doesn't budge. Arizona starts to put her hands up

459

but stops when she sees her sister isn't moving.

Corky smiles. It's ugly and mocking. "You're embarrassing yourself, Boss."

I take a step closer. "Get off the table and put your hands behind your head."

Corky shakes her head and makes sort of a clucking sound with her tongue. "Still embarrassin' yourself. Why don't you take out your gun, Boss? You—"

"Get off the table and put your hands behind your head!"

Corky chuckles. Behind her, Arizona looks unsurely at the back of her sister's head.

Corky continues, feigning boredom. "You got your hand on it, all threatening like. You know you got probable cause to pull it, right? First, I kicked your ass." She lifts her thumb. "Then I hurt the bitch cop." Her thumb touches her index finger. "Then I threw the dough boy cop onto his windshield." She touches her middle finger. "I assaulted you with a garden hoe." She touches her ring finger. "And there's the whole reason you and your posse came after us." She touches her little finger. "Five pretty good reasons to draw your gun, but you won't, will you, Detective Reeves?"

"I said—"

"Is it because you ... can't? Is that it, Detective Reeves?"

A rush of ice-cold wind swirls through my head and my heart is thumping so hard it's got to be moving my jacket.

"Loving the look on your face, Sam. It is Sam, isn't it?" She grins. "Did I look that way when you said my name out on the street? Probably. Always unnerving when the cops call you by name." She bobs her eyebrows. "And now you know how it feels."

"Get off the table," I say, my voice sounding ineffectual.

"I followed your story every day after your shooting,

Detective Reeves. I love it whenever I see a Jew puppet gendarme fuck up. And I especially loved yours because I knew it was messin' with your mind—big time. Killing a little kid has got to do a number on you."

"Shut up!" I shout, taking a step toward her.

"Did a lot of reading on post traumatic stress down in the joint, probably enough to get a college degree. Ari and I both got diagnosed with it, see, way back in juvi and again in big girl prison." Corky wiggles her fingers at me and bugs her eyes. "We craaaa-zee, they tell us." She shrugs. "Maybe they're right. So I figured you're crazy too. Figured you'd never go back to work. Figured you'd have all kinds of head trips. I got to tell you, Detective Reeves, imagining how messed up you were made me giggle like a little kid."

I'm breathing as if I'd been running sprints. Where are Steve and Angela? Where are all the other cops? Why hasn't anyone found the kicked-in door yet?

"It struck me a little while ago, boss. You had every cause to shoot me when I threw your ass into that bitch puppet behind the house. Fact is, I was waiting for it when we were running away. But when I looked back, I saw the bitch poppin' a round. Not you. Then when I threw the pussy-looking cop on his windshield, you could have done me right then. But you didn't. Oh, you were touchin' your gun." She wiggles her fingers at me again. "Oooo, scary." She laughs. "But the threat was as impotent as you."

An image streaks across my mind of my father's angry face looking out at me through my computer after I had told him I wasn't carrying my weapon. *"Son, it is time to suck it up. I understand what you went through after your last shooting, and I understand you not wanting to carry a weapon, but if you are going to go out there on the frontlines, your fellow officers and the public expect you to take with you all the tools necessary to protect them."*

I slowly straighten from my crouch, letting my hand drop away from my Glock as the weakness washing through my body a moment ago dissipates. In it's place ... anger. No, not anger. Controlled rage. Rage at these two women. Rage at all the evil they have done in their stupidity. Rage that it takes words from this evil woman to snap me back to reality.

I can feel adrenaline pumping through my muscles now. Or maybe it's chi power. Or maybe it's "I'm sick of pussy footing around with these bitches" power.

"One last time, Corky," I say, stepping at a right angle to put her and her sister in a straight line so I only have to deal with one at a time. Corky smiles, her eyes large with excitement—or insanity. "Get off the table."

"White power, Jew puppet," Corky says, reaching behind her with her right hand. "Ari baby," she says over her shoulder.

"Show me your hand!" I shout, taking one more step toward her, almost close enough to grab her.

"Now, baby!" Corky shouts, dropping over onto her side on the embalming table.

It takes a hair of a second for me to switch from Corky's actions to her sister's. Arizona has picked up the embalming machine. The two-foot-high, foot-and-half-square unit is full of fluid. Still, she gives the heavy container a good heave.

I've always been good at bobbing and weaving and never have those things been more important than when evading a three-gallon embalming machine. It sails past my right ear and crashes to the floor, the glass portion exploding across the con-crete, spreading shard and liquid in a small wave that crashes against the wall next to the double doors.

"Damn," Corky says, scooting calmly off the table, her arm still behind her. "Can't count on baby sisters for nothin'. I got to do everything. Here you go, Boss. A fine glass of embalming fluid for you."

She thrusts a drinking glass full of a pinkish colored liquid at me. I snap my arms up to cover my face. The content of the glass splashes against my chest, forearms, and neck.

I barely see Corky moving in on me before I'm overtaken by the embalming fumes. I start coughing but manage to thrust my hand out and slash a vertical tiger claw where I last saw her forehead down to where her mouth should be. Her scream is music to my ears. Still unable to see, I throw a hard cross punch but it hits only air.

Hands on my arm pulling me. I yield to it and drive in with my shoulder. It hits a body and I hear a yelp, Arizona I think. Still unable to see, I reach out and grab something soft, round, and big. I squeeze it with all my might and then rip it back and forth to a god-awful scream accompaniment better than heaven-sent harp music.

Then my feet slip out from under me.

My eyes are burning and my throat is on fire, but my training kicks in and I reflexively yank the big screaming woman around so I land on her with my pointy elbows and hard knees, a nifty surprise technique I've taught for years. "Use the attacker as a mat," I tell my students, "and land on them with your pointy hard things.

My "mat" groans loudly but a kick to my ribs—special delivery from the other woman—sends me rolling and I don't stop until I'm on dry floor. I'm just far enough from the big puddle of embalming fluid that my eyes start to clear. I can make out

Arizona trying to get up but the fluid is ultra slick and her feet slip, one going right and one going left. She is nearly in a full split before she plops over onto her butt.

"Get up and go, Ari," Corky snaps at her. I take advantage of the pause to strip off my soaked jacket and heave it away from me. My eyes clear a little more, but my throat is still on fire. Here comes Corky, like an enraged bull with deep scratches down her face. It doesn't look like any of them caught her eyes.

I dive for my jacket and in one smooth motion swing it up and into Corky's chest. Cursing, she flings it away from her, takes two more steps toward me, but suddenly snaps her head back as the fumes from my coat find her eyes and throat. Seizing the moment, I scoot forward and jam my left foot in front of her ankle to trap it, and grab her "Harley Davidson" belt buckle. As I pull on the buckle, I whip my right heel behind her knee and yank it toward me.

I've done this takedown technique on lighter students in class and against a skinny guy on the street, and every time the knee collapsed forward and the person crumpled to the floor. But Corky's weight, street savvy, and upper body mass makes things a little less clean. For about three seconds I think she isn't going down, but then her big leg starts to collapse while bending to her right at the same time. Once I'm sure her weight has shifted enough to fall, I scoot my cute self out of her downward trajectory.

But Corky somehow manages to thrust with her other leg to dive away from where she would have fallen next to me. She crashes into a metal bookcase, pulling it and all the things displayed on the three shelves onto herself.

I leap to my feet just as Corky untangles from the chrome bookshelf. Out of the corner of my eye, I see Arizona finally get up on unstable feet. Corky twists quickly toward me and flings something—a red box—straight at me. I barely snap up my forearms and turtle my head when it hits my left arm and envelops me in an ashen cloud.

Wait. Ashen? Ash? Funeral home? Damn!

My eyes are tearing badly, but I can make out that my shirt and arms look as if I've been cleaning my chimney. I brush frantically at my chest and spit some out my mouth. The red-wood box lying at my feet is covered in Asian calligraphy and a painting of a flying dragon.

My God, I'm covered in Asian.

I think of Mai and wonder what she's doing.

Another waft of embalming fumes hits me and my eyes are again burning and my throat feels like it's been rubbed down with coarse sandpaper. Prep rooms are normally ventilated when transferring embalming fluid from the machine into a body. Under normal conditions, the fluid isn't exposed to the air. But presently there is a small lake on the floor and my clothes are saturated with the stuff.

My first training coach and I once found ourselves in the middle of an outlaw biker bar over in North Portland where the two of us were facing about twenty-five drunken, leather wearing, hard ridin' tough guys who wanted our badges and shoulder patches to decorate their uniforms.

"Why did we back out of there?" I asked my coach, after he had pulled me out the door and into the safety of our car where we waited for reinforcements. In my young rookie mind, the police should "never back down, never withdraw."

My coach, Davey O'Brien, smiled at me, and said, "I'm only half Irish but my daddy is one hundred percent. He took me out for burgers one time when I was about ten, and a bunch of thugs started bullying everyone in the place. My daddy took my hand and scurried us out to the car. He must have seen the disappointed look on my face because he ruffled my hair, and said, "Davey, lad, a good retreat is better than a bad stand."

Well, since poor to no vision and an inflamed throat count as a bad stand, I'm outta here. Watching the women as best I can, I take one sidestep toward the door with my left foot and suddenly I'm looking at the ceiling moving away from me. I hit the floor on my tailbone, which sends an angry curse to my brain. I stepped in a small rivulet of the embalming fluid.

Corky is up and moving hurriedly past me. She bounds over the stream and grabs Arizona's arm. "Come on, Ari," she says, and they're out the door before I can get to my feet. I take a step after them and again my shoe slips but I manage to remain upright. This stuff is slipperier than black ice. I swipe the sole of my shoe several times on a dry section of the floor and test my footing. Feels solid. With a dry section of sleeve, I dab at my mouth where I feel and taste ash.

In the event the sisters decide to ambush me, I make quick-peeks around both sets of doors. The inner room and the hall are clear but the small door across the way is open.

Another door.

*　*　*

"What is this place, Cork?" Arizona asked, her voice sobbing in the dark.

"A basement. Try to find a switch ... here it is." A fluorescent light sputtered to life on the low ceiling, only one of the three long bulbs working.

"But the cop can see us," Arizona whined, looking around at the disarray of boxes, old broken coffins, a half-dozen gravestones, and a washer and dryer. Along the far wall, a coffin had been positioned at the end of a long felt putting green so the golfer could aim at a small hole at the base of one end of the casket.

"He knows we're down here and we can't see shit without it on. And stop your damn crying would you?"

"I'm so scared, Cork," Arizona sobbed, as she tenderly touched her left breast. "I've been shot and he practically tore off my boob. It's the same one he punched in the house. It hurts so much. And my stomach hurts where he kicked me."

No longer listening, Corky moved toward two closed doors.

"What is it, Cork? Where do you think they go?"

The older sister opened the door on the left, looked in, and gestured for her sister to follow. "Come on," she said, stepping over an old bicycle lying on its side and scooting out of the way a grey cracked coffin lid. She tried to move a box but it barely budged. "Help me move this under the window."

"You think we can get out such a little opening? Won't there be cops outside?"

"It leads out under a hedge. See the trunk of it right there? It's the only chance we got. Get out the window, lay low under the hedge, and make a break for it when the moment is right." Corky extracted a cell from her pocket. "Here, the throwaway. You know what to do tomorrow morning and when to do it." When her sister looked at her dumbly, Corky grabbed a wad of her jacket and hissed. "Don't mess this up, Ari. You understand? Remember why the call needs to be made. Don't mess it up. Colonel White is counting on us. We'll be famous."

"I understand, Cork. But you will be there, Cork. You will be there, right?"

Corky stepped up on the box, unlatched the cobweb-covered window and shoved it up. Dirt sprinkled down on her hands.

Arizona frowned and shook her head. "Why are you telling me all this?" She looked at the window opening and then at her sister. "I think I can get through it, but you're bigger than me. I don't think—" She snapped about and looked out into the dimly lit room. "Hear that, Cork?"

"Hurry," Corky said stepping down. "He's coming." She took her sister's arm and guided her up onto the box. The window was slightly above her shoulders. "On three, jump and get your arms and your boobs through the opening. Grab one of the bushes and pull yourself and I'll push you."

Arizona looked at the window. "It's going to hurt my boob. The cop practically tore it—"

"You got one chance, baby," Corky whispered, squeezing her arm. She leaned in and kissed Arizona. "I love you."

Arizona looked at Corky, her face understanding. "You talk as if—"

"Ready?" Corky nudged her sister in front of the window. "Stick your hands out and grab the outside ledge. Good. When you're through far enough, grab the trunk of the hedge." Corky clasped her hands and lowered them next to Arizona's closest leg. "Put your foot into my hands. Good. Okay one ... two ... three. Jump."

*   *   *

I'm moving along the wall, stepping over typical basement crap, typical for a funeral home, anyway. I keep spitting out pieces of ash, and I can't get the taste to go away. I can feel it on my face and see it all over my chest, arms, and hands.

I can hear the sisters but I can't see them. Corky says something about making a call tomorrow morning, not to mess it up, and it would make them famous. I hear, "Colonel White."

There they are.

"Freeze!" I shout, nearly tripping over a pile of stained and tattered sheets. The sisters are in a little storage room. Corky is pushing Arizona's big butt through a window.

"Pull, Ari, pull," Corky shouts, as I move to the doorway. Arizona's feet disappear.

"Officer needs help in here!" I shout at the window. "Suspect just came out the west basement."

Corky bounds over a bicycle, rushing me like a hard-driving linebacker. I sidestep her, but I don't kick because my shoes are still slippery with embalming fluid. So I rip another claw across her face as she blasts by. Nailed her too. She stops and spins around, her hand reaching shakily toward her face. Now the four vertical claw streaks I gave her upstairs have four horizontal ones overlaying them. Tic-tac-toe anyone?

She picks up a black leather doctor's bag and hurtles it at me. Again, my bobbing and weaving work pays off and it flies by me and crashes into a door to another room. The bag opens on impact and several chrome embalming tools spill out, any one of which is capable of cutting flesh, live as well as dead.

The impact pushed the door inward a ways. It's a bathroom, a blue painted-over window on the back wall, cleaning bottles and brushes on the floor, and a thick-as-syrup stench.

Corky lowers her head, but I can still see her hate-filled eyes. The lone, fluttering fluorescent ceiling light is behind her but those eyes reflect illumination from someplace bad. It chills my bones.

"It's over, Corky," I say, knowing I'm wasting my breath.

"Your sister's going to get caught outside and you'll never escape from here."

She lifts her head high enough to look at the ceiling but her eyes never leave mine. Her body is rigid, fists clenched. "I will never stop fighting you and those you work for. I will never stop fighting against the pandering to the muds in this country, the Mexicans, the niggers, the goddamn Jews. White people built this country with muscle and sweat, and I will fight until my last breath to get it back for us."

Anger fuels bad decisions, so to rev her up another notch, I say, "Uh, I might be wrong, Corky, but I think millions of black slaves did quite a bit of building too, and let's not forget the thousands of Chinese who built the Transcontinental Railroad, and, oh yeah, I do believe the Native Americans lived here long before the white man arrived."

She steps toward me and I lunge into her with three hard and fast punches into her gut. She belches a loud groan and bends forward clutching her stomach. I simultaneously slap my left hand onto the back of her head as my right cups her chin. I crank both counterclockwise to apply the principle of "where the head goes the body follows." The move forces her to corkscrew down onto her back next to the entrance to the bathroom. I grab a wad of her mullet close to her scalp and rotate my hand with a snap of my wrist. My move flops her over onto her belly, all the while she screams from the pain and fights to wrench my hand away from her scalp.

She grasps one of the embalming tools scattered on the floor from the overturned box. It's about six inches long and looks like a thick chrome hypodermic plunger, but with a ring on each side in which Corky has inserted her fingers. She rolls onto her side and swings it at my closest leg. I release her hair and snap my leg out of the way just enough that the instrument only snags some of my jeans as it streaks by.

She extends the weapon toward me and scoots herself back into the doorway. She gets to her feet. "I just attacked you with a weapon, Detective Reeves," she says, with a grimace. "You got probable cause to use your gun. Why don't you pull it out, huh?" She stabs the weapon at me, though she is three feet out of range. "Come on," she says, jabbing it again. It's not loaded with a needle but it's tapered to a blunt point that could penetrate flesh. "Pull it out and show me, Boss." She laughs ugly, and for a second I think the foul smell coming from the old john is really coming from her retched mouth.

The window behind her has been painted over, but fluctuating blue and red lights from outside find their way through where the old paint has chipped off. Finally, the posse has arrived.

Corky takes a step back into the room and begins to shut the door. "Excuse me, officer, I got to take a piss."

I charge her, my forearms in front of me like a shield. I don't know what she expected but she startles, lowering her weapon and looking behind her as she back peddles all the way into the room. My shoulder sends the door banging into the wall and the impact from my forearm shield sends her into the one under the window. I pin her weapon hand and arm against the wall with my shoulder. When she plunges her other hand into her pocket, I grab the forearm. A hard knee strike into her thigh brings forth a moan, and a second one makes her cry out and sag.

She begins to slide her pinned arm down the filthy wall, which brings me in closer to her. When she tries to bite the side of my face, I jerk my head away then return it hard and fast into her nose.

"Yes," she says nasally, as if getting head butted was something she wanted. She sneezes blood onto the side of my neck and face, and whispers, "Do it again, Boss. I like it."

She jerks her weapon arm straight down. I was strong pushing her arm into the wall but her sudden change of direction makes me tilt to the side.

Her street experience shows. She takes advantage of my momentary off-balance to push off the wall with her foot and shove me with her entire body. I stumble back two steps and hit the partially open door, slamming it shut. We're in a darkened disco now, the outside police lights strobe blue and red throughout the interior, making our every move jerk like an old-time movie.

Corky's nose, lips, and jaw are coated in blood, her white T-shirt and open blue windbreaker splattered with it. She smiles, her teeth bloody, her eyes excited, deadly. She drops the embalming tool into the toilet water.

"Prefer this," she says, extracting her left hand from her jeans pocket and snapping her wrist to release the blade from its black handle. "It did a job on the nigger and the raghead. Now it's going to do one on you." She tucks her bloody chin and looks at me almost flirtatiously. "Unless you're going to shoot, Boss."

Her knife is a Benchmade, a Gerber maybe, the blade about five inches long. Good quality with at least two kills in its history. The blade moves in a small teasing circle, the police lights reflecting intermittently off it. Now it's moving in a figure eight.

All I got to do is pull my Glock and send her to Hell. Justified in the eyes of the law, justified by the department brass and troops, and justified by the good citizens—most of them anyway. But they aren't the one pulling the trigger, they aren't the one watching the life ebb out of a set of eyes, and they aren't the one who has to deal with the nightmares that follow. Isn't the first kill the hardest and the next one supposedly easier? Whoever came up with that is full of it. Maybe someone sitting at home right now snacking on garbage food and watching TV could come up with a better one. Maybe—

The blade attacks.

I shield my face with my arms and lean to the side, banging my head against a white rectangle on the wall where a mirror had once been attached. The impact fuzzes my vision for a moment.

A burning sensation—I look down at a horizontal cut across my polo shirt—blood oozes from it. I look up to see Corky's ugly smile and the light-reflecting blade on a straight-line course for my face. I jerk my head away again and sidestep quickly, my hip striking the sink and my feet knocking over bottles and a bucket full of dirty liquid. Smells like ammonia. I snap my closest foot up between her legs and she screams in agony and twists forward. My female students have always said groin kicks hurt women too, but this is the first time I've tried one on the street.

I lunge forward and slam my palms against her weapon arm to pin it against her chest. She's hurting from the kick, but she manages to turn us around so her back is toward the door, her free arm pinned behind her. I drive her into it. She is snorting like a bull under the strain and with each exhalation she sprays me with her blood. I'd like to hit her again, but she is so strong I don't dare remove one of my hands from her arm.

My feet are starting to slide in whatever had been in the

knocked-over bucket. Trying to fight it. My right foot slides away from me and I nearly go down on my knees. I still have control of her arm, though my grip is more clinging than pressing. I struggle to regain my footing like a beginning skater trying to stand.

For a second I think I hear a police radio outside the door, then nothing.

Just as she did when I had her pinned on the wall a moment ago, she begins forcing her weapon arm downward, a direction hard for me to control. I take a chance and release my right hand and hammer the bottom of my fist twice into her shattered, bleeding nose. She falls back against the door, her scream abruptly changing into an awful sounding gurgle.

Now someone is pounding on the door from outside the restroom and the doorknob is rotating back and forth. "Sam? Sam?" Tad's voice, I think. I'm straining too hard to answer, as I struggle to control Corky's arm with one hand and squeeze her throat with my other. Blood squirts from her nose onto my hand and arm, and through it all she smiles, but with one less tooth.

Her eyes, with their strange illumination, shine with excitement. Arousal?

"Kiss me, boss," she gurgles. "Kiss me."

I start to squeeze her neck harder when from somewhere she finds the strength and leverage to spin me around. I hit the door with my right side. I still have her knife hand and it's pinned against my right hip. If I spin away from the door I might lose control of her hand. If I remain here, she can hit me with her free one. Just as I decide to twist away, she drives her weight into me with her shoulder, pinning me against the door.

Someone's beating on the other side of it again. "Sam!"

Angela's voice.

"I'm here," I call out, my voice strained. "I—"

Corky stops trying to free her arm and presses her face in close to mine. Her lips are blood-shiny and a bubble of mucous hangs from one nostril.

"You enjoying our date so far, Boss?" she breathes into my face.

Angela or someone tries to push open the door again, jostling us, but our combined weight against it prevents it from opening more than an inch before it slams back shut.

The point of her knife cuts my side. "Agh!" I cry out. Stings. Burns. She must have some flexibility in her knife hand. I push my side even tighter against her arm. I can feel her flexing her wrist trying to cut me again and—"Agh! Damn-it!" I shout, squinting my eyes from another burning pain in my side. I open them just as Corky's mouth presses against the side of my face.

"Kiss kiss," she sputters, again spraying blood onto my cheek. I can feel it running down into my collar.

When I was a rookie, I worked a couple days with a guy named Karp, a Russian guy who was ugly inside and out. We arrested a particularly belligerent man one night, and we had a hard struggle before we got the handcuffs on him. Handcuffs are never comfortable and, unless the officer double locks them, they will tighten every time the prisoner yanks against them.

Apparently, Karp took the man's resistance personal because after we got the guy onto the ground, he stomped on one of the cuffs, which imbedded the steel into the man's wrist cartilage. Hysterical with pain, the man pulled his hands out of the cuffs taking with them all the meat and flesh on the sides of his palms. Then we really had a fight.

I learned that day there is a point where a human will do anything to escape pain. I've reached it.

I snap the side of my head into her nose. She emits part of a scream, but I interrupt it with another headbutt to the same bloody, broken target. I've hit it so many times now most of her nose is lying against her cheek under her eye.

"Agh!" Razor-sharp steel slices across my belly. I slam my head into her face again, and again, and again.

She drops to her knees on the wet floor without making a sound, her chin resting on her chest. I still have hold of her knife arm. Blood pours down my forehead, into my eyes and over my nose into my mouth; some of it's mine but most of it's hers.

Sounds of someone kicking at the door. We're not against it now so they could just turn the knob. The door flies open, hits me in the butt, bounces back, and slams shut again. Knocked off balance on the slippery floor, I fall against Corky and for a moment lay draped ridiculously over her head and beefy shoulders, my right leg waving about in the air.

I grab the sink for balance, lower my leg, and start to push off Corky when I sense her doing something with her arms. "Aaagh!" I bellow from the intense burning sensation in my left calf. The bitch just cut me again. I was holding her knife arm so how did she ...

I made a white-belt mistake: She simply grabbed the weapon with her other hand.

The door flies open, bumps into my hip, and bounces back, hitting something with a thump instead of a bang.

"Ow! My leg," Angela cries out. "Damnit!"

Your leg? I want to shout. I manage to get enough leverage to push away from the sink and stand all the way up. Corky comes up on one knee and slashes at my upper thighs. I block it as hard as I can with my forearm, aiming for the radial nerve on the thumb side of her wrist. It's a chancy move against a blade, but it works and the knife flies from her numbed hand and stabs into the wall next to the toilet. It stays stuck for a second before dropping onto the wet floor. Still on her knees, Corky curses and thrusts her hand behind the toilet to retrieve it.

Somewhat stable with my left hand on the wall and my right on the edge of the sink, I chamber my knee high and stomp down hard onto her Achilles tendon. The foot collapses under my heavy stomp, no doubt tearing the tendon and breaking foot bones. Screaming all the way, she falls between the wall and the toilet.

I grab her trashed foot and yank her two hundred twenty pounds out of the corner so I can cuff her. When her head clears the toilet, she slithers and curls like an injured python and slashes at me with her recovered knife. I jump back clear of the weapon's arc and snap my shin into Corky's arm before she can slash back at me. The impact spins her around toward the toilet, and she again loses her grip on the blade. It spins away and comes to rest under the sink between bottles of 409 and Windex.

She hesitates for a second and then turns slowly toward me on her hands and knees, her bloody head down, but her flashing eyes focused on me. An injured animal is a dangerous creature. She lunges across the small space and attempts to tackle my legs. Corky's left hand misses me entirely but her right grabs a wad of my pant legs. When she starts to pull herself up, I whip a hammer fist onto the top of her head and she plops limply to the floor.

Incredibly, she starts to rise, but I knee drop the back of her skull, smashing her face straight down into the chemical spill. I press my knee down to pin her shattered nose, her ugly mouth, and her forehead into the floor. Then I club the side of her face with another hammer fist. And another. And another.

She's out. For a moment I think about dragging her over to the toilet, submerging her head to awaken her, and knocking her out again. But I don't. I'm not a savage.

I drag her toward the window wall a little so Angela can finally come in.

"You about done in here?" she asks. Sounds like something Mai would say.

I'm having trouble getting enough air and my head hurts so bad. A hand touches my shoulder.

Someone asks, "Why is the room tilting?" It's my voice. More hands ... holding me. Red and blue disco lights ...

Nausea.

Blackness.

CHAPTER SIXTEEN

Man-oh-man my bed is so cold. Wait, it isn't my bed. It's ... an embalming table and I'm naked as a porn star. The overhead light would be blinding bright if it wasn't for the fact I'm dead.

I'm dead? And I'm lying naked and about to be embalmed?

I sit up on one elbow and shield my eyes to see beyond the intense brightness. What the? People ... and they've formed a circle around my table. Can't see their faces—the light is so bright.

Down by my bare feet—yellow-bloody hair, blood-splattered black sweatshirt. Puke. And the pale young man standing by my right knee, the one dressed only in blue boxer shorts, his arms hanging limp at his sides with bleeding holes in his palms. Executioner.

Someone's moving toward me. Wish I could see the head. Long legs—tall—short bathrobe, one breast exposed. What is on her ... "Mooslum" carved into her breast and ... damn, her neck has been slit ear-to-ear.

Someone steps out from behind her. He's naked, and short enough I can see his face. Got a bleeding hole in his chest. "Jimmy! Oh. I'm so sorry. So sorry. So—"

"Sam?"

I tear my eyes away from the boy and look back at the woman. Still can't see her face. How does she know my name? Her's was ... Yolanda. Yes, Yolanda.

"Sam, you're okay now."

I'm okay? I'm lying naked on an embalming table, for crying out—

"Sam? Wake up."

LOREN W. CHRISTENSEN

Mai's brown and green-specked eyes looking into mine. She's wiping my cheek with a cool cloth.

"You were shouting," she says, her smile charging my batteries. "'Jimmy,' I think."

I look around. I'm in my bedroom, not the mortuary. No chrome, no bright light. No dead ...

Mai is sitting on the edge of my bed. "You confused?"

I nod, but am increasingly distracted by the pain in my forehead, ribs, stomach, calf.

"You have been home from the hospital for about three hours," Mai says slowly. It is eight in the morning. You were hurt arresting the woman. She cut you with a knife in many places. But none too bad."

"I have a different opinion," I manage, trying to scoot up a little. Chien hops up on the bed and puts her paw on my arm.

"Chien has been very worried. She sleep by your head all the time. Sometimes she would lift her head to see if you were awake yet. She went to use the box just before you wake up."

"Hey, buddy," I say, rubbing under her ears. "You worried about me?" She bumps her head against my shoulder a couple of times.

My head is clear now and I'm remembering everything: The ambulance ride to Emanuel Hospital; the doctors and nurses probing, scrubbing, and injecting; lots of brass and media around. Angela was there, so was Steve, and our new boss, Lieutenant Foskey.

Steve said Richard Daniels' neck cut was serious but he will make it. Foskey said Corky was in serious condition with a concussion, a broken ankle and a torn Achilles' tendon, and severely damaged nose. According to the doctor, my knife wounds could have been worse. My forehead was cut, and I got some good bone bruising, from head butting Corky's head and teeth.

Mai came to the hospital after Angela had called her. She found Mai's number in my wallet, a Saigon number. Angela said I owed her a lunch since the call probably cost twenty dollars.

I remember Mai squeezing my hand as tears rolled down her cheeks just before they wheeled me off to X-ray my head. They must have given me a sedative because after that I don't remember much other than vague images of Mai driving me home in my pickup.

"Lots of bandages," she says, pulling the blanket down to expose my torso. "They wanted you to stay for twenty-four hours but you made a big, uh, fuss. You were a fussy boy and you say you beat everyone up. When I tell them I was a nurse in Saigon, they say you can go. But I think they really did not want you to beat everybody up. Oh, and the doctor say you will live to love me very much." She smiles with a shrug. "I add the last part."

I laugh but stop abruptly. "Ow. Hurts my stomach and my side. You're right, they got me taped up pretty good."

Mai helps me slip on a red T-shirt. It's when she helps lower me back onto the pillow I notice the tears streaking down her cheeks. I take her hand into both of mine and rub it as her shoulders begin to tremble and her cry grows more audible. After a moment, she lies down beside me, careful not to bump any of my wounds. When I start to turn toward her, a ripping pain in my belly stops me, so I just pat her. Chien, her chin on my chest again, watches Mai intently.

After several minutes her body stills and her crying stops. "I was so scared when I hear Angela's voice on the phone. Even after her first words, 'Sam is okay,' I thought ... I was just so scared. I drove crazy to get to the hospital. A policeman stopped me because I did not stop for red lights too many times, but I was crying and when I told him where I was going, he drive his police car in front of me with his lights on and take me to you."

Grimacing, I turn enough to kiss her. When we finally break it off, I whisper, "I will live so I can love you very much."

She kisses me again, and says, "Works for me very much." When I start to laugh, sharp pains in my stomach and side scrunch up my face.

A man's laughter from the living room.

I come up on my elbow, groaning from the sharp bite in my side. "What ...? Is someone here?"

Mai rolls up and stands. "Oh, I forgot to tell you. Nate and Rudy are here."

"They are? Why didn't you tell me?"

She helps me to my feet. "I was busy crying, Sam. Angela was here too. But when you kept sleeping she had to go. She said she had to go to a, uh, I forget what you call it. When many people yell and wave signs."

"Protest. There is a protest today at City Hall."

She opens the bedroom door. "Yes, protest was the word."

Mai helps me down the hall and by the time I reach the living room I'm actually feeling a little better.

"Sensei," Nate says, getting up from the sofa. He bows.

"Sam!" Rudy half shouts, working his bulk out of the chair. "Lordy, I hear the other guy looks worse. Hard to imagine."

"Hope so. Sit, sit," I say, shaking his hand. I shake Nate's and I ease myself onto the couch near Nate. "So kind of you guys to come by. How long have you been here?"

"They both come almost same time," Mai says, sitting on

the sofa arm next to me.

"Heard it on the news this morning," Nate says. "Said you caught one of the women suspected in the racial murders. Said you got hurt."

Rudy nodded. "Attacked with a knife is what Channel Eight news reported."

I shake my head. "It was a nightmare. Never underestimate a woman's rage."

"Ooooh yes," Rudy and Nate say in unison, looking at each other.

"And you should not forget it," Mai says, with a gentle punch to my shoulder. When I overreact to it, Mai says, "You are not hurt there, sissy boy. Coffee, Sam? More coffee, guys?"

After Mai heads out to the kitchen, I stand and test my weight on my cut calf. "She did a number on me," I say, moving my arms around a little.

"You know, Sam," Rudy says, "When I was in Vietnam there were guys who seemed to attract shit, know what I mean? They always seemed to be in the middle of somethin' going down. If there was a sniper, they were in the line of the dude's fire. If there was a rocket attack, they were practically right under the incoming. If there were a bunch of guys drinkin' beer and a fight broke out, these same guys would get knocked on their butt because they were in the way. We called 'em 'shit magnets.'"

Nate nods. "The term is still used in Afghan, Rudy."

"I'm sure it is," Rudy says with a laugh, his belly moving under his white dress shirt.

I bend over to stretch my legs. I'm touching my forehead to my knee when I realize they both stopped talking. I look up to see them looking at me with smirks on their faces. "What? You guys think I'm a shit magnet?"

"Oh no no no," Rudy says, waving me off and shaking his head harder than necessary. "Just because you was only in my cab for five minutes before we was scufflin' with people trying to force their way inside. No no no, don't mean nothin'. Not even close to being a shit magnet."

Mai returns with a coffee pot and an empty cup. "I am out of the room for three minutes and the men are talking about shit and magnets."

"Thanks," Rudy says, holding his cup up for her to top it off. "So tell me, Mai, what do you see in this guy anyway?"

She moves over to refill Nate's. She scrunches her face, shakes her head, and says in feigned, heavily accented English, "Not too sure. He girly man. He's always getting beat up."

I start to laugh with them but stop when it tugs on my stomach bandage.

"Stitches hurt, Sensei?" Nate asks.

I look up at Mai as she hands me a cup. "I got stitches?"

"Yes. Sorry, I forgot to tell you. You sleep when they do it. Seven in your stomach and nine I think in your leg. Your side, they just do a bandage. Like your head."

I lift my hand to my forehead. It's a large rectangular pad. Hurts to the touch.

"What do you need, Sam?" Rudy asks. "Groceries? Medicine? I'd be glad to get whatever for you?"

"Thank you so much, Rudy," I say. "I think we're good. Plus, the more I'm up the better I feel. But man, the stitches and the bandages really tug on the ol' skin."

"I think you need a few minutes of meditation," Mai says, again sitting next to me on the arm of the sofa. "It would help you to re, uh, reconnect with yourself and help you see everything more clear."

I bump her leg with my hand, and smile. "Plus you want to show me how you fixed up the meditation area."

She shrugs. "Maybe."

Nate stands. "Well, I'll leave you guys to—"

"No, no," Mai says standing. "Join us. It is good that we are together. And good for your martial arts, Nate, and Rudy it is good for your ... let me see ... taxi cab driving."

Rudy frowns. "I don't know ..."

"I do know," Mai says, taking his arm and helping him get his bulk out of the chair. "You will like it."

"Oh Lord, every time my wife says that it means we're having cottage cheese and broccoli for dinner."

"Smart woman," she says, patting his arm.

"This looks great, Mai," I say, peering into the spare bedroom. It looks too small for three big men and a nearly six-foot-tall woman, but we all squeeze in and it feels ... comfortable.

Mai bought a low table made of a richly grained wood, on which she has placed a small bonsai evergreen tree, a stone bowl filled with white sand and an incense stick, and next to it three carefully stacked black rocks, all of which would fit in my hand. The top stone is shaped like a heart. She has set a small red Asian lantern on the right side of the table. On the wall above the table are two paintings, one a serene Buddha face, his eyes hooded in meditation and his mouth holding a slight smile. The other is Jesus standing on a high hill gazing out over a scrumptious green valley.

"I am glad you like it, Sam," Mai says, smiling happily. To the others she says, "The three rocks represent the dharma, which is Buddha's teachings, the sangha, which is the people who follow the teachings, and the Buddha, who was just a man, but a great teacher. To me, the three stones also represent the Father, the Son, and the Holy Ghost in Christianity." She retrieves two thick cushions next to the table and sets them in front of the altar.

"Sam, I think you might have to stand because sitting on a cushion might hurt your leg and your middle. Nate, would you please sit on this one? And Rudy, do you want to stand or would you be more comfortable sitting on the edge of the bed?"

"Oh, I could get down on a cushion okay," he says, chuckling. "But I would never get back up. Better sit on the bed."

Mai smiles and nods. "Sam, please stand with your feet almost together and your hands in front of you like this." She places the back of her right hand into the palm of her left, and settles them near her belly. "And touch the pads of your thumbs like this. Yes, very good. It is a standing meditation pose."

Mai crosses one foot in front of the other and sort of floats down onto her cushion.

"Lordy," Rudy says. "You drifted down as gentle as a falling snowflake. Just floated down. Lordy."

Mai twists around to speak to Rudy. "You must sit very tall with your legs together and your hands in your lap. Yes, very good," she says, patting his knee. She looks over at Nate who is actually sitting in lotus, each foot resting on the thigh of the other. "Very good, Nate. You do before. Okay, everyone. Close your eyes. This is a very simple meditation to make you get relaxed in your head and in your body. No peeking, Sam."

"I wasn't," I say like a child. Rudy chuckles.

"Please sit quiet for a moment," she says, "and feel your body. If you are comfortable, enjoy the comfortable. If you are uncomfortable, it is okay. Just experience the uncomfortable."

I haven't meditated standing before. I feel antsy and

twitchy, and I'm suddenly more aware of all the bandages on me and every little stitch.

"Sam, if you are uncomfortable, just experience it," Mai repeats softly.

I open my left eye a little and look down at the top of her head. I'm guessing she just said that because she knows I'm hurting, not because she read my mind as our father does.

"When you inhale," Mai says just louder than a whisper, "be aware of your breath filling your lower belly. Feel it center there for a moment before you slowly blow it out your mouth. As you do, feel your lower belly empty. Feel it get big from your air when you breathe in and feel your belly get small when you let it out." After ten exchanges, Mai says, "Now as you breathe, put your mind on your belly. Only your belly, nothing else. Feel it get bigger. Feel it get smaller. Get bigger ... get smaller ... get bigger ..."

I wasn't sure about standing meditation, but already I'm feeling a wonderful sense of calm wash over me. I can still feel my hurts, especially my calf and ... I can't think about them right now. Just focus on my belly, in ... and out ...

The slice across my stomach was creepy. Razor sharp steel *ssslicing* through my skin and my stomach walls and ...Oh man, got to think only about my breathing and my belly lifting ... and sinking. Lifting and ... Even with her arms pinned, Corky could still make those little nicks with the tip of the blade into my side. Damn, those hurt. Still do. What if she had been able to plunge it all the way in? A cold, heartless blade raping into my side, chipping a rib on the way to puncturing my liver, spilling its poisonous contents into my bloodstream ...

Stop! I mean, damn. Focus. My belly lifting ... lowering ... lifting ...

"Here's, the throwaway. You know what to do tomorrow morning." Corky's voice is unwelcome in my meditation. But she is persistent. I hear her urging her sister, *"You know what to do. And when to do it."*

Do what?

"Don't blow this, Ari. Remember when the call has to be made."

Call? What call? "Throwaway" must mean a cell phone, the kind you buy at a service station and grocery market. They can't be traced. *"Remember when the call has to be made."* Call. *"Tomorrow morning."* Today. This morning.

"Don't mess it up. Colonel White is counting on us."

Mess up the call? Colonel White?

"We'll be famous. Colonel White is counting on us."

I blurt out loud, "The rally."

"Sam!" Mai says, turning to look up at me. "What are you—?"

"Sorry, guys. Is someone special coming to the rally today? Does anyone know?"

"Yes, sir," Rudy says, looking happy to stand up. He pops his back. "Reverend Billy Souls will be there, of course, and the news said Reverend Doctor Rothman Sterling himself is comin'. Out of Chicago. Leader of so many black coalition groups I doubt he even knows how many. Never saw a camera he didn't like, no sir. Should be fun to watch him and Billy Souls do their best to get on the five o'clock news. My money is on the Reverend Doctor."

"Heard it's going to be big," Nate says, looking up at me. "Two or three thousand folks. They interviewed Billy Souls on Channel Six this morning, and he said you arresting the one sister didn't change anything. People still need to show their outrage at racial violence."

Rudy nods. "Channel Eight said pretty much the same thing. Supposed to be a big police presence there."

"Sam?" Mai says, trying to read whatever expression I'm showing. She stands, and touches my arm. Behind her, Nate gets up. "What is happening in your head?"

"The rally," I say. Everyone is looking at me with blank stares. "Arizona, the other sister, got away and I think she is going to the rally. And I don't think she's going to support the cause.

"I got to get down there."

*   *   *

Everyone protests at once. Rudy says I could reopen my wounds. Nate says even Apaches knew when it was time to rest, and Mai asks how could I even think of going when just minutes earlier she had to help me down the hall.

"I have no intentions of singlehandedly pushing the crowd back, but I can act as a spotter." Men being men, Nate and Rudy nod. Mai being a wonderful blend of mother, friend, and lover, folds her arms and shakes her head.

"I gotta go, Mai. I know her best. I know how she moves. I … It's my fault she got away. I gotta make it right."

She unfolds her arms and nods, though I can tell it pains her.

I look at Nate. "Can I use your cell? Mine got damaged." He retrieves it from his pocket and hands it to me. I poke the prefix number, but the movement of three nodding heads draws back my attention.

"What?" I ask suspiciously.

"I'll drive," Rudy says. "Sometimes cabs can get into places easier than civilian cars, or at least closer."

"No, Rudy. I can't place you ..." I start to say.

Mai ends the discussion.

"If you go, we go."

*   *   *

By nine twenty, the temperature was already in the high seventies on the way to the forecasted mideighties by late afternoon. It was much warmer on the cement and within the mass of people. The promise of heavy sweating didn't deter the fifteen hundred protesters who had gathered on the sidewalks and in the street at the intersection where Ocnod had been found dangling from the spider-armed lamppost.

People, about three quarters of them black, shook hands, hugged, took cell phone pictures of each other, and admired handheld signs. At nine thirty sharp, the Reverend Billy Souls, standing on a wooden box thoughtfully brought by one of his aids, lifted his hand to quiet the crowd.

"Let us lower our heads and pray for our friends Qasim Al-Sabti, known to those close to him as Ocnod, and Yolanda Simpson, a single mother of a newborn. Two fine people slaughtered by hatemongers, a sad, sad, reminder that racial hate, oppression, and persecution of people of color is still going on today."

A man's voice from somewhere in the center of the throng, shouted, "Why the po-lice let the one white bitch go? I'll tell you why, so she can keep doing what she been doing. The po-lice don't want the killing to stop." Many in the crowd murmured their agreement.

When the prayers were over, the people began moving south to Burnside and then west to Fifth Avenue, and then south for the twelve-block walk to City Hall. They moved slowly, chanting, singing, and capturing the event on their cell phones. They held their signs high for the news cameras, and for those who watched from the sidewalks and looked down from their office windows. Printed in angry black, some in blood red, the signs read:

NAZI SCUM OUT

FIGHT RACISM

STOP THE KILLING

TERRORISM STRIKES HERE

GOD LOVES ALL THE CHILDREN, RED AND YELLOW BLACK AND WHITE

BLACK POWER

ASIAN POWER

ARAB-AMERICANS UNITE

In the center of the march, a bulge of men, women, and teenagers wearing pink armbands, carried signs too:

I'M QUEER AND PROUD

GAYS FOR CHRIST

FAGGOT POWER!

STOP KILLING GAYS

Walking alongside the marchers, a black man in his forties with a three-inch-high greying afro shouted into a yellow megaphone, "We ain't gonna take it no more!" and the marchers shouted back, "We ain't gonna take it no more!" After a block the man with the megaphone shouted, "Hey, hey, ho, ho, racist scum have got to go," and the marchers repeated it. After two more blocks they began singing, "We Shall Overcome," stirring up emotions among the baby boomers not felt since the sixties.

Two police cars led the procession and two more followed

six blocks back. With everything going on, the downtown precinct commander decided not to take any chances, so he put six undercover officers in the march. The commander didn't tell the organizers because he didn't want to deal with, as he said, "The left-wing fruitcakes' usual accusations of police oppression."

All along the route the marchers called out to pedestrians of all races to join them. If they were black, the marchers shouted at them to join their brothers and sisters to stand up against white supremacists. When they joined the parade, they were cheered, but when they refused, they were booed. By the time the throng reached city hall, it had picked up another five hundred people, bringing the total to an official estimate of two thousand.

They gathered on the west side of the large structure where thirty steps, each about forty feet wide, led up to a wide landing and the main entrance doors. Every step was jammed with people. The crowd extended across the sidewalk and out into the street. Red, a tall redheaded cop in his midforties stood near the top of the steps where he could watch the speakers and still see the crowd. He wore tan khaki pants and a Hawaiian overshirt to conceal his weapon, and he carried a picture of Arizona in his pocket.

About ten steps down from him, wearing a black unzipped hoody, its hood up to hide her face, and a green T-shirt underneath with "USMC" stamped on the front, was Arizona, cautiously working her way up the crowded steps. After she stole the clothes out of a sleeping street person's duffle bag, she wondered if wearing the hood up might make her stand out in the heat, but she was relieved to see others with theirs up and some with bandanas over their faces so as not to be identified by the police.

She had joined the procession five blocks from City Hall and tried to blend in with the mob. She even sang "We Shall Overcome" with the marchers. A flier, someone handed her, said there would be fifteen minutes of speeches before Reverend Doctor Rothman Sterling spoke.

Five steps from the top now, she began moving from the crowd's center, to the left where a four-foot-high brick wall bordered the steps. She was careful not to make eye contact with anyone for fear she would be recognized.

"Hey! Hey!" Arizona half jumped out of her boots at the blaring megaphone on the landing just up from her. "Ho, ho. White supremacist scum has got to go!"

"It's okay, missy," a heavy-set black woman in a yellow top said, her smile wide and toothy. She touched Arizona's arm. "United we're strong. There's nothing to fear, now."

The woman's smile faded under Arizona's scorching glare and she snatched her hand back as if she had touched something foul.

The crowd roared back at the man with the megaphone, "Hey, hey, ho, ho. White supremacist scum has got to go!"

Instantly realizing what she had done, Arizona tried to soften her face with a smile. "Yes, ma'am, there's nothing to fear now." The woman nodded slightly and with uncertainty, and turned back to look up at the landing.

The heavily perspiring middle-aged black man with the megaphone continued the chant, pacing quickly back and forth on the landing, motioning for the crowd to return it louder and louder.

"Let it be heard throughout the city!" he screamed into the megaphone, his words coming out distorted.

"Hey, hey, ho, ho," hundreds of voices thundered between the buildings, "white supremacists have got to go!"

Like a frenzied cheerleader, the man scurried across the landing, his face glowing with excitement. He slammed his fist skyward and blared, "We ain't gonna take it no more!"

"Oh hell no!" the crowd shouted back, two thousand of them, and still growing.

Arizona looked at her watch and discreetly scanned the rooftops.

* * *

"Understand what you're saying, Reeves," Captain Tankersley, commander of the SWAT Division says. We're all in the cab and I'm pressing the cell against my ear to hear him over all the traffic noise as we near City Hall. "We got pics of the sisters and we know which one is still out there. But check it out, Reeves. As of zero eight hundred we've received thirty-one death threats on these reverend characters and two bomb threats, one on the Justice Center and one on City Hall. We're kinda hoping they follow through with the one on the Mayor's Office, know what I mean?"

We're at Fifth and Main, a couple three blocks from City Hall, and Rudy is pointing at a row of barricades across Fifth. I jab my finger at them to indicate I want him to drive up to them.

"I do, Captain. But I'm ninety-nine percent certain Arizona is going to do something involving a phone—maybe set off an explosive. And the target is Reverend Rothman Sterling. My gut's telling me I'm right."

"Copy that, Reeves. Be advised, we did a bomb check at zero seven thirty on City Hall, and the doggies came up with nothing, and we've had people posted on it since. We got sniper teams on all the surrounding roofs. We got undercover people and cameras up the kazoo. We're confident we can handle anything at this juncture."

A uniformed cop moves around the barricade and holds up his palms as we approach.

"Thanks, Captain. I got a feeling on this one. Be safe."

"Roger that, Reeves."

I lower my window and extend my badge at the young officer. "Let us through. How far can we go before we absolutely have to stop?"

The kid is sweating in his new uniform. "Oh, it's you," he says, his brow furrowed at the cab. "Saw you on the news this morning."

"How far?" I ask, stuffing my wallet back in my pocket.

"Block and a half. There's a row of City Bureau trucks blocking the way."

I nod and tell Rudy to slip us through the opening in the barricades.

"Smooth, Sam," Rudy chuckles. "Can you ride with me all the time?"

As luck would have it, there is an empty taxi parking space where the city trucks are blocking the street. I flash the coverall-wearing crew my badge and they turn back to talking in groups. Though we're a block away, we can hear the muffled sounds of a blaring megaphone and a chanting crowd bouncing off the buildings.

I'm still not sure what I'm going to do as the four of us head toward City Hall, Mai at my side, Rudy and Nate following. If I stay outside the crowd and look for Arizona, I might not be able to see her if she is deep in the throng. If I go into the crowd, I won't be able to see if she's watching things from outside of it.

Up ahead is the east side of City Hall, the sound of the crowd on the west side much louder now. The only people on this side are about a half-dozen officers posted around the pillars and two on each end of the property. Two shaggy-looking people sitting on the sidewalk hold signs demanding the mayor to legalize sleeping on the street. I know one of the officers on this corner and he nods as we pass.

"What are you going to do, Sam?" Mai asks.

"Remember in Vietnam when Father and I talked about our plan to go after those kidnapped girls, and about how, for much of it, we would be making it up as we go along?"

"And that is your plan now?"

I start to say it's the best I can do, but the roar of the crowd as we near Fifth Avenue stops me. I look up at the cement wall that's keeping people from toppling off the City Hall steps and falling several feet onto this north side sidewalk. All I can see are the tops of a few heads. Up the street, hundreds of people are spread out over the sidewalk and out onto Fifth Avenue, people unable to get onto the packed steps. An empty Starbucks grande cup hits the sidewalk in front of us, dropped from or thrown over the wall by some caffeinated person.

Normally, we would be able to walk right around the corner of the wall and head up the steps, but the overspill crowd makes it impossible. We head out onto Fifth Avenue and move around the rear of the crowd until I can see the front of City Hall.

There are easily two thousand people here, more likely twenty-five hundred. Some guy with a megaphone up on the landing is doing his best to work them into frenzy, and he looks to be succeeding. At least a thousand arms are holding up cell phone cameras to capture the moment for ... whatever.

"Thank you for coming," a little hippy girl shouts over the crowd noise, handing Mai a leaflet.

I read it over her shoulder. "Headline speaker: The Reverend Doctor Rothman Sterling."

"I'm convinced he's the target," I say. Nate and Rudy look at me. "You guys please stay here with Mai. If things get crazy head for the cab."

"Where are you going, Sam?" Mai asks holding my arm. "You are hurt. You should stay with us."

"I'm fine. Really. I'm just going to get a little closer so I can monitor things and report to my boss." Mai squeezes my arm, her head shaking. "It's okay," I say into her ear. I kiss the side of her face and look at Nate and Rudy. When they nod to indicate they'll watch her, I turn and move into the crowd.

*   *   *

I've been out of the car for about fifteen minutes now. My calf is telling me I should be lying on my sofa with my leg propped up, and my head and midsection are wishing my bandages and I were watching TV instead of zigzagging my way through a horde of screaming people.

So far three have responded to my "excuse me" with hard glares. I guess "we're not going to take it anymore" includes refusing to let white guys pass by them in a crowd. I keep moving trying to cause as little disturbance as possible.

I haven't even made it to the bottom step and I'm already doing some major sweating. It must be ninety on the concrete. Glad I didn't wear my good shirt since this polo is already damp from me and from all those sweaty bodies I've brushed up against.

Eureka! The bottom step. Now I only have to climb twenty-five or thirty more and get through a throng of folks already worked into an angry lather. I work my way to the left thinking it might be easier to move up along the wall than through the middle of the mass. It's theory based on nothing but I'm going with it.

A new voice on the megaphone. I look up at the landing to see a white guy, short hair, blue muscle shirt, and wearing a pink armband. He raises his arm for silence.

"Two weeks ago a group of rednecks attacked me in Forrest Park," he shouts, into the megaphone, pausing for dramatic effect as his eyes scan the faces. Then, like a television evangelist, he blares, "They blackened my eyes ... but it only gave me stronger vision." The gays in the crowd raise their banded arms, hooting their support.

I'm on the second step, moving laterally toward the wall.

When I don't hear anything for a moment, I look back up at the landing. The man has turned away from the crowd and appears to be heading into the building. But a few feet from the doors, he turns dramatically, shouting into the megaphone, "They broke my ribs ... but it only gave me a stronger heart."

Again, fists shoot skyward accompanied by a chorus of hoots, mostly from those with armbands. The man waits for the roar to subside, and then with perfect timing, he says, "I'm here to tell those cowards ..." He lowers the megaphone as he steps up to the edge of the landing, then raises it back to his lips, shouting, "I'm here to inform those redneck cowards ..."

"Tell 'em what it is!" a black man's voice cries out.

The man tilts the megaphone skyward, shouting into it so loudly it distorts the sound. "I'm here to tell those redneck cowards ... all they did was make me a stronger faggot!"

He jerks the megaphone away from his mouth, showing the crowd his proud and determined look, and punches his fist skyward, basking in the cacophony of cheers, applause, and whistles, this time from the blacks and whites as well as the gay group.

The wall is concrete, rough, and grimy, and there are splashes of color here and there where the maintenance people have scraped off most but not all of graffiti artists' work. Leaning over it I can see two uniformed officers manning barricades to keep Fifth Avenue traffic from trying to drive through the crowd.

I look back at the mass of sweating people all around me. A few feet away is a skinny, grey-bearded white man, old enough to remember the nineteen sixties, wrapped in an American flag. Judging by the bare hip peeking out between one of the folds, I think that's all he's got on. The woman behind him is working hard to balance a three-foot high cardboard Statue of Liberty perched on top of her head. A couple steps up from me, a bearded man dressed like Abraham Lincoln, complete with black tails and a stovepipe hat. He actually looks a little like Lincoln except he's a black man.

Up on the landing, an old Native American woman is now standing front and center, her white hair braided down to her rear, wearing a tan buckskin dress decorated with red, white, and blue beads. She's so frail it's all she can do to lift the megaphone to her mouth.

"What are you doin'?" a heavyset woman snaps at me when I slip between her and the wall after excusing myself.

"Just trying to slip by ma'am. Sorry. I hope you have a good day and a good time here."

Guess she didn't buy my fake smile, because she shakes her head and shoots me a look of disgust.

Strains of the Native American woman's haunting chant flows over the quieted crowd and into the high-steel canyons. "The heavens open up and speak to the spirits of our hearts and guide us in the way we should go."

I lost count of how many steps I've climbed now. At least ten, I think. It's hard to tell, but it looks like I might be about a third of the way up. A moment ago, a man and woman refused to let me by them so I flashed my badge. The man affected an even bigger attitude but eventually leaned away from the wall a little so I could squeeze by them, scraping my back on the gnarly cement wall. I best not flash the badge anymore. Could cause problems and I'm just a tad outnumbered.

"Our God created us all. Not just the Indian, not just the white man, not just the black man, Asian man, Arab man. We are not to judge how they all live, how they all are." She lowers the megaphone and flashes a two-fingered peace sign. The crowd applauds enthusiastically. And I move up two steps.

"She's not Apache but she's a good speaker."

I jump and twist around to see Nate just inches from me.

"Nate! What the—"

"Sensei, you're hurt, you don't have your gun, and you don't have a police radio. You must agree that that is the exception to the 'even a bad plan is better than no plan' rule."

I take his upper arm and turn us so we're facing out over the wall. "Nate, I'm on duty. You can't be next to me. I can't watch out for you and search the crowd for the suspect."

"Don't worry about me, Sensei. Do what you have to do. I'm just watching your six."

He's got my back. Oh man, one more thing. "Where's Mai

and Rudy?"

"Where you left them. I told them I had to go to the restroom."

I look down and across the sweating faces to where we were standing a few minutes ago. I don't see them. I scan the crowd in the street. Nothing. I check those people near the first step, then those on the next two steps, then those on the— There they are. One towering beautiful Eurasian woman and one roly-poly black man. Mai spots me, smiles, and gives me a little wave with her fingertips.

*　　*　　*

"OhGodohGodohGod," Arizona murmured as the crowd roar died.

The man pressed against her right side looked at her. "Everything all right, miss?" he asked.

Startled someone was speaking to her, and a nigger to boot, she turned away quickly, clutching her cell phone to her breast. For an instant she wondered how he could see her. Then just as quickly she thought of course he can, she's not invisible, though she was trying hard to make her two-hundred-twenty-pound self not noticed.

Oh, how she wished Cork was here. All night she worried the cop had killed Corky in the funeral home. But this morning she caught a glimpse of a newspaper, and there was Cork on the front page, and her own photo right next to her. Looked like the pics they took of them down at the joint when they got released. The huge headline said: "White Supremacist Killer Caught." In slightly smaller letters it said: "Sister Still Loose." She couldn't read below the fold. There's probably a bounty for her head. Yeah, a bounty and here she is in the middle of

Africa. I'm either brave or nuts, she thought. Maybe both.

She didn't know exactly when in the last few minutes she decided she would never make the call on the cell Cork gave her, but she knew it right now for sure. She didn't know why she wasn't going to do it other than she was tired of doing everything Cork wanted her to do. When she was with her sister, she just went along with whatever she said. But when she stopped to think about it some, doing what Cork wanted always got them into trouble. Of course, Cork always protected her when it did, taking care of her in juvies and, when they were older, taking care of her in the joint.

But she's not here now. Not here to tell her what to do. Not here to decide for the both of them. So now she had to do the deciding for herself. First time for everything, she thought.

Her first decision was not to make the call, the one to make all the cops leave from the rally and go to the fake bank robbery eight blocks away. She was to call nine-one-one and say two bank robbers had shot three people and taken some others hostage. Colonel White said the call would pull the cops away from guarding the "niggeroid." Pull them away so his people could "do what needs to be done, and do it with extreme prejudice," whatever that meant.

She unfolded the leaflet someone gave her. There's the guy's name. Reverend Doctor Rothman Sterling. Yes, he's the one. The extreme prejudice thing was about him, and it would "shock the world," Colonel White said.

There were lots of times when Arizona didn't get what people were talking about. Like now. How was shocking the world a good thing? Corky had always talked about a race war: whites against the muds. But Arizona never understood why that was a good thing either. Wouldn't a lot of whites die too?

And if whites were really almost a minority now, why would you want more of them to die?

She just had too many questions to go and do what Corky and Colonel White wanted. What she did understand was she didn't want to participate in any more killing. She still didn't like niggers, and she absolutely hated being surrounded by them. But to kill another one? Wasn't going to happen. So why was she here? Up until a few minutes ago she didn't know.

After she got out of the funeral home, crawled under those bushes, barely squeezed her bulk under the police car where she could hear two cops inside talking about fishing, crawled under a pickup and an SUV, she found herself between two buildings. There was less than five feet between the two, but it was enough space for her to hide under a stack of old tires. She lay there for at least two hours while creepy crawlies and night worms almost made her give up. Once she heard cops with dogs somewhere near, but they never came between the buildings where she was. Maybe they had already searched it before she crawled in.

She waited there until dawn. She hadn't heard any police radios for an hour, so she crawled out from under the tires and moved down the narrow alleyway until she came out onto a sidewalk. She headed toward the Willamette River and whatever bridge would take her over to downtown. It was on the steps to the Hawthorne Bridge where she saw the homeless guy sleeping. She swiped some of his clothing and left him with her filthy clothes.

She headed toward City Hall because, well, she was told to do it, which was the best explanation she had for coming here. But once she found the building and saw people setting up the speakers and stuff, something came over her to make her question what she was supposed to do.

Except in the last few days when she began to think about the killings and tried to understand their value in Colonel White's movement, she had never ever questioned anything Cork said. She had never questioned her when they were teens and would rob people—they were just trying to survive. She went along with her sister the time they nearly beat a wino to death just to see what it felt like, and when they dragged a nigger behind their car. She didn't like it, but she had learned not to question Corky. She went along when Cork planned how to stab the skinny bitch down in the joint, and when they hung the old man from the light pole and stabbed the raghead whore. But when they crucified Executioner, old feelings and new bombarded her brain.

She and Cork had about ten sets of foster parents when they were young. Her favorite was a woman, at least sixty-five, who was kind and gentle and never judged them. Daisy was born in Kentucky and lived there all her life until she came to Portland to see her dying sister. She stayed after the funeral and took in foster kids to earn a little money. She had a gift for taking care of them, Arizona remembered, and she and Daisy connected from the first day. Daisy often asked why the young girl did what she did, but Arizona couldn't answer.

One evening they were sitting out on the front porch sipping hot chocolate, and Daisy said to her, "Ari, there gonna be a time when you git all filled up with doing all this bad stuff. Thing is, real bad people never git full; they always have a big ol' hole in their dark hearts, which they try to fill by hurtin' folks. I know you bein' a good person deep inside your heart. I kin see it in yuh. I don't think you kin see it yet, but one day you're gonna, and it will happen when you get full of doing these bad deeds. You'll be so full you won't want to ever do them agin. In fact, you're gonna want to do good things for people."

Sounded goofy at the time, but now, maybe that's what she's feeling now. Full.

She was four steps from the top where some fat man was talking now. Yelling was more like what he was doing. Think he was introduced as Billy Souls. Got to be fake but still a good name for a preacher.

Some of these niggers acted like they're giving up a kidney or something when she mumbled excuse me and slipped between them and the wall. A couple of them spun around and acted all put out, but when they looked at her they moved over a little. Maybe her hood scared them or her size.

Arizona looked out over the crowd across the steps to the far wall and at those below her and out on the street. They're all here because of what me and Cork did, she thought, all those things we did for the cause. Thecausethecausethecause. Why does stuff have to be so complicated? Either the cause was way over her head or the cause was the dumbest thing ever. Well, right now she thought it was the dumbest thing ever, and it was just plain bad.

And she was full of being bad. Now it was time to do good.

She looked up at the rooftops and saw policemen up there with rifles. Down below on the other side of the wall there were more police. She started to turn back toward the front but stopped. That man down below her—about fifteen steps or so—squeezing by people along the wall. Wasn't he ... ?

Shitshitshit. It was the cop from the funeral home.

He looked up and his eyes found hers.

*   *   *

"Tankersley."

"Captain, Sam Reeves. I've spotted the suspect. She's above me a few steps, but with this dense crowd she might as well be two blocks away. I don't have the number to the command post. Can you have them contact their plainclothes guys and tell them to look for me along the north wall about a third of the way down from the top? I got a bandage on my forehead."

"Standby, Reeves."

Holding my phone to my ear, I squeeze by another obese woman, all the while keeping my eyes focused on Arizona. After we made eye contact, she's been trying to move up the stairs faster. Now it looks like two black guys are getting in her face.

"We hate our enemies ..." Reverend Billy Souls' voice booms through the megaphone. "... so we don't despise ourselves. Without enemies, there is no us."

I'm almost by the heavyset woman when she turns abruptly and blares, "Who you pushing? Touch me again and I'll throw your white ass over this wall."

Souls' voice bounces off the buildings: "We loathe and kill off our enemies ... to avoid feeling the pain about what they represent in ourselves."

"Sorry, ma'am," I say. Nate is one step down behind me. "Ma'am, I need to get up—"

"What you *need* is an ass whuppin from this here grandmother. I don't stand for having hands put on me."

A woman standing a couple people over to my right moves into my peripheral. "Why don't you just land in one place and stay put?" she snaps, grabbing my arm and fixing me with a no-nonsense motherly look from under the brim of her purple church hat. I sense Nate stepping protectively up to me.

"I'm good, Nate," I say over my shoulder.

Church Hat tugs my arm. "I've been watching you for the past few minutes, watching you move around like you have ants in your britches." I let her turn my body, but I keep my eyes on Arizona who just turned away from a man who has been yelling at her. I can't hear anything over the crowd and the damn megaphone.

"Those who hate," Reverend Billy Souls' voice blares, "look for two things in their targets: people who are easily identifiable, like black folks ..."

"You listening to the man, son?" Church Hat asks.

" ... and people who won't retaliate, people who are seen as having less power."

A man's voice shouts angrily from off to my right. "That's bullshit! Any of these white motherfuckers want to see how powerless I am?"

"I agree with the brother," another man's voice shouts from somewhere down the steps. "I personally ain't gonna stand by and let whitey kill me and my family."

Arizona has moved away from the man but I can see his mouth still ripping into her. She is nearly to the landing.

I look at my cell. Where is the captain? I can see Nate out of my periphery looking all about. I know he feels the crowd's mood change too. I look back to check on Mai but the mass is in constant flux and I don't see her.

"You listening to me?" Church Hat asks.

The first woman says, "I think you were right about ants in his pants, Sophie."

I look away and see a man a couple of steps up looking down at me. At least it looks like he is. He is wearing ultra dark wrap-around sunglasses. Damn, looks like the actor Michael Clarke Duncan's bigger brother. Black overshirt, black slacks, and a week's worth of whiskers. Got to be three hundred pounds, at least.

Reverend Billy Souls' voice: "I am deeply humbled and most honored to introduce a man who has done more for black folk across this great country of ours than—"

Souls is introducing the guest speaker. I got to move. "Excuse me ladies, I got—"

"Reeves, you still there?"

I plug my other ear. "I am, Captain."

"Listen. Red Berkley is smack in the center of the sweating mass and closest to the landing. You still next to the north wall?"

"I am."

The captain says something I can't make out. Must be talking into a radio or another cell. "Reeves, Red wants you to raise your hand and open and close your fist several times."

I pull away from the ladies, much to their angry curses, and do as I'm told, looking a whole lot strange to the two women. Nate looks at me questioningly.

"Red sees you and he's moving toward you."

"So with great pleasure and humility, it is my great pleasure to introduce the Reverend Doctor Rothman Sterling!"

A thunderous explosion of cheers, whistles, and applause.

I press my cell hard against my ear, and shout, "I'm trying to head up the stairs, Captain. Tell Red to go toward the landing by the wall. The suspect is wearing a black hoody and it's up over her head. She's big, two twenty at least."

"Hold on, Reeves." I hear the word "hoody," then, "Reeves, Red sees her. He's working his way over there."

I pocket my cell and squeeze between the wall and two teenage girls. I'm so glad it's my right side bandaged because my left one is getting some serious abrasions from this wall. The girls, both white, look at my bandaged head and giggle. Thank you, ladies. I'll be here all evening.

"Evil comes in many forms." It's a new voice coming from the megaphone. Not as booming as Billy Souls' or as deep. It's more soulful and as rich as Martin Luther King's. "In this darkest hour in Portland, Oregon we ..."

"You want to push *me*?" the Michael Clarke Duncan-looking guy booms. His head is huge and his face wet with perspiration. He is one step up but even if he wasn't he would still tower over me. I can see my puny two-hundred-pound self, reflected in his sunglasses.

"Look, pal," I say, feeling ridiculous having to look nearly straight up at him. "I need to get to the top to—"

"You going to push *me* to get there?"

"Look, Michael, I'm sure you're very proud of your hugeness and you have used it for years to get your way, but I really need to get by." Okay, not the best calming technique, but I really dislike big in-your-face ass clowns like this guy.

"You shaking now?" he asks, apparently missing my sarcasm and the "Michael" thing. "Or do you only push old women?"

"Hey, man," Rudy says, stepping up to us. Where did he come from?

"Who you calling old, Godzilla boy?" Church Hat blares, her glaring indignation steaming off of her.

I look quickly for Mai and spot her a couple steps down and three or four people deep into the crowd. A couple of brothers are blocking her way and appear to be trying to charm her. She's shaking her head and looks to be getting miffed. A woman blocks my view for a hair of a second and when I see Mai again, she's grabbed the arm of one of the men and is spinning him into his friend. They bang torsos. Before they can separate, she is zigging and zagging her way toward us.

The Reverend Doctor's voice rises and reverberates off the columns. "It gladdens my heart to see so many people here wanting change, but it saddens me there are a couple of million others out there in Portland who are maintaining the status quo."

"You need to back off brother," Rudy says to the big man.

"Oh hell no," Godzilla booms, glaring at Rudy like he's a slug on his shoe. "We got us here another Uncle Tom. Another cracker want-to-be."

Nate has moved up beside me. I sense more than see him extract something from one of the big pockets in his cargo pants. His war club is too big to conceal so what is it?

"Look, man," Rudy says. "You clearly got an agenda, but don't you agree we're all here today to put an end to this kind of ..."

"Back off, Oreo," Godzilla booms.

I flash my badge at the big man. "This has been fun and everything but I'm going around you. Try to stop me and you're going to jail."

He moves fast for a T-Rex, but I manage to block about ninety percent of his one-handed shove. The ten percent that catches my chest sends me back against the cement wall. Before the impact fully registers in my mind again how rough cement and tender flesh are not good bed fellows, Nate moves by me in a blur, streaking low toward Godzilla's legs. My first thought is he's going for a knee catch to yank the big man's legs out from under him, and my second thought is Nate would have an easier time yanking the roof off of City Hall.

But he's not shooting in for a knee catch. Instead, he drops into a side horse stance, one foot two steps higher than the other and his rear hand up to shield his head, as his lead hand whips into an arc. He is holding something but his hand is moving too fast for me to see it. Whatever it is smashes against Godzilla's left kneecap, the sound, like a large chunk of thick ice breaking on a frozen lake. The huge man emits a God-awful roar and slow-falls to his left, taking down half-a-dozen shouting people with him.

"Your path is clear now, Sensei," Nate says, matter-of-factly, stuffing whatever it was back into his pants pocket.

Rudy and I look dumfounded from Godzilla, who is curling into the fetal position with his huge hands cupping what used to be his kneecap, to Nate, and back to Godzilla again.

"What happened?" Mai asks, stepping between Nate and me and looking a little out of breath.

I look up at the landing just as Arizona steps up onto it.

*   *   *

I don't know what the Reverend Doctor said but it's getting a thunderous roar from the crowd, some of it cheers, some of it boos. No, not boos, but angry shouts. The crowd is pressing in tighter. I'm working my way up the steps and fighting for every one. I'm about six from the top.

Arizona is still standing there watching the Reverend and glancing nervously at the crowd. What is she going to do? I look back down and see Mai, Nate, and Rudy staying a few steps away as I asked. Telling them to stand fast would be ignored but telling them to give me space to do my police thing seems to be working.

There is Red looking at me. He is about three steps down and a few steps to the right of Arizona. He tilts his head toward Arizona and lifts his eyebrows. I nod and point to a spot just below her on the steps. "Meet me there," I mouth.

I turn quickly toward a sudden roar from the center of the crowd—shouting, shrieking, scuffling, flailing arms. Some of the mass around the problem presses back, forcing several people to stumble and fall to the steps and others to fall over them. On the far side of the crowd and down on the sidewalk, a dozen black-uniformed riot cops stream around the south wall of the stairs and begin working their way up.

I squeeze by two young men, both wearing their jeans below their butt cheeks and exposing plaid boxer shorts. The one closest to me turns around and acts like I just slapped his auntie.

Flapping his arms as if he's about to take flight, and with far too much indignation and grimacing, he says, "Who you fuckin' pushin'?"

Sick of all these bonehead obstacles, I say, "It would be ..." I smack my palm against his upper chest with a loud slapping sound, just as I taught the academy a few days ago, "you the one I'm fuckin' pushin.'" I take advantage of his startled look, and quickly push/pull his shoulders to spin him around. I two-hand push him into his buddy.

But his buddy sidesteps out of the way so my guy bangs into a group of schoolgirls, who act like they just got the cooties from him and push him all the way down onto the steps. His buddy, built like a spider with impossibly long legs and arms, draws his fist back about three feet behind him and launches a haymaker that would shatter his hand bones should he connect. Of course, it wouldn't do my mug any good either.

I swat it aside, quickly lift my knee up high, and drop the tip of my shoe onto his belt buckle, which has somehow been securing his low-slung jeans around his upper thighs. My plan was to strip his pants down to his ankles so I could bump him and make him trip over them, but the toe of my running shoe must have caught a button on the front of his boxers because I stripped them down to his ankles too.

No need for me to follow up on the guy because the burst of laughter and pointing fingers from those around us, and the over-the-top screams from the schoolgirls are doing more to him than any martial arts technique would.

Up on the landing, Arizona has pushed her hood off her head. She is looking over at the Reverend Doctor who is shouting into his megaphone for the crowd to "Calm down," words that have never calmed down anyone, ever. Two news cameramen are now on the stage filming whatever is happening in the center of the crowd, which judging by the shouts and screams has worsened.

I turn to check on Mai but several people have filled in behind me again, blocking my view. I don't see Nate either, but there is Rudy ripping into the kid I pantsed. My new friend doesn't tolerate fools.

Shouts and fast movement to my right. Two people, an older white man and a twenty-something black man, are down on the steps thrashing and smashing in a furious brawl. A foot from the crowd connects with the black man's head.

Screams. Pushing. Another fight erupts between three, no, four people.

The Reverend Doctor's voice shouts into the megaphone: "Friends! Friends! Friends!" I don't think that's going to work either.

I see Red moving up on the stage, and there is Angela right behind him. I was wondering where she was.

Two more steps to go.

A swarm of bodies—probably a surge from the fight—bang into me and send me painfully into the wall. "I don't have time for this," I growl, and push off the barrier hard, sending several people stumbling only to be shoved back by others. I scoot quickly out of their way, push a cursing woman aside, and step up onto the landing.

Arizona flings Angela off her arm as if she was a clingy child and drives her big fist into Red's chest, sending him stumbling back.

Twenty feet away, the Reverend Doctor turns to look at them. "Who are these people?" he asks through the megaphone. He looks over at his handlers who are gathered behind one of the big pillars off stage left.

"Get off the landing, Reverend," I shout at him. "Get off now!" He looks at me and sees a madman with a head bandage, and doesn't move.

Oh man ... The scene below me is a raging sea of chaotic movement: swells of people moving this way and that way, screaming, shouting, and limbs flailing, and political signs and water bottles flying through the air. On the far side of Fifth Avenue, streams of riot police officers move around the wall and into the crowd. Along my wall below, about twenty officers form a V-wedge formation and begin moving people as a blaring police PA system orders them to disperse in an orderly fashion. Don't think it's going to happen today.

Red is down but he's managed to grab Arizona's big leg. She punches his arms, screaming, "Let me go! I have to ..."

"It's over, Arizona!" I shout grabbing her thick shoulders

from behind. I snap a sidekick behind her closest knee and yank her shoulders straight down. When she lands on her butt, I jerk her right arm behind her and crank it into a shoulder lock. "Understand, Arizona? It's over. Now lay down on your front and ..."

Bam!

I turtle my head.

"Shots fired!" Red shouts into his lapel mic. He scrambles to his feet.

I don't know what direction it ...

Bam!

Cement explodes off of a pillar near the building's double wood doors.

With my attention on the gunfire, Arizona easily pulls away from me, rolls up onto her feet, and takes off toward the Reverend Doctor, who is looking all about, his face screwed up in confusion. One of the cameramen has dropped to one knee, aiming his camera at the mass of people who have abruptly quieted and frozen in place, except for their heads jerking about like nervous chickens. The other cameraman is moving quickly across the landing and filming the now crouching Reverend Doctor.

I take off after Arizona, managing to grab the back of her hoody, but she shrugs her shoulders without missing a step and I'm left holding only her sweatshirt. Still running, I fling it aside and reach for her again.

Bam!

The running cameraman screams, and is flung backwards, and shards of the camera lens spray through the air like casted diamonds. He thumps heavily onto his back with part of the camera eyepiece imbedded into his eye. His shattered camera clatters to the cement.

I reach desperately for Arizona's shoulder again. To my right, an ear-numbing wave of sound reverberates off the face of City Hall.

My hand closes around a wad of her shirt just as her arms encircle the still crouching Reverend Doctor. I cock my hand back to slam a hammer fist into the side of her neck to knock her unconscious ... I hesitate. Something tells me I might be wrong.

Bam! The side of Arizona's head disappears in a spray of blood and hair, and chunks of brain and skull.

"Wha—" I stagger back ... I don't understand ... Arizona drops onto her butt, her legs bent awkwardly underneath her. Her hands fall onto her heavy thighs. She looks as if she is meditating until her smashed head drops onto her chest. I see a shiver run through her body and then she is still.

Movement to my right. "Get the reverend off the stage," Angela shouts running toward me.

"Yes," I say, and we grab the Reverend Doctor's arms and scurry him toward stage right.

Bam!

Dust and chunks tear from a column a few feet to our left. The three of us tuck our heads reflexively as if it would protect us. Hands reach for the Reverend Doctor as we slip behind one of the pillars.

Bop! *Bop*! *Bop*! *Bop*! *Bop*! *Bop*! *Bop*!

"Sweet Jesus!" Angela shouts, squeezing her eyes shut and pressing her back against the ornate cement. The portable radio on her hip is going nuts with chatter.

"Different weapon," I shout. "Ours ... I hope."

Five seconds pass, ten. "Target neutralized," a mellow, cool voice says on Angela's radio. "All units be advised, the shooter is down. The shooter is down. Stay alert. There might be others."

"The blood, hers or yours?" Angela asks, looking at me for the first time.

I feel my wet face and neck. "Hers," I manage, thinking how close the bullet came to hitting me.

A new wave of sound washes across the landing—shouting, bodies hitting bodies, an echoing voice barking commands on a police PA system.

I quick-peek around the pillar. "Red's in trouble," I say, and take off in a sprint across the landing to where a frenzy of people are kicking the downed officer and beating him with signs.

I drive a front kick into the chest of a man kicking Red's inert head. The impact sends the man tumbling down steps. A young woman clubs Red's legs with a sign that reads, "Can't we all just get along." I move toward her, but her legs suddenly disappear from under her and she lands hard on her side—Mai. She smiles at me and pushes the woman away with her foot.

Angela grabs a middle-aged man who tries to leave after stomping Red's stomach but he sends her stumbling away with a hard push. I take a lunge step into him and hit his gut with four rapid punches. When he starts to upchuck his breakfast, I whip a hard slap into his ear, sending him tumbling down the steps. Screw police brutality. I'm pissed.

"His gun's gone," Angela shouts over the din, kneeling beside Red. "You okay, baby?" she asks tenderly. I take a knee on the other side of him.

The big man's eyes flutter open. Long pause as Red assesses himself, then, "That would have to be a no, Angie."

"Officer down," she says into her radio. "We're up on the landing on the west side of City Hall. And all units be advised an officer's gun has been stolen."

Red starts to say something, grimaces, and tries again. "I ... pulled my weapon when the first shots rang out. I think ... the crowd thought I was the one trying to shoot the reverend."

"We got medics coming, Red," Angela says, patting his shoulder. "Hang tight. You'll be fine."

"You get the suspect?" Red asks, squinting up at me. His eyes widen. "Damn," he says. "You hurt, Sam? You got blood all ..." he reaches for his chest where he was kicked and breaks into a ragged cough.

"Yeah, we sort of got her," I say. "But the sniper finished her and SWAT finished him. I touch my fingers to my face. "Blood's not mine."

"Rough way for me to pick up some overtime," Red says, closing his eyes. His left one is quickly swelling.

Angela gently shakes his shoulder. "Stay awake, Red. You might have a concussion in your brick of a head. No sleeping allowed." When his eyes start to flutter, she says, "Hey, remember when I was your trainee and we got a call on the loony guy who ate part of his bathroom mirror?"

Red starts to chuckle but his groan pushes it away.

Angela pats his shoulder. "He ate like a whole square foot of it. Remember? And while we were waiting for the ambulance, you asked him if he'd 'like a nice glass of Windex to go with that?'"

I stand and look down at the wide expanse of steps. Most of the mob has fled or been forced off the steps and out onto the street by the riot cops. Three or four hundred insistent rioters are in a standoff with a disciplined line of officers out on Main Street. There are one ... two ... three ... four people down on the steps, each has people tending to them. Way off to my left I see several cops escorting at least a dozen people in handcuffs. The jail bus is likely parked around the corner.

Angela, kneeling by her old training partner, looks over at Arizona, who is still sitting on her twisted legs with her hands in her lap. Her back is drenched in blood and it's pooling about her butt. She looks less like she's meditating now and more like she's—just dead. The cameraman is lying twisted on his back, the camera eyepiece protruding from his eye, making him look like a sleeping jeweler. A half-dozen people crouched behind the pillar stare at the bodies, not sure what they should do.

A couple of white teenagers scurry up the steps, one of them giggling, both filming the bodies with their cell phones.

"Get the hell out of here!" Angela bellows at them, "before I stomp on your cells and drag your skinny asses to jail."

"Nate and Rudy are down there," Mai says, pointing toward the street as she kneels beside Red. "In front of Starbucks."

My two new friends are holding a squirming guy down on the sidewalk. A couple of officers are rushing over to them. Two thoughts: I hope they don't search Nate, and I wonder if Rudy used his eyelid technique.

"I used to work in a hospital," Mai says to Red. "Tell me where it hurts."

He looks at her, grins. He might be hurt but he's still a guy.

I look back at Arizona. "I could be wrong, Angela ..."

Angela looks up at me. "What?"

"I don't know. I'm not sure, but ... the way she grabbed the reverend ... I think she was trying to protect him."

*   *   *

There is a solemn, thick stillness now on the west side of City Hall. Angela, Mai, and I are standing together at the bottom of the steps, and Nate and Rudy are a few feet away watching the two EMT crews load green body bags into the back of ambulances. A few pockets of people are clustered here and there, talking in hushed voices. Several news crews are filming and interviewing various police officials and black community leaders.

It's half past noon and the sun bouncing off the sidewalk is intense. The streets are still blocked off and will be for several hours as the police piece together the crime scenes here at City Hall, and the surrounding areas on Main Street. The shooter set up on the Third floor of the Walla Walla Building, one of the original structures built in the late eighteen hundreds and one of only three historical buildings in this area. I'm told he was dressed casually in khaki shorts and a Hawaiian shirt, and armed with a scoped M-14. The SWAT snipers separated him from his head.

I touch Mai's arm. "Angela and I have to go up to Detectives and give them our statements. You need to come to give a statement as to what you saw up on the landing."

"No problem," she says, sounding tired.

"Did you get hurt, Mai?" Angela asks.

She shakes her head. "Just ... I do not know. Long day and I am tired of people hating people just because they are different. It happens too much in Vietnam and it happens too much here. So sad."

The three of us, as if on cue, look up at the landing by the doors to City Hall where yellow crime tape flutters in a light breeze.

"Is it over?" Mai asks, rhetorically.

No one answers.

EPILOGUE

Dakota Ruth, one of the detectives pulled from her normal duties to work the City Hall investigation, is taking Mai's statement on what she saw of Red's beating. They are sitting at my desk while I write my report in Foskey's office. Mine is straightforward: I went, I saw, I did, and for once I shouldn't be in trouble. But I still have the night before to answer for. Specifically, why I didn't wait for backup before entering the funeral home. Why I didn't pull my weapon.

My weapon. I could have pulled it in the funeral parlor; I could have fired it. Will I get challenged about it? Hard to say. Some cops might wonder but the Chief's Office is probably glad I didn't. Whenever a cop shoots someone, it's always bad PR no matter how justified. One less thing as far as the Chief's Office goes, and the fact no one got hurt but Corky and me, makes it all good in their eyes. They might even say I made a good decision.

But I'll know why I didn't and I got to deal with it. Could I have saved Angela from getting struck with the bat? Would BJ have gotten slammed on his car hood? Was it my fault?

As I get up from Foskey's desk I hear Dakota thank Mai for helping today and then half jokingly ask if she had ever considered being a cop. Mai looks up at me as I walk out of the office, and goes, "Hmm."

"Hmm?" I say.

"Uh oh," Dakota says with a smile. "Did I touch on a sensitive subject with you two?"

I shake my head. "I was just thinking with Mai patrolling the mean streets it wouldn't take long before all the bad guys were fleeing to Canada."

The detective smiles, but the smile dissolves into a slight frown. The way she is looking at us—scrutinizing us, really—makes my heart skip a beat. I don't know her well but I've heard she is a tenacious investigator, with an eye for the smallest details. She normally works the Assault Unit but is often loaned to Homicide when there is a heavier than normal influx of cases.

She smiles a little and moves her finger from Mai to me and back to Mai again. "Are you guys like ...?"

"We met because of my father," I say quickly before Mai says anything. "It's a long story."

Dakota nods, her brow still furrowed. "I see. I was thinking about the Portland State shooting a couple of months ago." She begins rolling her pen over and under each finger, her eyes following it but not really seeing it. "The sniper turned out to be female Vietnamese. Someone got to her before we did and tore her eyes out of her head." Her eyes never leave the pen rolling across her fingers. When it reaches one side of her hand, it reverses and heads back. "We also found a young Vietnamese man on PSU's skybridge. He had been beaten to a pulp. They were both alive but we couldn't get them to talk. They still haven't.

"Also there was a Vietnamese woman beaten and thrown off or fell from the skybridge. DOA. She was linked to a killing that went down around the same time—a restaurant man who was linked to Vietnamese organized crime with ties to Ho Chi Minh City. Interesting."

The detective glances at Mai again and when she looks

back at her pen, Mai shoots me a frightened look. I shake my head. I hope she knows it means to keep quiet.

Dakota continues musing. "We figured the whole thing was a rival gang beef. The press thought so too, and people mostly shrugged the thing off after a few days. I remember reading a couple of editorials written by citizens who argued that since the police couldn't clean up the gang problem in Portland, maybe the solution was to put all the rivals into the baseball park, lock the doors, and let them shoot it out."

"Good idea." I smile.

Dakota tosses the pen on the desk and looks at us. "I didn't work the case but I was around the guys who did. I remember them talking about a name confusion when they were handing out diplomas at the graduation. They think it's possible the intended victim of the shooter was really a student named Nguyen. Same as you, Mai."

"I force a chuckle. "Same as a quarter of the population in Vietnam."

Angela walks in and nods to Dakota. "Hi, Dakota. You get pulled for this one?"

The detective looks away to Angela. Did she notice the cold sweat above my mouth? "Hey, Ange. Whenever and wherever there is a mess it seems."

Angela nods. "I heard the captain asking upstairs if anyone had seen you."

Dakota scoots her chair back and stands. "Better get up there then." She looks at Mai. "Thanks much. Later, Sam." She's out the door.

"Red is going to be okay," Angela says, heading toward the coffee, oblivious to Mai and me exhaling our tension. "But he's going to be healing for a long while. Richard Daniels is doing fine. And get this. An emergency room doc said his heavy jowls saved his life. If he had been leaner, Corky's knife would have likely cut something critical." Her eyes smile a little. "So much for getting the Fat Dicks to diet now. Oh, the bad news is BJ has a broken back. I don't know to what extent, but I did hear the prognosis is he will be able to walk. I guess he was headed home in his unmarked and heard all the action on his police radio. Since he was close, he decided to do some actual police work."

Angela tries twice to pour herself a cup of coffee but her hands are trembling so much she sloshes most of it on the counter. Mai moves quickly to her and gently takes the pot and fills her cup halfway. "More, and I think you burn your fingers," Mai says. Angela's nod is both an acknowledgement of Mai's wisdom and a thank you.

Angela sips a little and sets the cup down. "Police coffee tastes like Yak shit," she says. I say there is probably an interesting story as to how she knows such a thing, getting half a smile from her. "I want to go home and stay there this time," she says. I start to tell her we'll give her a lift but then I remember my truck is at home.

We look at each other for a moment, and I know she is thinking about the narrow alley with Puke. I don't know who moved first but we go in for an awkward but sincere hug. On her way to the door, she stops next to Mai and touches her shoulder. "Watch over him. He has a tendency to get into trouble."

A minute after Angela leaves, Foskey comes in. "Filled in Deputy Chief Rodriguez," he says. "He was most impressed and very happy about our unit's performance. He was especially impressed with what you did, and I wouldn't be surprised if he'd put you up for some kind of a medal. Maybe. He said he still has to run defense when the Chief inevitably asks why you and the others went into the house when you had it contained for a SWAT entry, and why you went into the funeral home alone."

I nod, remembering an old story about a prolific bank robber back in the nineteen fifties named Willie Sutton. After he was captured, a newspaper reporter asked him why he robbed so many banks, Sutton replied, "Because it's where the money is."

I try to contain myself but I'm too tired to control my mouth. "It's because that was where the bad guys were." He half smiles—he gets the reference—and tells me not to say that should I have to go before the chiefs. Good advice.

Foskey called up to Detectives and got a guy named Thompson to give Mai and me a ride home. He's a quiet guy, for which I'm grateful since I've told my story a half-dozen times already. On the way home, I start to poke Mark's number but he calls first. Everybody is reading my mind these days. He says he saw the news and called Anderson, the Public Information Officer, to get a rundown. I give him an abridged version of our involvement. He tells me he's still my boss and he is ordering me to get a lot of sleep. When I ask about David, he doesn't say anything for a few seconds. Finally, with a choked voice he says the doctors don't know how long David will be in a coma. The injury is severe and it's just too hard to determine right now.

I have a flash of satisfaction that two of the guys who beat my friends are dead but then I feel guilty for feeling it. Normal reaction to an abnormal event, Doc Kari would say. It still feels wrong. I tell Mark I'll call later to set up a time when Mai and I can take him to dinner.

I call Nate.

"Hey, Sensei. Rudy and I are having a beer at my house. Root beer for me, I swear."

"Good to hear, Nate. I'm proud of you. Put me on speakerphone, please."

"You're on, Sensei."

"Hi, Rudy. I just wanted to thank you two for what you did today. You made a difference and you kept people from getting hurt. You put yourselves at risk—which by the way meant you disobeyed me—but—well, you had my back, thank you."

"Craziness for sure, Sam," Rudy says. "I'm still shakin'."

"Thank you ..." Nate pauses for a beat. "Thank you, Sensei. That means ... a lot to me." I know he's thinking about what happened in Afghanistan.

Mai leans in to speak into my cell. "Hi, guys. I want to cook a traditional Vietnamese dinner for you and your wives."

"Invitation happily accepted, Mai," Rudy says. "Thank you. But please, no low calorie food."

"It already low calorie, Rudy," she says. "Vietnamese food very good for you."

"May I bring my war club, Mai?" Nate asks.

"Speaking of that, Nate," I say. "What did you hit the big man's knee with at City Hall?"

Two seconds of silence, then, "A Nerf ball."

Best to leave it at that.

*   *   *

It's noon. Twenty-six hours since City Hall. At least I think it's the next day. It could be two days later. What I do know is it's been a long time since I've slept so soundly, and without nightmares. Mai isn't in here, but her pillow and her side of the bed are still warm. It's a comforting feeling. I hit the restroom, slip on my jeans and T-shirt, and start to head out the door. I move over to the window instead. I open the mini blinds a little and squint into the late morning sun. It's going to be a scorcher.

It's a beautiful day, and it's hard to imagine the bloody battles of the past days actually happened. I gaze out at the deep green lawns, towering fir trees, blooming roses, and kids down the street shooting baskets, and I struggle for reality.

Ocnod and Yolanda, Puke and Executioner, the wino, Arizona, the TV cameraman, the sniper, and I haven't heard how many deaths there were in the crazy mob at City Hall. All because of hate. Brainless, stupid, ignorant hate. There will be some peace now—temporarily anyway.

I hope the investigation of the sniper can lead to the arrest of Colonel White. If it doesn't, he will be made a hero among his weak-minded followers. If it does, he will be made a martyr and considered a political prisoner by those outside and a leader by those incarcerated with him. Until a nonwhite gang member sticks a fork through his heart.

Ignorance begets racism. It's like a bumper sticker I saw after the terrorist flew jets into the Twin Towers and the pentagon. It read: "I learned everything I need to know about Islam on 9/11." Holding such a belief has to be the epitome of ignorance. Gluing your ignorance onto your car bumper for the entire world to see is a close second.

Am I racist? I like to think I'm not, but I know I've had my share of ignorant moments, like when I told Angela I didn't think of her as being Black. And, as a policeman I'm constantly up against the stereotype of violent minority gangs. It's sometimes hard to look at a group of Black or Hispanic men without suspicion. Whatever the reason, I must take responsibility and be mindful. One day at a time. Be in the moment, as Father always says.

Someone said racism won't go away until everyone on the planet is of mixed race. But what about prejudice against religion, sexual orientation, the elderly, and so on? I don't know. Much to think about.

I hear Mai laughing from somewhere in the house. I head out the door.

She hears me come into the dining room and turns away from the PC to smile at me. On the screen our father shoots me a military salute. "You are finally awake, sleepyhead," Mai says. She looks up at the clock. You sleep fourteen, no, thirteen hours."

"That's why I had to pee so badly," I say, pulling a dining room chair over next to hers. "Hello, Father. I hope you're well."

He nods. "Mai told me of your last few days."

I shake my head. "I'm so sorry she has been involved in all this ..."

"No need to apologize." He studies me for a moment, then, "How are you doing?"

If I were to tell him I'm fine, he would know I'm lying. He knows how I'm doing; I think he just wants to see how I answer.

"Well. My friends say I'm a shit magnet, which I can no longer deny." He smiles, as he, too, has been a magnet all his life. "By the way, a detective who interviewed Mai made a connection to her last name and the University shootings. I diverted her by saying Nguyen is a very common name. That and the general opinion that it was a gang war might waylay any connection to us."

"Did you handle the shit?" He clearly isn't falling for the distraction.

"Yes he did, Father," Mai says before I can answer. "He was amazing."

"She is your number one fan," Samuel says, with a twinkle in his eye. "From *Misery*. You see the movie? Stephen King wrote the book."

"I did," I say quietly. "I ..." Father tilts his head a little and his eyes smile.

I look down at my hands but I know he is looking at me. He knows.

His voice is gentle, urging. "Some say the lies we tell our friends and our family are nothing compared to the lies we tell ourselves."

I look up into eyes that are so knowing, so wise, so filled with love for his family. Sometimes I think those eyes know me better than I know myself.

I say, "I think the lies we tell others have greater repercussions."

"Hmm. How so?" Those knowing eyes.

I look over at Mai's puzzled expression and back to Father. He's waiting, as if he has nothing but time. Or he's waiting for me to grow a pair.

I exhale a long breath I wasn't aware I was holding. "Okay."

"What, Sam?" Mai asks, touching my forearm.

I look down at my hands once more. "I haven't been carrying my gun at work."

"Sam." Her whisper is heavy with disappointment. Father's expression remains the same.

"Not the first few days, anyway. Then I carried it, only because I thought someone at work would notice. But I didn't put a magazine in it. I carried it unloaded. After a while I somehow got the courage to put a mag in it but I didn't jack a round into the chamber. Still haven't."

Father doesn't look surprised because ... he probably isn't.

"I'm sorry. I lied to you, Father, and to you, Mai. I lied to a lot of others too: my shrink, the Deputy Chief, and to the detectives I work with."

I think about Lawrence getting thrown off the balcony, BJ getting his back broken on the hood of his car, Angela struck with a bat in the alley, and the protracted fight in the funeral home that allowed Arizona to escape. What if she hadn't had a change of mind about killing the reverend?

"What if there were no 'what-if' questions?" Father asks.

"What?"

"Life does not always do as we expect. Maybe the outcome would have been better if you had used your gun. Maybe it would have come out worse. We do not know. What we do know is you betrayed the trust of the people who count in your life. How do you feel?"

"Like shit."

"Good. You see, if you did not feel like shit that would not be good. Now, what is important is what you will do about it?"

"I think ..."

I search Father's eyes for disappointment. I don't find it. I don't see it in Mai's either.

"Will you tell them?" Father asks. "The other police officers. Will you tell them what you did?"

I lean back from the screen. Oh. I ... I don't know. If I go back on the job I have to tell them, and I can't go back on the job unless I can ... If I can't even say it, how can I do it?"

"I cannot answer that for you, Son. I can tell you I am happy you told Mai and me. That is a start. I can also tell you to be diligent in your actions. And I can remind you of something I have told you before. They are words Buddha said twenty-five hundred years ago. 'Do not dwell in the past, concentrate the mind on the present moment.'" He doesn't say anything for a several seconds, then, "The rest is up to you."

Mai takes my hand into both of hers. I watch her thumb caresses my fingers.

A silent minute passes, maybe five.

"Son." I look up at him. "You have a bandage on your head."

I laugh at the unexpectedness of the comment. So many times he has chewed me out or given me something to ponder, only to follow it with humor.

I touch the bandage. "I, of course, know this."

"Sam has lots more," Mai says, sounding proud of my wounds. Has she forgiven me so quickly? I don't deserve her.

"Yes, your biggest fan," he says, smiling at her. "Tell me, Sam, have you and your martial arts students or you and your police friends ever compared injuries and scars?"

"Oh yes. And I've had the most almost every time." Oh man, dumb thing to say considering his torso is marred by multiple bullet-wound scars, old knife slashes and, most horrifically, whip marks on his back from his years in a North Vietnamese prison. When he waves me off, I know he just picked up on my thoughts.

"Have you heard of *kintsugi*, Son?"

I shake my head.

"It is Japanese. It is the art of fixing broken pottery. It dates back to the fifteenth century when an emperor, I do not know his name, commanded his craftsmen to develop a more artful way of mending broken pots. Up to then they used a sort of metal staple, you see. With the development of *kintsugi*, they found a beautiful way to mend cracks and complete breaks with a mix of gold dust and glue.

"Over time, the Japanese came to love and even cherish the imperfection of broken pottery fixed this way. They see it as a creative addition to the pottery piece's story—its life story."

We look at each other for a long moment as I roll the concept around in my mind. I've been sitting with my hands on my knees. Mai slips hers under one.

"Father," she says, squeezing my hand, "I think you and Sam have much gold-dust glue in your bodies."

Father nods almost imperceptibly, his eyes never leaving mine. "*Kintsugi* works internally as well, Son."

"*Cám ơn*," I whisper, with a short bow.

"You are quite welcome. Just understand it might take awhile for the glue to set." I nod.

He looks at Mai. "Mai tells me she is having a good time there."

"It has been action packed," I say.

"No sunbathing or feeding squirrels in the park?"

"Sam fight a killer dog in the park," Mai says excitedly.

"Long story," I say when he frowns.

"Okay. So tell me, Son. Would you like to have more company?"

I look at him wondering what he's talking about ... "Wait," I blurt excitedly. The twinkle in his eyes gave him away. "You're coming here? To Portland?"

"My master's brother lives in California, in San Francisco's Chinatown. It is imperative I find him. I'd like you to accompany me."

ACKNOWLEDGMENTS

Many thanks to my family, friends, and colleagues who made this book possible: Publisher David Ripianzi for his encouragement and vast knowledge of the business; Leslie Takao for her sharp editing and insight into the characters; Carrie Christensen-LCSW-R for her help with the psychologist's scenes; Snake Blocker for his knowledge of Indian culture and weapons; Kevin Faulk for his expertise about the Afghanistan war; retired Detective Steven Russelle for helping with the house search scene; Pastor Medford Keith Foskey for teaching me about funeral homes; and Lt. Col. Dave Grossman for helping with Nate's guilt issues.

And as always to Lisa Christensen, my best friend and wife, for her encouragement and willingness to hear me read my day's writing, even after her exhausting workday.

ABOUT THE AUTHOR

Loren W. Christensen is a Vietnam veteran and retired police officer with 29 years of law enforcement experience. As a martial arts student and teacher since 1965, he has earned a total of 11 black belts in three arts and was inducted into the Masters Hall of Fame in 2011. As a writer, Loren has penned more than 45 nonfiction books, including over two dozen books on the martial arts, and dozens of magazine articles on a variety of subjects. He has starred in seven instructional martial arts DVDs. *Dukkha Unloaded* is his third fiction book in the Dukkha series. Loren W. Christensen can be contacted through his website at www.lwcbooks.com.